Jame crouched in the dark, shivering. Where was it now? A rustle, a scrape of scales on stone . . . it was coming after her.

With a choked cry she whirled and leaped. Her fingers caught at the rough stone blocks and she scrambled blindly upward until one hand closed on a wooden beam. She was hanging there when a dazzling light seemed to explode in the room.

"Well!" said a voice. "No one's ever done *that* before!"

Jame saw Penari standing below with a torch in his hand. Behind him, light gleamed on a huge mound of flesh, white, convoluted, and quivering with lidless eyes.

"Too bad it's you, boy," Penari said. "Monster hasn't been fed so far this month."

GOD STALK

"It's become increasingly hard to do anything new in the high-fantasy field, but there's still a big difference between those who can only reheat the same old stew and those who take full advantage of all that's been done before to brew up a fresh mix. Hodgell proves with this debut novel to be in the latter group."

—*Publishers Weekly*

GOD STALK

P.C. HODGELL

BERKLEY BOOKS, NEW YORK

A portion of this text previously appeared in
an altered form in 1977 in the book
Clarion Science Fiction edited by Kate Wilhelm,
Berkley Publishing Corp., N.Y.

This Berkley book contains the complete
text of the original hardcover edition.
It has been completely reset in a typeface
designed for easy reading, and was printed
from new film.

GOD STALK

A Berkley Book/published by arrangement with
Atheneum Publishers

PRINTING HISTORY
Atheneum edition published 1982
Berkley edition/August 1983

For information address: Atheneum Publishers,
122 East 42nd Street, New York, New York 10017.

ISBN: 0-425-06079-9

A BERKLEY BOOK® TM 757,375
Berkley Books are published by The Berkley Publishing Group,
200 Madison Avenue, New York, New York 10016.
The name "BERKLEY" and the stylized "B"
with design are trademarks belonging
to Berkley Publishing Corporation.

PRINTED IN THE UNITED STATES OF AMERICA

For Mike

With affection & gratitude

CONTENTS

BOOK I: TATTERS OF DUSK

BOOK II: CROWN OF NIGHTS

BOOK III: SHROUD OF DAYS

PRINCIPAL CHARACTERS PAST AND PRESENT

In the Kencyrath

Jame
Tori: *Jame's twin brother*
Marcarn (Marc) of East Kenshold: *Jame's friend, an aging Kendar*
Ishtier: *Highborn priest of the Three-Faced God in Tai-tastigon*
Anar: *Jame's former tutor, a scrollsman and Ishtier's younger brother*
Ganth Gray Lord: *Ganth of Knorth, once Highlord of the Kencyrath, who was forced into exile and supposedly died crossing the Ebonbane*
Torisen Black Lord: *Ganth's son*
Gerridon, Master of Knorth: *the arch-traitor who, some 3,000 years ago, sold himself to Perimal Darkling in return for immortality*
Jamethiel Dream-Weaver: *Gerridon's sister and consort*
Anthrobar: *the scholar who copied that portion of the Book Bound in Pale Leather which the Kencyrath used to reach Rathillien*

At the Res aB'tyrr

Tubain: *the innkeeper*
Abernia: *his wife*
Cleppetty: *the Widow Cleppetania, cook and housekeeper*
Rothan: *Tubain's nephew and heir*
Ghillie: *Rothan's younger cousin, the inn's hostler and musician*
Taniscent: *a dancer*
Kithra sen Tenzi: *a maid, formerly of the Skyrrman*
Sart Nine-toes: *a guard*

From Skyrr

Marplet sen Tenko: *keeper of the Skyrrmann inn*
Niggen: *his son*
Bortis: *a hill brigand in Marplet's pay, the sometime lover of Taniscent*
Harr sen Tenko: *the Skyrr representative on Taitastigon's governing council (the Five), Arribek sen Tenzi's political rival, Marplet's brother-in-law*
Arribek sen Tenzi: *the Archiem or ruler of Skyrr*

From Metalondar

King Sellik XXI
Prince Ozymardien: *Sellik's cousin, owner of Edor Thulig (the Tower of Demons)*
Thulig-sa: *Ozymardien's pet demon, used to guard Edor Thulig*

In the Kingdom of the Clouds

Prince Dandello: *heir to the Throne of Clouds*
Sparrow: *one of his attendents*

In the Temple District

Dalis-sar: *a Kendar drafted as the sun god of the New Pantheon; Men-dalis's father and Dally's foster-father*
Gorgo the Lugubrious: *once an Old Pantheon god of rain, now a New Pantheon god of lamentations.*
Loogan: *Gorgo's high priest*
Abarraden: *a fertility goddess of the Old Pantheon whose eyes Penari stole*

In the Thieves' Guild

Theocandi: *the Sirdan or lord of the Guild*
 Canden: *his grandson*
 Bane: *his pupil*
  Hangrell: *a would-be follower of Bane*
Penari: *Theocandi's older brother, Jame's master*
Men-dalis: *leader of the New Faction, Theocandi's rival*
 Dally: *his half-brother*
 The creeper: *his master spy*
Galishan: *master of the Tynnet Branching District, Melissand's lover*
 Darinby: *a journeyman*
 Raffing: *an apprentice*
 Scramp: *an apprentice from the Lower Town*
 Patches: *his sister*
Tane: *a former rival of Theocandi, the Shadow Thief's first victim*
Shadow Thief: *a temporarily detached soul used as a demon assassin by Theocandi*
Melissand: *a famous courtesan*

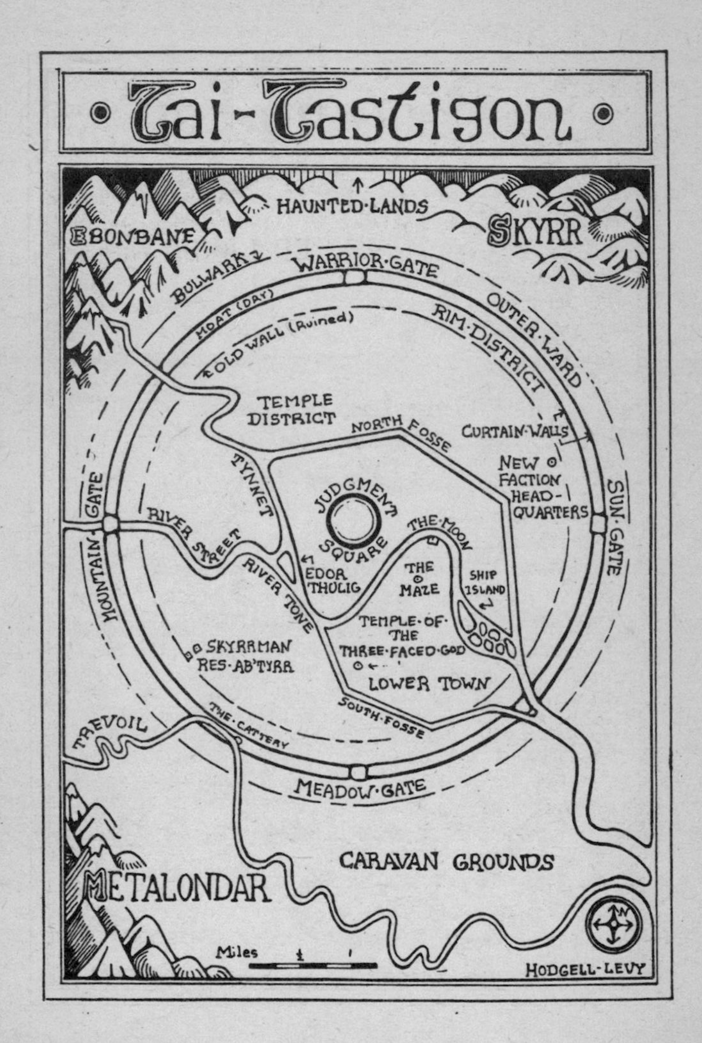

Tai-Tastigon
HAUNTED·LANDS
EBONBANE
SKYRR
BULWARK
WARRIOR·GATE
MOAT (DAY)
OUTER·WARD
OLD WALL (Ruined)
RIM·DISTRICT
TEMPLE DISTRICT
NORTH FOSSE
CURTAIN·WALLS
NEW FACTION HEAD-QUARTERS
TYNNET
JUDGMENT SQUARE
MOUNTAIN·GATE
RIVER STREET
SUN·GATE
THE·MOON
EDOR THULIG
RIVER TONE
THE MAZE
SHIP ISLAND
TEMPLE·OF·THE THREE·FACED·GOD
SKYRRMAN RES·AB'TYRR
LOWER TOWN
SOUTH·FOSSE
TREVOIL
THE·CATTERY
MEADOW·GATE
CARAVAN GROUNDS
METALONDAR
Miles
½
1
N
HODGELL-LEVY

The Eastern Lands
THE KEEP
THE HAUNTED LANDS
PERIMAL DARKLING
THE BARRIER
SKYRR
TAI-TASTIGON
THE EBONBANE
METALONDAR
EAST KENSHOLD
TAI-TAROSOLOFF (ruined)
EMMIS
BEN-AR CONFEDERATION
RIVER TONE
END-ISCAR
TONE MOUTH BAY
LEFY
TAI-ABENDNA
RIVER WEIR
TAI-WEIR
RIVER SONDRE
TAI-THAN (ruined)
TAI-SONDRE
THE EBONBANE
MILDARIEN PENINSULA
CAPE OF THE LOST
THE BAY OF BENITAR
FAR ISLES
N
Miles 50 100 150 200 250
LEVY-HODGELL

GOD STALK

BOOK I

TATTERS OF DUSK

CHAPTER 1

Out of the Haunted Lands

THE HILLS ROLLED up to the moon on slopes of wind-bent grass, crested, swept down into tangled brier shadows. Then up again and down, over and over until only aching muscles distinguished between rise and descent, climb and fall. A night bird flitted overhead. Jame paused to watch it, thinking enviously of wings. For a moment it showed clearly against the moon-silvered clouds, and then the wall of mountains to the west swallowed it. How near the Ebonbane seemed now that night had fallen. The range loomed over her, an immense presence filling half the sky, blotting out the stars. Two weeks of walking had at last brought her out of the Haunted Lands into these foothills, but that in itself was no help. Clean earth or not, this was still a wilderness. What she needed now was civilization—even a goatherd's hut—but something, and soon.

Thin, high voices called to each other behind her. Jame caught her breath, listening, counting. Seven. The haunts had found her trail again.

She tensed to run, then forced her weary muscles to relax. Flight would only weaken her. Besides, they seemed to be keeping their distance, an odd thing after so many days of close pursuit. Should she finally turn on them? They were well spread out, tempting targets for their wounded prey . . . ah, but what good would it do to kill something already dead? She would make one last bid for life, then, Jame thought as she started up the next slope. If only she could reach shelter before her strength gave out and they overtook her.

Then, suddenly, there was the city.

Jame stared down at it from the hilltop, hardly trusting her eyes. It lay well below her, cradled in the curve of the foothills as they turned to the southeast. Even from this distance, it looked immense. The outer circle of its double curtain wall was miles from edge to edge; the inner seemed to strain under the pressure of the buildings it contained. Gray and silent it stood between mountain and plain, a stone city that appeared in the cold moonlight to be more the work of nature than of man.

"Tai-tastigon!" Jame said softly.

Behind her, the wailing began again, then faded away. In the silence that followed, a cricket chirped tentatively, then another and another. The haunts had withdrawn. Not surprising with the city so near, Jame thought, rubbing her bandaged forearm. They had followed her far beyond their own territory as it was, drawn on by the blood-scent. She shivered, remembering that first encounter in the Haunted Lands before the burning keep. Dazed by fire and smoke, she had turned to find a dark figure standing behind her. For a joyful moment, she had thought it was Tori. Then she was down with the foul thing on top of her, its fetid breath in her face.

Jame looked at her hands, at the long, slim fingers and at the gloves hanging in shreds from them. Each ivory white nail lay flush with the skin now, its sharp point curving halfway over the fingertip. They looked almost normal, she thought bitterly. Trinity knew what the haunt had thought when those same nails, fully extended, had ripped the rotting flesh from its face.

Not that that would stop such a creature for long. Even if she had killed it, nothing stayed dead forever in the Haunted Lands, just as no one could live there unprotected without changing as the haunts, once ordinary men, had changed. That was the curse that the Kencyrath, Jame's own people, had let fall on the region when their main host had withdrawn from it long ago. No longer maintained by their will, the Barrier between Rathillien and the shadows beyond had weakened. Perimal Darkling, ancient of enemies, now gnawed at the edges of yet another world, poisoning the land, sucking health from the air. Still, it would have been much worse if a handful of Kencyr defenders had not remained, Jame thought; it was worse now that they were all dead. She, the youngest and last, was getting out none too soon.

Or perhaps not quite soon enough. Though the Haunted Lands lay behind her, she could feel their evil growing in her bandaged arm even now.

It had taken her some time to realize that the wound was infected. Injuries rarely took such a turn among her people, for as a rule Kencyrs either died outright or healed themselves quickly and well in the deep helplessness of *dwar* sleep. Jame had hardly slept at all in the past fortnight. Such endurance was another trait of her kind, but it also had its limits. She was perilously close to them now. There was some time left, however, enough, with luck, to find help in the city below . . . if the city could provide it. There it lay, Tai-tastigon the Great, just as the Scrollsman Anar, her old tutor, had once described it. Only one thing was different: nowhere below was there a trace of light—not a watch fire on the walls, not a street torch, not even the dim star of a candle in some indistinct window. All was dark, all was . . . dead?

Memory shook her. Two weeks ago she had climbed another hill, had found another mass of buildings spread out lightless, lifeless below her. The keep. Home. But not anymore. *He* had called her tainted, a thing without honor, and they had driven her out. But . . . but that had been years ago, she thought in confusion, one hand pressed against her forehead, against the ache of thwarted memory. Where had she been since then? What had happened to her? She couldn't remember. It was as if the frightened, outcast child she had been had run over the hills into the mist and walked out again half-grown to find . . . what? The dead.

But not all of them.

Abruptly, Jame swung down her pack and began to burrow through it, throwing its contents right and left until only three objects remained inside: a book wrapped in old linen, the shards of a sword with the hilt emblem defaced, and the small package that contained her father's ring, still on his finger. Tori, her twin brother, had not been among the slain. If he had escaped, as she desperately hoped, let him call her honorless when she put sword and ring in his hands for she would accept such a judgment from no one else. "No, my lord father, not even from you," she said in sudden defiance, looking back the way she had come.

Far to the north, green sheet lightning played across the face of the Barrier. A wind was rising there that would topple the keep's burnt-out towers and whirl their ashes southward—after her. Jame paled at the thought. Hastily, she shouldered the pack and set off down the hill toward the city, trying to fix her mind on the hope that Tori had come this way before her, but all the time tasting ashes on the wind.

A LONG, GENTLE SLOPE stretched from the edge of the hills to the first out-work, an earthen bulwark of alarming size but overgrown with feather weed and breeched with many deep fissures. On the other side, the land ran down at an increased angle to the foot of the outer curtain. To the right, a ramp made of rubble work ascended to a gate set high in the wall. This structure and the half-ruined bulwark suggested a city once heavily fortified but now secure enough to neglect its own outer defenses. Perhaps this confidence had been misplaced, Jame thought as she trudged up the ramp. Perhaps those proud towers seen first from the hill and now so close at hand were nothing but shells, gutted and empty, the home of rats and moldering bones. Anar had not said so, but then neither had he mentioned the unnerving lightlessness of the city. The gateway rose dark and vacant before her. Nothing moved there but the weeds between the paving stones as they nodded in the wind.

Inside, the land again dropped sharply away, this time into a broad, dry moat. A bridge spanned it. Jame crossed and found the city gates on the far side gaping open without a guard in sight. She entered the city.

At first the way seemed clear enough. The avenue was broad and straight, lined with high walls set with many iron-barred gates. These opened into private courtyards and gardens, all dark and deserted. For several blocks Jame walked along this open way, and then the road disappeared under the remains of a gatehouse set in an ancient wall. On the other side lay the great labyrinth of Tai-tastigon.

Within six turnings, Jame was utterly lost. The streets here were laid out like an architect's nightmare, swerving drunkenly back and forth, intersecting at odd angles, diving through tunnels under buildings and sometimes ending abruptly at the foot of a blank wall. Nor were the buildings more reassuring. Tall, narrow, pinched in aspect, they presented face after withdrawn face to the street, each one locked and sealed into itself, all indifferent to anything that passed before them.

Jame prowled on, more and more ill at ease. The wind whimpered about her, rattling grit in the gutter, setting a wooden sign to creaking fitfully overhead. There was still no trace of light, no sign of life; and yet the more she saw, the more convinced she became that this was no citadel of the dead. There were indications of age all around her, but little of decay. Occasionally she even saw a flowerpot on a high window ledge and once a banner restless in the wind, showing golden patterns to the moon. Clearly, if the people had left, it had been very recently; but if they were still here, they were deliberately keeping very quiet.

Or then again, perhaps not. As she rounded certain corners, the wind bore, or seemed to bear, not only dust and scraps of paper to dance about her feet, but snatches of sound. Several times she stopped short, straining to catch a thread of song or chant distorted by distance; and once far, far away, a voice laughed or cried, impossible to tell which, before it too dissolved into the rush of the wind. Was anyone really there? Something like the patter of small, running feet made her start more than once, and a dozen other lesser sounds niggled at her attention, but not one ever quite emerged from the harping of the wind. Nerves, Jame told herself at last, and went on.

Her thoughts kept returning to the city gate, now far behind, standing open to the Haunted Lands, to the coming storm. If only she had barred the way, but how—and against what? Her arm throbbed. Strength was leaving it, would soon leave her. It was foolish, of course, to think that a closed gate could shut out the wind; and as for the haunts, surely they had withdrawn. There was nothing else out there to follow her, she told herself firmly. Nothing. It was only because the pursuit had been so long, so bitter, that she felt even now that she was not free of it.

Then the sound of falling water reached her, and she went forward eagerly into a small square where a fountain played merrily by itself. This was the first clear running water Jame had seen in weeks. She welcomed its coolness as she scooped it up with one hand to drink, then splashed more on her heated face. Her arm also felt hot. Gingerly, she unwound the makeshift bandage, hissing with pain as skin came away with the cloth. Beneath, the teeth marks still showed clearly, white-rimmed against a darkness that had spread out from them like some kind of subcutaneous growth. Her fingers twitched briefly. There was still life in them, but it was no longer entirely her own. Jame swallowed, tasting panic. She had suddenly realized that if the healing process was delayed much longer, she might have to choose between her arm and the living death of a haunt. Oh for the chance to sleep, but not here, not out in the open. She must find shelter, must find . . . light?

Yes! Jame sprang up, staring. On the other side of the square, under a shuttered first story window, was a bright line. She crossed over to it and scratched on the windowframe. The light at once went out. All the other cracks, she now saw, were stuffed with rags from the inside. In fact, every nearby door and window was similarly secured. If this was true throughout the city, then the people were indeed here after all, but they were in hiding, barricaded inside their homes. Therefore, whatever it was that they feared, that all of Tai-tastigon feared, was out here in the streets—with her.

Jame stood very still for a moment, then cursed herself with soft vehemence. Fool, to have let her attention wander. For the first time since entering the city, she opened all six senses fully to it, and what they told her chilled the fever heat in her veins: she *was* being followed—no, stalked—and it had nothing to do with the Haunted Lands or the keep, whatever she had done there. No, this threat was new, and its source already far too close for comfort.

Then the pattering sound began again. Before, confused with distance, it had woven in and out of her hearing; now it was rapidly growing not so much louder as more distinct, like the approach of rain over hard ground. Jame couldn't tell from which street it came. When the noise seemed almost on top of her, out of the corner of her eye she glimpsed something white running close to the ground. She spun to face it, but already it had gone to earth. In the sudden silence, a pair of yellow, unblinking eyes stared at her from the deepest shadows of the street that led eastward.

A cat, Jame thought with relief.

She had actually taken a step toward the thing when she saw the cracks. They were coming toward her down the moonlit side of the roadway past the yellow eyes, shoving some cobbles apart, uprooting others. At first their progress was slow, almost tentative; but as they entered the square, the multitude of small cracks abruptly combined into five major fissures, which lunged forward, splitting everything in their path.

Jame backed up rapidly. She neither knew what would happen if one of those cracks opened under her feet nor particularly wanted to find out. Turning, she fled westward. The quick footsteps followed her, and after them came the crack of cloven stone.

She took refuge in a doorway. There were the eyes staring at her from across the street, and the lintel over her head split in two. She fled again. The labyrinth should have been her ally, but turn and twist as she would, she could not lose her pursuer.

Then, suddenly, the eyes were ahead of her.

Jame darted down a side street and skidded to a stop. Before her, in the shadow of an ornate gateway, lay a broad, inky pool of water that stretched from wall to wall. She was about to splash across it when something huge surfaced with an oily gurgle. For a second, moonlight glistened on a broad, leathery back, and then it was gone again.

From behind came the sound of splitting rock. It had almost overtaken her. Swallowing hard, Jame stepped back and waited. A moment later, as the water again broke open, she sprang forward, one foot coming down on the sleek back, the other on the far shore. The fissures, however, plunged straight into the pool. For a heartbeat nothing happened, and then the waters went mad. Spray lashed the walls, soaked Jame as she shrank back into the archway. For an instant, she thought she saw a huge, blind head rearing up, gape-jawed against the moon, and then it was gone. The water gurgled down into the cracks. The pool, it seemed, had been all of an inch deep.

Across the wet cobbles, Jame once again met the yellow stare. For a moment their eyes locked, then the thing turned and rapidly pattered away. It ran not on paws but on small fat hands like an infant's, and no shadow kept pace with it on the moon-washed pavement.

When it was out of sight, Jame turned to regard the gateway. It was set in a high wall, which extended a considerable distance in both directions and appeared to set off an entire district from the rest of the city. Beyond the gate, the shadows cast by overhanging buildings lay black and unbroken across the way until far ahead faint lights appeared suspended in the gloom. The air that breathed in Jame's face was heavy with incense. She hesitated, then drawn by those distant lights went warily forward into the shadows.

It was not as dark inside as she had expected. Here the buildings fit together like a gigantic puzzle-box, interlocking in the oddest ways and yet each standing by itself with no shared walls. Moonlight filtered down from above. This, in addition to her excellent night vision—the racial legacy of far dimmer worlds than Rathillien—brought Jame forward until she came to a street where light spheres hovered at intervals by the walls.

She had had to force herself to get this far. Out in the city, her sixth sense had merely tingled with the presence of those odd beings that had stalked her. Here, she flinched under waves of raw force that gained strength with each step that she took into the district. All around her, a hundred, a thousand hearts of power were beating feverishly in the night. Anger, defiance, and fear—gigantic, inhuman—crashed down on her rapidly weakening defenses. The ground and air seemed to shake. I'm a mouse caught in an earthquake, she thought in sudden panic, shying back against a wall. It vibrated under her hand. Those beings whose home this was had no thoughts to spare an uninvited guest. They could crush her flat and never know that they had killed. She must get out.

Jame fled back the way she had come, blindly, headlong.

Just when she felt that she must stop or die, the gate to the district appeared before her. Gasping, she threw herself down on the damp pavement beyond it. After a moment, she sat up unsteadily and leaned back against the wall, cradling her injured arm.

Fool, fool, fool, to spend her dwindling strength so recklessly. Soon she might call on it in her need and none would come. Already she had forfeited her sixth sense, temporarily deafened by the unheard cacophony that she had just escaped. Was this the way she always behaved, rushing about like a total lack-wit? What a cursed nuisance to have mislaid so much of her past . . . or to have had it taken from her.

"Damn," she said suddenly, lowering her head onto her arm.

She must be mad to joke about that. Lost, lost, all those years, her home, her family, almost herself. It wasn't the frightened child she remembered who must cope with this night-stricken city but the stranger that child had become. All she had now were shreds of her Kencyr heritage. Very well. She would cling to them and, idiot that she apparently was, force herself to be wise, to conserve her strength. She got carefully to her feet, then froze.

The wind was turning. Fitful gusts of it, foul with the breath of the Haunted Lands, brushed past her face, toyed with her hair. The gate to the north was open. Through it had come the outriders of the storm, but who could say what might follow in their wake? Jame shivered and turned away. Stepping over the still quiescent fissures, she walked hastily southward along the wall with the wind catching at her heels. She did not look back.

At length, the winding roads brought her to the edge of a vast open area where every street in the city seemed to meet. Jame walked out into it toward the large marble throne at its center, glad for such freedom after so many dark ways, glad even for the boisterous wind, which here had still more of the clean western mountains about it than the northern wastes. A flash of white caught her eye. A flurry of papers was bounding toward her across the pavement before the wind. All whirled past except one that plastered itself against her boot and refused to be shaken free. She peeled it off. It was covered with marks that she recognized as Kessic, the common-script of Rathillien. It read:

NURK LURKS IN DOORWAYS.

Who or what, Jame asked herself, is a nurk?

Curious to see if the other blowing papers carried the same message, she caught as many as she could. Some did, but most were as different as the languages in which they were written. After five minutes, Jame had collected specimens of Nessing, Globvenish, Skyrr-mir, and several other even more exotic tongues. She had also been warned away from streets, alleys, squares, rooftops, and even window ledges each with its own peculiar occupant. It seemed that no place out-of-doors was considered safe, although from what exactly she had no idea until one paper, covered with lines that looked like an incredibly complex knot hacked apart at random, announced quite simply:

BEWARE THE DEAD GODS.

The wind snatched the paper away and sent it tumbling off after the others. Jame let it go. Gods? Caught in the grip of the Kencyrath's own deity, it had never occurred to her that other people might think there was more than one. *Gods?* Was that what these Tastigons called such creatures as the baby-handed beast and the puddle-dwelling leviathan, for surely there was nothing else half so odd loose in the streets tonight. She began to laugh at their foolishness, and then stopped abruptly, catching her breath.

Another voice had cut across her own. For a moment Jame thought she had imagined it, but there it was again, faint with distance, screaming. Before the second cry died away, she was running toward the mouth of the street from which it had come. In her haste, she did not see the small dust devil that had momentarily caught up the last of the loose papers and was now traveling slowly after her across the flagstones, against the wind.

The narrow ways closed about her again. She paused at a

crossroads under a hollow crown of arches, unsure of which way to turn, then plunged into the right-hand street as the shriek sounded again, much closer this time. Broad ribbons floated from the upper windows here, silently braiding and unbraiding themselves in the air, masking the entrance to the alley until Jame was almost on top of it.

Inside, an old man was backed into a doorway, gripping his staff and snarling toothlessly at two young men who stalked him. As Jame entered the narrow lane, he shrieked again. There was no fear in that sound, only pure, frustrated rage, reinforced by the heavy stick, which he swung with unexpected vigor, causing his assailants to leap back. Youth and endurance, however, were on their side, as would be the final victory if only they were patient. Their aged prey knew this all too well, as his impotent fury showed. So did Jame.

Without thinking, she darted forward and, with a Senethar fire-leaping kick, neatly dropped the attacker on the old man's right. The second man spun about to find his friend crumpling to the ground. He didn't see Jame, who was already parallel to him in the shadows, poised to strike again. The blow never fell. As Jame paused in surprise, the man stared wildly past her, apparently at nothing, then turned and bolted. Another figure detached itself from a doorway farther down and fled after him, glancing back with a pale, horror-stricken face. Then both disappeared around the far corner.

Jame had actually started after them when a wave of dizziness struck her so suddenly that she thought the cobbles had lurched beneath her feet. When her mind steadied, she found herself clinging to a doorpost for support, with the old man gleefully hammering on her shoulder and repeatedly shrieking, "Run, you buggers, run!" almost in her ear.

"Eh, that was smart work," he said, turning to Jame at last, his cloudy eyes almost luminous with delight. "They'll think twice before bothering old Penari again. But who are you, boy? What's your name?"

"Jame . . . Jame Talissen," she stammered, automatically giving a name that, up to that moment, she had not remembered she possessed. "But I'm not a—"

"Talisman . . . Talisman," the old man repeated querulously. "Odd name, but then you Kennies are odd people. You are Kencyr, aren't you? Ah, you can't fool me, boy, not with that accent; but then it would never occur to you to try, would it?'' All his wrinkles suddenly slid into an expression of extreme craftiness. ''You're a Kencyr, and that means you're so honest it probably hurts. Come see me later, boy. I may have a job for you.'' And with that he scurried off down the alley, leaving Jame half-collapsed on the doorstep, weakly finishing the protest he had not waited to hear.

The effort brought dizziness surging back. Jame fought it desperately, feeling control begin to slip away. Images flashed through her mind: the darkened keep, faceless figures in the gloom, the snap of . . . twigs? no, of fingers breaking.

''No!''

It was her own voice, echoing sharply back from the opposite wall. Once again she huddled on a doorstep in a silent city, near the body of the man she had just struck down, far from the northern wastes and their vengeful ghosts. Trinity, another slip like that and she would be gone for good. Forget the past, she told herself; it could no longer hurt her without her consent, but the present, ah, the present could kill.

Somewhere, something was burning.

Jame's head jerked up. The alley was clouded with smoke. Ten feet away, the body of the fallen man had begun to burn.

Numb with shock, she watched as tongues of thin blue flame licked up around the still form. The skin on the back of the outflung hands blackened and fell away. The hair went up in a sudden blaze, revealing for a moment a beautiful heliotrope tattoo behind the left ear blooming in the heart of the flames. Garments, skin, muscle, and bone, each crumbled in turn as the black, greasy smoke rolled upward, teased a few feet above the body by the sudden presence of a small whirlwind in the passageway.

Then Jame saw that a large, indistinct form was taking shape before her, and without consciously willing it, she found herself on her feet again, pressing back into the shadow of the doorway. A vague head-shape on top of a long column of smoke swayed back and forth at the level of the shuttered second story windows. There was also the hint of a very long tail, defined only by a small cloud of soot that swept from one wall to the other, leaving dust devils in its wake. The creature fed slowly, sensuously, then belched and wandered off down the alley, leaving behind only ashes and a greasy spot on the cobbles.

At that point, it didn't matter to Jame if this was a god, an hallucination, or the local form of street sanitation; she was out of the alley the way she had come before the creature had turned the far corner.

Beyond, the wind stopped her. It had risen again and now came in sharp blasts that lifted the ribbonlike banners away from the walls and set them to warring in midair, one side of the street against the other. Ruby and amethyst veined with gold burned in the cold moonlight; silver flashed against emerald and turquoise. Then all colors dimmed. Tattered clouds, forerunners of the storm, had crossed the moon's bright disc. Behind them, rolling down from the north, from the keep, came the mighty storm-rack.

Jame stood shivering in the blast. She tasted ashes, felt them gray on her face, her lips, a death-mask for the living; but *Nothing stays dead forever,* whispered a thin voice in her mind. She dragged a jacket sleeve over her face, as though to wipe off the skin itself, and felt suddenly naked. Without her sixth sense, numbed as it still was, how could she know what even now might be searching the darkness for her? The gate to the north was open. Beyond the city, beyond the hills, among the toppled towers shadows were stirring, crawling, snuffling along the trail of blood and guilt. *He* would follow, for there were things he would want back from her, things he would come great distances to reclaim. Even now she thought she heard his tread. It shook the ground.

Dreams, all fever dreams, Jame told herself desperately, making one last effort to break free.

But the ground still shook.

It was as if something very heavy had been dropped some distance away. There was another vibration, and another and another, evenly timed, forming a slow, ponderous beat of increasing strength. It was getting closer. Then Jame saw a strange sight: all the banners down the street were tearing loose and coming toward her. They seemed, by the shape they had assumed, to be plastered against a huge form, but she could see nothing behind them. A fourth story balcony crumpled against the wall. Ribbons caught in the wreckage. Then, briefly, moonlight flooded the street once more, and Jame saw dust mushroom up around a large, circular patch on the ground. The stones beneath her lurched again. When the next footprint appeared, twenty feet closer, she saw the cobbles at its center sink a good three inches into the earth.

She was just thinking in a numb sort of way that whatever else this thing was, it was damned heavy, and wondering what, if anything, she should do about it, when the bone-jarring beat suddenly picked up speed and the dust surged toward her, leaving a trail of crushed stone in its wake.

"Oh, *no,*" said Jame out loud, and bolted.

She turned left at the crowned crossroads and raced on into the city through streets that echoed with her passing, around corners, under walkways, and finally over the river by a stone bridge, which gave a fleeting glimpse of steel gray water and boomed behind her as the other swept over it.

All too soon, the air began to burn in her lungs and her eyes to blur. She was running quite blindly, near the end of her strength, when her foot struck something and she fell. Training made her roll over outstretched arm and back rather than sprawl, but the pack jolted her spine cruelly, and as she came up again, her legs gave way. The thing must be almost on top of her. She scrambled to her feet, gasping and half sick, but driven by the pride of her warrior race to meet death honorably.

To her amazement, nothing happened.

The pursuer was indeed there, hardly five paces away, sweeping first one way and then the other as piles of debris, boards, and fragments of masonry all turned to powder under the heavy tread. It seemed to be pacing rapidly back and forth before her, turning with an abruptness that suggested bafflement rather than some elephantine attempt at cat-and-mouse, almost as if it had run into a barrier even more invisible than itself. Then, without warning, the huge pug marks turned and stalked back the way they had come.

Jame found herself face down on the pavement without distinctly remembering how she had gotten there. There were bits of broken cobblestones pressing into her cheek, and her knees hurt badly. That was it: the ground had seemed to leap up at her, and she had gone to meet it—knees first, by some miracle, not straight down like a diver. As her heart slowed, she sat up unsteadily and rested her forehead on her aching knees for a long moment. Then she looked up.

The street about her was strewn with rubble and lined by

empty, half-collapsed buildings. Moreover, the farther ahead she looked, the worse the general decay became, until the roadway itself at last wholly disappeared under the debris that had flaked away, scablike, from the rotting façades that overlooked it. It was like standing on the edge of some great urban sore, born of an unknown and unmentionable disease whose symptoms were ruin and desolation. Not only that, but the source of infection itself was close by . . . and it was still very, very active. Jame had thought her sixth sense numb, and perhaps it still was to such small teasings as she had experienced before, but this was altogether a different matter. She could feel the power flowing about her—cold, deep, impersonal—like a mighty river that wears the rocks in its bed to pebbles and eats away its banks. Now it began to find channels through her own mind. Unable to run, she turned at bay, at last drawing fully on that core of resistance bred into all her kind by long exposure to powers beyond their control. One by one, her mental barriers went up.

The effort left her spent, almost stripped of her will. As if in a dream, she felt herself rise and walk, drawn toward the source of the power even as its currents buffeted her. The mounds of earth and debris loomed before her. She began to climb, sneezing at the dust from boards that disintegrated under the weight of her hand. Splintered wood, chunks of plaster, a broken clay doll, and then she was on the crest, staring down at the temple.

It rose tall, stark and windowless above a sea of ruins. Those buildings farthest from it still contrived to stand; but the closer they came, the more total was their collapse, until those that had once stood beside the temple itself were now reduced to bulwarks of dust piled high against its gleaming flanks. Nothing entered that poisoned circle by choice. Bats sheared away when their flight brought them too close. Rats swarmed through the buildings beyond, but none descended into that greater desolation. Nothing moved there that the wind had not touched, and even it seemed to sicken and die in the presence of that sullen edifice, whose shadow alone had crumbled granite and reduced mighty oaken beams to a handful of dust.

The source of all this destruction, the temple itself, was not large, although it gave the impression of occupying a great deal of space. Jame knew instinctively that its interior would also seem immense, just as she knew, without ever having seen anything like it before, to whom it was dedicated.

This was a dwelling of the Three-Faced God. Torrigion, That-Which-Creates; Argentiel, That-Which-Preserves; Regonereth, That-Which-Destroys: names rarely spoken outloud and never all at the same time, names whose very mention could bring down a power that few men could now control and whose potential even for casual destruction was all too clearly shown by this graveyard of homes and hopes. This and none other was her own god, the one who had taken the Three People—Arrin-ken, Kendar, Highborn—and made them one against the enemy from outside, Perimal Darkling, Father of Shadows. For thirty millennia, three thousand years on Rathillien alone, the Kencyrath had fought the long retreat from world to world, down the Chain of Creation, waiting for their god to manifest himself through them in final battle. Chosen they were and proud, but bitter, too, over long delay, and angry that, the task being set, their god had apparently left them to accomplish it alone.

And finally, for what? A lie?

The power that flowed around Jame now, she suddenly realized, was different only in degree, not kind, from that which she had sensed in the puzzle-box district and again in the streets among the so-called dead gods of Tai-tastigon. Was there only one god, as all Kencyrs believed, or many? If the latter, then her people had been cruelly deceived for longer than one could bear to think. Had the Kencyrath been used? Very well. It had been created for use—but not to serve a lie. Honor would not endure it, nor would Jame. The mere suspicion of betrayal—now, when she most needed all the reassurance that her Kencyr heritage could give—acted on her like the deadliest of insults. Fists raised, wrists crossed, she silently challenged the temple before her: let it be war, then, until the truth was known. It was a mad gesture, as mad as to spurn the one place in this haunted city where she could be sure of help; but she was beyond reason now. Let it be war, or at least a clean end far from this seething abscess of divinity. As she turned away, darkness fell again and did not lift. The storm had broken at last.

MEN SAID AFTERWARD that no blacker night had ever fallen

on Tai-tastigon. The wind roared through the city, ripping up slates, clawing at the houses until those within feared that not a wall would stand until morning. They thought they heard voices wailing high above the earth, and those who peered out swore that they saw terrible things as the north wind, the demon wind, bore southward the nightmares of a dying land.

JAME STUMBLED ON, wrapped in feverish dreams, oblivious to the chaos around her. It seemed to her that she was back in the keep, a child again slipping silently through the hallways, looking for something. It was very late. If anyone saw her, there would be hard words in the morning, especially if *he* learned of it; but she was too anxious to care. It was important that she find . . . what? Her feet were very cold, and the night was very dark. Nearly everyone must be asleep. Jame hurried on, wondering why she was so nervous, wishing she could remember what she was searching for. Then, suddenly, she knew. There was a space beneath a certain staircase, a favorite hiding place, and she was not looking for something but someone. Tori. There were the stairs now. Why was she so afraid to look beneath them? It was what she had come for, wasn't it? A dark recess, and in it, yes, a dim figure.

"Tori?"

No response. Jame crouched lower, peering into the shadows, then jerked back with a hiss. Oh God, Anar. Pressed against the far wall, she fought down nausea. No time for that now. She must look in all the places that Tori might be, hoping desperately that he would be in none of them.

The dead were everywhere, huddled in doorways, crumpled in corners, stretched out on the floor as though trying to crawl to safety, tendons like taut wire along the bone, bones held together with a bit of skin and desiccated flesh. Jame made herself look into every face that sword, fire, and decay had left recognizable. She knew them all but never found the one she dreaded most to see. But if Tori wasn't here, where was he? Once Anar had told her that if she walked long enough to the south, she would come to another sort of land where the wind smelled sweet and the soil was untainted. Tori had heard that story, too. Was that where she would have to go to find him?

She was still looking for Tori; but now there was a pack heavy on her back and she was trying to find her way out of the keep. Something had frightened her—no, she had done something terrible, and now she must get away. But where was she? The passages wound on and on, twisting, turning, leading nowhere. Had she lost her way? No, don't even think that. Keep going keep going keep going . . .

There was someone walking behind her.

You were gone so long child; now will you leave us again so soon? It was Anar's voice, faintly mocking, hardly more than a whisper.

What? No word for your old tutor? Look at me, child.

She would not. No one at the keep had been kinder to her, but never again did she want to see that face from the dark of the recess.

Then she heard other voices echoing in the hallway behind her. At first they were only a soft-textured murmur, one sound running into another, but then strands began to separate. An accent here, an inflection there . . . Jame felt her heart lurch. They were all coming. Shambling feet scraped on the floor, rotten clothing ripped as bodies stumbled against the rough stone walls, but the voices that called to her were sweet and wheedling.

Where are you going, child? Come back to us. We love you.

But once they had let her go easily enough, Jame thought bitterly. *He* had said that she was tainted, a thing without honor, and they had let him drive her out into the wilderness. Now they said that they wanted her back. It was a lie, of course, but to what purpose? Then she knew. They wanted her to hesitate, to delay because *he* was coming, too, coming to get her, coming to make her pay for what she had done.

She heard his footsteps overhead.

I must run, Jame thought wildly, and found that she could not move. The crash of iron boots grew louder. He was coming down the stairs from the battlements.

"It's a dream, all a dream!" she cried out loud in helpless protest.

For an instant, the city street again lay before her, with a metal sign high overhead banging against the wall. Then it faded into the keep's upper corridor. A black figure strode down the hall toward her, brushing aside the indistinct crowd that swarmed there, crumbling flesh from bone with his touch. Three broken arrows still nailed the gray jacket to his chest. His mutilated hand reached for her.

Child of Darkness! The voice was the sound of bones grinding, cracking. *Where is my sword? Where are my . . .*

"FATHER!"

The hated word stopped him.

Nothing stays dead forever: but "I gave you fire!" she cried at him, at them all. "Fire and final rites, such as I could manage. Even when your hands twitched in my grasp. Even when I saw your dead eyes open. Did you *want* to become haunts?"

They stared at her. She could read nothing in their faces. Then they were covered with ash. They were falling apart.

"Nooo!" she wailed, clutching at them, seeing her childhood again in flames.

The wind whirled them away.

Her legs betrayed her, and she went down, too spent to remember her bad arm until she tried to break her fall with it. Pain dazed her, spiraled her senses toward darkness. "Don't go!" she heard someone cry. "Don't leave me alone, not again!" Yes, it was her voice, but this time no one answered. For a moment she clung to the image of that empty hallway, the last of her old home that she would ever see. Then it too slipped away.

The cobbles beneath her hand were hard and cold, glazed with ice from the bitter rain that had begun to fall. She lifted her face to it. It seemed to wash away everything—icy street, shuttered windows, even, at last, itself. Jame let them all go. Numbly, like a sleepwalker, she rose and stumbled on, beyond guilt and grief at last, moving blindly forward until the night swallowed all.

CHAPTER 2

The House of Luck-Bringers

THE FIRST THING Jame saw upon opening her eyes was the cat. It was rather hard to overlook, being very large, very close and, in fact, very solidly sitting on her chest. They stared at each other. It yawned, showing white teeth and a great expanse of pink ribbed gullet, then snuggled down with its nose tucked under her chin and one forefoot resting firmly in the hollow at the base of her throat. This made it somewhat hard to breathe. Jame raised her hand to shift the paw, then froze, staring at her arm. It was not only still there but almost healed, with nothing but white scars to mark the injuries that might well have cost her both limb and life. *Dwar* sleep had come in time after all.

For a moment, sheer relief made her almost dizzy. Then she began to wonder where she was and how she had gotten there.

From what Jame could see, she was lying on a cot in a small room, at the other end of which was a narrow doorway blazing like the mouth of a furnace with the level rays of the rising sun. The light made her eyes ache. She shut them for a moment, then craned backward until above and behind her a window framed with ivy leaves came into sight. Toward one edge, suddenly appearing in silhouette as a gust of wind pushed back the greenery, were several small stone heads, all frozen in fits of mad laughter.

That stirred a memory.

Jame relaxed, trying to remember what had happened after her awakening in the rain. She had slept again and dreamed that she was walking—well, clearly she had been, although out of all that time only one image remained: the façade of a house covered with small figures carved in full relief that gamboled up the walls, clustered around the windows, and clung together under the eaves, all looking like deformed children, all making gestures that bordered on the obscene. The door had opened at her touch. And beyond it? Think. Yes, now bits of it came back: a room full of faces, of eyes wide with fear staring at her. After that, it had been like sinking into deep water, alone at first but then the familiar forms had begun to slip past in the darkness, faces, hands, hair, touching, clinging, dragging her down beyond light, beyond life . . .

The beams overhead had white roses painted on them against a cerulean blue ground. They were not part of any nightmare, past or present. Why then was it so hard to breathe?

Oh, you fool, thought Jame. It's that damn cat.

She was trying to dislodge the beast, who only responded with a loud purr, when a woman darted into the room crying, "Boo, you great lump!" and heaved it off her chest onto the floor, rump first.

"Oh, the wretch!" the newcomer exclaimed, shoving the offended feline out of the room. "I'm only gone a minute, a few seconds, and he comes sneaking in. You haven't been smothered, have you? I mean, it would be a bit much after surviving the Feast of Dead Gods to be done in by Mistress Abernia's pet tabby, wouldn't it? I'm Taniscent, by the way—Tanis to my friends." She perched on the edge of the cot and leaned forward eagerly. "Well? Don't you want to ask where you are?"

"I seem to remember lots of tables and men with ale mugs," said Jame slowly. "Everyone stopped drinking when I came in, though. Is this an inn of some sort?"

"Yes, the Res aB'tyrr—that is, the House of Luck-Bringers—and as for stopping, aiee! Some of our patrons were like to drop dead of fright when you opened that door, and the rest nearly jumped out the windows. If you hadn't gone down in a heap a moment later, there wouldn't have been a full bladder in the house."

"I'm sorry I broke up your party. But what about my arm?"

"Oh, that was a proper mess," said Taniscent with relish. "The healer said it would have to be amputated—bitten off, preferably, if we could find someone with a suitably tame demon—but while Tubain was trying to make up his mind, it began to mend. Damnest thing he'd ever seen, the healer said; but then he'd never tended a Kencyr before. Thirteen days it took. Yes, you've been asleep that long."

Jame's startled reaction to this was cut short by the appearance of a large, dark form in the doorway. After several moments of maneuvering, it came edging sideways over the threshold and turned into a big-bellied, bald-headed man.

"Every year those frames get narrower," he said cheerfully. "So you're with us again. We'd begun to worry. I'm Tubain of Endiscar, your host. Be welcome to this house and peace be yours therein."

"Jame of the Kencyrath. Honor be to you and to your halls."

"Kencyr! Well, now, so the healer was right. We don't see many of your kind here these days except for those bound for East Kenshold or west over the Ebonbane. Where did you come from? Where are your people?"

"My people are dead." The words came flatly now, a mere statement of fact. Already the nightmare images were fading and so, she suddenly realized, was the room about her. I'm slipping again, she thought with a flicker of panic, and fixed her attention on Tubain's broad, bland face. "I came from the north."

"No one comes from that direction," the face said decisively. "The fever must have confused you. You must have come from East Kenshold. On this side of the mountains, there's nowhere else . . ." nowhere . . . nowhere . . . nowhere . . . a word echoing in the distance, then dying away. Jame slept again.

IT WAS NOT A CAT that woke her the second time but a great clatter. She opened her eyes just in time to see Taniscent scoop a small bronze mirror off the floor, toss it on the opposite cot, and run out in a flurry of bright shawls, not noticing that her new roommate was awake. Jame stared after her. When they had first met that morning, she had assumed that Tanis was at least in her thirties, but how could the girl who had just rushed out of the room be more than nineteen? Perhaps *dwar* sleep had dulled her senses . . . or perhaps not. After all, she had accepted far stranger things without question on that first night. But there would be time for answers later; now what she wanted was food, for the long healing process had left her desperately hungry.

She sat up carefully, then swung her feet to the floor and, after several tries, succeeded in standing up. There, that wasn't so difficult. With fresh confidence, she took a step toward the door, only to discover that the folds of her overgrown nightgown were snugly twisted around her legs. She stood there swaying for a moment, then lost her balance altogether and came tumbling down on the opposite cot.

A face stared up at her from the mirror beside her hand. Was that really what she looked like, all sharp lines and huge, silver-gray eyes? Certainly, no one would ever call those features beautiful, Jame thought ruefully; but were they really enough like a boy's to have fooled that old man in the alley? Well, maybe, with all that long black hair out of sight under a cap. It was a very young face, and a defiant one, she thought with an odd sense of detachment, but frightened too. And those extraordinary eyes . . . what memories lived in them that she could not share? Stranger, where have you been, she asked silently. What have you seen? The thin lips locked in their secrets.

"Ahh!" said Jame in sudden disgust, tossing away the mirror. Fool, to be obsessed with a past she couldn't even remember. But all that was behind her now. A new life had begun, and with it came at least the prospect of food. Spurred on by her growing hunger, she soon managed to untangle the gown and then set off gamely for the door.

Beside it, crouching darkly in a corner beneath a wall vase full of flowers, was her knapsack.

The sight brought Jame up short. It seemed to have been

waiting for her, patiently, dull malignancy gathering in its dusty folds. I haven't outrun anything, or left anything behind, she thought bitterly. For two weeks she had carried the relics of her past, known and unknown, on her back like a deformity. Even now they were part of her, and so were those lost years, whatever terrors they might have contained. The latter were beyond her reach now, but as for the pack and its contents, she must find a safe place to hide them as soon as possible. Then, forcibly putting all of this out of her mind, Jame lifted the hem of her gown and unsteadily left the room.

Outside, an open gallery stretched some ten paces in either direction, connecting the north and south wings of the inn. Below, one story down, was a courtyard bounded on the far side by a stout wall. From below came the pungent odor of manure and the sound of hooves shifting on straw, mingled with a more distant clatter of pots and a sudden whiff of something cooking. Whatever the latter was, it smelled delicious. Jame was trying to locate the source when there was a crash somewhere nearby, closely followed by an angry shout. A tall, aproned woman emerged from a side door to the left holding a piebald cat at arms' length, dropped it on the pavement and stalked back inside.

Ah, the kitchen. Now, how to get down to it?

At the northern end of the gallery she found a broad flight of stairs angling around the sides of a square well. Trailing skirt gathered up in her hands, Jame cautiously started down the steps. All went well at first, but halfway to the bottom, her foot caught in the hem and she found herself falling. Instinctively, she curled into a ball and finished her descent in this manner, in no immediate danger of breaking anything but under the distinct impression that she was renewing every bruise she had ever had in her life.

She was stretched out on the tiles at the bottom gathering her wits and admiring, in a rather dazed way, the carved rafters high above, when a head blocked her view and demanded, "Are you *quite* finished?"

"Y-yes, mistress," said Jame, staring up into the hard, bright eyes of the woman from the courtyard. "I ran out of steps."

"In well-regulated households," the irate voice said, "invalids do not come casually tumbling downstairs. And I'm the Widow Cleppetania, cook and housekeeper . . . not the mistress."

"And I'm Jame of the Kencyrath," the other replied rather sharply, "not an invalid."

The widow snorted. "I'll believe that when I see you stand up."

Jame did, very slowly and painfully, clutching at the night-gown as it tried to slip off both shoulders simultaneously.

"Humph!" said the widow, not quite so harshly. "If you can walk, you can eat. Come along, young lady, and be fed."

Jame followed her into the kitchen, a high-vaulted room with three fireplaces, two of which had large kettles hanging on rachycrokes over the flames. The one on Jame's right as she entered contained boiling water, and behind it she saw a tiny scullery tucked under the stairs. The pot to her left, which hung between the kitchen and the main hall, gave off the marvelous odor that had drawn her from the gallery. The widow gestured her to a seat on the raised hearth of the third fireplace, whose back was to the courtyard. Jame sat down beside it, grateful for the warmth of its flames, while the widow ladled broth into a bowl.

"Watch your mouth," she said, giving her the steaming porringer. "It's hot."

Jame ate, too hungry to be careful or even to mind the burned tongue that her first taste gave her, while the widow finished sweeping together the remains of a dish and then returned to the bustard, which she had been preparing on the central table. The kitchen filled with the fragrance of thyme, basil, and rosemary. She was dicing figs when Jame finally put the bowl aside, scraped clean.

"Cleppetania . . ."

"Call me Cleppetty," said the widow, reaching for a beaker of white wine. "Everyone else does."

"Cleppetty, what is the Feast of Dead Gods?"

"Ha!" She started to flourish the vessel, remembered just in time that it was nearly full, and put it down with a thump. "I told Tubain that only ignorance or imbecility could have brought anyone out on such a night. The Feast of Dead Gods is what I expect you narrowly missed becoming. Once a year, on Autumn's Eve, all the gods who've lost or outlived their worshippers come back from wherever it is they've been and spend the night wandering the streets. Some are harmless enough, but most are hungry and out hunting for sacrifices—which is fine if they happen to relish potted begonias, but not so good if their people were fools enough to raise them on baby's blood or virgin's hearts. It's said they can't enter any building without an invitation, but most Tastigons seal up their windows and doors on that night just to be sure. Not Tubain, though; it wouldn't be hospitable, he says."

She snorted, reached for a spoon, and began to stir the mixture so energetically that part of it flew out of the bowl. "It would have served him right if something big, red, and ravenous had strolled in that night instead of you. That man and his hospitality! We would have been ruined years ago if it were not for Mistress Abernia."

While she had been speaking, the piebald cat had furtively slipped back into the kitchen and was now sitting beside Jame, cleaning itself. Another cat joined it, and then Boo. Jame watched them, digesting this information, while the widow seized the bustard and began to cram stuffing into it as enthusiastically as if it were a defunct enemy being dealt the final insult.

"Cleppetty . . ." she said at last, very slowly. "If there are so many dead gods here, how many live ones are there?"

"Why, hundreds, thousands." The widow stared at her over the carcass. "Bless you, child, what island of the moon did you come from not to know that every god in the Eastern Lands has a temple here? Tai-tastigon is the holy city of them all. That's why things are so strange here sometimes: we're not just god-ridden, we're overrun. Everyone knows that except, apparently, you. Now, is there any other common knowledge I can astound you with?"

Jame considered this for so long that the widow, after a moment's wait, went back to her bird. There were any number of questions she would have liked to ask about these gods, but she hardly knew how to frame them and was, moreover, rather afraid of the answers she might get. Better let them wait, she decided, as Cleppetty maneuvered the bustard onto a gridiron and started toward the fire with it, her back arched against the strain.

"There is one thing," she said, getting out of the way as

the woman bent to fit the iron into its fireside slots. "About Taniscent . . ."

The widow froze, one side still unsecured. "What about her?"

The sharpness of her tone startled Jame. "Well," she said hesitantly, "this morning I could have sworn that she was about thirty years old. But now, just a few minutes ago . . ."

Cleppetty dropped the rack. The bustard plunged into the fire in a fountain of sparks as cats scattered in all directions (except for Boo, who only tucked in his paws), and the widow dashed out the door shouting, "Tanis, you damn fool!" Jame heard her thunder up the stairs and along the gallery as she tried to rescue the bird from the flames. She was still trying when Cleppetty stalked back into the kitchen, seized a pair of tongs, and rolled the singed fowl out onto the hearth. She regarded it balefully for a moment, then turned sharply to Jame.

"There's a drug called Dragon's Blood," she said in a hard voice. "It temporarily restores youth—or the illusion of it—but the more often you take it the more you need, and the faster you age between times. Tanis started using it four years ago when she turned twenty and thought that age was ruining her dancing. Now she takes it because of that worthless lover of hers, who I suppose she's with now. If this goes on much longer, she'll destroy herself. I'm telling you this because we care for each other here, and that poor, foolish child needs all the help she can get. Remember that."

Then they heard heavy feet stamping into the hall, and someone shouted for food.

"Customers already!" Cleppetty surveyed the kitchen with despair, taking in the burnt bustard on the hearth, the mound of broken crockery still on the floor, and the piebald cat on a high shelf, peering warily around a china plate that had already begun to teeter ominously.

"What an afternoon . . . for you too, now that I think of it. Back to bed with you and let me salvage what I can of the day; and the next time you come downstairs," she shouted after Jame as she started carefully up the steps, "*please* do it the regular way."

AFTER THAT, Jame recovered rapidly. In a few days, she was

running all over the inn, as bright-eyed with curiosity as a cat; but for all her pleasure at finding herself in a new, intriguing situation, she did not forget what brought her to this city in the first place. Now that she had seen Tai-tastigon, however, she realized that it would be virtually impossible to find news of her brother in so large and complex a place. Anyway, if Tori had come this way, he probably hadn't stayed here long, not with the Riverland—the home of the Kencyrath on Rathillien—waiting on the other side of the Ebonbane. She would have to follow her brother there, Jame decided, if they were ever to meet again on this side of the pyre.

"But how do I get out of the Eastern Lands?" she asked Cleppetty.

"Just now," said the widow, "you don't. The mountain passes snowed in a week ago and won't clear again until the spring."

"But surely there are other routes."

"Once, yes. Folk used to go overland around the Ebonbane's southern toe, but now the Mildarien Peninsula is infested with haunts—and worse. As for the sea lanes, an early storm season has closed them, too. Every year we get more and more sealed off. Someday the routes westward will disappear altogether, but in the meantime if you meant this to be a short visit, your timing's as skewed as your sense of direction."

Jame's first impulse was to set out anyway—southward, perhaps, in search of a ship willing to dare the Cape of the Lost in storm season. The psychic attraction that held the Kencyrath together tugged at her. Once she would have yielded to its pull without a second thought, but now she found herself hesitating. After all, her full strength had not yet returned, and she must not foolishly endanger the ring and shattered sword, her brother's lost birthright, which she would be carrying to him. No, she must wait either until she was completely fit again or spring made travel less hazardous. After all, what were a few more weeks or possibly even months when it had taken her years to fight her way back to that terrible homecoming at the keep? The world of her people would open up before her soon enough, she told herself. Her task now was to prepare herself for it.

Meanwhile, life at the inn whirled along, each day repeating the basic patterns and yet improvising on them endlessly. Cleppetty set the pace. Every morning she started out by scrubbing the kitchen, the tiles of the great hall, and the floor of the side room where those too drunk to go home the night before had been dragged. Then there was the marketing, then the cooking, which kept her in the kitchen all afternoon. By early evening, the central cauldron was full of soup or stew and all available surfaces were covered with brie tart, humble, galantine, and eel pie, haslet for the hunters, leek dishes for the lustful as well as meat laid out ready for the spit and an odd assortment of other viands depending on who was in town for what religious festival. Then the customers began to arrive. From early evening until the late watches of the night, the inn filled with clatter, song, and ceaseless shouts for wine. Every third day, the widow baked bread, spreading flour all over the north wing with the vigor of her kneading. Every seventh day she did the wash.

As soon as Jame was strong enough, she began to help whenever Cleppetty and the others would let her. At first, this was mainly in the kitchen. Cleppetty had a minor talent for theurgy, and, with her book of common household charms, could do a number of handy things such as kindling a fire with its own ashes, making broken china whole, and raising bread in half the normal time. At the end of Jame's second active week at the inn, she suddenly found the book thrust into her hands.

"Now let's see you try," the widow said, plopping a lump of unleavened dough down on the table before her.

Jame hesitated. Many of her people had such talents if not far greater ones, but those that did were feared and often compelled to enter the priesthood. Apprehensively, she recited the charm. It usually took Cleppetty half an hour to ready her bread for the oven; Jame's rose in five minutes. When the widow sliced into the baked loaf, however, they discovered that its sudden expansion had been due to the growth of rudimentary internal organs.

That was the end of Jame's apprenticeship in the kitchen. From then on, she helped with the laundry, washed dishes, and assisted in the great hall every night.

Tai-tastigon, by daylight, was a quiet place as far as she could tell; but as dusk crept through the streets, strange new sounds and smells took root in the shadows and grew. As she darted between the tables under the three great chandeliers, Jame often heard the distant clamor of some religious festival or glimpsed the bizarre costumes and gilded faces of the celebrants themselves as they entered the Res aB'tyrr to drink a noggin to luck before some important rite. Once they brought with them a silent woman clad only in golden ornaments. Ghillie, the hostler, pointed her out to Jame, whispering that she was to be their sacrifice. Jame thought he was joking until she met the woman's haunted eyes across the table.

And so the days passed. The people at the inn continued to treat her well. Tubain was always courteous as, indeed, he was to all who entered his establishment. Cleppetty remained brusque but not unkind. Rothan, Tubain's nephew, was friendly enough but rather pompous as befitted the inkeeper's heir. More observant or less tactful than the others, Rothan's young cousin Ghillie made the mistake at first of teasing Jame about her hands, and got the scare of his life when she nearly went for his throat. Luckily, he was a light-headed, good-natured boy and soon forgot the entire episode. As for Tanis, she was delighted to have a roommate patient enough to listen to the tale of the endless fluctuations in her affair with Bortis, a handsome, arrogant bandit, come down from the hills to winter in the city.

The only member of the household whom Jame did not come to know was Mistress Abernia. Tubain's wife never left her own chambers in the south wing. Jame heard her from time to time shrilly berating her husband for some outrageous piece of generosity or other, but never saw more of her than a shadow cast on a closed curtain, gesticulating wildly. No one would (or perhaps could) tell her why Tubain's wife lived in such seclusion.

Nor was this the Res aB'tyrr's only mystery. Of more pressing concern was its relationship with the establishment across the square, an inn called the Skyrrman, run by a native of the Tenko canton of Skyrr named Marplet. Ever since her arrival, Jame had been puzzled by a series of small, unpleasant events at Tubain's hostelry. One morning, for example, she came down to find Rothan and Ghillie grimly scraping excrement out of the mouths of the b'tyrr figures on the front wall. Another day, someone tossed a sealed jug over the wall into the inner courtyard where it shattered, spraying Cleppetty's newly washed sheets with urine. It didn't occur to Jame to connect these events with the Skyrrman, however, until one afternoon something flew through the window and landed in a heap on the table that she was scrubbing. It was the piebald cat. Patches of its fur had been burned off and three of its legs were broken as well as its neck. Then Jame heard Marplet's household rowdies out in the square, laughing.

A black rage rose in her. She dropped her washrag and sprinted for the door, only to be jerked back on her heels as Cleppetty grabbed her collar from behind.

Half-strangled, she heard the widow's harsh, angry breath in her ear and, through clearing eyes, saw Rothan and Ghillie on the other side of the room, both obviously furious but doing their best to ignore the taunts now being shouted in the square. Tubain had simply disappeared into the cellar. Then the voices outside faded into the distance, and Cleppetty let her go.

"Why?" she demanded hoarsely, one hand on her bruised throat. "We should all have gone after them. Why didn't we?"

"Child, if you have any friendship for us at all," said the widow, "don't ask . . . and above all, don't interfere." With that, she turned and stalked back into the kitchen.

Jame stared after her. Bound by the Kencyr law of hospitality, she must obey; by that same law, however, the honor of the household had become her own, to defend or forfeit. But how could she defend what she didn't understand? The sudden passivity of her new friends, whom she didn't believe to be cowards (except, perhaps, for Tubain), baffled and unnerved her. And that wasn't the worst of it, either. Cleppetty and the others knew exactly what was going on, Jame realized suddenly with growing dismay, and had probably known since well before her arrival. But they hadn't told her. Why? Because, for all their friendliness, they still didn't trust her. Because she was an outsider. Again.

At first, she pretended that it didn't matter. After all, these people had a right to their secrets and no reason as yet to trust her with any of them. But as the days passed and Marplet's growing, unexplained harassment brought the others closer together in their passive resistance, she felt her own exclusion more and more. It reminded her all too vividly of life at the keep. For the first time, she realized how much being a full member of this household mattered to her, and how much she needed it.

I've got to belong someplace, she said to herself one day, and if not here, where?

She was lying on the warm tiles of the north wing roof, four stories up, looking out over the city. Ivory spires rose in the distance, tipped with light as the sun began its slow tumble down the far side of the Ebonbane. Night always fell quickly in Tai-tastigon, and with its fall the city sprang to life. Jame longed to be down in those convoluted streets, sniffing out their secrets. She had not forgotten the subtle lure of the maze, much less the gods of Tai-tastigon and the challenge she had issued because of them before her own temple. But Tubain had requested that she not leave the inn at all. He seemed to think that if she ever did, she would become instantly and irretrievably lost. Regarding the darkening tangle of streets below, Jame thought wryly that he might well be right; but the day might come when she would have to risk it. As much as she liked these people, she couldn't stay here indefinitely on mere sufferance. If matters didn't improve soon, she would have to slip the silken collar of Tubain's concern and disappear into the night, as alone and friendless as she had come.

Below, someone made a remarkable noise, half-gurgle, half-squeak. Looking down, Jame saw Tubain at the rail outside Taniscent's room, staring up at her. There was so much horror in his expression that she promptly slithered down the tiles, jumped to the second story roof and, catching the eaves, swung down to the gallery floor beside him.

"What's wrong?" she demanded, sudden eagerness sharpening her voice. Was he at last going to take her into his confidence?

"You could have broken your neck!" the innkeeper said, almost incoherent with agitation. "What were you *doing* up there?"

"Oh." Damn. "I was looking at the city. Why would anyone have laid out the streets in such an insane jumble?"

"Well," said Tubain, making an obvious attempt to regain

his composure, "it's partly intentional and partly not. You see, we're rather prone to disasters here, natural and otherwise. Old buildings are always getting knocked down, washed away, or trampled flat, and new ones rise wherever there's room. But that's the least of it. Ever since Tai-tastigon was built back in the days of the Old Empire, folks in these parts have loved puzzles. Once their whole culture was built on them, social conventions and all, and the highest form of art was the labyrinth. Of course, things have changed a lot here since then, but some folk still hold to the old ways. For example, when the Sirdan Theocandi of the Thieves' Guild came to power, he reconstructed part of the Palace into a perfect maze; and old Penari lives in the heart of one so complex that its own architect lost his way trying to get out and was never seen again."

That latter name made Jame start. "This Penari . . . who is he?"

"Why," said Tubain, surprised, "the greatest thief in the history of Tai-tastigon, which is as much to say in the world, and the only man ever to know all the streets of the city. The Temple District is his manor, but he's not very active or much seen these days. Where did *you* hear of him?"

Jame hesitated, then told the innkeeper about the incident in the alley. Tubain's eyes grew wide as he listened.

"For fifty-six years," he said at last, "ever since that man stole the Eye of Abarraden under circumstances that weren't just difficult, mind you, but physically impossible, every thief in the guild has dreamed of becoming his apprentice. For fifty-six years! And on your first night in the city, he makes you the offer. By all the gods, *that* will make some faces red at the Palace, the Sirdan's not the least."

"Do you mean to say," said Jame, quite horrified, "that he was offering to teach me how to *steal?*"

"Why, what else, and why not? Nearly everyone in Tai-tastigon does or has or wants to. It's fine work, I hear, if you can get a good master and, of course, don't get caught." At that moment Cleppetty called him from the kitchen door. He excused himself and trotted off, saying, "Penari, eh?" out loud to himself. "Just think of that!"

Jame did, long and seriously over the following days.

Meanwhile, she continued to room with Taniscent, but began to find this arrangement increasingly unpleasant. Soon after her arrival, Cleppetty had wrung a promise out of the dancer never to use Dragon's Blood again. This was a relief of sorts, but it didn't save Jame from the days of brittle smiles that followed nor the nights of hysterical weeping when it became clear with the wearing off of the drug that Tanis had paid all too heavily for those brief returns to her lost youth. On the other hand, Jame was keenly aware that she herself was not the most desirable of chamber-fellows; her own sleep still brought her dreadful shapes, and she would often wake with a start, unsure if the voice she had heard cry out was her own. On such nights she would take a blanket and go up to the fourth story solar to sleep, if she could, and often to wake in the cold dawn with Boo snuggled warmly against her.

This large, empty loft soon became her refuge from the tensions of life at the inn. As a rule, no one bothered her there, since the whole area was much too open to serve either for storage or guests. Here she at last found a hiding place for her pack, behind some loose stones in one corner, and also the necessary open space to experiment with the Senethar training patterns.

She often wondered who had taught them to her. When her brother Tori had first begun to learn the arts of war all those years ago at the keep, she had begged to be taught them, too. Her plea had been flatly refused. And yet now the knowledge was there, as she had discovered in the Haunted Lands. It was wonderful suddenly to have the benefit of such training, but frightening too not to know where it had come from or what other skills she might have brought out of those lost years.

The incident with the bread had shaken her badly. She was different, she always had been, Jame thought, staring blindly at her hands, and her father had not been able to accept it. *Shanir, god-spawn, unclean, unclean* . . . words out of the past, shouted at her from the keep gate. That had been soon after her nails had first worked their way to the surface. How her fingertips had itched, and what a relief it had been (as well as a surprise) when the sharp points at last broke through the skin. Nail-less until then, unlike everyone else at the keep, she had been proud of her new acquisitions. The horror and disgust of the others had bewildered her. Jame realized now that they had been afraid, frightened of what she was, of what she might become, although no one had ever made it clear to her exactly what that was. Would her people always react to her this way? If so, what sort of a fool was she to long for them, for the unhappy home she had lost? A Kencyr fool. Well, now she had six months to learn if she could make a life for herself apart from the Kencyrath.

But days passed, and Jame remained an outsider at the Res aB'tyrr although virtually a prisoner within its walls. As this confinement became more and more burdensome, she spent longer periods in the loft, working eventually with the Senetha dance patterns that corresponded to the four Senethar types of combat, discovering as she went which ones she knew. Earth moving, fire leaping, water flowing, wind blowing . . . the second was still almost beyond her in her weakened state, and the fourth (assuming she knew it all) quite impossible, but it pleased her to at least have made a start. So she kept pushing at the limits of her knowledge and endurance, both to expand them and, often, simply to wear herself out. Exhaustion made sleep easier and certain thoughts less gnawing.

One morning a few days after Winter's Eve, she was doing the kantirs of a fourth-level water flowing pattern when she saw Ghillie, upside down from her position at that moment, staring at her open-mouthed around the newel of the spiral stair.

"Ee!" he said when she stopped rather suddenly, her back arched in a curve that from his position must have looked almost impossible. "Why didn't you say you were a dancer?"

Jame straightened, grinning, and turned. "'Ee' yourself," she said. "I didn't because, strictly speaking, I'm not. This is a kind of fighting practice. But what are you doing up here at this hour? I didn't expect to see you until afternoon after last night's debauch."

"Aunt Cleppetty got me up," said the boy ruefully, *"and* gave me a fine lecture on disappearing before all the guests were in bed. She also told me to tell you that she's going marketing just now and wants you to go with h—hey, watch out!"

But Jame was already past him, boots in hand, ricocheting down first one stair and then the other toward the front door where Cleppetty waited impatiently, a shopping basket on her bony arm.

THEY CROSSED THE SQUARE with Jame hopping on one foot, trying to get herself shod without falling down, too excited even to notice the derisive hoot from the door of the Skyrrman that greeted this performance. At the southwestern corner of that inn, piles of bricks, dressed stone and timber—all waiting to be hoisted up to the unfinished fourth story—were spread out on the pavement, partly obstructing the side street. Cleppetty marched straight through these, looking neither right nor left nor—more to the point—up, where a heavily laden sling swung creaking in the breeze. It was typical of Marplet sen Tenko's attitude toward the general public that he should permit such a thing to hang there apparently unattended, and typical of the widow's attitude toward Marplet that she should completely ignore it. As for Jame, only stubborn pride carried her after Cleppetty through that sinister shadow as a gust of wind made it shift on the ground and set the supports high above to groaning.

Then it was behind them, and they had turned onto the small street called the Way of Tears, which ran along the west side of the Skyrrman, past the gate to its inner court and the back wing that housed the servants' quarters. Here a slim, black-haired girl leaned out of a window to stare down at them. Jame, her mind still on falling objects, almost shied before she saw that the other's hands were empty and her expression showed only curiosity. For a moment their eyes met. Then the road twisted away behind the inn, and the bief contact was broken.

Tai-tastigon by daylight proved to be a much different place from the one Jame remembered seeing on her first night. Now, instead of dark, empty ways, the streets were full of life. Men hurried past, intent on their own business. Women leaned out of upper windows to gossip with neighbors across the way, while lines of wet laundry flapped languidly between them. Children, playing in the gutter, stopped to watch and giggle as a stray dog urinated on someone's pet geraniums. All that was mysterious or menacing seemed to have vanished or to have grown as pale as the moon set high against a bright, late morning sky.

Then they passed under the arch of an old gate into a tangle of backways. The main streets had been confusing enough, but here even the residents seemed to rely heavily on members of the Pathfinders' Guild, who hawked their expertise at every crossroad. Those who weren't willing to pay a guide's fee had scrawled directions to themselves all over the walls. One had even anchored himself to his own front doorknob with a string, which stretched along the pavement for five blocks before ending suddenly in the middle of an intersection, the victim, perhaps, of some indignant guide.

Jame was just thinking that their route couldn't possibly get any more complex when the widow dove into yet another maze-within-a-maze composed of dank, rapidly narrowing lanes. Caught between claustrophobia and wall-slugs, Jame was almost ready to retreat the way they had come (assuming she could find it) when they suddenly emerged from a crack between buildings into a small square bustling with people: the vegetable market, reached by some arcane shortcut.

While Cleppetty shopped, Jame wandered around the stalls and carts, admiring the great piles of produce. She noticed that two municipal guards armed with the usual iron-headed truncheons were also on the prowl, presumably looking for thieves. It didn't occur to her that they might actually find one until a boy suddenly winked at her across a stand and made a potato disappear into his pocket as if by sorcery. Jame thought of those iron-bound clubs and went on to the next stall without a word.

Barring that incident, nothing disturbed the general air of normalcy about the market; and even the theft, in an odd way, seemed a natural part of the scene. Sitting on the edge of the central fountain with her fingers dipped in the cool water, Jame wondered if the exotic image she had built up of Tai-tastigon had anything to do with the true life of the city. Once a year, perhaps, the very stones went mad, but was the rest of the time passed like this, in steady industry spiced with nocturnal revels for those who desired them?

She was still wondering when someone shrieked.

Jame's head snapped up. She saw a gnarled farmer drop the turnips that he had been showing to a customer and snatch a broken scythe out of his cart. God of her ancestors, he was coming straight at her. The end of a blue ribbon curled over his arm as his blade leaped up. But surely that first wild cry had come from behind her, Jame thought in confusion, springing to her feet; yes, there it was again not ten feet away, mixed now with a great splashing. She twisted about and saw a heavyset man festooned with blue ribbons charging at her through the fountain. He was brandishing a short, sharp sword.

For a whole second, Jame simply froze, paralyzed with amazement. Then she dove for cover under the bed of a tomato cart and came up again on the far side. Cleppetty, who had taken refuge in a doorway, reached out and pulled her into the recess. Together, they watched the fight.

The two men met almost on the spot where Jame had been standing, but they did not remain there long. Step by step, the older man with the scythe was forced backward. He used his improvised weapon well, swinging in tight, vicious arcs that hissed and flashed in the sun, but he was at a disadvantage: his adversary, while a hopeless swordsman, had the dubious fortune to be completely berserk.

The farmer's ramshackle cart was close behind him now. Beyond both men and wagon, Jame saw the guards watching with interest.

Then the older man's foot came down on one of the turnips he had dropped, and he went over backward, crashing into the cart with such force that the near wheel fell off. A torrent of vegetables cascaded to the pavement. The swordsman sprang forward with a triumphant shriek, only to stagger and fall himself on the treacherous footing. He tried to get up again and again, foam dribbling down his chin, too deep in madness to remember his weapon or look where he put his hands or feet.

The farmer rose slowly, carefully, and picked up his scythe. He touched the edge once as though to be sure of its keenness, then stepped toward the fallen man through the field of squashed vegetables. The latter rose to his knees, his voice a squeal of frustrated rage. The sound stopped abruptly as the blade caught him under the chin. Something went flying through the air and landed wetly on top of the pile of tomatoes before Jame. She stared at it. The eyelids were still fluttering. Then the farmer stalked over, grabbed the thing by the hair, and walked off with it.

Cleppetty left the doorway, muttering savagely to herself, and half dragged Jame through the wagons toward the fissure by which they had entered the square. Looking back, Jame saw the tomato-seller examine his produce, throw two into the gutter, and carry several others to the fountain. He was washing them when the wall cut off her view. The murmur of renewed business followed them for several turnings into the dank nest of lanes.

"Cleppetty . . ."

". . . think they'd have more self-respect than to do it in public," the widow was saying to herself in tones of profound disgust and unusual directness. "Some people have no sense of propriety. And what a mess . . ."

"Cleppetty . . ."

". . . no consideration for others, either. At least I got the salad makings before . . ."

"CLEPPETTY!"

Jerked to a halt by Jame's sudden stop, the widow turned and glared at her. "Now what's the matter?"

"Cleppetty, what *happened* back there?"

"If I tell you, will you stop yelping at me and get a move on? We've lost enough time already. Besides, you're standing in a puddle."

And so she was. Boots squelching loudly, Jame followed the widow out of the tangled maze, several times treading on the older woman's heels in her impatience. Cleppetty, however, said nothing until the road widened and they were walking side by side again.

"Those men!" she said, beginning with a sort of explosion. "Their sects are involved in a temple war. The ribbons prove it's a legal one, and so, having paid for it, they've the right to do whatever they want or can to each other, anywhere, anytime."

"Legal? Paid? To whom?"

"Why, to the Five, our governing council." She gave Jame a sharp, sidelong look. "Surely you've at least heard of that."

Jame nodded. Ghillie had mentioned it several times, but never this business of warfare in the streets, which was odd, given his taste for the sensational. "It's made up of King

Sellik's representative, the Skyrr Archiem's, and three that the city guilds choose themselves, isn't it?''

''Of course,'' said the widow, ''and they need money to pay for the guards, themselves, and especially the city charter. Tai-tastigon is half in Metalondar and half in Skyrr because of the River Tone, you know (or do you?), and must pay for the privilege of belonging to neither. So the Five levy taxes and license violence. As for the wars, there are four kinds.'' The basket handle slid down to the crook of her elbow as she brandished a knobby finger in Jame's face. ''One: private, for individuals and families. Two: trade, for merchants. Three: temple, for religious fanatics like those two oafs back there. Four: guild, and very messy those can get, too. You may yet see one for yourself if the Sirdan Theocandi of the Thieves' Guild loses any more of his people to that Tai-abendran upstart, Men-dalis. Praise be that my sister's daughter's son is well out of it back in Emmis.''

''Your—uh—grand-nephew is a *thief?''*

''Oh aye, and a good one too, I'm told . . . and we shall never get home if you keep stopping like that.''

''S-sorry,'' said Jame, making a fast recovery. ''But why do the citizens put up with it, I mean with madmen lopping heads off in the streets and ruining merchandise? Those two back there might have killed anyone, including me.''

''That,'' said the widow, ''was because you were unlucky enough to get caught between them and fool enough to stand there gaping until they nearly ran you down. You seem to have a knack for that sort of situation, by the way, which I hope you will in future try to control. As for the rest of us, the more wars there are, the less we have to pay in taxes. So we take an occasional risk. There are worse systems.''

At that point, they turned yet another corner, and Jame recognized the Way of Tears with Marplet's wall stretching out on her left. Cleppetty, like a horse nearing the stable, picked up speed. Jame was fairly trotting to keep level with her as they approached the corner. Her sodden right boot kept slipping down, however, and she entered the square as she had left it, hopping on one foot, this time tugging the boot off. Cleppetty was already among the brick mounds, several paces ahead of her. The servant girl Jame had seen at the window was just turning away from the fountain, an ewer full of water clasped carefully in her arms. She looked across at the two from the Res aB'tyrr, and the pitcher slipped out of her grasp.

Then time seemed to slow for Jame. She saw the ewer falling, falling, and the girl's face distort with a look of horror. She was staring not at Jame and the widow but above them. Simultaneously, Jame heard a rush of air overhead and saw the shadow of the sling darken across Cleppetty's shoulders. The ewer was falling, falling, and she was springing forward. Bare toes and shod dug frantically at the cobbles. Her hands struck the widow's back, and they were both falling, with Cleppetty propelled ahead, her hands in the air, her basket flying away . . . and the ground leaped up at Jame's face.

The ewer shattered, cobbles bit into her cheek, and then the sky fell.

Bricks crashed to earth all about her in a deadly hail, smashing on impact, filling the air with flying shards. One grazed the arm that she had flung up to protect her head, numbing it at the elbow. Far away, a woman began to scream. Then something all too close struck the ground with a resonant boom, making the pavement pressed against her face jump. There was another crash, even nearer, and then nothing.

Jame thought she must have gone deaf. A moment passed, however, and through the savage ringing in her ears she heard dust rattling down, the fountain splashing, and then, nearby, Cleppetty's oh-so-welcome mutter, no louder, no more or less indignant than ever.

She carefully unwrapped her arms from about her head. The right was still partly numb but moved without difficulty. Not so her leg. Looking back, Jame saw the last object that had fallen. It was a beam, some ten feet long and nearly a foot square at the head. The first end to hit had gouged half a dozen cobbles out of the ground; the second had smashed into a pile of bricks, fragmenting the first seven layers. Her bare foot was wedged between pavement, girder, and the two surviving tiers of bricks.

The widow was kneeling beside her now, but her words were only noises to Jame, for she had just heard something else, high above, which seemed to thicken the blood in her temples and pull her head back as though it were on strings. Niggen, Marplet's ungainly son, was leaning out of the third story window, where the tackle rope had been secured, snickering.

He stopped abruptly when he saw Jame's face.

The killing madness had come on her too suddenly to be checked or controlled. She was still thinking quite clearly, but only about how to get to that window, to get at that toad-faced boy, and what she would do then with red hands, red nails. But first one had to be mobile. She began to pull at the trapped foot. Something gave in the ankle, and then it was free. She tried to stand. Far back, behind the madness, there was pain, but now only a certain weakness registered, which must be kept in mind lest it betray her. Someone was saying, "Stop it stop it stop it," over and over again, and then a hand gripped her hair, jerking her head around.

Eyes stared into her own, inches away, and a voice demanded, very distinctly: "Do you want to destroy us all?"

Jame blinked. It was Cleppetty, her face dirty and scratched. Over the widow's shoulder, she saw Ghillie and Rothan running toward them across the square.

"All right?" The widow gave her a light shake. *"All right?"*

Jame nodded, speechless.

Cleppetty sighed and let go of her hair. "Good. Now come along home, child. There's nothing more to do here, and you're hurt."

The cousins had reached them by this time. Ghillie made a gesture as though to help Jame, but Rothan, for once showing more sensitivity, stopped him. They walked back to the inn with Jame a little apart from the others, limping badly. No one said a word, not even the servants who had appeared in the door of the Skyrrman. Certainly, no one laughed.

Once inside the Res aB'tyrr, however, the silence broke. As Jame slowly pieced her senses back together, she found herself seated in the kitchen with Cleppetty bent over her ankle and everyone else crowded around them, talking furiously.

"Did you see . . . did you hear . . ." someone was babbling in the background. ". . . could have been killed," said another voice, nearer, angrier. "I tell you, this time they've gone too . . ." "Just cuts and a pulled muscle . . . then why . . . I don't know." Ah, Cleppetty and Tubain, coming rapidly into focus.

"Kencyrs are odd people," the widow was saying, quite clearly now, "and this child is odd even for a Kencyr. Just look at those . . ."

Jame closed her hands with a snap and thrust them out of sight behind her. "Why did you say 'Do you want to destroy us all?' "

Everyone in the room spun around and stared at her.

The corpse has sat up on its pyre, she thought grimly. Hurrah. "Why did you say that?"

"Well?" Cleppetty glared at Tubain. "Are you going to tell her? She's earned the right to know."

The innkeeper raised his massive shoulders and let them drop again in a gesture of complete helplessness.

Cleppetty snorted explosively. "Very well," she said. "If you won't, I will. The sum of it is that we're involved in an undeclared trade war with Marplet sen Tenko. It began about a year ago when he started to build the Skyrrman, which he had no right to do in the first place since Tubain here has the tavern charter for the whole district. We went to the Five to protest and were sent to the Skyrr representative, Harr sen Tenko. He wouldn't even see us."

"Even if he wasn't the most corrupt magistrate in the city," said Rothan, "his wife wouldn't let him. We found out afterward that she's Marplet's sister."

"It gets better," said a mournful voice under the sideboard, where Ghillie had gone to earth to avoid being trampled by Cleppetty.

The widow snorted again. "You may well say so. After that the goading started. It looked odd to us from the start, and so we held back—a damn good thing, too, because pretty soon we noticed that every time Marplet's lot tried to start a fight, there were always one or two guards lurking around just out of sight. So that was it, then: Marplet had bought them; and if we reacted, they would swear before the Five that we had started the trouble in the first place, had in fact begun an undeclared trade war, and so as the instigators would have to pay. Wars are expensive. The fine for an illegal one would ruin us—*will* ruin us, if we fall into Marplet's trap. Now do you understand?"

"I . . . think so," said Jame. "But why didn't you tell me this before?"

"He," said the widow, jabbing a finger at Tubain, "didn't want you caught up in it. He seems to think that if he ignores it, the whole thing will dry up and blow away. Well, it didn't blow away, it fell down—and the gods know what it will do next. *Now* will you take this business seriously?" she demanded, turning on the innkeeper. "*Now* will you admit that something has to be done?"

Throughout this tirade, Tubain had been leaning against a post of the cellar door with his eyes closed, like a small boy pretending to be asleep in a room full of bogles. Now that they were all staring at him, he opened them, said with great dignity to no one in particular, "I'd better go check those new hogsheads," and disappeared down the basement steps.

"He won't even *talk* about it!" Cleppetty exclaimed, hoarse with exasperation. "Mind you, he's a good man—one of the best—but there are some things he simply can't face, and that doesn't make it any easier on the rest of us. If you stay here, child, you'll have to be especially careful because you seem to attract violence and have a potential for it that, I think, will mean disaster for someone sooner or later. That's the trace of far-seer in my family speaking. Take it for what it's worth. But remember, it would be a poor return for Tubain's hospitality to pull the inn down on his head.

"Right. That's enough of that," she said, clapping her hands. "The rest of you, scat. We all have work to do and no more time to waste."

After the others had left, Jame stayed in the kitchen for a while with her foot in a basin of cold water, surrounded by a growing cloud of cinnamon, ginger, and galingale as Cleppetty attacked the ingredients of a goat's heart pie. Then Tanis, who had been out, burst into the room and so embarrassed her with praise that she was forced to flee. Although her ankle throbbed savagely with every step up to the loft, she was almost dizzy with relief. The waiting was over. She would not have to leave the inn after all. For as long as she needed it, she had a home.

And yet, somehow, that wasn't enough.

Sitting on the ledge, looking out over the city, Jame considered this. A home, yes, but the inn could never be her whole world. She had too many questions that could only be dealt with out there in the labyrinth of Tai-tastigon, questions that no outsider could hope to answer. Only when she knew the city could she hope to know its gods. She must find a way into the heart of this larger society—as she had into that of the Res aB'tyrr—and how better than by joining the city's most powerful guild?

But to become a thief! No proper Kencyr would even consider the idea. But hadn't she been told often enough that she wasn't proper and never would be? She would probably go through life as she had begun it at the keep, with only a precarious toehold in the world of her people. Honor alone—as the Kencyrath understood it—kept her secure, and only a scrollsman or a priest could tell her if such a thing as an honest thief was possible. The spirit of the law would undoubtedly be outraged, but if the letter remained intact . . .

Jame suddenly grinned. It seemed she had already made up her mind. In the morning she would first seek her priest's blessing (ha!) and then the killer-maze that Penari called home. If she survived both, it looked as if the Kencyrath was about to acquire its first official thief.

CHAPTER 3

Into the Labyrinth

THAT NIGHT JAME slept deeply and was pleased to find in the morning that her ankle had all but healed. After she had worked the last bit of stiffness out of it, she went down to the kitchen to inform the household of her plans. She expected opposition. Instead, ''I've seen this coming for a long time,'' said the widow as she cut generous slices of bread and cheese and put them into a knapsack. ''You're not the sort to relish life in a cage.'' Tubain also made no protest but was clearly upset as he intercepted her at the front door and furtively slippped three silver coins into her hand. She thanked him with a quick smile and left the inn.

Marplet sen Tenko was sitting in a window of the Skyrr-man smoking a long-stemmed pipe.. His big tiger-tom, Fang, crouched beside him on the sill. As Jame crossed the square, both the innkeeper and the cat watched her with almost the same expression, calculating, self-confident, and faintly amused. Neither would relish a quick kill, she realized with sudden insight. This man would toy with the Res aB'tyrr as long as the game entertained him and not a moment longer. Still, his mocking gaze teased the flicker of an answering smile from her, and she saluted him formally with raised fist and open hand, as one does an acknowledged enemy on the eve of battle. Then she left the square.

Her goal was the house of her god, where she meant to ask the priest if she could join the Thieves' Guild without a fatal loss of honor. The many gods of Tai-tastigon had made her question the very foundation of the Kencyrath, their belief in the Three-Faced God; but as she had realized the night before, she could no more separate herself from all aspects of her culture than step off the edge of the world. That was clear to her now, far clearer, unfortunately, than the location of the temple. On impulse, she set off toward the rising sun.

The streets unrolled before her, twisting back and forth under a bright winter sky. They rarely led due east. Realizing that she was not going to get anywhere in a hurry, Jame began to enjoy the challenge of these tangled ways. Some streets were quiet, lined with handsome houses or the back walls of gardens; others bustled with brightly clad crowds, through which peddlers strolled, hawking fermented mares' milk and honeyed locusts, while bands of penitants trotted past chanting their sins in unison. But best of all, in Jame's opinion, was a nest of spiral lanes, each arm of which was devoted to a different sub-chapter of the Glovers' Guild. Here she saw gloves made of leather, linen, and silk dyed all shades of earth and sea, their cuffs sparkling with jewels or heavy with shining threads. It was an elegant pair of black kidskin that she finally bought, however, joyfully spending all the money that Tubain had given her. With gloves on, her differences would not be so apparent. The idea delighted her.

Beyond the glovers' lanes, the buildings began to grow progressively larger and shabbier. This looked promising, she thought, remembering the abandoned structures around the temple; but while there was a growing tinge of darkness in the atmosphere, it was nothing like that which surrounded the dwelling-place of her god. Then she came to the crest of a small hill and found herself looking down over a narrow canal at the charred ruins of the Lower Town.

In a city as thick with gods as Tai-tastigon, only the practice of keeping such beings confined to their sanctuaries made a normal life possible for their mortal fellow citizens. Occasionally, however, one did escape or "come untempled," and that was what some people believed had happened to the Lower Town. At any rate, six years before it had become evident that something that had no right to be there was at large in this rich district; but since no one knew its name, there was no way to drive it out. At last those who could had left the area, putting their homes to the torch behind them. Even this last attempt at purification by fire had failed, however, and the destitute had thus inherited what no one else would have.

This, at least, was the story that Ghillie had told Jame. She didn't know how much of it she should believe, but there was undeniably something wrong here, even after all these years. As she passed more and more of the blackened buildings and the hovels that had sprung up like sickly growths in their shadow, she found herself moving warily, her sixth sense prickling, as though she had invaded, in its absence, the den of some unknown and unimaginable . . . *thing*.

It was a strange place to hear the sound of rushing water. Drawn by it, Jame continued eastward until she came to a low section of the Old Wall at the end of a street. Beyond it, there was a sharp drop down to the floor of the Rim, that relatively new district that circled the city between the old and inner walls. Some ten feet below her, a cataract of water roared out of a vent in the wall, holding a rainbow captive in its spray.

"Is that the River Tone?" she asked an old man who was standing nearby, watching the waterfall.

"Nay. That be the sewer outlet."

"But the water is perfectly clear!"

"'Course it is," he said, spitting down into it. "Old Sumph and his priests see to that. We puts it out, they takes it in. Eats shit, does old Sumph—among other things—and loves it. You don't believe me, go over to the inner wall sometime and have a look 'cross at his backside."

Jame reflected that whenever she asked about the gods of Tai-tastigon, she always seemed to find out more than she wanted to know. But if this old man liked being informative . . .

"Can you tell me," she asked him, "where to find the Temple of the Three-Faced God?"

His shoulders stiffened. When he turned, she fell back a step, thinking from his expression that he meant to strike her.

Instead, he spat on the ground at her feet and hastily shambled away.

What an odd reaction, she thought, watching him go. Some people, apparently, liked her god even less than she did. Nor was the old man unique. When Jame put her question to other residents of the Lower Town, most were too frightened to say anything, and some became violent. All she found as the day slid down into dusk were hostile looks, incredible squalor, and more sickly or deformed children than seemed possible. Quite a number of these urchins took to following her until, by the end of the day, she found herself at the head of a ragged, hobbling parade, unsure if she should walk slower so as not to tire them or run away from the lot.

However, the problem disappeared along with the children as the sun dipped behind the Ebonbane. Everyone was seeking shelter, Jame realized, and all around her the few feeble lights were flickering out. Clearly, this was not a place to be out in the streets after dark.

Her wandering had by now brought her to the Tone, running swiftly in its deep bed, and hearing faint music ahead, she set off along its left bank in the growing gloom.

Across the river stood rows of shining houses similar to those that once had filled the Lower Town. Beyond them, farther upriver, were the islet estates of the very rich, cradled between the arms of the Tone, separated by canals.

Music came from some of these gleaming isles, but not the boisterous strains that had first reached Jame in the darkness of the Lower Town. These she continued to follow as the two branches of the river drew closer together until the farther one disappeared behind the flank of a large, narrow island ringed with a marble wall in the likeness of a ship's side. Ahead, looming against the Ebonbane, was a huge white structure with mastlike spires from which streamed banners of scarlet and gold. The grounds around it swarmed with people costumed and plain, rich and shabby, all dancing together in the mad grip of carnival, drunkenly singing the praises of the Sirdan Theocandi and the great, the wonder thieves of Tai-tastigon.

Jame walked on along the far bank, listening, looking, catching delight like a heady perfume borne on the air. It was a long island. At its point the walls rose in a jutting prow set with the figurehead of a woman triumphantly brandishing a severed head in either hand. Their stone beards curled down her arms and the swift waters of the Tone creamed about her bare feet as though the island were surging onward into the heart of the city.

A block beyond that Jame crossed a bridge and turned back. She had gone down the other side of the island almost as far as the stern when out of the corner of her eye she saw something pale falling. There was a loud splash below, closely followed by another, as a young man on the opposite bank dove into the river, fully clothed. She saw him surface, his arm wrapped around something, and begin to struggle across the current toward her side. The racing water would have borne him away if a man on the quay below had not thrown out a line and several others run down the steps to help pull him in.

"Is it another one, Tob?" a latecomer called as he darted past her.

None of the straining figures below had time to answer: they were hauling first the pale object and then the young man up onto the dock. Jame saw that the former was the naked body of a boy. His white skin was oddly marked as though someone had drawn the diamonds of a game board on it and blackened every other one. Then she saw that the dark areas were not skin at all but rather the lack of it.

"Aye," said a bitter voice from the midst of the group bending over it. "Another one." And they all looked up at the Sirdan's palace.

Upstream, the shadowy form of a man stood at the railing of a balcony suspended over the water. He was looking down at them.

The swimmer stood, white shirt plastered to his ribs, and stared back. For a moment the tableau held. Then one of the men coughed and began to struggle out of his coat. They carried the draped corpse up the steps and away, leaving the young man to glare upward a moment longer before he turned to follow them. He passed Jame without noticing her, blinded with anger. She saw him cross one of the catwalks back to the island, then turned away and walked on.

The music died away behind her, and the lights grew dim. A chill wind was blowing off the mountains, pushing at her back. She suddenly felt very cold and tired.

THE REST OF THE NIGHT was spent in following first the Tone and then the Old Wall away from slums and mansions alike and in several hours of sleep snatched on someone's second story balcony.

Hovering near the wall a few feet from where Jame had taken shelter was one of the strange light spheres, which she had first seen in the puzzle-box district. She woke in the gray dawn at the sound of a voice and saw the globe darken. Below, a black-robed man paused under the next light and extinguished it too by murmuring, "Blessed-Ardwyn-day-has-come" in a bored monotone. He disappeared into the morning mist, banishing the puffs of light as he went.

Jame breakfasted on the cheese and bread that Cleppetty had provided, then swung down to the street.

She had decided not to return to the Lower Town. Even though the violent reactions of the people there had convinced her that the temple of her god lay somewhere nearby, she no longer trusted herself to find it blindly. Better to retrace the wanderings of that first night . . . if she could. Consequently, Jame now followed the Old Wall northward to the Sun Gate. From there, a two-hour's walk along the curving streets of the Rim District brought her to the Warrior Gate, now standing firmly shut against the Haunted Lands, the Feast of Dead Gods being long past.

Like all Kencyrs, Jame had received extensive memory training as a child. She knew the lengthy epics of her people by heart and could recite genealogies of leaders and important people stretching back thousands of years. This, however, did not help her greatly with visual images. It was midafternoon before she found the little square with the fountain and only recognized it because of the network of deep cracks that ran through it. Jame followed these westward until they ended suddenly before a familiar gate.

Now she had a choice. Before her lay the puzzle-box, more properly known as the Temple District, which she had previously entered and left by the same route. In that respect, it was a dead-end. Still, she felt drawn by it and curious to know if her earlier impression had been correct. Perhaps she had overreacted. Perhaps these so-called gods were not the threat that she had at first believed. At any rate, it now occurred to her that, to the best of her knowledge, none of the people she had questioned so far about her own god had been priests. That was excuse enough. Bracing herself, she stepped through the gate into the Temple District.

Moments later as Jame walked through cross-currents of incense, hearing the drone of chants on all sides and seeing the tangle of buildings that stretched out of sight at each crossroad, she reluctantly faced the truth. Although the feverish beat of power had now sunk to a steady pulse, it was still undeniably there. The threat was real after all. Damn.

The sound of loud voices nearby broke in on her thoughts. On the steps of a small temple, a round little man in hieratic garb was arguing vehemently with a plump old woman.

"What do you mean, 'No'?" he was saying angrily. "What sort of answer is that?"

"An honest one," the woman retorted, brandishing a fistful of delicate bat bones inlaid with silver under his nose. "Now see here: I don't read these things for the fun of it. You ask me 'Will all be well'; the bones tell me that all won't. There the message ends. But as a far-seer I can tell you this much more: a deadly force is all too near you even now and will come nearer still. You will provoke it; and what it begins, you will finish. There, priest. You wanted your fortune told. Now I wish you the joy of it." With that, she turned and flounced down the steps.

The indignation went out of her gait before she reached the bottom, however, and Jame suddenly found herself looking down into a pair of worried eyes. "Foolish as he is sometimes, he's not a bad man," the old woman said to her in an undertone. "Spare him if you can." Then she scurried away.

Jame stared at her for a moment in amazement, then shrugged. Far-seers had no great reputation for sanity. On impulse, remembering her errand, she went up the steps.

"Excuse me, sir," she said to the priest, who had turned back to his sanctuary and already had one step over the threshold. "Can you tell me where to find the temple of the Three-Faced God?"

The little man spun about. Jame had just time to note the desperate unhappiness in his face before he shrieked, "Heretic!" and struck out wildly at her. As she swayed to avoid the blow, her half-healed ankle twinged in warning. Without thinking, she followed the path of least resistance, which happened to be over the guard rail, down five feet, and over backward into a puddle. A burst of laughter greeted this performance and one of the men who had stopped to listen to the previous altercation shouted, "Well done, Loogan!" after the priest, who had already disappeared. "All hail Gorgo the Lugubrious God!"

"Loogan, huh?" said Jame under her breath as she got to her feet, flushed with anger. Then she limped back the way she had come, ignoring the jeering spectators.

Her temper had cooled somewhat by the time she reached Judgment Square, that vast open area with the Mercy Seat at its center. On this visit, Jame found it full of people. As she threaded her way through the crowd, fending off peddlers, she marveled at how different everything was from the first time she had seen this place. Then, as she approached the Mercy Seat, she saw that it too was no longer empty. At first Jame thought that the figure lolling on it was an effigy of some sort, then that it was a sleeping man clad in a tight black garment which, oddly, seemed to be moving. It wasn't until she was quite close that she saw the darkness was not cloth at all but dried blood and flies. The man's skin, still attached at the neck, hung over the back of the Seat like a strangely shaped cloak. Under the dangling right hand, someone had scrawled in chalk:

> Steal a peach, steal a plum,
> See to what your carcass comes.

Greatly sobered but undeterred, Jame continued on. After all, that would never happen to her, although it gave her a jolt to think that the thief in the stone chair had probably once said as much to himself.

On the far side of the square, she found what looked like the right street and soon confirmed this by coming to the crowned crossroads. Not far beyond that was the River Tone and the bridge by which she had crossed it. On the opposite side her troubles began again, for this was the area through which she had raced so blindly and one street was no different from any other to her. Dusk was falling too, bringing the prospect of another cheerless night in the open. Discouraged and footsore, she sat down on the edge of a small fountain in a dirty little square to eat the last of her food. Without provisions or money she would soon have to start home, perhaps to mount another expedition later—although it was clear to her now that she might spend the rest of her life bumbling around these streets without coming any closer to her goal. Perhaps it was time to admit that the labyrinth had defeated her and her plans.

To the west, the sun had slipped behind the Ebonbane, kindling veins of fire in its snow-locked passes. Jame was gazing up at the mountain peaks dejectedly when she suddenly remembered the Res aB'tyrr's loft with its fine view of the city. That was what she needed now: height. She jumped up and eagerly scanned the surrounding roof lines. There were several tall buildings visible above the houses bordering the square, but one soared above the rest, its upper stories still flooded with light above the growing sea of shadows. That was the one.

Moments later, Jame stared up at its crumbling façade. The door was bricked shut. She swung herself up onto the portico roof and pulled the rotting boards away from a second story window. Inside, light filtered through cracks and down the stairwell revealing a wilderness of dust and decay. She went up the steps quickly but with care, for many of them were rotten, until a collapsed flight some seven stories up blocked her way. From there, she went out a window and up the side of the building for the last twenty feet, gouging fingerholds through the sour plaster to the lath.

When her hand finally closed on the eave trough, she pulled herself onto the roof. She was climbing up the steep slope, eyes fixed on the tiles before her for rotten spots, when a foot suddenly appeared almost under her nose. Something gave her shoulder a strong push, and she found herself slithering down the incline, nails scrabbling for a grip. Then her foot came up against the gutter and the descent stopped. Heart hammering, she looked up. A young man clad all in white was smoothly crab-stepping down the roof toward her. Two other men watched from the ridge.

"If you do that again," she heard herself say in a remarkably conversational tone, "I shall fall off."

"That's the idea," said the descending man with an angelic smile, and he reached out toward her again.

Jame seized his wrist and pulled. Over-balanced, he

pitched forward past her into space. She released her first hold and grabbed for his jacket as he shot past. They both went over the edge. Jame's free hand caught the gutter and then nearly lost it again as the other's suddenly arrested weight wrenched at her muscles. She hadn't come up here to kill or be killed, Jame thought savagely, wondering which shoulder would dislocate first, and damned if she would let either happen through some stupid accident—although from the way her companion was dangling, it wouldn't surprise her if she had inadvertantly hanged him with his own collar.

Two heads appeared above, silhouetted against the sky.

"Well?" she snapped.

A minute later all four of them were sitting on the roof, feet braced against the gutter, panting. The two rescuers seemed the most shaken of the lot, and Jame's erstwhile assailant the least. The latter was in fact still staring down into the void like a man entranced.

"That's the closest I've ever come to going over," he said at last in an awed voice. "I almost wish you'd let me fall."

"I suppose we could try again," said Jame, anger giving way to curiosity. "Do you often go around pushing people off roofs?"

"Oh, all the time. Only citizens of the Cloud Kingdom are welcome up here and, of course, their guests. Incredible . . . just incredible . . ." He leaned forward, causing Jame and the man on his other side to grab his flowing sleeves simultaneously. "I've seen a hundred, a thousand fall, and each time it seems to take longer. Seconds, minutes, hours . . . twisting, turning, dancing in the air . . . marvelous!"

"Messy too, I should think, when they hit the ground."

"Oh, I never watch that long." He sat back and looked at her with wide admiring eyes. "No one has ever come so close to sending me over before. You must be an unusual person. You're sure you won't let me push you off? Well, in that case no one else shall have the pleasure. Come to court some day soon and I shall have Uncle grant you the freedom of the skies."

With that, he bowed to her, rose, and seemed to float up the incline. All three men had just disappeared over the ridge when Jame remembered her mission. Eagerly she examined the patterns of the city below, but nowhere in the deepening shadows was there a sign of that desolate circle, those cold white walls.

"Hey!" she called after the trio, and the fair head popped back into sight over the ridge, looking disembodied.

"Yes?" it said, hopefully.

"I'm looking for the temple of the Three-Faced God. Do you know where it is?"

"Oh." Disappointment washed over the features. "Sparrow will show you." And it vanished again.

"*Hey!* When I come to court, who shall I say invited me?"

"Why, Prince Dandello, of course," the voice drifted back. "The Cloud King's nephew."

"No, I don't know why the groundlings won't discuss your god or, for that matter, the priest Ishtier," said Sparrow, waiting on the crest of a gambrel roof for Jame to scramble up to him. "They're a fat-headed lot from what I've seen; though mind, I've never had much to do with them. Born in the clouds, I was, and here I'll die—barring accidents—without ever touching the ground."

Without warning, the wiry little Cloudie launched himself down the far side of the roof toward a projecting cornice, bounced off the top of it, and easily cleared the eight-foot gap across to the opposite roof. Steeling herself, Jame followed him. They had come quite a distance across the labyrinth by now with comparative ease. Obviously, this was the right way to travel for anyone with good nerves, although not even these saved Jame from a quick spasm of fear as the street flashed past beneath her, some forty feet below.

"Two things, though," said Sparrow as she caught up with him several houses later. "They do tend to treat anything they don't like as if it doesn't exist, and I think the Townies blame your god for whatever it was—no, *is,* that's happening to them. We Cloudies haven't been overjoyed either, what with the way these roofs have disintegrated. You'd never believe it, but this was a flourishing neighborhood six years ago. Now watch your step. We're getting close."

The warning was necessary. They had reached the edge of the temple's greatest influence, as the condition underfoot clearly showed. Jame went first now, picking her way carefully, hearing plaster rattle down inside as boards groaned under her weight. Then there the temple was, tall, stark, ghost-pale under the new moon. The power that flowed continually out of it buffeted her, but at the same time she felt the attraction of that monolithic structure, the sure, arrogant claim of the force that dwelt within its walls on her, body and soul, as a Kencyr. For a moment, Jame hesitated. Then, "Damnation," she said and, with a gesture as foolhardy as it was defiant, threw down all her mental shields. The power claimed her instantly. She forgot her guide, her resentment, everything as it drew her down from the rooftop, across the graveyard of dust, and into the dark doorway.

The moment Jame crossed the threshold, the maelstrom seized her. It seemed to her dazed mind that two currents flowed through the twisting corridors, the greater bound outward, the lesser on either side of it whirling inward along the walls toward the temple's heart. She was spun forward, whipped around faster and faster until her shoulder crashed into a door and it gave way, spilling her sideways onto a tesselated floor.

Her senses ringing in the sudden lull, she stared numbly at the patterns beneath her hand. They spiraled in toward the center of the chamber. Her eyes followed their curve to the foot of the statue there on its raised dais, then up that towering, black granite form to the three faces of her god. The aspect of Regonereth, That-Which-Destroys, was turned toward her, its features obscured with marble carved veil-thin. Lower down, one hand reached out and upward through a fissure in the masonry as though beckoning. Each long, scythe-curved finger was tipped in ivory, honed and gleaming.

Ishtier, Highborn priest of the Kencyrath, stood in the shadow of his god, watching her with hooded eyes. His nearly fleshless lips were raised in a faint smile, and tongues of power from the outer corridors licked eagerly past her, spiraling into the center. She got quickly to her feet.

"Who are you?" It was a thin, dry voice, not exactly rusty but like the hinges of a door infrequently opened.

"Jame of the Three People."

"That is but half a name. Tell me the rest."

"With respect, my lord, it does not concern you." She did not realize until she saw his slight smile deepen that he had asked and she replied in High Kens. More power swirled into the room, tugging at her mind. It was getting harder to think.

"Very well . . . for now," the priest said, "Why have you come?"

Jame tried to answer, struggling with the unaccustomed clumsiness of mind that prevented her from shielding herself against this man. Much more of this and not even her namelessness would protect her.

"I-I want to join the Thieves' Guild," she said, hating herself for the stammer.

"You, a Kencyr, wish to steal? You would sell your honor so cheaply?"

"I would sell nothing!"

"Then you are a fool," said the priest coldly. "Nothing comes without a price . . . not even this conversation."

Jame caught her breath as power whipped past her face. A second bolt of energy clipped her shoulder, numbing it and spinning her around. Two more quick blows took her off-balance again. Her jacket had begun to smolder. She ripped it off, twisting desperately, futilely, to avoid the invisible assault. Ishtier watched, the thin smile again on his lips.

"Dance, fool, dance," he said softly.

Sudden anger made Jame reckless. Defiantly, she raised her clenched fists in challenge, not to the priest but to the statue towering above him. "Lord, a judgment!" she cried to the three faces of her god.

Ishtier drew himself up with a hiss of outrage. Then, abruptly, his expression changed. *"Steal not from your own kind,"* said the god-voice through his unwilling lips. *"Do with others what you will, so that it be done with honor, until in your thoughtlessness you destroy them."* The voice ceased. Wiping spittle from his face with a shaking hand, Ishtier said hoarsely, "There, brat. You have the answer you sought. Now get out."

Jame bowed and went, not trusting herself to speak. She had her answer indeed, ambiguous in part as it was. Now it was time to go home.

The moon rose over her shoulder as she walked westward, thinking over the day's events. Twice within the last few hours a priest had humiliated her. She had never liked the breed anyway, not since she had realized as a child that it was because of a priest that Anar had gone mad. It had taken a continual effort to protect the keep from the deadly influence of the Haunted Lands. Before Jame's time, this had been the responsibility of the scrollsman's older brother, a priest of great power and knowledge; but one night this man had fled with a female companion, leaving his inexperienced kinsman to assume the terrible burden alone. By the time Anar had become the twins' tutor, his mind had already begun to crumble under the strain. Soon he was more like a child himself, except that he still kept their home safe and continued to do so until sword's edge and arrow's point had destroyed everything for which he had sacrificed so much.

Indeed, it was a terrible thing to wield the power of a Kencyr priest, to stand between the people and their god. The best, like Anar, were often destroyed by it, while others became so warped in time that allowances had to be made for them, even with the rigid structure of the Kencyrath.

Jame, however, forgave nothing, especially not now, now that she had met Ishtier. Old grief and fresh resentment kept her simmering all that long walk home until, in the early hours of the morning, she turned onto the Way of Tears beside Marplet sen Tenko's inn.

There was a burst of raucous laughter from the courtyard of the Skyrrman as she approached its gate, and a slim figure darted out into the street ahead of her, closely pursued. Cloth ripped as hunter and hunted converged. The slighter of the two reeled into the opposite wall, clutching the remains of her bodice over small white breasts. Jame saw that it was the black-haired servant girl. Niggen was standing in the middle of the road with the torn fabric in his hand, giggling.

Before the boy even realized that she was there, Jame had spun him around. The heel of her palm caught him under the chin with a blow that snapped his head back and practically lifted him off his feet. A moment later, it would have been hard to say who was more startled—the men at the gate, Niggen on the ground spitting teeth, or Jame herself, who had acted purely on instinct.

"If you touch that girl again," she said to Marplet's son, "I shall gladly knock out whatever teeth you have left."

Not until she was crossing the square toward the Res aB'tyrr and heard someone shouting for a guard behind her did she realize what she had done. Marplet had his excuse at last.

"I'm sorry," she said, pulling her cap off in contrition to the astonished Ghillie who met her at the door. Then she turned to face the small group approaching her from the Skyrrman.

Marplet was in the lead, with two burly guards behind him, and Niggen trotting eagerly at his side. The innkeeper stopped short, however, when he saw Jame's face framed with her mane of black hair. For the first and last time, she saw him pale with anger as he turned on his awkward, bewildered son.

"Do you mean to say," he demanded, pointing at her, "that you were beaten by that . . . that *girl?* You spineless booby!" Without another word he whirled and stalked back to the Skyrrman.

The guards looked at Jame, at each other, then shrugged simultaneously and walked away.

"Something told me you were home," said Cleppetty wryly behind Jame. "Come and have some supper."

By then, it was very late. The widow had apparently been in bed before the disturbance but showed no sign of returning to it even when Jame had finished her bowl of warmed-over stew.

"Can't sleep yet," she said in answer to Jame's question. "I'm waiting for something."

"What?"

"With luck, you'll never know."

But Cleppetty had hardly finished speaking when a shriek brought both women to their feet. It came from across the square. Jame was halfway out the front door when the widow grabbed her arm and hung on grimly.

"Let me go!" she cried, trying to dislodge the older woman without hurting her. "I said I'd break that slime-ball's teeth if he hurt that girl again, and so help me God I will!"

"It isn't Niggen," said the widow. "Did you seriously think that Marplet would accept an humiliation like that without revenging himself on someone? Wait."

They stood listening to the cries until the door of the Skyrrman suddenly opened and a figure was thrown out. Even then Cleppetty wouldn't let Jame move until it had staggered halfway across the square toward them. Then they both ran out and helped the sobbing, half-naked girl into the kitchen where the widow brought out a jar of ointment and began to dress the whip cuts on her back. Fortunately, the girl was more frightened than hurt, but there was still a great deal of blood, wailing, and general mess before Tubain arrived in his night-shirt to survey the damage.

"Tuby," said the widow, "we will have to keep her."

From the moment the innkeeper had entered the room, he had been surreptitiously trying to leave it again. At Cleppetty's words, however, he suddenly stopped fidgeting and looked squarely at the weeping girl for the first time.

"Of course, we will," he said.

Jame wondered if she herself had been adopted in a similar fashion.

The bandaging done, Ghillie and Jame helped the newest member of the household up to Taniscent's room. They had just tucked her in and quietly retreated to the gallery when the dancer herself slipped into the courtyard below through the side gate. Ghillie took one look at her and fled. Clearly, something had upset Taniscent badly, and Jame, meeting her at the head of the stair, immediately learned what it was. After weeks of cooling ardor, Bortis had finally called her an old hag and gone off with a fifteen-year-old from the next district.

Jame nearly said "good riddance." Instead, respecting Tanis's distress, she concentrated on putting her friend to bed. This proved difficult. She was just beginning to think that she would have to sit on the dancer until she settled down when the widow's voice rose from the courtyard in an exasperated shout:

"Now listen to me, all of you: Shut up and go to sleep!"

"Yes, Cleppetty," six voices meekly chorused from all over the darkened inn.

Taniscent sighed and closed her eyes. With kohl running down in streaks to puddle beside her nose, she looked, if not haglike, at least thoroughly grotesque, and closer forty years old than twenty-four.

Jame took a blanket and lay down on the gallery floor. It was hard to believe that the long day was over at last. She had a premonition that she had started something—several things—during the course of it that might have alarming consequences later, but was too tired to sort them out now. Besides, here was Boo, lumbering out of the shadows purring loudly. Knowing that if she didn't humor him the cat would probably sit on her face, she opened the blanket and let him curl up inside it against her. Dawn was just beginning to touch the eastern sky as she fell asleep.

CHAPTER 4

The Heart of the Maze

"PENARI!"

The echo cracked back from the stone walls of the entrance way, unsoftened by any furniture or trappings.

"Where are you? It's me, Jame . . . the Talisman!"

Something rustled in a far corner, disturbing loose debris with scurrying claws. There was no other response.

"Damn," said Jame.

She was standing just inside Penari's home, that huge, circular edifice known as the Maze. It had been easy enough to locate from the rooftops, but now that she was here it was obvious that her problems had just begun. Many thieves before her had matched their wits against this intricate building, searching for its heart; only a handful had ever been seen again. That was what she must risk now if the old thief would not even come out to greet an invited guest. With a sigh, she resigned herself to the inevitable.

Three doors opened off the entry hall. Jame tied the end of a large spool of thread to the post of one, kindled the torch she had brought with her, and crossed the threshold. Inside, the confusion of small rooms and narrow passages began at once, choking off all outside light and sound within a few turnings. Still and close as the ways of a tomb it was, and very like being buried in one. Leaping torchlight held back the darkness, but between its flickers the walls themselves seemed to close in.

Surprisingly, there were several small streams running through the building and a number of stairways going up but none leading down. Jame wandered about the ground floor, shouting at intervals but still getting no response. Then she began to climb. The levels became less complex the higher she got, although there was still no way to tell exactly where she was at any given moment. Penari's hidden apartments could be anywhere. By the time she reached the fifth and final level, her thread, voice and patience were all beginning to run out. She had just decided to give up when the floor underfoot suddenly gave way.

She fell, the thread snapping, the torch plummeting down ahead like a falling star. Then it vanished. A moment later, the water slammed into her.

Black, choking, not alone . . . her hand found the edge of the pool, and she pulled herself out in a near panic, barking her shins on the rim without even noticing it. Behind her, something surfaced with a liquid chuckle and dove again.

Jame crouched in the dark, shivering, listening. What had she just escaped? Where was it now? If only the pool would confine it. A rustle, a rasp of scales on stone . . . it was coming after her.

She sprang up and backed away. A wall brought her up short. Eyes were no use in this almost tangible darkness, but her ears caught the sound of something very large, very heavy, fumbling at the pool's rim, slowly drawing its immense bulk out of the water. The close air filled with a thousand small noises, multiplying as the walls gave back their echo. With a choked cry she whirled and leaped. Her fingers caught at the rough stone blocks and she scrambled blindly upward until one hand closed on a wooden beam. She was hanging there in midair when a dazzling light seemed to explode in the room.

"Well!" said a voice. "No one's ever done *that* before."

As her vision cleared, Jame saw Penari standing below with a torch in his hand. Behind him, light gleamed on a huge mound of flesh, white, convoluted, and quivering. Pink, lidless eyes stared back at her over his shoulder.

"Too bad it's you, boy," the old man said, "Monster hasn't been fed so far this month."

"From what I can see, Monster hasn't any teeth."

"Being a moon python, he doesn't need 'em," said Penari with more loyalty than truth. "Twenty years ago he had a fine set."

"I'm sorry I'm late," said Jame, rather incoherently. "I was ill. Uh . . . if I come down, will I get eaten?"

"After scaring the poor bugger half to death? He'd be more likely to throw up on you . . . or on me," he added, glancing up mistrustfully at the swaying head.

Somewhat reassured, Jame dropped to the floor. Leaving the giant snake to recover himself, Penari led the way through a bewildering series of corridors to the heart of the Maze. To Jame's surprise, this one large room occupied the whole core of the building, extending from the second level basement up to the ceiling of the fifth floor. Spiral stairways led from the bottom, where they stood, to screened alcoves and shelves of books and scrolls that extended up out of sight into the shadows. A huge chandelier full of guttering candles provided the chamber with its only light. Wax from it dropped steadily on the red and gold patterns of the carpet and on a massive table laden with manuscripts. Everywhere there were rich things dimly seen and covered with dust.

Penari showed her the various entrances to the central room and took her out into the Maze to demonstrate how one reached the outside world from each. He apparently expected her to remember every unmarked turn after one sight of it. When he had trotted her from cellar to attic and back, the old thief fished a small greasy coin out of his robe and gave it to her saying, "Right. Now go buy a pig for Monster's dinner."

For the next few days, Jame went to the Maze early each morning, after a night of helping at the inn, and for the next six or seven hours ran errands for Penari. She began to wonder if she had misunderstood the nature of the job that the old man had offered her. Then, on the fifth afternoon, Penari snatched up his staff and went with her when she left the Maze. They turned north at the gate, east at the Tone, and soon were in sight of the Sirdan's Palace, already gray in the dusk, rising up behind its exultant figurehead.

The outer courtyard was again full of lights. This time, however, they shone on the nightly thieves' bazaar, where the spoils of the day were being sold or bartered to the sound of ferocious haggling. Jame felt many eyes on her as she followed Penari through the crowd. Word must have gone before them, for as they entered the Guild Hall, all faces turned in their direction and many voices stilled. The Guild secretary was at his post beside the throne dais with a small group of people waiting to see him. Penari cut in at the head of the line, drawing Jame after him.

"This is the Talisman," he announced, presenting her. "I want to enroll him as my apprentice."

The secretary peered at Jame, his face an odd mixture of bewilderment and suspicion. "Master Penari, this is not—"

"A Kencyr? Of course it is. You think I'd trust my secrets to any of this rabble? Go on, Master Secretary, record it. Under Guild law, no one can dictate my choice, or interfere with it once made—as much as some might wish to."

The triumph in his voice was unmistakable, and so was his determination. The secretary shrugged and wrote in the huge book on the table before him.

"Talisman," he said to Jame, "do you swear to obey the laws of the Thieves' Guild of Tai-tastigon, to uphold its institutions, to conduct yourself to its credit and to that of your master?"

"I so swear."

"Very well. Bare a shoulder—uh—'boy.'"

One last chance, Jame thought. If this fails, I give up. And she stripped off both tunic and shirt.

The secretary looked stunned. Penari, however, after a moment's impatient wait, picked up the brand—red with ink, fortunately, not heat—and pressed it against her skin, muttering something about dithering officials.

That was it, then. He's too blind and I'm too flat, she thought despairingly, and put her clothes back on.

The episode was apparently over as far as Penari was concerned, for he was already halfway down the hall when she turned to follow him. A hand on her arm stopped her. The nails of the index and middle fingers were filed to sharp points. A man with almost luminous gray eyes set in a dark face was looking down at her. "Someone wants to see you," he said softly. The grip on her arm tightened, meaning to hurt, succeeding. "Now."

"Go along, Talisman," her new master called back from the doorway. "Give my regards to Theocandi!" And he disappeared, fairly gurgling with some secret mirth.

The dark man released Jame's arm and signaled her to proceed him. They went through a door behind the secretary's desk and beyond that into a narrow, winding passage. It was rather like being back in the Maze except that here the halls were richly appointed and she was being followed by this . . . person, whose gaze, sliding insolently over her body from behind, made her feel acutely self-conscious. Then the corridor opened into a small, tapestry-hung audience chamber. The Sirdan Theocandi stood on the far side of it, waiting. Even without Penari's parting words and the heavy chain of office that this sharp-featured old man wore, Jame would have known him from the authority—one might even say the arrogance—of his stance. She saluted him warily with crossed wrists held low, but not the open hands of friendship.

"So," he said in a flat, cold voice, not bothering to acknowledge the greeting. "Penari has at last taken an apprentice. Let us hope he has chosen wisely, for himself *and* for the Guild."

"I hope to serve him well, m'lord," Jame said, wondering if she had been summoned merely for a lecture. Somehow, she didn't think so.

"There are many ways in which to serve. Some are more advantageous than others."

Ah-ha! "And what might those be, m'lord?"

"A clever person can find them out." Confidence now ran in a strong current beneath the icy surface of his voice. Forty years of power and easy victories showed in his disdainful assurance that he could buy whatever, or whomever, he wanted. "There are secrets . . ." he began, but at that moment the drapes to one side parted and a boy came quickly into the room, holding a scroll.

"Grandfather, look at this," the newcomer said eagerly.

For an instant, Jame wondered why the boy's pale features were so familiar. Then she remembered: that was the frightened face she had seen in the alley the night Penari had almost died. The boy felt her eyes on him. He turned, saw her, and promptly lost what little color he had.

The Sirdan, however, was too angry to notice this interchange. The boy's intrusion had set him badly off stride for reasons that Jame could not even guess. "We will continue this discussion later," he said curtly to her, still glaring at his grandson. "Now go."

"Very well, m'lord. Oh, by the way," she added, turning at the door. "My master sends his regards." She sensed his wrathful eyes on her back as long as she was in sight.

Walking out through the hall, Jame considered the growing complexity of her situation. It was obvious now why Penari had chosen her, a Kencyr, to be his apprentice. After decades of pressure to make him reveal his secrets, he had taken revenge on them all by choosing to confide not only in an outsider but in one whose very race was to him a guarantee of her incorruptibility. Just now he had thrown her to Theocandi in hopes that the Sirdan would break his teeth on her. That he had not was only the first warning that little from now on was apt to be as simple as her new master seemed to think. As a further token of this, what in all the names of God was she to make of Theocandi's grandson, that pleasant-faced boy who had stood by watching while two pug-nasties had tried to kill an old man?

She was descending to the courtyard when something warned her that she was being followed. The dark man came down the steps toward her, flanked by three others as richly clothed as he, in shades as sober.

"There's a meeting at the Three Legg'd Dog in an hour," he said to her as he passed. "Be there."

He and his companions were several steps below Jame when she said, quietly, "No."

Those unnervingly bright eyes turned back to her, lighting up even more with incredulous, pleased surprise.

"What did you say?"

"I said, 'No.'" Automatically, she noted the position and postures of all four, the flash of a knife hilt sheathed in one man's boot, another in his comrade's belt, and took an unobtrusive step back to the stairwell. "I belong to the Guild now and as such owe loyalty to it and to my master," she said. "No one said anything about jumping when *you* whistle."

"Quite right, too," said a new voice from the foot of the steps. A young man clad in royal blue stood there watching them. "No one owes Bane anything he can't exact by force," he said, still speaking to Jame but watching the four. Two others had come out of the crowd to stand behind him. Am I being defended? Jame wondered, unexpectedly amused, but then decided that she was more the excuse than the cause for this confrontation. The role didn't appeal to her.

"Carry on, gentlemen," she said to the gathering at large and walked past the lot of them into the bustle of the market before anyone had a chance to react.

The young man in blue caught up with her several blocks later, on the south bank of the Tone.

"That was rather remarkable," he said, falling into step beside her. "It isn't often that anyone stands up to Bane, especially without support. You must either be extremely brave or phenomenally stupid."

"Mostly the latter, I think, in conjunction with being very Kencyr."

"Really? Someone told me that, but I didn't believe it. Is it true that you people don't come from Rathillien at all, and that you're able to touch minds with animals, and that you can carry each other's souls?"

"More or less," said Jame, smiling at his sudden eagerness. "Also, some of us can't endure sunlight—although I can; and most of us are left-handed—although I'm not. By the way, you may not remember it, but I think we've met before. About a week ago, weren't you the one who dove into the river after that boy?"

The light went out of his face.

"I thought so. Who was he?"

"No one knows," he said with growing bitterness. "So many young boys come in from the provinces looking for someone to sponsor them in the Guild. Bane can pick and choose. To be fair, I don't think the Sirdan approves, but he has very little control over his so-called pupil. Theocandi's general edict has protected your master so far, mostly because Penari has never much interested Bane. You, however, apparently do—and that can be very dangerous."

"Wait a minute. Go back a bit. Why should the Sirdan protect Penari? I got the impression that they don't like each other."

"Nor do they, but Theocandi has to have some guarantee that no one will beat the old boy's secrets out of him"—they'd kill him first, thought Jame—"and besides, differences notwithstanding, brothers have to stick together, the way Mendy and I do."

"Now let me get this straight; Penari is Theocandi's brother . . ."

"Older."

"And you're Men-dalis's?"

"Younger. Right. The name is Dallen, incidentally—Dally to you." For the first time since the mention of the flayed boy, he smiled. His face was surprisingly youthful. "You really don't know much about current events, do you? I wonder if you have any idea what kind of a situation you've walked into."

"If I did, I probably wouldn't be here. And speaking of walking, are we bound someplace in particular or are you just looking for a nice stretch of river to pitch me into?"

He laughed. "I don't think I could if I wanted to. No, I just thought it would be a good opportunity to introduce you to some of the other 'prentices at the Moon in Splendor down the way. It's as close to neutral ground as we have left in Tai-tastigon; and since your master hasn't taken a side yet, you probably won't want to at first either."

"Not until you've had a chance to recruit me for your brother, you mean."

"But of course," he said, with an ingenuous smile.

THE MOON WAS A LARGE, brightly lit inn facing the Tone and River Street. Inside, the noise was deafening. Wall to wall, the great hall seemed to be cobbled with the heads of apprentices, with a few older journeymen thrown in and one young master holding court in a far corner. Jame's companion was greeted with a roar of welcome and not a few eyes turned toward her, openly or covertly. She had the sense of being sized up from all directions and found reassuringly lacking. Room was made for them at a center table.

"I don't see any women here," she said in an undertone to Dally, taking an offered seat.

"Very few have been permitted into the Guild since Theocandi came to power. He doesn't think much of female thieves, which is idiotic considering the great ones we've had in the past. At any rate, no one can accuse you of getting in under false pretenses."

"I should hope not, but if anyone says anything about having made a clean breast of it, there's going to be bloodshed."

At that moment, a wizened monkey of a boy scrambled up onto the tabletop, upsetting tankards right and left, and rose unsteadily to his feet. Those whose ale hadn't been spilt raised a derisive cheer and some began to clap.

"No, no, no!" the boy screeched, waving his hands. "No dancing tonight, 'least not 'til we've welcomed our new member. You, Talisman, stand up. Fellow lunatics, Master Penari's new 'prentice!"

There was another cheer, as derisive as the first, but somehow tinged with uncertainty as well. They hadn't made up their minds about her, Jame thought, bowing to them. Among her own people, such hesitancy would quickly be followed by a challenge, and so it was here, too.

"The measure, the full measure!" someone shouted in the back of the room and many eagerly took up the cry, all hesitation gone.

The "full measure" arrived. It was an enormous flagon that must have contained over a gallon and a half of ale. Regarding it with dismay, Jame said "Propose something else."

"Well! What else can we pr-pr-propose, eh?" The boy threw a broad wink at his audience. "Something reasonably simple . . . like maybe fetching us the Cloud King's britches."

"All right," said Jame.

Dally choked on his beer. "Talisman, you loon," he gasped between bouts of coughing, "Scramp was only teasing you!"

"And I've paid him the compliment of taking him seriously, or as much so as anyone can. See you later."

She was gone before he could react, leaving behind a small but rapidly spreading ripple of shock.

Behind the Moon in Splendor was the house of an obscure lay brotherhood whose members, for reasons best known to themselves, spent their lives pushing a boulder up a ramp and then letting it fall from a considerable height on a bound chicken. In the course of a day they usually disposed of nineteen or twenty birds in this fashion. The sound didn't carry far, but one could distinctly feel the floor shake inside the Moon, and sometimes a dish fell off the wall.

Dally had anxiously noted two such tremors since the Talisman's departure, and now here was another one rattling the cups on the table. He was furious with himself for having brought her to this place instead of to his own faction's haunt, where he at least had some control over Lower Town trash like Scramp. If anything happened to his new friend, he would take it out of that wretched boy's hide. For the hundredth time, Dally wondered where the young Kencyr was.

Most Tastigons who knew anything about the Kencyrath thought of it as an exotic oddity. They laughed at Kencyr claims to a home-world other than Rathillien, and as for Kencyr beliefs, how could any reasonable man even consider monotheism, much less warnings that some monstrous evil lurked all around the Eastern Lands, waiting to devour them? You humored people like that, especially if they happened to be the finest warriors around, but you didn't always take them seriously.

Dally, however, did. The Kencyrath had fascinated him since childhood. He had always longed to meet one of its people; and tonight he finally had, only to lose her again in a matter of minutes. This Talisman seemed an unlikely figure when set against the magnificent, vaguely sinister forms of his imagination, and yet perhaps not so out of place among them after all. He hoped desperately that he had not seen the last of her.

"I see you waited for me," Jame said, slipping onto the bench he had kept vacant for her. "Here." She tossed the bundle of cloth across the table to Scramp. It was a pair of trousers, made of rich fabric but much mended. "I'm afraid the only proof of ownership I can offer is that patch on the back," she said as the little Townie held them up so the people in the rear who had stood up on their benches could see. "But if any of you gentlemen think I had time to embroider the royal crest there, you don't know much about needlecraft. Just the same . . ." the noise level was on the rise again, excitedly overleaping her voice ". . . *just the same,* I should tell you that I didn't steal these pants. The Cloud King gave them to me."

And that was exactly what had happened. On climbing to the inn's roof, Jame had been amazed to find Sparrow waiting for her. It seemed that when she had not appeared in court within a few days, Prince Dandello had sent out scouts to look for her; and it was her erstwhile guide who had spotted her first, entering the Moon with Dally. He had escorted her to the Winter Quarters, which were across the river in the loft of an abandoned house. There His Spacious Majesty had been pleased to give her not only the coveted freedom of the skies but also an old pair of pants when she explained her need of them.

She tried to tell the other apprentices all this; but Scramp, after listening with incredulity for a moment, stopped her short by suddenly bursting into laughter. That set off the rest of the room. Only Dally saw Jame's face go white and understood why.

"Scramp, my dear lad," he said quickly with an unmistakable note of alarm, "there's one thing you must never, ever do in dealing with any Kencyr, and that's even to imply that he or she isn't telling the truth. It simply isn't healthy."

Scramp took this warning, if not seriously, at least enough so to sit down and temporarily shut up. The racket soon regained its normal tone. Jame relaxed slowly. The violence of her reaction had surprised her, almost as much as the realization that so many of her new colleagues were not prepared to take her or her concept of honor seriously. There might well be trouble over that later; but if so, it could be dealt with when it came.

"Do you suppose," she said rather plaintively to the room at large, "that I might have a drink now? A *small* one?"

A moment later seven noggins had appeared on the table before her, and an untold number were still on the way.

"Welcome to the Thieves' Guild," said Dally with a grin.

BOOK II

CROWN OF NIGHTS

CHAPTER 5

Winter Days

DALLY SLID TO the right, feinting, then lunged. Jame pivoted to meet him. Her left arm jerked up as she tried to snare his knife in the full sleeve of her d'hen. For a second the blade caught in the tough, mesh lining, then he twisted it free and jumped back. Hissing wickedly, her return strike skimmed the front of his tunic.

"Not bad!" he said, maneuvering warily at arm's length. "You're fast enough, but you always hold back. Come on, let's see some aggression!"

Back and forth they went over the flagstones of the Res aB'tyrr's courtyard, circling the well, avoiding the mound of manure that Ghillie had just mucked out of the stable. It was three and a half weeks after Winter's Eve, and the late afternoon air was growing chill, but still the lesson continued.

"C'mon, attack, attack!" Dally gasped, leaping in with a lateral strike, which Jame neatly blocked. "What's the matter with you?"

"I don't like knives!"

"Well, you've got to learn how to use one anyway, unless you want every flash-blade in town picking on you. You can't take them all on bare-handed . . ."

Jame, with a frustrated growl, drove her knife between two flagstones and sprang at him. A moment later, Dally found himself disarmed and face down on the pavement with the pile of manure inches from his nose and his right arm locked in a most uncomfortable position over his head.

". . . then again," he said in a muffled voice, "maybe you can."

"Am I—uh—interrupting something?" said an unfamiliar voice tentatively.

"I am, I think, about to be stood on my head in a dunghill," said Dally, wriggling futilely. "By all means, interrupt, interrupt!" His arm released, he scrambled to his feet, then froze, regarding the boy at the gate with disbelief.

"Canden, the Sirdan Theocandi's grandson, isn't it?" Jame said. "Meet Dallen, the brother of Master Men-dalis."

The kinsman of the Guild's two bitterest rivals bowed to each other warily. Neither seemed quite sure what to do next.

"Cleppetty's just baked a damson tart," said Jame, amused. "Come in, both of you, and have some."

"It really was you in the alley that night, wasn't it?" Canden asked as he perched on the south hearth, gingerly juggling a slice of pastry. "I thought you were a ghost god. You gave me a real scare turning up at the Palace like that."

"I'll bet I did, and for all I know, you deserved it. What in all the names of God were you doing, hiding in the shadows while those two pug-nasties tried to murder your grand-uncle?"

"Oh, they wouldn't have hurt him." Canden gave Dally a quick, nervous glance. "It was all a trick, you see. In another minute I was supposed to jump out of the doorway and save him, thereby winning his gratitude and maybe a chance to become his apprentice . . . or so Grandfather hoped. I told him it wouldn't work, but he never listens to me. Now he's furious with me for failing and with you for being successful, but I don't care. In fact, I'm glad," he said with sudden, desperate defiance, quite losing control of the tart, which slid off his knee onto the floor. "I don't want to be a thief or trick Grand-Uncle Penari out of his secrets or be the next Sirdan when Grandfather dies. No one seems to understand that."

"Wait a minute," said Dally, startled out of his suspicious silence. "I thought Bane was Theocandi's chosen successor. After all, he's the old man's only pupil."

"Normally, that would be true, but he was forced on Grandfather by his father, Abbotir of the Gold Court, just before the Guild Council meeting six years ago in return for political support. The funny thing is that I don't think Bane wants to be a thief either. He has his own interests, his own . . . amusements. Three weeks ago, on Grandfather's name-day, his followers made me watch while he mutilated that child. The things they did to him before he died—and after . . ." He shuddered, then suddenly looked up. "I would have come sooner if Grandfather hadn't wanted me to, but to spy, to betray . . . that can't be what friendship is for . . . can it?"

Dally, who had been listening first with suspicion, then with embarrassment, now looked at that young, pleading face and said warmly, "Of course, it isn't."

At that moment Cleppetty appeared at the hall door. She stopped short, staring first at the half-empty pastry tin and then at the sticky mess on the floor at Canden's feet. In the midst of this explosive pause, Dally stepped up to her and gravely kissed the tip of her sharp nose. Then with one accord he and Jame bolted out the street door, dragging Canden with them.

"Well," said Jame several blocks later when they had stopped running, "now that you gentlemen have arranged things so that I can't go home for a few hours—or maybe a few days—how do you suggest we spend the rest of the afternoon?"

"I hear that the Askebathes' temple has been desanctified for repairs," said Canden eagerly. "They might let us in to have a look around . . . if there isn't something you'd rather do."

"Why not?" said Dally, smiling at the boy. "We're free until this evening and can pay our respects to my father while we're in the district."

"Is he a priest?"

"No. He's Dalis-sar, the sun god of the New Pantheon."

Jame grinned, remembering how she reacted the first time he had sprung this bit of information on her. All she could think of to say, in a tone of profound confusion, had been, "How did *that* happen?" "Oh, the usual way," Dally had said lightly. "My mother was a handmaiden in his temple in Tai-abendra. Actually, I wasn't born until after she'd left to marry a local tradesman, but she arranged for my adoption so I and Mendy, who's a true god's son, would be full brothers." "Handmaiden" was the usual clerical euphemism for a temple prostitute.

So they visited the house of the Askebathes and then that of Dally's father. Jame was unable to see much of anything in the latter because of the blinding light cast by the wheels of Dalis-sar's war chariot. Today it was especially bad, Dally told her, because the god himself was standing in the golden vehicle.

"It would be even worse," he added, "if he were facing us directly. Instead, yes, he's still glaring back over his own shoulder. That's been going on for a good six years now. No one knows why."

Jame herself could see neither god nor chariot because of the glare. When she held up her hands to blot out the heart of the fire, however, it seemed to her that behind it was not the rear of the temple but the city itself, as though seen from a great height, with the details of the Lower Town preternaturally distinct.

But the sanctuary was alive with more than radiance. Anger shook the air like the steady, immense rumble of a volcano, penetrating flesh, jarring bone, yet unheard. It was the darkness at the heart of the light. Once Dally had proudly told Jame that, like all the deities of the New Pantheon, Dalis-sar had once been a man, and that man, a Kencyr. She had smiled at the idea of a monotheist being drafted as a god. Now, however, the cold darkness of that rage, so like her own the day the beam had fallen, left no room for doubt. Shaken, she left the temple, her fingertips on Dally's arm, for the brightness had left her temporarily blind.

Outside, all was enemy territory. She had never felt it so much as now, walking sightless and vulnerable between the two young men. The gods of Tai-tastigon were all around her. The shadow of their power brushed her mind in the red-shot darkness. If any of them, even Dalis-sar, proved to be real in the same way that her own god was, she would have to admit that the entire culture and history of her people—thirty millennia of hardship, sacrifice, and honor—were built on self-delusion. But how did one go about proving the entire populace of a large city wrong; and if she failed to do so, how could her faith in her own heritage, in herself, remain intact?

They were passing the temple of Gorgo the Lugubrious. Speculatively, Jame looked at it, blinking away the last of her blindness.

Canden left them at the district gate, and Jame and Dally walked on, discussing their new acquaintance. Dally clearly wanted to take the Sirdan's grandson at his word, but felt he owed it to his brother to keep some suspicions alive. Jame, who as yet had no stake in Guild politics, smiled at her friend's reluctant caution.

They arrived early that evening at the headquarters of the New Faction, a fortresslike house near the Sun Gate in the Gold Ringing District.

"One has to make a good impression," said Dally as he escorted her through the richly appointed corridors. "It isn't easy, though, competing with a man who has the whole Guild treasury as his privy purse."

Men-dalis received them in his private study. It was the first time the leader of the New Faction and Master Penari's apprentice had met. Dally watched them both eagerly, noting the graceful formality with which they exchanged greetings. All was going well, he thought.

Jame would have agreed—at first. As fair as his brother was dark, blessed with sapphire blue eyes and movements a dancer might envy, Men-dalis was without doubt the handsomest man she had ever seen. The very room with its rich furnishings of blue and silver seemed to take on an added luster from him. No one would ever doubt that this indeed was a true son of Dalis-sar, Lord of the Golden Chariot.

He began to speak of his plans for the Guild after the Grand Council awarded him the sirdanate that coming winter. Jame had heard them all before from Dally, but never so glowingly described. The eloquence of the speaker first tugged at her imagination, then swept it forward into a bright, nebulous future compared to which Theocandi's forty year regime seemed the merest dross.

Then, abruptly, something brought her back to the present with a start. A face was peering over Men-dalis's shoulder. Far back in the shadows of the room, perched on the edge of a table like an escaped gargoyle, was a tiny, skull-faced man. His hands, more bone than flesh, lay twisted together on bony knees under a sharp chin. His expression, which only her

Kencyr eyes could have seen in the dark, was one of unalloyed malignity.

Soon after that, Men-dalis's monologue ended and they were graciously dismissed. Jame, glancing back from the doorway, saw the New Faction leader already deep in conference with the man from the shadows, who, she suddenly realized, must be the head of his spy network, a man known in the streets of Tai-tastigon only as the Creeper.

"Dally . . ." she said as they left the house. "Would you say that I frighten easily?"

"Gods, no. Why?"

"Your brother scares me. I think he might be capable of anything."

Dally looked startled, then said, "Of course he is!" and launched into an enthusiastic description of all the glorious things that Men-dalis would do when he had power. Jame tried to listen, but her mind only saw that radiant, preternaturally handsome face, cheek to cheek with a living death's head, whose eyes, pools of hatred and envy, had not once left Dally's face.

MEN-DALIS DID NOT REQUEST that Jame visit him again. Clearly, he did not attach much importance to her and was content to win her loyalty, if at all, through Dally.

Theocandi also kept his distance, but with less indifference. Through Canden, Jame learned of the life-long rivalry between the Sirdan and her new master. Theocandi had always been jealous of Penari's reputation and raged at his older brother's refusal to envy him his own position and power. All his life, the younger brother had tried to excel the elder—in skill, arcane studies, renown—and always he had failed. Now in the evening of his days, nothing was more important to him than mastering the secrets that had always made Penari superior in all things that had ever really mattered to either of them. In the end, however, Theocandi could not believe that Penari would give what he considered to be family secrets to an outsider. Consequently Jame was left alone, for the time being at least.

Meanwhile, she, Canden, and Dally were getting on splendidly together. Dally, too good-natured to hold his suspicions for long, had taken an almost fraternal interest in the younger boy, while Jame responded to his loneliness, so reminiscent of her own at an earlier age. She also discovered that Canden had in him a spirit of inquiry not unlike her own and a fascination with the past that if anything surpassed his mistrust of the present.

"Do you know what the oldest building in Tai-tastigon is?" he asked Jame one day. "That temple of yours. As far as I can tell, it was here before the city walls went up, before the Old Empire was established, before the Kencyrath itself even arrived. How is that possible?"

"Maybe the scrollsmen and Arrin-ken know who built it," said Jame. "I don't. Every time we've had to shift worlds, though, the temples have always been waiting for us. The one here is probably as old as Rathillien itself. The other Tastigon priests don't even like to acknowledge its existence."

"Maybe that's why they chose a different part of the city for the Temple District," said Canden thoughtfully. "I've heard that there's another even larger Kencyr temple to the south, in the ruins of Tai-than."

He talked a great deal about this lost city, the great southern capital of the Old Empire, whose decaying towers no man had seen in half a millennium. An expedition was currently being organized to search for it, and Canden desperately wanted to be part of it. It was an announcement of these preparations that he had brought to show his grandfather the night he had interrupted the old man's attempts to bribe Jame. Theocandi would probably never have let him go anyway, but now he was too incensed by the boy's failure in the alley even to consider it. Jame felt responsible for all this. Trying to make it up to the boy, she gave him her friendship and, in an attempt to placate Theocandi for his sake, passed on to him some of the things that Master Penari taught her.

None of these could be classified as a secret. In fact, nothing she had learned so far seemed to fit into that category, and Jame was beginning to wonder if the old man meant to keep his own council after all. This disappointed her, of course, but on the other hand the training he was prepared to give her left neither time nor grounds for dissatisfaction.

Eventually, Penari introduced an intense course on the rules of Jame's new profession, however, which gave her hope that her lessons were about to move in new directions.

She learned that everything an apprentice stole over a certain value became the property of his master, whose duty it was to send the booty to one of the five Guild courts, each one of which was specialized in a different kind of merchandise. There it was assessed and the length of time determined for which its possession was punishable by law. This crucial time, called the period of jeopardy, began as soon as the object came into the apprentice's hands. In Tai-tastigon, possession was the sole proof of guilt. Complicity was sometimes punished as well, but only if the accused had been in physical contact with the stolen article. Penalties ranged from fines to the loss of a finger, hand, or the whole of one's skin, for robberies involving undue violence or the injuring of a guardsman. The worst punishment of all—public flaying preceded by whatever mutilations a mob of concerned citizens could inflict—was reserved for anyone who tried to assassinate one of the Five or a Guild-lord.

Hearing this, Jame's eyes darkened with memory. Not long before, an embittered young journeyman had attacked the Sirdan in the Guild Hall itself. It would be a long time before she forgot that pitiful figure, already blind, tongueless, and castrated, writhing under the knife and cauterizing irons on the Mercy Seat.

Realizing that he had lost her attention, Penari ended his lecture with a snarl. Scooping a handful of gems out of a desk drawer (along with several marbles and a mouse's skull), he threw them down on the floor before her, then immediately swept them up again and demanded to know exactly what she had seen. This was an old exercise between them, and Jame usually did very well at it. Today, however, she could only name eighteen out of thirty or so stones. Various things were distracting her, not the least of which was Monster, who had fallen asleep with his head balanced precariously on her shoulder.

Penari, thoroughly exasperated by now, snatched up the large translucent rock he used for paperweight and threw it, nearly braining them both. Upon extricating herself from the python's sleepy coils and recovering this stone, Jame suddenly realized that it was not the piece of quartz she had always taken it for. She was in fact holding an enormous uncut diamond, the Eye of Abarraden itself.

That day's lesson ended with Penari sending her out into the Maze with instructions to find her way from one point to another and, on returning, to describe to him turn for turn where she had been. She went, knowing that the old man would detect any mistake in her eventual recitation instantly. The same was true when he had her go out to memorize sections of the city. He would name a street and ask her how she would get from it to another, sometimes insisting that her route lie over the rooftops or even through the houses themselves as if she were escaping from a very determined pursuer. In the course of these games, she had suddenly realized something very odd: for her master, Tai-tastigon was the same, structure by structure, as it had been when he had first gone into seclusion over fifty years before and nothing would convince him otherwise. This knowledge cleared up some of her confusion. It didn't help much, however, when he made her describe routes through areas long since reduced to rubble by one of the city's numerous disasters and subsequently rebuilt. Today, she was happy enough to contend only with the Maze and did so well in it that Penari, mollified, let her go early.

Standing on the threshold, turning up the collar of her d'hen against the cool evening air, Jame reflected that she was receiving an education every bit as eccentric in some ways as it was excellent in others.

A tall figure passed by the end of the street, instantly recognizable by his cream-velvet d'hen. Jame called after him to wait, and a few minutes later she was walking westward beside Darinby, a journeyman of Master Galishan. Darinby was one of the Guild's finest, a true craftsman with family tradition behind him and glory ahead according to most savants, who predicted that he would soon become the Guild's youngest master. Jame had always admired his skill, style, and integrity. He was the sort of thief she hoped to become if the length of her stay in Tai-tastigon permitted it; and it pleased her very much that he in turn seemed to like her. They walked on together, discussing the upcoming Guild elections.

"No, I haven't chosen a side," said Darinby, "and probably won't either. Theocandi's too corrupt for my taste, and Men-dalis is too ambitious. My master will probably support the latter—if he can get his mind off M'lady Melissand long enough—but you and I, Talisman, should be glad we've no voice in the matter.''

''Huh. Sometimes I wonder if anyone else realizes that.''

''Your position *is* rather peculiar, isn't it?'' he said, smiling. ''Strictly speaking, Penari has no more power than Galishan, just one vote out of a hundred among the landed masters for their two representatives; but others will be swayed by his decision, and you're the only person in the city close enough to him to influence it. Bad times are coming. I don't envy you, Talisman, no, not at all.''

They parted at the Serpent Fountain.

''Oh, by the way,'' the journeyman said, stopping suddenly and turning back toward her. ''There's a rumor that since you enrolled at the Guild Hall, Bane has given up young boys. I should walk wary if I were you, Talisman.''

She watched him go, his d'hen glimmering in the dusk.

Wind devils whirled about the fountain, mixing its spray with the thin rain that had begun to fall. Jame spun about. Surely someone was watching her. Often over the last few weeks she had felt the sudden chill of eyes but never seen the face behind them. No more so now. Darinby's words, however, had unlocked a memory. The first time her flesh had crept this way had been in the Sirdan's Palace, walking down a corridor with the whisper of footsteps behind her. Names of God, but her nerves must be raw. The square was empty, its shadows tenantless. She set out for home briskly, not deigning to look back.

IT WAS MID-EVENING when Jame reached the Res aB'tyrr after a breathless game of Follow-my-lead across the rain-slick rooftops with a trio of Cloudie friends. The first thing that struck her as she opened the kitchen door was the uproar within; the second was a large, half-roasted goose. Her immediate impression was that someone had thrown the fowl at her. Then she realized that the headless creature was in fact under its own power and making a very credible attempt to escape. After several hectic moments of being hauled about the courtyard, frequently off her feet, she finally pinioned the greasy, squirming carcass and marched it back to the door.

Inside Kithra—formerly of the Skyrrman—was struggling to hold down the lid of a pot from which a score of naked chicken wings protruded, flapping madly, while Cleppetty pursued an escaped quail about the kitchen with a broom, and Ghillie, huddled in a corner, frantically read names out loud from a book of household exorcisms.

"Look under fowls, not fantods," gasped the widow, flailing away determinedly. "You brought it home, you get rid of it!"

Ghillie flipped over several pages and began to read again, even faster than before: ". . . Afanci-Ainsel-Allisoun-Assgingel . . . ah!"

A wind full of chittering sounds rushed through the kitchen and up the three chimneys. Cleppetty's bird plopped to the floor. Kithra's kettle stopped jumping. And the goose suddenly went limp in Jame's arms.

"Ah, indeed!" said the widow with satisfaction. "But, oh, what a mess!" She ruefully surveyed her once immaculate kitchen, spattered now with fragments of pastry, goose, and bits of stuffing.

"So this is how you amuse yourselves when I'm not around," said Jame, dropping her now inert captive on the table. "What happened?"

"Bogles," said Cleppetty succinctly. "And this is nothing: you should have been here when the pigeon pie decamped. Now upstairs and off with that shirt, missy; you're better basted than that damned bird."

The gods of Tai-tastigon were for the most part properly templed; but now and then, presumably when they slept, wisps of power escaped. These sometimes attached themselves to passers-by and were carried out of the District to become the dreaded bogles—malignant, mischievous, or simply mindless impulses that would wreak havoc until the speaking of their proper name dispelled them. Nothing had ever followed Jame home—nothing would have dared—but Ghillie, clearly, had been less fortunate.

As she changed clothes up in the loft, Jame heard clapping and cheers from across the square. Though still not completely furnished, the ground floor of the Skyrrman blazed with light. The uproar receded, leaving behind the sound of a harp running thoughtfully through its trills. Jame listened, hardly breathing. The master harpist was playing well tonight, more than living up both to his reputation and to the staggering sum that Marplet sen Tenko must have paid to bring him upriver from his home in Endiscar to perform here. With such competition, it was hardly surprising that the Res aB'tyrr was almost deserted tonight and had been for the last two weeks. The music ended, its last note dying away into silence before the storm of applause began again.

In a dark, third story window of the Skyrrman, a shadowy figure raised its hand to Jame in a mocking salute. She returned it, one palm down in the Kencyr fashion to show appreciation, and then descended to the kitchen.

"We're still being watched," she said, reentering the room. "This time by Marplet himself, I think. Why do you suppose they do it?"

"The gods only know," said Cleppetty, scraping food off the wall. "Why, for that matter, have they been making a list of our patrons this past fortnight, and what business has our precious Bortis at the Skyrrman?"

"Bortis?" It took Jame a moment to remember Taniscent's former lover.

"That's right," said Ghillie, coming in from the courtyard with a bucket of water, which he poured into the scullery cauldron as Kithra stoked the fire under it. "In case you haven't noticed he practically lives there now."

"Something's up, all right," said the widow, sitting back on her heels. "But what? Marplet's well on his way to ruining us as it is, what with all his grand, imported talent. Of course, he can't keep it up forever, even with his brother-in-law's support; but if we lose enough business long enough, Tubain won't be able to renew our charter when it falls due come Spring's Eve . . . and if he can't, Marplet will snatch it up as fast as hot bricks in a blizzard. Without that bit of paper, the Res aB'tyrr has no legal protection. It will be the end of us. Surely that should satisfy him."

"But it won't," said Kithra suddenly, her voice hardening. "He played cat-and-mouse with you, and the mouse drew first blood. After what happened to Niggen, his pride is at stake now too. No, he won't be so easily satisfied."

Jame was inclined to believe her. If anyone knew the workings of Marplet's mind, it was his former servant. Kithra had come from her home in Tenzi canton a year ago to work at his inn, and by dint of some very skillful seduction had finally ended up in his bed. This should have greatly improved her social position, but she had reckoned without Marplet's intense misogyny. Her ploy had only earned his contempt. The girl's hatred for him now, after the way he had expelled her, was frightening in its intensity. Just the same, it had not taken the edge off her natural ambition. Jame believed she was currently trying to decide if it would be more advantageous to marry Rothan, become Tubain's mistress, or take on both roles simultaneously. She looked at Kithra askance, wondering just what her attack on Niggen had unleashed on this normally tranquil household.

And then there was Marplet sen Tenko. Slowly she was beginning to understand him better—the love of perfection that had led him to construct his inn so slowly, using only the finest materials; the almost feline quality of mind that allowed him to take such pleasure in his many schemes; his shame at having to call that lump of flesh Niggen his son. She could almost feel the sense of anger and betrayal that gripped him each time he saw that ungainly boy in his perfect house. What she did not feel, strangely enough, was any sort of personal animosity toward her whenever their eyes met across the square.

"Female or not," Cleppetty had said in grim amusement when she mentioned this one day, "now that he's taken your measure, I think he's rather come to like you. You'd look better sitting on his hearth next to that mangy tomcat of his than Niggen does, and more natural than you do here, for that matter. A tiger cub in a field of tabbies, that's you."

"Meow!" Jame had said, and rolled Boo over on his back.

Now she folded up her sleeves and helped the others scrub down the kitchen, half listening to their talk, thinking her own thoughts. Finally the inn closed its doors for the night.

Up in the loft, on the edge of sleep, a sudden coldness jolted her awake, made her throw back the blanket and stand staring out. The Skyrrman was dark. She was alone and yet, somehow, as beside the Serpent Fountain earlier that evening and a dozen times before that, she was being watched.

Are you thinking of me, butcher of children? she asked the night. I am of you. Thought crosses thought, like steel in the dark. Why can't you leave me alone . . . and why am I afraid that you will?

The rain had turned to snow. White crystals fell on her black hair, on bare arms and breasts. Shivering she lay down again, wrapped in her blanket, but did not sleep until the eastern sky was tinged with light and cocks had begun to crow at the edge of the city.

CHAPTER 6

Water Flow, Fire Leap

MID-WINTER'S DAY ARRIVED, cool and clear. Jame, Dally, and Canden went to Judgment Square to see the apotheosis of the Frost King, but were driven to the rooftops when fighting broke out between two factions in a temple war and the crowd panicked. Up on the tiles, Jame first had the pleasure of preventing her friends from being thrown off and then of presenting them to Prince Dandello, who had come with his retinue to see the rites. The bloodshed below, however, made the prince ill, and he soon left. The other three soon followed.

They were becoming a common trio, one the Guild had trouble understanding. But then they understood little when Jame was in question. By now, she could open any lock in the city, go anywhere like a shadow in the night, and reach anyone from a guild lord in his hall to the meanest beggar in hiding for his life. But still her new talents made her uneasy. The closer she came to actual stealing, the more she wondered how it would be possible to abscond honorably with someone else's property, despite what Ishtier had told her. And so she hedged. The apple vendor missed the rottenest of his wares from the bottom of the pile; the nobleman, surrounded by his retainers, discovered that the smallest button on his trousers was inexplicably missing. And now a rich merchant went his way, unaware that deft fingers had slipped into his pocket, found the least valuable coin there by touch alone, and triumphantly carried it off. Surely not much honor was risked by such trifling thefts as these.

"Just the same," said Dally, looking doubtfully at the tin coin that she had just dropped into his hand, "they'll never understand it at the Moon."

Jame smiled ruefully. She knew only too well what her reputation was now that she had gone for weeks without matching the exploit of the Cloud King's britches, which had brought her into the Guild with such fanfare. The other young thieves conveniently forgot that none of them had accomplished much during their first six months or, for that matter, in their first year. For Penari's pupil, however, things were different. With such a master, she must command respect or deserve contempt; her peers had left her no middle ground.

But that trial would soon be over. Winter would now be sliding down toward spring, and it was time that she make plans to leave Tai-tastigon. Her smile faded. She had suddenly realized that she didn't want to go.

There were several reasons for this, she realized later. For one thing, she hated to leave without somehow having proved herself worthy of Penari's instructions. For another, she was hardly closer to solving the mystery of the gods than she had been when she first came. And then there was the Res aB'tyrr. The business of the charter must be settled by Spring's Eve, so come what may, she would be on hand for that. But if Marplet failed in his current scheme, he would simply launch another, and another, and another, until one succeeded or he, somehow, was stopped. It was impossible to see how this business would end. Moreover, if Kithra was right, Tubain would have her (Jame) indirectly to thank for anything unpleasant that befell him from now on. It was hardly honorable to desert him now and yet how could she commit herself to a campaign that might drag on for years if Marplet found it sufficiently entertaining?

But there was more to her hesitation even than this. She was no longer sure that she should rejoin the Kencyrath. She was remembering more and more of life at the keep: her father's ill-will, her brother's disapproval, all for something she couldn't help, for a cruel trick of heredity. It was said that there was no greater punishment for a Kencyr than to be cast out, denied any place among his people. But was that really worse than a shadow existence, permitted on sufferance alone to sit at some stranger's hearth? She didn't know. What had been true at the isolated keep might not be so in the Riverland. Still, as she sat on the loft's window ledge that night, more and more the face of the Kencyrath bore the features of Tori, her twin brother, whose love for her, however strong, had shone but feebly beneath the weight of his prejudices.

There was a burst of applause from the inn across the way, which quickly settled down into rhythmic clapping. Harpists were popular in Tai-tastigon, but a good dancer even more so. Jame thought of Taniscent in her lonely room below, hiding that wrinkled face and prematurely aged body from even the kindest of eyes. Once her talent might have saved the inn. How much that thought must prey on the former dancer's mind now God alone knew.

Cruel, cruel city with its gleaming snares and velveted claws, its eyes that shone up steadily at her even now, watching, waiting. And this was the place she thought to call her home? Yes. Its temper suited her. She could make her own way here and never think of the past again.

But was that possible? Perhaps . . . if she really knew what she was turning her back on. However, not only had several years fallen out of her own life, but she had learned not long ago that she didn't even know any recent Kencyr history. It seemed, for example, that the host of the Kencyrath had suffered a major defeat some thirty years ago, which had resulted in the exile of Ganth Gray Lord, its greatest Highborn. Dally knew this much, but little more. It had been a long time since news had moved freely across the Ebonbane—which probably, Jame thought, was why her own people had never learned of these events. Nonetheless, hearing of them now, she felt more cut off from her heritage than ever and even less inclined to abandon it without knowing what she was giving up.

But was the knowledge worth the pain that gaining it might cost?

And what about the ring and broken sword? They must be

gotten to her brother somehow, if only by messenger. Maybe Tori would even prefer it that way. But who could she trust with such a mission . . . assuming she could bring herself to delegate it at all.

Round and round her thoughts went—to go, to stay—and to make matters worse, she must decide soon. The passes usually cleared soon after the Feast of Fools, which took place just after Spring's Eve, and remained open until the Feast of Dead Gods at the end of the summer. This year, however, the readers of bones had predicted a remarkably short season, lasting perhaps a matter of weeks or less. When the high passes unlocked, she must go quickly or not at all.

Dawn surprised Jame, with no decision made. The widow, coming down early on a baking day, found her already up to her elbows in dough and pummeling away at it with all the frustrated energy of a mind at war with itself. Wise Cleppetty set to work without a word, and between them they soon plunged the kitchen deep into a floury fog that did not lift until late morning. Then came the baking, then the scrubbing, all in silence, all at a pace that even the tireless widow began to regret. She was just beginning to wonder, rather desperately, if she was about to be launched into spring cleaning two months early when Jame suddenly put aside her apron and left the inn.

The widow collapsed into a chair. "Don't ask!" she told a startled Kithra.

Jame found herself walking eastward with no clear idea of where she was going. On Armorers Row, a display of daggers laid out on black velvet caught her eye, reminding her of her aversion to knives. That was another mystery rooted in the past. Was she never to understand the reason for that either? On impulse, she picked up a knife, closed her eyes, and tried to remember.

Nothing came.

Sudden anger rose in her. Dammit, she wouldn't go through life without a past, forever a stranger to herself. Fiercely, she summoned all her will and threw it against the barrier in her mind. The ornate hilt bit into her hand. The sounds of the market fused into a dull roar. For a long moment she was alone in the red-shot darkness behind her trembling eyelids, and then she saw the room.

It was huge, its upper regions lost in shadows. Figures moved about her, indistinct, all eyes and gleaming teeth. One of them held up something. A cloak made of black serpent skins sewn together with silver thread. They put it on her bare shoulders . . . heavy, heavy, and the tails, coiled together beneath her chin, twitched. She was climbing a stair. The snake heads thumped on each step at her heels. He was waiting in an alcove, the shadows a mask over his ravaged face. A white-bladed knife slipped from one cold hand to another. She went on, clutching it, up toward the doorway barred with red ribbons, toward the darkness beyond . . .

"Hey!"

Her eyes snapped open. A shop boy was standing in front of her, scowling pugnaciously.

"You wanta buy that?" he demanded.

She dropped the dagger and walked blindly away. Her head throbbed. The hall, the man on the stair! Red ribbons, she vaguely remembered, were usually for a lord's wedding chamber, but the Serpent Skin Cloak and the Ivory Knife, surely they were things of legend. She thought of her mother, that strange, beautiful woman whom her father had brought back one day to the keep out of the Haunted Lands, out of nowhere. The others had thought her mute, for by day she never spoke, but at night her daughter had often awakened to the sound of her voice, reciting the ancient stories or singing songs that had been old when the Kencyrath was but new-founded. That was how Jame had first heard of the cloak, the knife, and the Book Bound in Pale Leather.

It was no use, she thought: fact would not separate from legend. But still, where had that hall been and who, in all the names of God, had she been climbing to meet, knife in hand?

The parapet of the Old Wall stretched out before her. Below, beyond it and the curtain walls, the caravans were gathering on the southern plain for their dash across the Ebonbane in the spring. To leave Tai-tastigon, to remain—either way, it couldn't hurt to make some inquiries.

The rest of the afternoon did little to ease either her growing headache or her mind. The first caravan-master she spoke to told her that the fee for anyone joining his convoy at Tai-tastigon was thirty-five golden altars. "If the price were any lower," he said, giving her a shrewd look, "we'd be overrun with thieves joined up for the pickings. It's no good trying to cross on your own, either; those hills will be thick with bandits come the thaws. No, without my help or that of my colleagues, you'll never see the other side."

"What about the sea routes?" Jame asked, stung by his smug air.

"These days, that's for those who don't care what they pay, or if they arrive. You've heard of dead water? Hit a patch of that some dark night and you sink like a brick—ship, cargo, and all. The straits are rotten with it. You don't believe me? Go ask in any port and check the fares too, while you're at it. Mine will look like a bargain after that."

"Well then, couldn't I work my way across? I can be a first-rate cook by then, and I'm already a fair hostler."

The master laughed. "All such positions were filled weeks ago, boy, but if you wouldn't mind working in another sort of position . . ." His hand dropped to her knee.

"Think about it, you scrawny bastard!" he shouted after her a moment later. "No one else will make a better offer!" And with that he retreated into his tent, gingerly feeling his jaw for loose teeth.

Unfortunately, the master was right. His two colleagues asked forty and forty-five altars respectively, and both laughed at her request for employment. Discouraged, she started home on the path that ran along the outer face of the bulwark. It had never occurred to her that passage would be so expensive or—worse yet—honest work so hard to find, though she cursed herself now for not having realized that the shortness of the season would affect both drastically. She had virtually no money of her own. Another thief would have stolen what he needed; but even if Jame had been in the practice of taking valuable things instead of trinkets, she would still have had too much respect for her oath not to turn them over to Penari. Although he and Tubain kept her in pocket money, neither paid her for her work—which was only fitting since one had agreed to train her without the usual fee and the other was giving her free room and board. She had counted on striking a bargain with the caravan-master and working for whatever she couldn't pay outright. It seemed now that she must either come up with the whole sum or a new plan if she really meant to leave in the spring.

Just then she came to a brook cutting through the bulwark and realized with irritation that she had missed the cut that led to the Meadow Gate. There were, however, other ways to enter the city. She followed the stream until it disappeared behind a gate in the outer curtain wall, then climbed the steep, lichen-covered stairs to a postern high in its outer face. Inside, a rope walk stretched across the dry moat to a minor gate set in the inner wall. Below, on either side of the swift water, were the kennels, catteries, and mews that catered to the sporting element among the city's rich folk.

Jame was two-thirds of the way across when she happened to look down and saw a man walk up to a small back-water carrying a weighted sack that appeared to be moving. He threw it in. Instantly such a feeling of panic swept over her that she almost fell. Close, wet, no air . . . she scrambled over the guide rope and dove clumsily. It was a long way down. The water hit her like a body blow, driving air out between her teeth. My God! she suddenly thought, halfway to the bottom. Do I know how to swim? At any rate, she clearly knew how to sink and was rapidly doing so in water that proved surprisingly deep and shockingly cold. Weeds rippled in the current below. Among them nestled many small sacks, only one of them still moving. Fighting down the panic that beat at her, she unsheathed the knife that Dally had insisted she carry and slashed open the bag. A small, furry body wriggled frantically through the slit. They swam upward together and surfaced gasping. The man on the bank stared at her open-mouthed as Jame waded ashore holding the shivering ounce cub.

''What in Perimal's name did you think you were doing?'' she demanded, nearly inarticulate with delayed shock and rage.

''Drowning it, of course,'' the man said, still staring.

''Why?''

''Look at its eyes.'' Jame did. They were wide with fear and opaque as milk opals. ''Blind,'' said the man regretfully. ''Born that way, poor mite. We kept it an extra month hoping they would clear, but this afternoon Master said, 'Right. Dispose of it.' So here I am, and there it is.''

''How much?''

He looked at her, puzzled. She forced herself to clarify.

"How much do you want for it?"

"Well now," he said, rubbing his chin, "although it don't look like much now, that's a Royal Gold, one of the rarest cats there is. If it were sound, Master would ask two hundred altars for it or more, but blind . . . well, Master is a hard man. He'd rather destroy it than ask less."

"I'll get the money," Jame said, knowing she spoke nonsense. Two hundred altars was more than half the price of Tubain's seven year charter, enough gold to keep the inn affluent for three seasons. Still, desperation drove her to repeat, "I'll get it, somehow."

The man looked at her, at the trembling cub in her arms. "*Well* now," he said slowly. "It seems to me that the tyke might as well disappear into the city as into that pool, though Master would ruin me for sure if he ever found out. I'll tell you what: promise never to tell how you came by him, and he's yours."

There was little that Jame would not have promised at that moment. It was only as she hurried away, slipping her prize inside her d'hen for warmth, that she realized there was no way she could ever prove that the cub had not been stolen.

THE SUN SET behind the mountains as Jame walked quickly through the curving streets of the Rim. She was still very wet and fast becoming bitterly cold in Tai-tastigon's sudden twilight with the cub a shaking morsel of ice against her right breast. The mind link she had shared with it in that moment of crisis no longer seemed to exist, although the beast clung to her as tightly as before, its small claws pricking her through her shirt. Perhaps it would return. Now all she felt was the cold and the same vague sense of being followed that had haunted her for so long that she now virtually ignored it. Besides, the inn was just ahead, on the other side of that gatehouse set in the Old Wall. Soon there would be warmth, supper, companionship . . .

In the shadow of the gate's arch, blocking the way, stood three men. The largest was Bortis. He smiled disagreeably but with satisfaction when he saw her and said: "I've a message for you, thief. You aren't to go home tonight . . . nor ever again if you're mindful of your health."

"Oh?" Jame said, bidding for time to rouse her half-frozen wits. "Who shall I thank for this kind warning?"

"Let's just say a friend, and you needn't bother to try going another way. All roads are closed to you tonight. Your friend doesn't want you hurt, but if you should be so ungrateful as to ignore his advice, well, something unpleasant might happen to you." His smile broadened. "In fact," he said softly, "something may happen to you anyway."

Jame took a quick step backward. With her right arm immobilized by the cub, she couldn't fight effectively against such odds. Her only chance lay in flight. Then, simultaneously, she saw Bortis look over her shoulder and sensed too sharply for any doubt that someone was behind her. She whirled. Bane stood there, smiling at her.

"Well, well," he said, regarding the young ounce. "Mother and child. Very pretty. Gentlemen, this lady would like to pass. Have you any objections?"

Bortis grinned and lunged. Bane pushed Jame out of the way and side-stepped. The edge of his left hand cut down on the other's wrist as he shot past. He was behind the man with his right forearm across his throat before the bandit had time to recover. Bane's left hand, now free, came up from his belt gripping bright steel. With a gesture of great delicacy, he pricked Bortis's right eye.

Bortis staggered against a wall with hands to his face. The other two men recoiled from him, too shocked to press the attack.

"Shall we go?" Bane said to Jame, bowing. "Theocandi's spies heard that there might be trouble here tonight," he said as he escorted her to the gate of Res aB'tyrr. "I thought I'd come to see what was brewing. Shall I stay in case there's more excitement?"

"No!" said Jame. Her stomach twisted at the thought of Bane involved in the hostelry's affairs, even of him setting foot inside its walls. "No thank you," she repeated, trying to be more courteous. "We'll cope . . . Bane, I don't understand you at all."

"You only think you don't," he said with a lazy smile. "You know me as well as you know yourself. Go in, m'lady. Your lips are blue with the cold." And he drew a fingertip down her cheek, turning the sharp nail edge to the jawline where it left a thin line of blood.

Cleppetty was at the kitchen table, chopping meat. For a moment she simply stared at the bedraggled, apologetic apparition that had materialized on her doorstep with dripping clothes and a smear of blood on its face. Then she advanced on Jame purposefully. Minutes later the young ounce was snug in a nest of old aprons by the fire, and Jame, having been shaking out of her wet garments and into a blanket, was sitting beside it, looking rather dazed.

The widow thrust a cup of hot spiced wine into her hands, waited until she had drunk half of it, and then said: "Explain!"

Jame did. Just as she finished, Ghillie and Rothan came in. Rothan was glaring into space with bloodshot eyes, making little whuffling noises deep in his throat. Ghillie, on the other hand, seemed half wild with joy even though his lip was split and bleeding freely.

"You should have seen him!" he crowed. "They said we couldn't pass, we objected, one of them hit me, and Rothan here went at them like a bull with a bee up his butt. It was glorious!"

"Wait a minute," said Cleppetty. "Who are 'they'?"

"Why, some of Marplet's pug-nasties, of course, too far from home to be protected by their precious guards. Oh, we've waited a long time for this! You should have been there with your skillet, Aunt Cleppetty. All we needed to make it perfect was a few cracked skulls."

"I may crack some yet," the widow said, regarding the capering boy balefully. "This doesn't sound good." She went to the door and shouted for Tubain, Kithra, and Taniscent.

"Kithra's out," sang Ghillie, trying to induce Jame to dance with him. "So is Taniscent. I saw her leave with Bortis."

"Bortis!" said Tubain, entering from the courtyard. "When did she start seeing him again?"

"Just about the time he settled into the Skyrrman," said the widow. "I thought you knew. Ghillie, you monkey, calm down. What will the customers think?"

"There aren't any."

"*What?*" Cleppetty advanced on the boy menacing. "None?"

"Look for yourself!" he cried, ducking behind the still immobile Rothan. "The hall is empty."

At that moment, Kithra burst into the kitchen through the street door. "They're stopping them all," she gasped. "They tried to stop me too, but I got away and ran."

"*Who* are they stopping?" Cleppetty demanded. "We're all here now but Tanis."

"Why, the customers . . . all our regular people."

"Of course, Marplet's list!" said Jame. "Now he's making use of it, but to what purpose? Surely he doesn't mean to blockade all the streets until Spring's Eve."

"He may not have to," said the widow grimly. "Ghillie, Rothan—wake up, you great lump!—go watch the main approaches to the square. Tuby . . . bless us, where is the man?"

"He went out the courtyard door, madam," said Kithra tactfully. "I think he's gone to warn his wife."

"Hmph! Well, let him go. In these lands, we don't tie our leaders to trees and keep them on the battlefield. Kithra, stay with me. We've got water to draw, just in case. You, missy," she said, turning to Jame, "get some dry clothes on fast and come back down. I've work for you, too."

Jame dropped the blanket and, naked, darted up to the loft. When she came down again, hastily belting her spare d'hen, Cleppetty was waiting with Boo and the sleepy cub in her arms.

"Here," she said, handing both over. "Take them up to Mistress Abernia. They'll be safe there as long as the south wing stands."

Jame crossed the courtyard and climbed the stairs with her charges, conscious with each step of a growing excitement. At last, after nearly five months at the inn, she was about to meet its termagant mistress.

Light shone around the edges of Abernia's door. Jame scratched on its panels tentatively, then rapped with her knuckles.

"Who is it?" the shrill, familiar voice demanded.

"It's Jame, mistress. Cleppetty sent me." She could hear the sound of breathing now, down by the keyhole, and below, the widow's urgent voice barking orders.

"Please, mistress. I've brought the children."

The door opened abruptly, light streaming around the broad figure on the threshold. A powerful hand scooped both the ounce and the cat out of Jame's arms. The door slammed in her face.

"I gather you met her," said the widow drily as Jame reentered the kitchen, looking dazed.

"I-I think so . . . Cleppetty, am I losing my mind, or was that Tubain dressed up in . . ."

"Hush!" The widow glanced hastily out the door to be sure that Kithra was still at the well. "The mistress was already here when Tubain first gave me a home at the Res aB'tyrr. I discovered her secret by accident and have helped to maintain it ever since as it's clear that Tubain needs her. She can face things that he can't, and on her own ground she's a regular lion. Nobody else knows about this, not even Rothan, but it occurred to me tonight that someone else should, in case of an emergency. That's you, for lack of anyone more sensible."

"I'm honored . . . I think."

"You are," she said with a sudden smile. "Now help me get these kettles filled."

But there was no time. Ghillie burst into the kitchen followed by Rothan. "Marplet's men are coming!" the boy gasped. "*All* of them. Rothan figures thirty; I saw closer to fifty. Shall we bar the door?"

"No," said the widow after a moment's rapid thought. "Whatever they have planned, they'll be looking for an excuse to make it seem spontaneous. The fewer opportunities we give them to complain, the better."

"So what do we *do?*"

"Wait."

They stood at the kitchen door, listening. Outside, the sound of voices, shouting, laughing raucously, was coming closer. Jame and Ghillie ran to the front windows. Men were entering the square from all directions, calling ironic greetings to each other as though they had met there by chance. The fur-trimmed clothes of some betrayed them as brigands from the hills, doubtless colleagues of Bortis, while Jame recognized others as members of Tai-tastigon's true criminal class, guildless men who would do anything for a price. A loud, mock debate ensued over which inn should be patronized. Ghillie and Jame retreated precipitously to the kitchen just as the front door crashed open and the first of them came tramping into the hall, shouting for the best wine in the house.

"Now what?" said Ghillie, white-faced.

"We serve them," said Cleppetty grimly, "or rather you three do. Kithra stays here with me. They may have special instructions about her." She jumped down from the bench she had been using to reach a high shelf and handed Jame a small black bottle. "Put three drops of this in every tankard. That should confuse them some."

"Confuse" was a mild word for it, Jame thought as she and the others plunged down the steps to the cellar with their first load of empty vessels. Not long ago, Ghillie's girlfriend had teased him into trying some of Cleppetty's special medicine, and he had spent the rest of the day watching green marmosets scamper across the ceiling. Still, three drops wasn't much per glass, and it was a very small bottle. She climbed the steps, two tankards clasped by the grip in each hand, and her courage quailed at the roar that came crashing down to meet her.

The next two hours were a nightmare. Jame, Rothan, and Ghillie were kept continually in motion carrying food and drink to the clamorous mob and suffering everything it could provide by way of pinching, tripping, and general insults. The interlopers were still playing the part of rowdy but otherwise normal customers, except that they missed no opportunity to criticize either the food or the service and got excessive pleasure out of assuring Jame and the others that all accounts would be settled at the end of the evening. The little bottle was long since empty. Some men had taken to staring into space, grinning idiotically, but the majority seemed relatively unaffected.

"How long can this go on?" Ghillie gasped as he and Jame collided on the stair.

In the hall, someone started shouting for Tanis.

"That's done it," said Cleppetty, looking out the kitchen door as the noise grew to a steady, pounding chant.

"Madam, it's all right!" Kithra called from the back door. "I just saw her come in."

"What good is that?" Jame said to the widow. "She can't dance."

At that moment, Taniscent herself entered through the curtains below the minstrels' gallery. Candlelight shimmered on her translucent garments, on skin glowing with scented oil, and the crowd roared at the sight of her. Jame felt her mouth drop open. She thought she had never seen the dancer look more beautiful, or so young. Beside her, the widow growled deep in her throat.

"Sixteen years old, seventeen at most," she said. "How much Dragon's Blood did it take to do that, and who gave it to her?"

Taniscent mounted the table under the central chandelier, the applause of the audience dizzying her with delight. Oh, it was every bit as wonderful as Bortis had promised. This was where she belonged, where she would stay forever. Briefly, she wondered where her handsome lover was and why he had left her to wait for this moment of triumph alone. She would tease him about that later. Now, she would dance as she had never danced before, glorying in her remembered skill, in the youth that again burned so hotly in her veins.

Jame watched, entranced. She had forgotten how good Tanis was, or what enthusiasm she could draw from her audience. But although the men cheered, there was something half-mocking, half-expectant in the echo, and an undercurrent of pure cruelty. Turn, bend, glide . . . the sensual dance went on, separating planes of sense, merging them again in the flickering light . . . and then the change began.

Jame blinked. What place had lines in the lovely face, or flecks of gray in that dark, lustrous hair? Cleppetty gripped her arm fiercely. The waist seemed to be—no, *was* thickening, the slim ankles likewise. Breasts, glossy with oil, began to sag under the diaphanous fabric. The note of the mob had also changed. Hisses and jeers now interlaced the applause, growing in volume. The sound broke Taniscent's trance of movement. She faltered, looked down in bewilderment at the malicious glee on the faces below, and then caught sight of her own hands where the veins now ran blue and prominent under the skin. With a wail of horror, she fell to her knees. Ghillie and Jame ran to help her, elbowing a way through the jeering crowd to get her to the kitchen. Behind them the tumult grew.

Cleppetty was putting on her hat and cloak. "Take her up to her room," she ordered Kithra, then turned to Jame. "Ghillie says that you know how to dance."

"I know the Senetha. D-do you mean you want me to . . ."

"That's right. I'm going out of the district for help, and we've got to buy time either until I return or they get enough wine in them to reinforce the drug. Thank the gods they mean to drink all they can before the burning starts or we would have been finished hours ago."

"B-but Cleppetty, what if they don't like me?"

"That we'll have to risk. Put on one of Tanis's costumes and stand on your head if you have to, but *keep their attention.*" And with that she disappeared out the street door.

Jame stood there gaping after her for a second, then turned and fled up to Taniscent's room with the voice of the mob loud behind her.

KITHRA HAD THE DANCER in bed and was trying to keep her there. Ignoring them both, Jame burrowed into the chest at the foot of Taniscent's bed, throwing gaudy clothes right and left. Was there anything there that wouldn't fall off her the first step she took? A long black scarf, a pair of diaphanous trousers . . . she tore off her clothes, put the latter on with her own belt to hold them up, slipped the former around her neck, crossed it over her small breasts, tied it in back. One hurried step toward the door and the thought stopped her as though she had run into a wall: one does not dance the Senetha barefaced in public. Someone had told her that emphatically, many times. The half-memory of a face formed, was scattered by a flicker of pain. She snatched up another gauzy scarf. Knotting it around her head like a semi-transparent blindfold, she went out onto the gallery. The wind brought to her the rising clamor from below.

Inside the great hall, chaos reigned. Half the men at least seemed finally to have succumbed to Cleppetty's little black bottle and were either staring into space or stumbling about wild-eyed. Marplet's household toughs were trying to organize them. Then one man more clear-minded than the rest jumped onto the center table, waving a blazing brand. Jame darted into the room. Vaulting onto the table, she caught the man with a fire-leaping kick squarely in the stomach. He disappeared off the other side, doubled up in mid-air, his torch flying. There was a moment of startled silence as audience and would-be performer stared at each other. Then, taking a deep breath, Jame gave the assembled ruffians a full, ceremonial bow. Hesitantly, she began to dance.

The quavering notes of Ghillie's flute came down from the minstrels' gallery. He had never played for her before and, having no idea what tune to use, had settled for Taniscent's favorite. Worse and worse, Jame thought despairingly, trying to adapt to it. All she needed now was to remind her audience of how different this was from Tanis's usual, provocative performance. In fact, the Senetha was so different that Marplet's bullies were probably still watching her only because they hadn't figured out yet what she was doing.

But the essence of the dance is concentration. Long practice soon made Jame forget her nervousness, and she began to flow through the patterns, feeling the power build in her, around her. There was more of it than she had ever sensed before, dancing alone in the loft. It came from all sides, from the men who watched her open-mouthed. Hunger lay naked on every face. For a moment, the rawness of it took Jame's breath away, and then something deep inside her responded. With a gesture at once reckless and exultant, she clothed herself in their desires. This had happened before, would happen again. In the utter intimacy of the dance, she gave each man what he wanted most, took from him all that he could give without the touch of hand or lip.

Then one by one the upturned faces fell away. In the darkness that followed, golden-eyed shadows whirled with her. *Priestess,* they whispered in her ear, *Chosen of our Lord, feed on us and give us food. Dance!* And she danced—in joy, in terror, touching and touched—until all sound faded and she was alone.

When Jame regained her senses, she was kneeling formally on the table. The room was empty except for the widow, who sat watching her intently.

"What time is it?" she asked, stretching with unaccustomed sensuousness.

"Nearly dawn. You've been sitting like that for hours."

Memory returned in part with a rush, freezing her in mid-gesture. "What happened? Did you get help . . . or was I so bad that they all jumped out the windows shrieking?"

"I found a pair of guards who would come, all right," said the widow, "but when we got here there was nothing for them to do. Everyone was gawking at you. Then, when you bowed and sat down at the end, it was as if they couldn't see you any more. Damnedest thing I've ever seen. We would have had them staggering all over the inn, hunting for you, if I hadn't promised that you'd dance again tonight."

"Oh, Cleppetty, no!"

"Oh, child, yes, if you don't want another riot. But don't worry," she added, grinning fiercely. "We can lay in another supply of black poppy milk by then, though I doubt if you'll need it. You surprised me, missy. I don't know how you did it, skinny thing that you are, but you seduced every man in the room . . . and some women too. Not even Taniscent ever did that."

"Tanis! I'd forgotten about her. How is she?"

"Gone. Kithra left her untended to see how you were doing, and she slipped out. Betrayed, ruined, and replaced all in one night—no wonder she ran away. We'll get her back, though. Whether she dances here or not, this is her home, and now she'll need us more than ever. What you need is sleep. Tomorrow—or rather later today—we'll see about a better costume for you, one not quite so likely to fall off. Now don't make faces at me, missy; like it or not, you've got a new career on your hands.

CHAPTER 7

The Feast of Fools

THE NOTE WAS written in the flowing script on a piece of the finest cream parchment.

> *The dancer B'tyrr* [it said] *will present herself at Edor Thulig during the Feast of Fools to perform before His Glory, Prince Ozymardien of Metalondar*

"Well," said Tubain, reading over Jame's shoulder, "I suppose it was likely to happen sooner or later. His Glory is always interested in anything unusual, and that's you."

"Very flattering, I'm sure," said Jame with a grimace. "Just the same, I don't much care for the tone of this thing. He seems to expect me to come running with my tongue hanging out because he's deigned to whistle for me."

"When you're the richest man in Tai-tastigon, maybe in all the Eastern Lands," said Cleppetty from the top of the ladder, "you make assumptions. Here, catch."

She tossed down a ball of ribbons, which dissolved in mid-air into a mass of multicolored streamers fluttering down indiscriminately onto the two below, the nearest table, and into an early patron's bowl of soup.

"Damn!" said the widow, and came clattering down.

"Such a pity too," said Tubain, mournfully still staring at the note, oblivious to his sudden, garish splendor. "Just when things were going so well."

"What's he talking about?" Jame asked the widow as she helped her collect the ribbons. "Does my prospective host do after-dinner card tricks or is he just an avid anthropophagist?"

"Worse," said Cleppetty grimly. "He collects things. Jewels, furs, ivory, people. Last year, for example, he took to wife the most beautiful virgin in the Eastern Lands—and rumor has it he's kept her just as received. In a collection like his, you understand, there's no place for a damaged article."

"How frustrating for her."

"As you say, but the point is this: if you dance particularly well before him, he's liable to collect *you.*" She called Ghillie to help her shift the ladder to another part of the hall. "At any rate," she said, climbing it again with a handful of loose ribbons, "you've got until tomorrow to decide. He should at least pay well . . . provided you ever get out to spend it."

Jame watched as she reached the level of the b'tyrr figures and began to blindfold each one by stretching a ribbon across its eyes and securing it on each side with a nail. In view of their talismanic function, this struck Jame as a thoroughly inauspicious procedure. All over town, however, the minor tutelary figures were being treated in much the same way, while in the Temple District priests went about their evening duties with as great a pretense of normalcy as possible. They, like everyone else, were waiting for midnight and the Feast of Fools, that annual leap-day no calendar ever showed for fear the gods would discover its existence and spoil the fun. It seemed rather churlish not to let the faithful b'tyrr in on the secret, but there it was: one couldn't make exceptions.

The B'tyrr, the Talisman—now she was called "luck-bringer" in two languages, neither of them her own. Jame smiled ruefully. What a contrast to her own full name, which she never used.

"Hullo!" Dally called from the doorway. "Ready to go, or are you still needed here?"

"Cleppetty?"

"Go, go," came the answer from above. "The work is well in hand for once."

"My jacket is in the loft," Jame said to Dally. "Come up and see how much Jorin has grown." Without waiting for an answer, she darted up the steps. He overtook her on the last turn of the spiral stair, and they tumbled onto the loft floor together, laughing. Across the room, near the place where the knapsack still lay hidden, two sleek heads raised inquiringly, the milk opal eyes of the ounce cub gleaming above and behind Boo's round face.

"He's grown, all right," Dally said, bending down to stroke Jorin, who responded with one of his most unfeline chirps of pleasure. "Pretty soon he'll be too big for the loft. A pity you had to stain his fur, though; the markings were beautiful."

"Altogether too beautiful," said Jame wryly. "A common tawny I can explain, but not a Royal Gold. Someone would be sure to make trouble. There's been no trace of the mind-link, though. Maybe it will take another crisis to reestablish it, or maybe it's gone for good. That might be just as well."

"I still don't see why," said Dally. "It doesn't seem right to be ashamed of a gift like that."

Bitterness twisted Jame's smile. Why indeed? What was it that made most of her people so fear those old abilities and physical traits, which, if legends spoke true, all Kencyrs had once shared? That question lay at the heart of her expulsion as a child from the keep. With an effort, she put herself in the place of that man, her own father, who had stood at the gate, shouting curses after her.

"I suppose," she said slowly, "that it's partly because we no longer trust anyone to use such gifts properly. Of course, the ability to touch minds with an animal isn't all that threatening, but what about those who can weave dreams or whose blood, once tasted, binds a man body and soul? Our history is full of strange people, Dally, with stranger powers. One of the strangest is the Master. When that man fell, it was as if we all had fallen, even those who fled out of his power into Rathillien. That was when honor became such an obsession with us . . . and when we began to fear all Kencyrs who, like the Master, had special gifts that might be turned to the service of the Enemy."

"Wait a minute," Dally protested. "That happened nearly three thousand years ago when the Kencyrath first came to this world, didn't it? But just now you spoke of this Master, whoever he is, as if he were still live."

"So he may very well be. After all, he betrayed his people and god to Perimal Darkling in exchange for immortality."

"This is no good," said Dally, shaking his head. "You've got to tell me this story properly or not at all."

Jame hesitated. Few outsiders knew the full history of that treacherous act, which had nearly shattered the Kencyrath's spirit forever, but then Dally, as Dalis-sar's stepson, was to some extent a member of the family. Abruptly she knelt, closed her eyes, and began to recite:

"*Gerridon Highlord, Master of Knorth, a proud man was he. The Three People held he in his hand—Arrin-ken, Highborn, and Kendar—by right of birth and might. Wealth and power had he, and knowledge deeper than the Sea of Stars. But he feared death. 'Dread lord,' he said to the Shadow that Crawls, even to Perimal Darkling, ancient of enemies, "my god regards me not. If I serve thee, wilt thou preserve me, even to the end of time?" Night bowed over him. Words they spoke. Then went my lord Gerridon to his sister and consort, the priestess Jamethiel Dream-Weaver, and said, 'Dance out the souls of the faithful that darkness may enter in.' And she danced. Two-thirds of the People fell that night, Highborn and Kendar. 'Rise up, Highlord of the Kencyrath, said the Arrin-ken to Glendar. 'Your brother has forfeited all. Flee, man, flee, and we will follow.' And so he fled, Cloak, Knife and Book abandoning, into the new world. Barriers he rasied, and his people consecrated them. 'A watch we will keep,' they said, 'and our honor someday avenge. Alas for the greed of a man and the deceit of a woman, that we should come to this!'"*"

"Ouch," said Dally. "I'm sorry I asked. But what were those three things that got left behind?"

"The Serpent-Skin Cloak, the Ivory Knife and the Book Bound in Pale Leather. The third was the greatest loss, I'm told. Nobody ever dared to memorize it, not at least since a priest named Anthrobar turned his brain to a cinder simply by trying to copy the damn thing—and to make matters worse, his partial transcript, which is what we used to get to Rathillien, disappeared soon after our arrival."

"In other words, you're stranded here without it?"

"That's about it . . . and nice quiet neighbors you've found us too," said Jame, with a sudden grin. "Blood feuds every other day, wars on the weekends, and our wretched god sitting on top of the whole mess. With your luck, you may even get the Tyr-ridan before we're through with you."

"The what?"

"The Tyr-ridan. It's another reason why mind links and what-not are considered ominous. You see, the more old abilities one has, the closer one is to the godhead itself."

"What's wrong with that? The closer the better, I should think."

"Not with our god it isn't. Remember, we haven't even been on speaking terms for the last twenty thousand years or so. When it wants something done, it simply manifests itself in some unfortunate Shanir—that is, one of the old blood, of the old powers. Creation, preservation, destruction . . . sometimes one attribute shows up in an individual, sometimes two, or even all three under different circumstances. Things tend to happen around the Shanir. Worse, when all three aspects of the god are present at once, each one concentrated in one of three Shanir known collectively as the Tyr-ridan, the final battle with Perimal Darkling is supposed to occur."

"But surely you should be looking forward to that," Dally protested. "After all, it will be the culmination of your destiny."

"When the Master fell," said Jame, "I think a lot of our people lost faith in their destiny altogether. But listen, we'd better get going." She eased her d'hen out from under the two cats and stood up. "Canden will think we fell down a privy hole on the way."

They descended and crossed the hall.

"Don't forget," the widow's voice called from on high, "you're to perform here during the Feast. Anytime will do."

Dally saw his companion grimace. "You still have reservations about dancing, don't you?" he said as they crossed the square.

"Yes, more so all the time. I can't get over the feeling that I'm abusing a great and terrible ability, although what its proper use is I can't guess. I knew before that the Senetha was a way of channeling power—all Kencyrs use it to generate the force behind the Senethar in combat—but this . . .! Dally, it's frightening. Somehow I'm vampirizing my audience, men and women both. I don't like what that does to me . . . or maybe I like it too much."

"Well, it should be some comfort to know that no one can remember afterward exactly what they see when you dance," said Dally. "I can't, anyway. You'll have to admit, though, that this forgotten talent of yours chose a lucky time to surface."

That, indeed, was true. Not only had it been instrumental in saving the inn that night some eight weeks before but since then it had caused a remarkable change in the financial condition of the Res aB'tyrr. Two days ago Tubain had renewed the tavern charter and returned with a little sack containing fifty golden altars, which he had presented to her rather sadly, knowing what she wanted them for.

Marplet, with a somewhat whimsical air, had since offered her as much a week if she would work for him; and Jame had surprised herself by turning him down with sincere thanks. She now knew that she had the rival innkeeper to thank for Bortis's absence. Some said that the maimed brigand had been driven away because he had disobeyed orders. Jame suspected, however, that Marplet had done it to protect her, since Bortis clearly blamed her more than Bane for what had happened to him. In a way, Jame thought, Marplet himself was acting much like his former henchman in transferring his hostility from her, its proper object, to poor Tubain.

"Why do things always get so complicated?" she said out loud, interrupting Dally.

"It's a confusing system, all right," he said, adding, "the Thieves' Guild, I mean," when he saw her puzzled look. He had, she realized, gotten off on an altogether different topic.

"Most people don't realize that there are actually two elections," he continued. "In the first, late this coming autumn, the landed masters choose their two representatives for the Guild Council. In the second, next Winter's Eve, the Council votes for the new Sirdan. The bribery market is very lively already. Even Mendy is making arrangements with someone very important for a big loan, although I shouldn't think," he added loyally, "that he'll have to buy as many people as Theocandi will. But you see, all this makes a lot of extra work for the spies and, well, the Creeper told me yesterday that he couldn't spare men any longer to search for your dancer friend. I'm afraid there's nothing more we can do. She's probably dead of old age by now anyway. I'm sorry."

"Well, you tried," said Jame. "Word may come yet through other channels. Meanwhile, it mustn't ruin our holiday. After all, by this time next week I may be gone."

Dally bit his lip at this, but said nothing.

Soon after, they met Canden in Antiquarians' Row, where the Tai-than expeditionary headquarters were located, then walked north together. Canden talked with great enthusiasm and considerable expertise about the maps that he was helping to collate for the expedition's leaders, the renowned explorer Quipun of Lefy. Jame gathered that Quipun had given this task to the boy originally to keep him quiet, but suspected that he was now beginning to realize his eager young helper's potential.

They came to the River Tone and walked along its bank, buying from street stalls fresh grilled shrimp and venison rolled in almond dust. The setting sun cupped between the white slopes of Mounts Timor and Tinnabin spilled its crimson light down the hidden paths by which the first caravan would travel the next week. For the first time, the imminence of her departure struck Jame. It seemed impossible that she would be leaving so soon with so many questions still unanswered and her researches in the Temple District barely begun. She hadn't even really decided what it would be like to rejoin her people. Since the night of the near-riot, events had simply carried her forward, smoothing the way to a leave-taking that now seemed all too sudden. She almost wished that something would happen to prevent it.

Just then, Edor Thulig, the Tower of Demons, came into sight on the left. Its foundations rested on the largest privately owned island in the city, which lay between arms of the River Tynnet and the River Tone. The high wall that girt it was topped with barbed spearheads and torches that threw their light on the swift water below. Its gate, however, was open, revealing the full sweep of the stairs that reached from the Tone's edge to the threshold of the Tower itself, and there too the doors gaped wide. Inside, firelight set monstrous shadows leaping over the ceiling and walls of the vaulted entrance way. Outside, obsidian sheathed walls soared up one hundred and fifty feet to the clawed toes of the four stone demons whose interlocking wings encircled the top of the edifice. Above their outthrust heads was a band of high, clear windows, this time of richly hued glass, and finally the stone tracery of the dome under which Ozymardien's great collection was kept.

"There'll be quite a party up there tonight," said Dally, staring up at the stained glass level.

"I suppose so," said Jame. "I've been ordered to attend it."

She told them about the summons. They both agreed that, intriguing as the opportunity was, it would be wisest to forgo it. At this, Jame merely looked thoughtful, and Dally, regarding her with sudden apprehension, quickly proposed that they see the Feast in with a glass of ale at the Moon.

The tavern was swollen with apprentices, but a friend of Dally's named Raffing called them over to a side table where he and several other of Master Galishan's pupils, including his roommate Scramp and Darinby, were sitting.

"Lit up like a shrine and open as a whore's legs," a lanky, pimple-faced thief was saying. Jame recognized him as Hangrell, the apprentice of a rather disreputable master, whose territory abutted the Lower Town on the west. "He's mocking us, he is. Tower of Demons indeed! Everyone knows he only has one."

"One is quite enough," said Raffing with a grin. "Look at its record: in the thirty years since the Tower was raised, no thief has gotten so much as a clay pot out of it yet."

"Exactly what does the Prince's pet devil do?" asked an apprentice new to the city.

"Mangles souls," said Darinby laconically.

"But how?"

"How do you think? Look over there." He pointed to a small table in the back of the room where a single man sat facing the wall. His shadow was black on the stones before him, all except the shadow that should have been cast by his head. Then there was nothing. His hair seemed to be falling out in strips with the skin still attached. Underneath, the flesh was brown and wrinkled as a rotten potato.

"Poor old Jubar won't be with us much longer," said the journeyman dispassionately. "He ran into the demon up in the lit levels during the last Feast of Fools. The idiot thought that because the gods slept, so would Thulig-sa."

"Why didn't it?" Jame asked.

"You don't outwit a demon that easily, or any other being with even part of a human soul. Gods never have them, their worshippers know better. But a true demon has only victims, and therefore needs a soul as badly as we do bones. Some tear off whatever they can get through the shadow, like Thulig-sa; others suck it dry, bit by bit, like the Lower Town Monster. Either way, it means a slow, withering death for their prey."

"Sometimes not so slow," said the pimple-faced apprentice with a sly smile. "Remember Master Tane."

"Here now," said Darinby sharply. "That was never proved. *You* remember present company, Hangrell."

They all looked at Canden, who was staring fixedly at his cup.

"Just after the last Guild Council," said Dally in Jame's ear, "the Sirdan's chief rival died suddenly. Theocandi was suspected of using soul sorcery—a shadow thief, to be exact—but as Darinby says, it was never proven. Speaking of souls," he said out loud, "don't the Kencyrs equate them with the shadow too?"

"More or less. With us, though, both are more . . . uh . . . detachable. Some of the Highborn and, I think, all of the Arrin-ken, have the ability to carry other Kencyrs' souls. The only advantage this seems to have, though, is that a man who has voluntarily given his soul into someone else's charge is very hard to kill."

"That sounds desirable, anyway."

"Not always. We like to keep death as an option."

"Sometimes it's easier than running away," said Scramp.

"Your terms are beginning to confuse me," said Darinby, as though Scramp had not spoken. "What's an Arrin-ken?"

"The first of the Three People, our judges. The priests give the laws, the scrollsmen record them, the Kendar enforce them, and the Arrin-ken temper them . . . or at least they used to. Two thousand years ago they got disgusted with the rest of us and withdrew to consult. As far as I know, they're still at it."

"For two thousand years?"

"Time doesn't mean much to that lot: they're as close to immortal as makes no difference. I didn't say, you know, that they were human. In fact, they look rather like big cats—tiger size—can move things without touching them and, on occasion, have been known to walk through stone walls. The rest of us used to be much closer to them physically and mentally than we are now."

"Marvelous!" said Scramp with a giggle. "I love bedtime stories. Tell me, have you ever seen one of these beasties?"

"I think I have," said the new apprentice unexpectedly, "or at least its tracks. Anyone who's ever lived on the slopes of the Ebonbane can tell you about the Mount Timor Cat and how it's outwitted generations of hunters. It's even been known to help caravans caught by the snows."

Scramp snorted. "I liked the first story better," he said. "It sounded more . . . convincing."

Jame regarded the little Townie thoughtfully. She was fairly certain that he had been trying to gain acceptance among the others all these weeks by baiting her—the only one more an outsider than himself—so she had tried to be patient. There were, however, limits.

"One would almost suppose," she said mildly, "that you didn't think I was telling the truth."

Scramp gave her a quick, frightened look. Unlike some of his colleagues, he had never underestimated this odd, silver-eyed creature—but he also knew that whatever level of impudence he reached he must then maintain, if he was not to lose everything he had gained. Even now, he could feel the men at the other tables watching him out of the corners of their eyes, silently goading him on.

"What does it matter if you are or aren't?" he said, wondering if his voice was really as thin as it sounded. "Who are you anyway? The penny pickpocket. The rotten fruit thief."

There was dead silence. Everyone was staring at them now, all pretense of indifference gone. For a moment, the Talisman's eyes went very hard and metallic. Then, slowly, they cleared.

"Not a very distinguished record, is it?" she said in a brittle voice. "Still, there's a little time left to make amends. Your master Galishan holds the Tynnet Branching District, doesn't he?" Darinby nodded, suddenly very serious. "Very well. With your permission, I hunt there tomorrow night . . ."

"Don't say it, don't say it," Dally plead.

". . . in the Tower of Demons."

Men-dalis's brother put his head on the table and groaned. Outside, bells began to ring, people to shout, fireworks to explode. Inside, everyone except those at his table stood up and, to the horror of the innkeeper, began with great solemnity to smash the furniture.

The Feast of Fools had begun.

FROM GATE TO GATE, Tai-tastigon blazed with lights. The midnight sky bloomed suddenly with scarlet flowers, emerald vines rising, golden fountains dripping fiery sparks on the rooftops below. Candles thronged every window. Bonfires threw their fitful glare on the façades of houses, on the fantastic figures that leaped and whirled around them. Down River Street came the effigy of a major fertility god borne on the shoulders of its shouting worshippers. Its priests ran on ahead with robes tucked up, snatching flowers from passersby, weaving them into garlands, and dashing back to throw them over the figure's jutting phallus. Those who followed loudly kept score. In all that great, exulting city, only the Temple District was dark, and now the Lower Town as well where no joy ever survived the fall of night.

Two figures stood in the shadows on the shore of the Tynnet, across the water from Edor Thulig.

"If anything happens to you," one said with considerable violence, "I'll break that Townie's neck."

"No, you won't," said the other. "You know perfectly well that he didn't push me into anything that it wasn't already in my mind to try. I've had a good master, Dally. He hasn't asked for anything but loyalty, and it won't disturb him at all if others call him a fool for having bothered with me. Just the same, the man who stole the Eye of Abarraden deserves better than a petty larcenist for an apprentice. Anyway, maybe I'll feel better about leaving Tai-tastigon if I can do it with a bang."

"It may be with a loud screech if Thulig-sa gets its paws on you," said Dally gloomily. "That is, of course, assuming His Glory doesn't add you to the jade screens and stuffed fantods first."

"Don't worry," said Jame with a grin. "I'd look silly under a bell jar. Just pass on my message to Sparrow, if you can find him . . . and Dally, if something should go wrong, please be kind to Scramp. You don't know what it's like always to be an outsider."

Before she realized his intent, Dally caught her by the arms. His kiss was so sudden and fierce that for a second she thought her front teeth would be knocked down her throat. Then he was gone. She stared after him, incredulous, then pushed the incident to the back of her mind. Putting on her dancer's mask, she crossed the bridge.

Inside the outer wall, beyond the open gate, a wilderness of white roses glowed faintly in the darkness. Jame followed a tesselated walk through them to the still-unguarded river steps. There really was something arrogant about all this openness, she thought as she climbed the steps, a kind of contemptuous challenge thrown down to the whole mad city, now reeling into its last four hours of carnival. The passage way was some thirty feet long and lined with a mosaic of Metalondrian devils doing unspeakable things to intruders. Ahead, an open hearth fire roared up the central well of the tower. No one, guest or servant, was in sight, all having long since either mounted to the upper levels or retreated into the honeycomb of rooms between the outer wall of Edor Thulig and the inner one of this shaft.

Jame started cautiously up the spiral stair. The wind, whistling in the open door, rose with her, tugging at her cloak, running cool fingers over what skin the Senetha costume left uncovered.

The costume . . . what a time they had had making it. Tight black cloth, some leather, much skin showing in unexpected places . . . how pleased Kithra had been with it in the end, and how shocked the widow was. Jame hardly knew what to make of it herself except that, for what she did, nothing else would serve. And she had worn something like it before. She was sure that part of her mind remembered where and for what purpose when she danced, but that knowledge always slipped away again when the trance ended. It was the trance itself that worried her now. If it fell on her again, here, she would be stripped of all control while it lasted. Anything might happen. Too late to fret about that, however; here was the end of the stairs and the threshold of the demon's true domain.

The lit levels varied from three to five. Ceilings differed in height, stairs sprouted in odd locations, passageways—all gleaming white—dipped and swirled in a more or less concentric fashion. It was not a true maze in the Tastigonian sense, but it was designed to confuse anyone in a hurry, and doubtless had done so many times in the past. Light spheres illuminated every corner, throwing multiple shadows at Jame's feet.

Several times as she prowled this area, fixing its major patterns in her mind, she heard something moving stealthily behind her but tried to ignore it. With the Prince's invitation but none of his property in her possession, there should be no danger. That would come soon enough.

Guests were normally conducted through this region blindfolded. One broad staircase led from the upper level to the chamber above where, from the sound of it, the party was still in progress; none, however, gave access to the servants' quarters below in the honeycomb. Intermural stairways must service that. When she had satisfied herself as to the area's layout, Jame fitted together bits of metal taken from various pockets in her cape and clipped a thin, strong rope to the resulting spidery form. Then she opened a window and stepped out onto the broad shoulders of the southern stone demon.

The wind buffeted her in savage gusts, filling her cloak, making it tear at her shoulder. She released it. It whirled away, a boneless night bird homing. For a moment it was hard to stand. Then came a lull. Jame swung the grapnel cautiously, paid out more line, and threw it upward. It disappeared over the balcony railing above. She tested it, took a higher grip on the rope. As her feet left the stone image, the wind came again, pushing her sideways into space. Far, far below, the spear-lined wall, the steps, the river. She began to climb. An immeasurable time later, her hand closed on the railing. She stepped over it into a pool of ruby and amethyst light on the balcony floor. Inside, there was a burst of laughter and applause. Shadows moved across the magnificent windows, dark, very close. Jame retrieved the grapnel. The narrower floor of the upper gallery was perhaps twenty-five feet above her, forming a partial roof. She threw the hook over its railing and climbed quickly up. As she had suspected from the presence of this rim walk, both the outer tracery dome and the inner one of amber glass were fitted with sliding panels. One on the north side was partially open. Jame slipped through it into the heart of Prince Ozymardien's treasure trove.

The cavernous interior, dimly lit with spheres, suggested the nave of a cathedral in its dimensions and a museum in its content. The faint light fell softly on the sheen of silken tapestries, on the marble limbs of statuary arching out of the gloom, on furs, gem-encrusted weapons, ivory miniatures on black velvet, cups of gold, and feather capes, all spread out ready for the touch of their master's hand. Jame walked among them, marveling at their splendor. She longed to spend hours here simply looking when she knew that minutes must suffice. Then, on a little table just beyond an incredibly lifelike figure reclining on a couch, she saw what she had come for: the Peacock Gloves.

Everyone knew the story of the old man who had embroidered their high, shimmering cuffs with threads gleaned over a lifetime from the floor of the city's finest textile shop and how, when they were at last finished, the Prince had bought them for his new bride. The sum he had paid would keep their creator in luxury for the rest of his life, but it was a trifle compared to what His Glory must have spent on nearly everything else under this dome. Then too, the bride must soon have tired of them to have found their way here, to this forgotten table littered with cosmetic bottles.

Jame, however, thought they were the loveliest things she had ever seen. She was trying them on when behind her someone sighed. She whirled, and saw the figure on the couch change position. It was the princess, the virgin bride, fast asleep among the ivory warriors and the stuffed monstrosities.

Well, why not, Jame found herself thinking wildly. She's part of the collection too, isn't she?

She stood there frozen, waiting for the eyes to open, for the first scream. Nothing happened. Warily, she crossed over to the couch and looked down at its occupant. The princess lay curled on her side like a sleeping child. Her lips were slightly parted and her eyelids quivered, a hint of moisture on their long lashes. Over her stood the other, the predator come in from the night, tense, watchful, but slowly relaxing. Then with great care, she reached down and pulled the displaced sheet up over the sleeper's bare shoulder, turned, and silently left.

Down on the main balcony again, Jame disengaged the grapnel from above, caught it as it fell, and hooked it over the rail with the full one hundred forty feet of line dangling from it. The wind, even fiercer now, battered her. She checked the sleeves of her costume to be sure they covered the gloves' ornate cuffs, then, fighting down a sudden tremor of nervousness, reached for the catch on one of the tall, glowing windows.

OZYMARDIEN'S CHAMBERLAIN was thoroughly exasperated. Had he not transformed the entire upper chamber into this opulent forest glade? Did not the most beautiful courtesans and finest performers in all Tai-tastigon grace these silken bowers and cavort under the jeweled boughs where hidden birds sang so enchantingly? Was there not present everything that should promote a glorious celebration of this, the Feast of Fools? Yet there sat His Glory on the velvet sward beside a wandering brook of chilled wine, sulking, bored. It was so hard to find a genuine novelty to whet that jaded palate. Now, if that little tavern dancer—the Bitter? the Batears?—had come, there might have been some hope. But then again, probably not. What he needed was a miracle.

What he got was the thunderclap of a window slammed open by the wind and a slender figure standing on the sill, looking startled. On the far side of the tower, three other costly windows crashed shut, two of them shattering. The wind howled through the hall, lashing the artificial trees to frenzy, dislodging clockwork song birds, candied fruit, and dwarf musicians from their branches, overturning candles everywhere.

"That's not a woman, it's a natural disaster!" the Chamberlain's assistant cried, making a futile grab at a passing marzipan thicket. "Somebody, quick—catch that oak!"

The figure from the window was walking across the room through the clusters of shrieking courtesans. It stopped before the Prince, bowed and, with no prologue whatsoever, began to dance. The wind still roared, the flames leaped, but bit by bit the human clamor died away as all watched, hypnotized. To the Chamberlain, it seemed as if he was no longer in the Tower of Demons at all but in another, larger chamber with darkness pressing tangibly, obscenely against the windows. There was a curtained bed decked with red ribbons. A figure danced before it with a white-bladed knife in its hand and something like a pallid, five-legged spider crawled feebly across the floor toward it. Then both the vision and the memory of it were gone. The dancer was walking back to the window by which she had entered. His Glory, suddenly coming out of his trance, began to clap wildly, ecstatically. The Chamberlain, with a great effort, took himself in hand.

"Put out those fires!" he ordered the guards, "and somebody, stop that woman!"

JAME, OUT ON THE BALCONY, heard the shout. She couldn't remember if she had performed or not and rather thought they were after her for breaking those beautiful windows. Either way, a quick retreat seemed in order. She grabbed the rope and swung over the railing. Fifteen feet down, a blast of wind caught her like the blow of a fist, knocking her sideways through a window onto the lit levels. The rope slid through her fingers. She crashed to the floor and lay there half-stunned in a confusion of broken glass.

From somewhere nearby came a confused mutter, as though many voices were whispering hoarsely together. Bruised and bleeding, Jame staggered to her feet. The rope was gone, either blown away from the tower or detached from above. Her first line of escape had been cut off.

The noise was getting closer, louder . . .

She must try to reach the spiral stair that circled down the tower's main shaft—but the stairway that would bring her closest to it was the same up which that abominable sound was coming. She should have left her soul with Ishtier, Jame thought wildly . . . but no: he couldn't be trusted to return it.

Should she wait for the Prince's guards to find her? Not that either—it would mean her skin for the theft of the gloves, even if they arrived in time. Think, fool, think . . . there was another flight of stairs on the west side of the tower. She backed toward it, extinguishing each light sphere as she came to it with a whispered "Blessed-Ardwyn-day-has-come." The sound faded, grew again, so confused by the strange turnings of the semi-maze that it sometimes seemed behind her, sometimes ahead.

It *was* ahead. She whirled and saw Thulig-sa coming at her around the curve of the passageway, a patchwork thing of stolen shadows exuding dull malice and hunger. A dozen piping voices accompanied it, all crying, "Run, thief, run!"

She ran. The darkened corridor swallowed her and her precious shadow, concealed them both as she darted into a side passage and stood there trembling, her back pressed against the wall. The demon rushed past in the dark, trailing the moans of its previous victims. Then she was out in the open again, racing along the western wall and down the steps. No time for the spiral stair now; no time for anything but the third escape route, which must be taken without pause for thought or fear.

The window stood open before her as she had left it. Without slacking pace, Jame was through it onto the shoulders of the stone demon, in the air, falling.

It was a very long way down. The wind spun her like a dry leaf, let go in time for her to see the spear-tipped wall, the steps, her own shadow leaping up to meet her on the torch-lit water.

It was like hitting a stone wall.

Deep beneath the surface, Jame fought for her life. The air had been slammed out of her, and the current was savage. She surfaced, gasping, went down again, and came back up. A bridge soared over her head, then another one. Any minute now she would either be dashed against the Guild island figurehead or swept past it into the white water of the channel. Someone was running along the bank, trying to keep up. Dally. It had to be. If he dove in now, they would probably both drown. Where the hell was . . .

Something splashed into the water just ahead. She made a wild grab, felt her fingers close on the rope and slide down to the cork-bound hook. On the upper span of the Asphodel Bridge, Sparrow (who, it seemed, had received her message after all) gave a triumphant whoop and braced himself to take the strain. A minute later, Dally hauled her up onto the quay. Leaning against him, she shook down her sleeves, held up the Peacock Gloves, and began to laugh hysterically.

If the sudden appearance of the Cloud King's britches at the Moon could have been said to have caused a stir, it would be hard to describe the reception of the Peacock Gloves. There was a moment of stunned recognition, then pandemonium. It was as if a great insult had finally been avenged, a haughty arch-enemy humbled, and every thief there was caught up in the wild exultation—all, that is, but one.

Ever since her arrival, Jame had been surreptitiously watching Scramp, whose miserable silence seemed louder to her than all the commotion that surrounded them both. Silently, she willed him to be sensible, to realize that for the first time in months nobody was goading him on, but she was the only one not caught by surprise when he suddenly pushed back his tankard, stood up, and, in a shrill voice, said, "I don't believe it."

The others stared at him, some puzzled, some beginning to snicker.

"I don't believe it," he repeated, louder, as though to blot out the laughter. "Either those aren't the real Peacock Gloves or you didn't get them in the Tower of Demons." He took a deep, shaky breath and said, very distinctly, "You're lying."

A look almost of physical pain crossed Jame's face. "Don't, Scramp," she said very softly. "Don't push. Please."

"You're lying!"

It was almost a shriek, like some small animal caught in a trap. He backed away from the table, knife in hand.

"C'mon, you—you coward!"

This time Jame followed him slowly, feeling sick. The smashed furniture had been cleared away, leaving an open space now ringed with shouting apprentices. As Jame entered the circle, she hesitated, then shifted her knife from right to left hand. Dally was appalled. Not only would this force her to depend on her weaker side, but it rendered her d'hen's full left sleeve useless for defense.

Scramp lunged. Cloth ripped as Jame sprang back. Forgetting the jacket's uneven construction, she had tried to block with her unpadded right arm. The boy slashed at her face, barely missing as she slipped aside in a wind-blowing evasion.

"Do something!" Dally shouted at her. Her reluctance to fight was so obvious that several voices had taken up Scramp's cry of coward.

"Damnation," said Jame in disgust and threw down her knife.

Scramp leaped at her, steel flashing. She caught his hand. The blade flew out of it as she twisted, and Scramp came crashing down. Pinned, he recanted, then burst into tears. The others rushed in on her cheering. At that moment, she would gladly have gutted the lot of them.

"Good work!" said the luckless Dally, coming up half-wild with relief, and received such a look that he fell back a step. A boy slid up to him through the crowd and tugged at his sleeve. He bent to listen to the urgent whisper, then turned quickly back to Jame.

"You've got to get out of here fast," he said in a low voice. "Someone told the guards about the gloves, and now there's a full squad converging on the Moon. Here—" He handed her the articles in question, which he had taken charge of when the fight began. "You'll be safe enough in the Maze, if you can get there. I'll stay and help confuse the trail."

"As you wish," she said coldly. "Just be sure they leave that boy alone." She disappeared out the front door, tucking the still-damp gloves in her wallet.

Penari's house was only about three furlongs from the Moon, and Jame usually reached it by going upstream a ways, then cutting due south. As she emerged from the inn, however, she found a brace of guards bearing down on her and so turned hurriedly down the side of the Moon, hearing a shout of recognition and the heavy clump of boots behind her as the chase was joined. The streets behind the tavern formed one of those sordid little tangles that all but those forced to live there and the guards assigned to the district soon learned to avoid. Jame, in fact, had never been through it before and soon found herself in difficulties, especially since the overhanging walls prevented her from taking to the rooftops. She could hear the guards behind shouting. Other voices answered them to the left and right. The squad had arrived in force and was closing in.

Ahead, the dirty lane branched in an unusual and rather slipshod way. Jame was reminded of a similar formation in the Maze, which she had often passed on her way to Point A, Master Penari's favorite intersection for some obscure reason and the one to which he most often had her find her way. If she were going there now, she would take the right fork, go past three alley mouths, turn left . . . well, why not? As she followed this course, she suddenly realized that each step of the way was recognizable. Looking up to the second, third, and fourth stories, even more familiar patterns abruptly emerged.

She was running now, aware of voices close behind her but too excited to care, when, rounding a corner, she crashed into something that she at first thought was a wall. Then it put out brawny arms and caught her on the rebound. Far over her head, a bearded face looked down at her, rather bemusedly.

"Pardon," it said in a remote, polite rumble. The language was formal Kens.

"H-honor be to you," she stammered in the same tongue, almost by reflex.

"Who speaks?"

"One who would have further words with you . . ." A guard appeared at the end of the passageway, came lumbering down on them. ". . . later. Meet me at the Res aB'tyrr in the Red Wax District." She ducked under his arm and ran. Behind, there was the sound of a mighty collision, then of two voices, one swearing luridly, the other rumbling an apology.

A Kendar! She remembered his counterparts at the keep, their gruff kindness to her despite her father's disapproval. How wonderful it would be to have one of her own kind for a friend again—if only he would accept her. This might turn out to be quite a special night after all. Then, as though in confirmation, she turned the last corner and saw, just as she had known she would, Point A in all its solid glory, the Maze itself.

Penari looked up from his overflowing table as she burst out onto a ground level balcony some two stories above him.

"Sir!" she shouted down, "I know the secret of the Maze! It's a street plan of the old city—all five levels of it plus the basements and sewers with walls instead of houses. That's it, isn't it? *Isn't it?*"

"Talisman," said Penari, "you may amount to something yet. Now come down and tell an old man how you young fools have spent the festival."

She did, in considerable detail, and concluded by laying the gloves on the table before him. It was the story, however, more than the plunder that delighted the old thief, as Jame had expected it would. Hence she was not surprised when, after chortling himself dry, he made her a present of the Peacock Gloves.

"Just take them over to the Shining Court and have Master Chardin assess them," he added. "Tell him to put the Guild dues on my account and don't you go strutting them in public until it's safe, boy. Remember that!"

She left him grinning to himself like some ecstatic death's-head and chanting, "I to the temple, you to the tower," over and over again with great satisfaction.

The Shining Court, fortunately, was near at hand. To her surprise, she found Master Chardin waiting for her in the hall, a robe thrown over his night shift.

"You think I could sleep through this racket?" he said, leading her into his brightly lit workroom. "You've set the Guild in an uproar, young man—again. No, don't apologize. It's the results that count. Now, let's see these famous gloves."

He took them, making soft, reproachful sounds at their dampness, and stretched them out under the multiple light spheres. As he examined them, Jame regarded him curiously. She had never met this thin, prematurely balding young man before; but like everyone in the Guild, she had heard much about him. He was perhaps the only one of Theocandi's appointed officials who would have nothing to fear if the present Sirdan was overthrown: Men-dalis would never be fool enough to dismiss anyone so supremely competent. No one, however, knew how Chardin himself would vote. He was a man who lived for his work, for the pure pleasure of handling the rich things that came into his court each day, and was known to be almost constitutionally apolitical.

"I'd value these at fifty-one, no, fifty-three altars," he said at last, straightening up. "That's five altars, three crowns Guild duty. You say your master will settle? Very good. He or you, depending on who keeps possession, will be at jeopardy for the next thirty days. Now, in case the Prince wants them back, what ransom?"

"No ransom," said Jame firmly, "No bids, either."

"How about rewards? There's an unconfirmed rumor that the Princess will pay very well for their return, perhaps as high as seventy-five altars. No? Well, I can't say that I blame you. Just look at that needlework, those colors . . . you've got a real prize there, my lad, one I wouldn't mind bidding for myself."

After a few more minutes of rapture on one side and quiet gratification on the other, Jame left. Homeward bound through the noisy, windblown streets, one eye wary for guards, she wondered about the Princess's offer. Had it been made, as Master Chardin had implied, without her husband's knowledge or backing? What funds other than the bride's portion of her dowry would be available to her? Not very extensive ones, probably. Seventy-five altars was a great deal of money, suggesting an unexpectedly ardent desire to regain her stolen property. It was unpleasant to think that she, Jame, had deprived that child of something so valued, when she had only meant to take a trifle; but would any real thief allow such considerations to distress her? Of course not. It was time, she told herself, to start acting like a professional; but oh lord, what would that giant Kendar think of all this?

Someone very big suddenly stepped out of the shadows, barring the way. At first she thought it was the Kendar himself, then, with greater alarm, that it was a guard. Neither, however, was the case.

"Lady Melissand wants to see you," said the burly apparition in atrocious Easternese. "You come."

Now what in all the names of God could the most famous courtesan in Tai-tastigon want with her? Jame was eager to get home and perfectly aware that the streets were no place for her tonight, but this brusque invitation (or was it a command?) also made her exceedingly curious.

"I'll come," she said, and followed her lumbering guide northward into the district called the Silken Dark.

The Lady Melissand managed a small, very select establishment just off the street of ribbons, where her commoner sisters plied their trade. On the outside, it looked like quite a plain, sedate house; inside, however, there was a lush courtyard garden with fountains, flowering trees, and birds of brilliant plumage flying about freely under a lacework dome. Bursts of laughter and an occasional moan came from both the shrubbery and the rooms above as Jame and her guide walked through the green shadows of the garden.

Melissand's apartment was in the back, opening onto the court. Someone inside was shouting angrily. As they approached, a man stormed out, nearly running into Jame. He gave her one furious look, then disappeared into the shrubbery. They heard him stumble, probably over someone's feet, and go out the gate cursing. Like everyone else in the Guild, Jame had laughed over Master Galishan's infatuation with Lady Melissand, but it had never occurred to her before now how agonizing it must be for so proud and jealous a man to fall so hopelessly in love with a woman whom any rival could enjoy for a price. She would have given much not to have him know that a fellow thief had just witnessed his frustration and shame. The apartment door was still open. She scratched lightly on it, then entered.

The Lady Melissand lay on a pile of satin cushions with a studied grace that went oddly with her exasperated expression. At the sight of her visitor, however, she instantly regained her poise and waved Jame to a seat opposite her. Trays of sweetmeats and thimbles of honey wine were offered, polite conversation was made, and then she settled down to bargain seriously for the Peacock Gloves.

"But how did you know I had them?" Jame asked.

"Ah, my dear," said the other archly, "I have spies everywhere. I know everything."

Jame wondered if she also knew that the articles in question were folded up in the wallet at her side. It seemed not. The bidding went from thirty altars to fifty, from fifty to seventy-five.

"You see, I've always wanted them," said Melissand, delicately nibbling on a candied tree frog, "ever since I first saw them. Yes, the old man offered them to me first, but then His Glory stepped in with a better offer behind my back. One hundred altars . . . you know, my dear, you have a most unusual face—such delicate bones, such unnerving eyes! One hundred twenty-five."

"M'lady," Jame protested, trying to stem this tide of unwanted offers. "You overwhelm me. I really must have time to think about this."

"Ah, but of course! How rude of me. Take as long as you like; but remember, I asked first, and can probably better anyone else's bid. In fact," she said, frankly appraising Jame, her smile deepening, "come back no matter what you decide."

"M'lady," said Jame rather desperately, "you'd only be disappointed. Contrary to popular opinion, I am *not* a boy."

"My darling goose," said Melissand, widening her eyes, "whoever said you were?"

THERE MUST BE SOMETHING IN THE AIR, Jame thought as she regained the street. First Dally and now this lady. Who next? Boo?

Meanwhile, there was the growing mystery of the gloves. She didn't believe for a moment that Melissand's interest was purely esthetic, nor, she was beginning to suspect, was the Princess's. It was time she had a closer look at these trophies of hers, but not so close to the courtesan's house.

Several streets later, after she had eluded one inept follower and a second very good one, Jame stopped under a streetlight and took out the gloves. They were indeed a masterpiece of needlework. Even in this dim light, the embroidered cuffs shimmered with the iridescence of skillfully blended colors. Each "eye" possessed subtle differences in shade and stitchery, each thread proclaimed different exotic origins and yet they merged harmoniously together. Perhaps beauty alone was at stake here. Such richness in color, texture, and weight . . . but what was this extra stiffness, here, inside the lining? Jame found where the inner stitching had been cut, and slipped her own gloved fingertips inside. Out came several sheets of very thin paper, folded many times. The waters of the Tone had done the ink little good, but enough remained legible—more than enough.

"The fool," said Jame softly to herself, looking over the intervening buildings at the dome of Edor Thulig. "The incredible, little fool."

THE ROSE GARDEN was as open and deserted as before. Jame hid her wallet, containing the gloves, under a bush, then followed the walk around to the back of the tower. Here, as she had expected, was another door, plainly intended for the servants' use. She scratched on it until a face appeared at the grate.

"I want to see the guard in charge of the treasure dome," she said. "Tell him it's about an article of clothing."

The face disappeared. A few minutes later, the door opened, and a handsome young man emerged. He grabbed Jame by the arms and rammed her back into the entry wall.

"You miserable little thief," he hissed in her face. "Where are they?"

"You damned idiot," she said, trying to get her breath back. "Aren't you in enough trouble as it is?"

He let her go and stepped back, glaring.

"I want to talk to you and the Princess. Kindly take me up to the dome."

He led the way up through the servants' domain without once looking back, his big hands clenched at his sides. There were several bad moments for Jame in the lit area: she had only guessed that Thulig-sa would not attack an empty-handed thief, however guilty. Fortunately, she was right. The party above had apparently ended after so many of its elaborate trappings had either blown away or burned up, and enough walls were back in place to give His Glory some privacy from the servants now busily cleaning up the mess. Jame could hear his shrill voice rhapsodizing over something or someone as she and the guard furtively climbed the last flight of stairs.

The treasure dome was much as Jame remembered it, except that candles now burned around the couch and the princess was sitting in the middle of it, hugging her knees. She jumped up at the sight of them and tried to assume an authoritative stance.

"I have the reward money here," she said, indicating a small casket on the table where the gloves had lain. "Did you bring them?"

"No, your highness."

The girl's eyes went wide with fear and despair, all pretense gone. She sat down abruptly on the bed. The guard swore under his breath. Stepping quickly forward, he stood beside the princess with his hands protectively on her hunched shoulders.

"Your highness," said Jame hurriedly. "I didn't come here for the money or to return the gloves, I played a dangerous game and have won, I think, the right to keep them—but nothing gives me the right to keep these." She took the letters out of her sleeve. Both the princess and the guard stared at her. "I thought you would feel safer if you could destroy these yourself," she said, putting them on top of the casket. "Please believe me, it was never my intent to cause you pain, much less to put your position here or more likely your very life in danger; but if you two must conduct an affair practically under His Glory's nose," she concluded in sudden exasperation, "will you kindly have the sense in future not to put everything down in writing?"

IT HAD BEEN A NEAR THING, Jame thought as she made her way through the crowd-choked streets, bound for home at last. It appalled her sometimes how easy it was to set such a train of events in motion. Cleppetty had been right about her talent for precipitating disasters, or at least near misses. This one, however, had come out reasonably well, if with some loose ends. Scramp's part in it still bothered her, but perhaps now that he had proved his courage by challenging her, the others would be more willing to accept him. And there was still that big Kendar to consider. It had been the height of idiocy, she now realized, to tell a stranger to cross half the labyrinth by night in search of an obscure inn. If he wasn't there when she got home, she would have to go out looking for him.

She had covered about a third of the way, taking a shortcut through the dingy back streets where many of the younger thieves had lodgings when, to her surprise, she came upon Raffing sitting huddled in a doorway, his head in his hands.

"What's the matter, Raff?" she said, stopping in front of him. "Too much young ale?"

He started violently. "Oh! Hello, Talisman. No, it's not that. Something terrible has happened. About an hour and a half after you left the Moon, Master Galishan came in, white as a priest's linens. Of course, he heard all about you, Scramp, and the gloves almost before he was over the threshold. That put the sauce on the capon good and proper. He hauled Scramp out of the corner, tore into him like a mastiff after a rabbit, and ended up by disowning him altogether."

"Oh," said Jame lamely. "I'm so sorry. How is Scramp taking it?"

"That's just it," Raffing said with a sudden shudder. "He's not. He came back to our room before me and—well—he hanged himself."

Several streets away, there was the sound of wildly discordant chanting. It grew closer, louder, faded as the mob of frenzied celebrants tumbled together past the end of the street, somersaulting down to the Tone where a good many of them would undoubtedly fall in and drown.

"Does his family know?" Jame said at last.

"Gods, no." Raffing glanced involuntarily up at the darkened window above him. "Thal's balls, Talisman, I've only just cut him down!"

"Do you know where they live?"

"As a matter of fact, yes. Why?"

"Take me there."

"Now? Go into the Lower Town at night? Well, why not?" he said with a semi-hysterical laugh, lurching to his feet. "I sure as hell can't go home."

The festival was dizzily spiraling down to its end. After nearly twenty-four hours of revelry, only the heartiest were left to celebrate, and they did it with the air of survivors in sight of rescue, dancing on the bodies of the fallen. The Lower Town itself, however, remained as it had always been after sunset: dark, sullen, menacing. Luckily, their destination was near the fosse that constituted the western boundary of the area. Not a trace of light showed about the house's sealed windows. After considerable scratching, knocking, and finally subdued shouting through the keyhole, the door opened a crack and a wizened face, a younger edition of Scramp's, peered out.

"Not so loud!" it hissed and withdrew. Jame followed. The door swung shut behind her, its lock clicking.

She was in a large room dimly lit with candles. Six children, all younger than the one who had opened the door, were sitting up in beds of various descriptions, staring at her. The mother, a plain but neatly dressed woman, stared too, her face expressionless. Jame cleared her throat awkwardly. Those seven young faces, each one a living portrait of Scramp at a different age, watched her as she told them about their brother. When she had finished, she brushed off a spot on the already clean table, took out the gloves, and laid them on it.

"You can do one of two things with these," she said to the oldest and apparently brightest of the children who, she suddenly realized, was a girl. "Sell them to Lady Melissand, who is willing to pay at least one hundred twenty-five altars, or give them to Master Galishan if he will promise to take one of you in your brother's place. She wants the gloves, you see, and he wants her. Tell her she'll be at jeopardy for the next thirty days . . . and be sure you get the money or the promise before she has a chance to examine them."

The girl nodded. "I'll go to the master tomorrow," she said, almost in Scramp's voice.

"Good. That will be best . . . and by God, if anyone bothers you, they'll answer to me for it."

Someone pounded on the door.

"Talisman!" It was Raffing, shut outside. "In Ern's name, open up . . . it's coming!"

"It?" Jame said to the girl, who only gave her a wild look in reply. A child began to whimper, then another one. She looked for a moment at the gloves lying in a pool of light on the table, then unlocked the door and stepped outside. It slammed shut behind her. Raffing, who had turned away for an instant to stare down the street, launched himself at it, to no avail. It would not open again that night, not even if Scramp himself were to come crawling home with his blackened face and swollen tongue to scratch at its charred panels. Raffing clawed at her arm, babbling something, then turned and ran. Jame stood in the middle of the street, watching the Lower Town Monster approach.

It was a darkness that crawled, a huge, sprawling form that seemed both to have and to refuse any given shape. The cobbles showed faintly through it, as did the walls beneath its questing fingers as they traced the outline of each door and window, probing delicately into the cavities where wood or stone had fallen away. Flat as a cast shadow it seemed at first, but then it paused and gathered itself like a prone figure rising on its elbows. There was the vague shape of a head, a face molded in darkness, unearthly, unreadable.

It was looking at Jame.

She stared back, wondering why she was not afraid. It was almost as if it wanted to tell her something. *Stand, stand, and let me touch* . . . but to be touched was to die the death of the soul. Slowly, she began to walk away. It followed her.

In eerie silence, at a walk, they went through the streets of the Lower Town. At the edge of the fosse, the pursuer stopped. Jame, standing on the opposite bank, saw it stretch out tentative fingers toward her over the water and lose them, as though the current ran on invisibly far above its natural bed. Then it withdrew, creeping soundlessly back into the darkness of the Lower Town. The muffled wails of children rose to meet it.

"Substance *and* shadow," said Jame softly to herself as she watched it go. "But whose soul, demon? I wonder."

It was nearly midnight by the time she reached her home district. The town had quieted down remarkably as the festival drew to its close, and the streets were nearly deserted. Very soon now the gods would wake, and no one with his wits still about him wanted to rouse their suspicions with any unusual commotion.

The Res aB'tyrr was in the process of closing up. Inside, a blizzard of ribbons fluttered down as Ghillie unmasked the b'tyrr, hiding for a moment the man sitting at a back table, the sole remaining customer.

He was every bit as big as Jame remembered. Massive shoulders, corded arms, hands twice the size of her own, dark red hair and beard shot with gray . . . at a guess, he was in his mid-eighties, late middle-age for a Kendar. Although he looked fit enough, Jame noted with concern that his air of remoteness had deepened. He was gazing sightlessly at the still full cup between his hands, oblivious to the cascading ribbons, to her, to everything.

"He's been like that ever since he came in," said the widow, emerging from the kitchen. "D'you think he's ill?"

"I—don't think so," said Jame. "Just exhausted, more

likely. Look at his clothes. He's come a long, long way, probably on foot.''

She went over to his table. ''All gates and hands are open to you,'' she said to him in formal Kens, then, in Easternese, ''Be welcome to this house and peace be yours therein.''

''Honor be to you and to your halls.'' The rumbled answer was uninflected, almost subterranean.

''Please.'' She touched his cheek with gloved fingertips. ''Come with me. I know where you can rest.''

He looked up at her vaguely, blue eyes like deep water under heavy brows, and shambled to his feet. Picking up his pack and a double-edged war axe with carefully sheathed blades, he followed her mutely up to the loft where she chased the cats off her pallet and made him lie down. He fell asleep instantly. She pulled the blankets over him, then withdrew to the opposite corner and sat down with Jorin curled up in her arms. The ounce began to purr, the man to snore.

Soon she would go downstairs and help the others, but not just yet. The events of the last twenty-four hours were rushing through her mind. She could no longer tell which were her responsibility, which the result of circumstances outside her control. She blamed herself for everything. Was it honor or pride that first made her accept Scramp's challenge, then humiliate him before all their peers? What *was* honor? What was she that lives should crumble so casually when she touched them? Bortis was perhaps as correct to blame her for his maiming as Scramp for his death or Taniscent for her shattered life. She no longer knew how to regard any of these events. And what, ancestors preserve her, would this man, this emblem of her people and past, think of them? She would tell him everything, Jame decided, all her fears, all her secrets. He would judge her. Then, for the first time in her life, she would perhaps know how to judge herself.

The sound of a bell made her start. Another joined it, then another and another, until all over Tai-tastigon they were in full tongue. A shriller, less musical note chimed in from below. The Feast of Fools had ended. Standing at the kitchen door with kettle and iron ladle, Cleppetty was helping to beat in the new year.

CHAPTER 8

Voices out of the Past

THE KENDAR WAS still asleep when, three days later, the first caravan left. On the fourth day he finally woke, but seemed even less interested in his surroundings than on the first evening when he and Jame had met. He would eat if watched but didn't seem to hear any questions put to him and spent most of his time either in sleep or mechanically polishing the blades of his great war axe.

"He worries me," said Jame with a frown, watching Cleppetty stir with a spring of lemon balm the warm wine she would presently take up to the newcomer. "It's as if all the spirit had been battered out of him."

"Maybe he's just weak-witted," suggested Kithra wickedly.

"No," said Jame. "As it happens, I've seen this sort of behavior, years ago, in my father's keep. It was a hard life there. After a while, some people simply gave up. Most of them asked for the white-hilted knife; but a few just sat down in a corner—so as not to be in the way, you see—and stayed there until they died."

"Are you saying that if our friend doesn't rouse himself . . ."

"He may well die," said Jame, taking the cup, "by passive suicide."

On the tenth and fourteenth days respectively, the second and third caravans left. From the loft, Jame watched first one and then the other ascend into the Vale of Tone by the River Road and vanish into the shadows of the Ebonbane. Word filtered back that they had come upon the remains of the first caravan just under the Blue Pass, scattered over a mountain field black with crows. Soon after that, snow fell among the peaks again. A few wagons, late for the rendezvous, had gathered south of the city, hoping to form the nucleus of a fourth convoy, but no one was optimistic now about their chances of starting. True to predictions, the season had closed after only two weeks.

It was an odd time for Jame. All plans gone awry, she lived without new ones, waiting to see if the Kendar would live or die. A shock of some sort might restore him to his senses before it was too late. If he really had decided to die, however, it was not honorable for her to try to thwart him. That he would eat at all under these circumstances both surprised and encouraged her, so she continued to do what she could, hoping that something would bring about a change.

Meanwhile, the Tower of Demons affair continued to have repercussions. The day after the Feast, representatives of Prince Ozymardien appeared bearing not only ten golden altars in a silken bag as payment for the B'tyrr but also a command that she dance before His Glory again. When it became clear that she would not, agents began to lurk around the inn, apparently looking for a chance to kidnap her. Luckily, none of them ever made the connection between Jame and the Senetha dancer. Surprisingly few people ever did. The B'tyrr did not perform again until the Prince lost interest and recalled his men.

Perfumed notes for the Talisman were delivered every day for a week from the Lady Melissand, whose interest had apparently survived her outwitting.

Less regular and far more irksome were visits from the guards, who searched the inn for the Peacock Gloves several times with a thoroughness that made Jame glad they were no longer in her possession. Afraid they would unearth the knapsack, she moved the Kendar's pallet over to the corner where it was hidden so that no one could get at it without shifting him. Few guards were so intrepid. One, whom Jame suddenly recognized as the man who had nearly caught her behind the Moon, regarded the sleeping Kendar so intently that for a moment she was afraid he would try.

"Doesn't look so good, does he?" he finally said. "Poor old Marc."

"You *know* him?"

"Sure—Marcarn of East Kenshold. I met him six, no, seven years ago when he and a bunch of other Kennies were sent to help us during the Lower Town disaster. Didn't recognize him at first in the alley that night, he was looking so patchy. I would have bedded him down in the guards' barracks, but he kept saying that he had to get to this place. So I brought him."

"That was kind of you. Did you . . . tell him why you were chasing me?"

"No," he said, eyeing her speculatively, "but I will when he wakes up if you don't tell me now where the gloves are."

"That won't do," said Jame firmly. "If he wakes, I'll tell him myself. But you may as well know that they aren't here anymore. My word of honor on it."

"Well, that's something," he said, looking more cheerful. "You can't blamc an old dog for wanting a bigger bone. After this, Talisman, a proper prize you'll make for the guard who catches you. Keep an old friend in mind if there's a choice, won't you? The name's Sart Nine-toes." With that, he gave her a clumsy bow and went tramping down the spiral stairs.

Later, Jame dressed for the one of the few new activities that occupied her these days. Once ready, she paused only to check the Kendar's condition (which remained unchanged) and to snatch up an old cloak, then she ran from the inn, bound at full speed for the Temple District.

Because this area was assigned to Penari, Jame had gotten to know it very well. As the old thief's apprentice, she had the right to steal anything there that she could get away with; but, to the great relief of the priests, she had not as yet exercised this privilege. Most of the local officials had stopped noticing her at all by now. They would have been far less at ease, however, if they had known why she continued to prowl among them day after day; bit by bit, she was beginning to solve the mystery of the gods of Tai-tastigon.

Early in her wanderings through the district, Jame had noticed that the most powerful of these beings were the ones with the most dedicated followers. This suggested to her that, here at least, faith might create reality. It was a beautifully simple solution and quite an appalling one from the standpoint of any Kencyr. After all, if this were true for the Tastigons, might it also be so for one's own people? In effect, had the Three-Faced God created the Kencyrath, or was it the other way around? If the latter, then the Three People had spent the last thirty millennia hag-ridden by a nightmare of their own making. Not only would this invalidate the very principles that justified their existence, but it would mean that they, not some cruel god, were responsible for the mess in which they currently found themselves.

Jame didn't want to believe this. Some instinct told her, however, that she had stumbled on at least one part of the truth, and she felt compelled to dig for the rest. As a result, she had begun a series of experiments in the Temple District on perhaps its most innocuous resident: Gorgo the Lugubrious. It was in front of this god's temple that she found herself some thirty minutes after leaving the inn and up its steps that she rushed, adjusting the hood of her cloak to overshadow her face as she went.

The outer room was empty, as was the tiny courtyard that opened off its far side. Wailed responses sounded dully through the wall to the right. The service was well underway. Jame paused to catch her breath, then slipped through the door into the chapel. This was a small room with a very high ceiling, completely dominated by the towering image of Gorgo set at its front. The god was represented as an obese, crouching figure, with the most sorrow-stricken face imaginable and unusually long legs, the bent knees of which rose a good two feet above its head. A steady stream of water trickled out of tiny holes in the corner of each green glass eye. Loogan the high priest was holding forth in front of it for the benefit of a small, dutiful congregation, all of whom were cloaked and hooded as though in the depths of mourning. Jame settled down unobtrusively on a back bench, mentally breathing a sigh of relief. He had only gotten to the fourth canticle of the creation ode: she was not too late after all.

The words of the service, uttered in a shrill singsong, scraped about her head. Many of them were pure gibberish, but there was some quite lovely liturgical story-telling scattered throughout, the relic, Jame believed, of an older ritual. There was no doubt that Gorgo was a god of ancient lineage, much come down in the world. Most demeaning was the hierarch, Loogan, whose every gesture and mouthed bit of nonsense seemed like a calculated insult to the dignity of his religion. Still, some vestiges of power remained in this room, enough to convince Jame that Gorgo might serve her purpose. She had already stuck a number of pins into layman and priest alike, hoping to determine exactly what Gorgo was and what relationship faith had to his existence. No pin to date, however, had been as sharp as the one she meant to use tonight.

Ah . . . Loogan had come to the tenth canticle, a hymn celebrating Gorgo's compassion for the sorrows of mankind. At this point, his assistant, hidden behind the statue, should throw a lever that would open the ducts to a reservoir on the roof and allow water to trickle down on the celebrants. There was a faint, mechanical creak. Loogan looked expectantly at the ceiling, arms raised to call down the benediction of tears. Nothing happened. The congregation stirred uneasily as their priest, his face a picture of anxiety, repeated the signal words. Again, the sound of the lever being thrown; again, no water. Jame stared upward intently. Was there a hint of mist gathering in the upper darkness? She couldn't tell. Damnation.

Loogan wearily dropped his arms and began the whole service over—as he must do until he got the proper results. Jame edged toward the door. The little priest saw her. The surprise mixed with growing anger in his face told her all too clearly that, despite her hood, she had been recognized. Hastily, she slipped out of the room.

Up on the roof, Jame removed the clumps of moss that she had used that afternoon to block the ducts. The pin had been too dull to provoke a miracle after all. Next time, she must try for something more conclusive, more spectacular, but now for some reason the whole business had left a bad taste in her mouth. She climbed down and set off for the Moon to wash it away.

"HAVE YOU HEARD THE NEWS?" Raffing shouted over the din as Patches, Scramp's younger sister, made room for Jame at the table. "Mistress Silver's idiot son has gotten himself caught for pickpocketing again. That's the third time since last Midsummer's Day."

"Will the Sirdan ransom him again?" asked the new apprentice.

"Oh, he'll try, if only for his mother's two votes, but the Five may not let him. Rumor has it that one of them—probably Harr sen Tenko—is thoroughly annoyed, and who can blame him? Three times!"

"It'll be the Mercy Seat for sure," said Hangrell with considerable relish.

"Don't you believe it. I say exile at most. Don't you agree, Darinby?"

"You're probably right," said Master Galishan's journeyman tranquilly. "Money has a loud voice in this town. Even so, Carbinia of the Silver Court isn't likely to thank Theocandi for anything less than a full pardon. She's never reasonable when that son of hers is involved. No, as long as the Five are adament, the Sirdan's support in that quarter is at hazard."

"Does he need it so badly?" Jame asked.

"Every vote will count this time. Let's see. Theocandi can depend on Abbotir of the Gold Court because of Bane, and probably on Master Chardin too. Men-dalis, on the other hand, will undoubtedly get the four Provincial votes. So far, then, it's a tie. Thulican of the Jewel Court will go with whomever looks best, probably at the last minute. Odalian, Master Glass, can be bought and so, I suspect, can the masters' two representatives. That's sixteen votes in all—ten for the five courts, four for the Provincials, two for the masters—and at least six of those will go to the highest bidder, who will use them to win the election. Money will be the key factor this time, make no error about that."

"Then it will be Theocandi," said Raffing with disgust. "He has the whole Guild treasury to draw on."

"He is also a miser," said Darinby flatly. "He may well be out-bid, especially if Men-dalis's mysterious backer can provide the funds. I wonder if we'll ever find out who he is."

"One of the Five is already helping Men-dalis by refusing to pardon Mistress Silver's son," said Patches suddenly.

Jame and Darinby looked at her approvingly, but Hangrell, smothering with jealousy, snorted contemptuously. "Speak when you're spoken to, girl," he said. "Who invited you, anyway?"

"Who, for that matter," said Jame softly, "invited *you?*"

Hangrell tried to meet her eyes and failed. Muttering some excuse, he left the table precipitously, pursued by jeers. Never a favorite, the lanky thief had recently lost even more credit through his efforts to worm himself into Bane's favor. He would not be missed at the Moon.

"What an alarming person you are, Talisman," murmured Darinby. "Still, it won't help our young friend here if you fight all her battles for her."

"I don't intend to. The next time someone tackles her, he may be in for a nasty surprise."

Patches grinned. She was still sore from her last Senethar lesson and looked forward to trying out her developing skills on someone without her instructor's uncanny reflexes.

"Besides," said Jame, ruffling the girl's sandy hair, "Half-a-noggin here is too clever not to make her own way once she's gotten a start, prejudices or no. As for the rest of this lot . . ." her eyes raked over the room, hardening, "the more afraid of me they are, the better. I'm tired of being underestimated. Now if you gentlemen will excuse me, I have a cat to walk."

Darinby caught up with her outside. "I'll go with you for a ways," he said, falling into step beside her.

"What's the matter, afraid of being attacked?"

"No, but you should be. Bortis is back in town."

"Oh?" said Jame lightly. "I didn't know he'd been away."

"You should have. He's a hill brigand, remember. Now that the season is over, he's in Tai-tastigon again, bragging about the massacre under the Blue Pass (for which, it appears, his band was largely responsible), and swearing vengeance on you for the loss of his eye. Oddly enough, it never seems to have occurred to him to blame Bane."

"Hmmm. Still, boasts break no bones."

"No," said Darinby darkly, "but other things do. You were saying a minute ago that you've had enough of being underestimated, which, I suppose, means of being a target for half the bullies in town. That, admittedly, is a problem, but it's one I expect you'll have all your life. Very few men are ever going to give someone as fragile-looking as you her due in anything. That may be one reason why Bortis can't accept what happened to him: even if you didn't wield the knife that maimed him, you were there, you were the cause. For men like him, Talisman, you're a baited trap. They'll never be warned off because they can't admit to any danger. On the other hand, frightening sprats like the regretable Hangrell isn't going to make you any friends either."

"You think I need friends like that?"

"No. You've been fortunate in your allies—and in some of your enemies too, come to that. After that run-in with Bane on the Palace steps, half the Guild must have laid bets that you'd be dead within a week. All I'm saying now is that while you may not be able to stop people from underestimating you, you must never underestimate them . . . especially when they've sworn to have your blood. Huh!" he said with a sudden, rueful laugh. "Harken to the sage. I didn't mean to lecture you, Talisman, only to speak a word of warning in what I'm afraid is still a deaf ear."

"Sorry, Darinby. If it will make you feel any better, I'll go on from here by the rooftops—where it's safe."

"You have an odd idea of safety," said the journeyman, watching her swing easily up onto a portico roof and from there climb to the eaves. "Watch out for loose slates."

Jame had, in fact, meant to go aloft as soon as she left the inn. She loved the rooftops late at night, especially when the full moon transformed them as it did now into a wild, mountainous country quite distinct from the world below. Here the wind hunted freely among the gutters and chimney pots, coursing down the sweep of a thatched roof, whistling to itself among the gables. Bits of straw were in the air. Tiles lost their grip and slid, clattering, into the void. A solitary Cloudie crouched on the opposite eave like a lesser gargoyle, fishing for some tidbit below with a grapnel much like the one Jame now always carried dismantled up her sleeve. The streets below glowed with light, with all the pageantry of the late night city. Not one in all that bustling crowd looked up; not one had ever seen the wild, lonely land above, the Kingdom of the Clouds where moon shadows raced.

Jorin was waiting impatiently for her. After checking Marc again, she and the ounce went down the back stairs together, hearing snatches of song from the great hall. They turned right at the old gatehouse into the rim road and followed its curve to the Mountain Gate. Beyond that, the foothills of the Ebonbane rolled on under the full moon.

They had come here every night for the last two weeks. In that time, the summer flowers had bloomed unseen, filling the darkness with their fragrance, while the cloud-of-thorn briers held up their impaled blossoms above tangled shadows. The berries beneath these fragile white flowers already glistened in the moonlight like dark drops of blood. Birds who had eaten them during the day clung to the spiked branches singing ecstatically on and on until their hearts faltered and stopped. Roe deer drawn down from the mountains by the lure of sweet grass drifted over the hills, making Jorin prick his ears and chirp eagerly. There was another presence in the hills that excited him even more, but of that Jame never saw so much as a shadow. She was simply aware on occasion of being watched and remembered the vague stories of a catlike creature, perhaps an Arrin-ken, that was said to live in the mountains above. The first time this happened, she had called to it with her mind as she did to Jorin, trying to reestablish the psychic link. The very quality of the silence that came in response, as though to a child who had spoken out of turn, had so abashed her that she had not tried since.

Instead, she and Jorin had gone on with the business that had brought them here in the first place: learning how to hunt. Night after night, they stalked rabbits, quail, and roebuck. Blind Jorin's ears and nose were keen enough to guide him toward the mark, but the quarry nearly always took fright long before he was in striking range. When it broke, Jame (who had been creeping up on the opposite side) would leap to her feet and try to turn it back toward the cat. They could sometimes keep it boxed between them for several turns, both chirping excitedly, but so far success had always evaded them in the end. Tonight, a doe bolted straight into Jorin, knocking him over, and then streaked off into the darkness with the ounce in wild pursuit. A few minutes later, he came trotting back, panting and obviously pleased with himself. It was all a game as far as he was concerned: the instinct to kill had not yet ripened in him. They drank at a mountain stream, then climbed the highest nearby hill to watch the sun rise over the eastern plain.

The sky had turned the color of wild honey. Golden light permeated the air, transforming the blades of grass that waved about them into a living bronze relief peopled with small animals and insects stirring after the long night. Far to the south, a gray-prowed rack of clouds sailed through the glowing air. Lightning flashed in its belly and the mutter of distant thunder reached them, but little rain would fall, for Tai-tastigon was experiencing days of growing drought. Below, the city rode at anchor in a sea of mist, pinnacles catching the clear light that was already turning the peaks above to rose.

It was time to be getting home.

They trotted side by side through the gray streets of the waking city. For the ounce, there was only the anticipation of breakfast; for the girl, as always the fear that someone from the nearby catteries would recognize the cub's quality through his stained fur and raise the unanswerable cry of thief. This morning they hardly met anyone, which made the shock all the greater when, turning under the old gatehouse, they found their way blocked by a single burly figure.

Jame had just time to note the eye patch and the broad, cruel grin when a footstep behind her made her whirl. Her raised forearm went numb with the blow but did not fully block it. The iron head of the club glanced off her right temple, seemed to lift her sideways off the ground. She was on the pavement with her back to the inner wall of the arch. There was a great roaring in her head, and blood dripped down on the cobbles by her hand. Jorin crouched before her, terrified. Someone was laughing. A dark form strode forward, bent and caught the cub by the scruff of its neck. Steel glinted. A knife . . .

Jame screamed and sprang. The old war cry echoed deafeningly off the archway stones. For a moment she saw Bortis's startled expression, and then he was gone. In his place, something cowered against the opposite wall, hands over its face, gurgling.

This time she did not hear the other man approach nor recall his presence until the back of her skull seemed to explode. She found herself lying face down on the cobbles without remembering having fallen. Two boots were very close to her face. He was standing over her, poised for the killing blow.

Rapid, heavy footsteps echoed under the arch, approaching. Something struck her left arm lightly. "Pardon," said a deep, preoccupied voice up somewhere near the ceiling, and the boots in front of her both left the ground simultaneously. Overhead, there was the sound of teeth clattering together, with a screech diced fine between clicks. The club fell, narrowly missing her hand. A moment later, some much larger object crashed to earth a good twelve feet away. The shriek, trailing after it, ended abruptly on impact. Large, gentle hands turned her over. The movement unleashed pain and red-shot darkness.

She was being carried . . . no, she was in the kitchen on the floor. The same hands were taking off her cap, probing carefully at the knot of pain beneath.

". . . would have cracked the skull if not for all this hair," a deep voice said.

Above, a bearded, frowning visage; beyond, other faces, another voice: "Did you see what that cat did to his face?"

"It wasn't Jorin!" Her own voice, shrill, wild. "It was . . ."

The Kendar's palm pressed lightly on her mouth. Over it, she saw Marplet standing at the street door.

"I'm sorry," he said, quite distinctly.

Darkness closed in again.

"IT WAS THE RATHORN BATTLE CRY THAT DID IT," said Marc, sitting down rather stiffly on the floor so she would not have to look up at him. "That sound would have raised anyone who ever fought under the Gray Lord up off a pyre, much less out of whatever fog it was that I'd managed to lose myself in."

"Well, all I can say is that you must have risen—or descended, in this case—pretty fast to have gotten to the gatehouse so quickly. What did you do, jump out the loft window?"

"No," said the big Kendar, quite seriously. "I climbed down two stories and then, to save time, fell the rest of the way."

Jame started to laugh, then stopped suddenly, making a grab for her head. This gesture also ended abruptly, with a half-stifled yelp of pain. She hardly knew which hurt more, her head or her arm, which was mottled black and blue from elbow to wrist and should by rights be not only bruised but broken. It was now four days after the attack. She had slept off the worst of its effects and was left only with a raging headache, occasional double vision, and a scar forming just under the hairline of the right temple that would be with her the rest of her life. She had gotten off far more lightly than she deserved, and she knew it.

"Maybe you should get some more sleep," said Marc, regarding her critically. "We can talk later."

"No, now—if you don't mind. I've too many questions hoarded up, and you know what a rocky pillow those make. Tell me this much at least: where were you going that night I ran into you in the alley?"

"I suppose I was trying to reach the caravan grounds," he said slowly. "I was going to take passage across the Ebonbane. Another journey. Sweet Trinity, how many there have been."

He was silent for a moment, his eyes fixed on memory. Jame, watching him, realized that her question had sent him much farther back in time than she had intended.

"Ah, it's a long road that I've walked," he said at last, quietly, as if to himself. "Mile after mile, league upon league. And when I first set out, I thought it would only be for a few days, just a little hunting trip by myself to escape the other boys' teasing. That was nearly eighty years ago. Even then I stood head and shoulders over all of them, too big a target for laughter to miss. It was quiet enough when I came back, though. The gate stood open. The guard lay across the threshold with his throat cut. Inside, dead, all dead, my lord, my family, betrayed by a hall guest who had opened the gate one dark night to tribesmen from the hills. I tracked that man down," he said, sounding almost surprised by the memory. "I took my great-grandfather's war axe, which the hall guest had stolen, out of his hand and split his skull with it. His kin hunted me through the mountains half that winter. I killed most of them. Ah, but it was a red, red time. Then I came south into the Riverland and grew to manhood there, searching for a Highborn who would give me hearth space, a new home to replace the one destroyed."

"Surely someone must have been willing to take you in," Jame protested. "After such a loss, it would only be fair."

Marc shook his head regretfully.

"Fairness isn't a consideration anymore," he said, "not, at least, for most Kendars. Too many holdings have been lost in recent years, too many lords killed, their people rendered homeless. The surviving Highborn can make their own terms now. The only choice for many of us is to become *yondrigon,* threshold-dwellers, in the house of some lord who often makes us pay our way by leasing us out as warriors, craftsmen, or scholars. Some of us go for years without seeing the threshold we supposedly occupy or gaining any pledge of eventual acceptance there. That was my situation. For thirty-six years, I soldiered from one end of Rathillien to the other as a yondri of the Lord Caineron. Not that I cared much for fighting; that winter in the mountains had taken away my taste for bloodshed. Few care to meet a man my size in battle, though, and it helps to feign an occasional berserker fit. Oh, I was worth something to my lord and hoped finally to win a permanent place in his household. The fall of Ganth Gray Lord changed all that."

"Ganth of Knorth?" said Jame. "Dally told me a little about him, but it was pretty garbled. Who was he, anyway?"

"Why, Glendar's heir, Highlord of the Kencyrath. He raised the central houses under the rathorn banner to fight the Seven Kings and would have won too if the border keeps had supported him, his allies had proved true . . . and he hadn't gone mad. Anyway, there was a pitched battle, defeat, and exile for the Gray Lord.

"I didn't fare much better. My Lord Caineron was slain in the fight and I was cast adrift again, no light thing for a man nearing middle-age. No Riverland lord would so much as look at me after that, so I came east. More than thirty years ago, that was. Harth of East Kenshold took me in, one more graying yondri to warm himself by his fire. Ah, he was a fine man, a lord of the old stamp. He only sent his threshold-dwellers out once, when the Five asked for help during the Lower Town crisis. Old Ishtier was high priest then."

"He still is," said Jame.

Marc stared at her. "But that was seven years ago, and he'd already been here a good twenty years before that! He must have refused recall again, Trinity only knows why. I shouldn't think that any priest would care to stay in this god-infested place beyond his term. Have they at least sent more acolytes to help him?"

"I don't think so. What happened to the ones he had?"

"All dead, drowned trying to round the Cape of the Lost in storm season, trying to get beyond the Ebonbane. We passed them coming out of the city as we marched in, but not a word did they have for us. I've never seen Kencyrs look so scared."

"That *is* odd. There's the Lower Town Monster, of course, but if it didn't panic me, why should it them? Do you know of any other reason?"

"None," he said, shaking his head in bewilderment. "After that greeting, you may be sure we kept our eyes open; but none of us saw anything but fire and street fighting, the Thieves' Guild having just been set on its ear by the last Council session and the assassination of Master Tane, the Sirdan's chief rival. No, all we got out of that trip were burns and a topic for five years of winter eves.

"Then one night the riders came down on us from the north, yes, out of the Haunted Lands. Three score of them there were, all in black, and they were Kencyr, though I've never seen their like before. Their armor was like something out of an old song, all hardened leather and steel, hacked and dented, and their swords were black with blood. They tore into us without so much as a word. We were fighting for our lives before most of us were fully awake, and a long battle it was, under torch and moon. They were devilish hard to kill. When we did draw blood, it ate into our flesh and pitted our weapons. They penetrated every room in the keep, had a look around, and then fought their way out again. And all that time their leader sat his brute of a horse on the hilltop, watching. Then the cocks began to crow. We saw their banner as they rode away, a black horse on a red field."

Jame whistled softly. "The device of Gerridon, Master of Knorth. Do you suppose that's who it really was?"

"If he got the immortality he was after, yes. But he's not

had everything his own way for all of that: his left hand was missing.

"At any rate, that's the last action I fought for my Lord Harth. He was a brave old man and stood with us shield to shield all that long night. Their blood was his undoing. I've seen men burned less on their own pyres. The horrible thing was that he lived nearly two years after that, the flesh slowly crumbling away from his living bones. When he finally died, his son told us yondri that we no longer had a place there. Six of us started out for Tai-tastigon. I was the only one who arrived."

Silence fell between them for a long moment. Marc stared at the floor and Jame at him, not knowing what to say. Then he gave himself a shake like a dog leaving deep water and smiled at her.

"Enough of that. They tell me below that you come from East Kenshold too, though I could have sworn I knew everyone there."

He undoubtedly had, Jame thought, and was perfectly aware that she had never crossed its threshold. This was simply his way of giving her room to maneuver around the truth if she wished to. It took a genuine effort not to do so.

"They say that because it's the only answer that makes any sense to them," she said. "In fact, I came down out of the Haunted Lands, from a keep near the Barrier."

Marc regarded her with amazement. "But the only thing up there is North Kenshold, and that was abandoned nearly three centuries ago."

It was Jame's turn to look confused. "Do you mean to say that my people weren't the original settlers? But then who in all the names of God were they?"

"Perhaps I know," the big Kendar said after a moment's hard thought. "You see, when the Gray Lord rode into exile, it was for the Eastern Lands that he was bound. But the report is that he died crossing the Ebonbane. Most of his people turned back then. A few went on, however, passing Tai-tastigon in the dark of the moon and were never heard of again—till now. Those must have been your people."

"But if that's true," Jame protested, "why didn't they tell me about it?"

"Ganth would have wanted it that way. When the Kencyr

lords, his own allies, let the Seven Kings strip him of power, he threw down his name as well, in a sense leaving it and his shame with them in the Riverland. His people, including your father, must have honored his wishes after his death. How many of the household are left?''

''Only myself, and possibly my twin brother Tori. Like you, I came back to a dead keep. Marc, what's a rathorn?''

''Why, it's something like a horse except that it has two horns, scale armor on its chest and belly, and fangs. Some of them also have a taste for man-flesh. Beautiful creatures they are, but nothing more vicious walks the earth—which may be why Glendar adopted one as the family crest when he took over from Gerridon.''

Jame had removed the loose stones in the wall behind her and drawn out the knapsack. Now the small, oblong package was in her hands, and she was gingerly unwrapping it.

''Does it look like this?'' she asked, holding out its contents to him on the cloth.

Marc examined the ring with its engraved emerald, which encircled what appeared to be a small bunch of twigs held together with brown parchment. ''Aye, that's the beast,'' he said at last, ''and this, I think, is the seal of the Gray Lord himself, lost these many years. But what's stuck through it?''

''A finger,'' said Jame, not looking at it. ''My father's. I tried to pull the ring off to take it to my brother. All the fingers on the other hand went as I was prying loose the sword hilt. I looked up into his face, and he was staring down at me—without eyes.'' She shuddered. The thing slid off the cloth onto her knee. Marc picked it up quickly and held it cupped in his big hands so that she could not see it.

''By rights, the ring and the sword shard should go to Ganth's son, Torisen Black Lord,'' he said thoughtfully. ''Your father must have been greatly trusted to have been given charge of such precious things. I don't really think you have to take the—uh—remains to him as well. A bit of fire would be best for them, and more respectful too. What's that other package you have in there—the big, flat one?''

''Oh, just a book I picked up somewhere. But what's this about a son? You didn't mention one before.''

''I gather he came as a surprise to a lot of people, turning up so long after his sire's death. How he made them believe who he was without seal or sword I don't know, but he did. Now he's the most powerful lord in the Kencyrath. Of course, all we ever heard at East Kenshold were rumors, some of them years old; but from the sound of them, it looks as if he's taken up his father's work. If so, there should be lively times ahead for us all."

"This Torisen . . . how old is he?"

"In his mid-thirties, I think," said Marc. "Why?"

"Nothing. Just a mad idea." A flicker of pain crossed her face, and she touched her forehead tentatively.

"That's enough for now," said Marc firmly, getting up. Something slipped out of his belt and fell to the floor with a clatter.

"Your friend with the incomplete foot must have been here," said Jame, picking up the guard's truncheon.

"Who . . . oh, Sart Nine-toes. No," he said, accepting it back, "this one is mine."

"What?"

"Well, it looks as if we're going to be here awhile, so I thought I'd better get a job. Sart suggested the guards."

"Oh, did he?" said Jame grimly. "I owe him for that." And then, much sooner than she intended, she told Marc about Master Penari, Ishtier's judgment, and the Talisman, watching anxiously for his reaction.

"You say a priest approved of this?" he said at last, looking puzzled. "Odd. Just the same, it could mean trouble. I've made a commitment to the Five that isn't easily broken, and you've probably done the same with your master. If we were sensible people, we would separate and stay out of each other's sight until it's time to leave this city. Are you a sensible person?"

"Hardly."

"Neither am I," he said with a slow smile. "We'll have to work something else out—later, when you've slept and I'm off duty . . . and by the way, your gloves will wear better if you cut slits in the fingertips. Good night."

She listened to him clump down the steps, and let out her breath slowly. The moment she had most dreaded was past. He knew the worst about her now, and it didn't seem to bother him at all. Either he was unusually tolerant or maybe, just maybe, it wasn't so terrible to be different after all. She would have to think about that.

The knapsack lay beside her, the small oblong package, rewrapped by Marc, on top of it.

Burn the dead, or join them.

"Father, let go," she said out loud in a low, exultant voice. "To ashes with the past."

CHAPTER 9

A Matter of Honor

THE WIDOW CLEPPETANIA was making humble pie. The pastry shell was ready. The sealed pot of wine, spices, and tripe had done ten hours worth of simmering in five with the aid of a simple spell, but the kitchen was wretchedly hot nevertheless. This was not a dish that she cared to make in midsummer. Mistress Abernia had specifically requested it, however, and would shake the rafters if it was not forthcoming.

Once, the widow would have told her to go bark for it.

Now, with the advent of the ambitious Kithra, she found herself doing all she could to keep Abernia's usual ill-humor from endangering her hold on Tubain. The possibility of having to call the new servant girl "mistress" was more than the widow could stomach. No, if Kithra must wed, let her have Rothan—who was already ears deep in love with her—and manage him until he came into his inheritance. Then Cleppetty and Abernia would step down, but not before.

"Allied to a figment of someone else's imagination," said the widow out loud with a grimace. "It could only happen here."

She retrieved the clay cooking pot from the ashes and

transferred the tripe to its pastry shell. Boo lumbered in from the courtyard, clamoring for the tidbits, which no one was supposed to give him. Cleppetty surreptitiously put a few choice pieces down on a saucer for him, turned back toward the south fireplace, and started violently.

Jame was sitting on the hearth.

"What are you trying to do," the widow half-screeched at her, "drive me into conniptions? Why can't you stomp through life like the rest of us?"

"Sorry, Cleppetty."

The widow gave her a hard look. "You're pale. Has your head started hurting again?"

"No, it's not that. I've just seen Taniscent. In the Lower Town. An old woman crossed the street ahead of me wearing Tanis's favorite shawl—you know, that ghastly orange and purple affair. Then she turned, and I saw that it was Taniscent herself. She looked nearly eighty, all wrinkled and blotchy—half-senile, too, I think—but she knew me. She ran, Cleppetty. She gave a panicky sort of bleat, and she ran."

"Well, what did you expect?" the widow demanded, floury fists jammed on her sharp hips. "The sight of anyone from the inn can only remind her of what she's lost. Anyway, even if that beating you gave Niggen did set the whole thing off, you didn't force that overdose of Dragon's Blood down her throat. She was a foolish, vain child and has only herself to blame. Still, she was, and is, one of us. What happened next?"

"I lost her," said Jame in disgust. "That district has been so warped by fire and decay that only those born there can master the heart of it now. Patches and her Townie friends have taken up the hunt. If they find Tanis and she isn't ready to come home, Patch says her mother will take care of her until she is. For some reason, that family seems to think it owes me something."

"That's just as well for Taniscent," said Cleppetty briskly, turning back to her pie. "You've done well, child. Now let matters take their course. Sooner or later, she'll come home . . . and an altered place she'll find it, too, what with Kithra and Marc in residence. Speaking of Marc, how have you and that big Kendar been managing? It can't be easy for a thief and a guard to share the same roof, much less the same room."

"Oh, it's not all that hard," said Jame, trying to adjust to this abrupt change of topic. "I'm only in danger from him when I have stolen property in my possession, so I never bring any back to the loft or into his assigned territory. I think he's even got used to the idea of a Kencyr thief."

"Well, why not? You've made the profession honorable. The Widow Cibbeth sends her thanks and blessings, by the way. The temple would have repossessed her godson by now if you hadn't retrieved his ransom from that pocket-picking Hangrell."

"I hate thieves who specialize in robbing old people," said Jame. "If nothing else, where's the skill in it? Oh, I know all guildsmen can't be as principled as Darinby, but it's still depressing to come across a specimen like Hangrell, whose highest ambition, apparently, is to become one of Bane's scrap-fed rats.

"But if the Talisman doesn't bother Marc, do you know who does? The B'tyrr. Cleppetty, have you noticed that he always leaves the room when I dance? That worries me. His moral sense is very good, far better than mine, and I hate to go against it. But Tubain still needs the B'tyrr, so I guess there's no helping that."

She was silent for a moment. The widow, watching her askance, saw the haunted look return to her eyes.

"Cleppetty," she said, raising her head suddenly, "do you remember what you said to me the day the beam fell, that sooner or later I would destroy someone? Was that someone Tanis, or am I still a danger to you, to Tubain, to everyone I love?"

Kithra's voice cut across the widow's startled response.

"Madam, come quick! It's Marc. I think he's been hurt."

Jame leaped up and was past Cleppetty out the door before she could move. Heavy feet tramped into the hall. A voice, vaguely groggy, said something about matching scars. The big Kendar was standing in the hall with Sart Nine-toes beside him and a blood-stained cloth wrapped about his graying temples.

"Just the same," he was saying cheerfully to Jame, "I bet I've got the bigger headache. After all, mine's the bigger head."

She brought him into the kitchen, made him sit down on the scullery hearth, and unwrapped the makeshift bandage.

"That's not too bad," said Cleppetty, looking over her shoulder.

"No," said Jame with relief. "More ugly than dangerous, I'd say. Just the same, you're going to be out of it a day or two, my lad."

They cleaned the wound and dressed it with a poultice of balm leaves steeped in wine. Then Jame took Marc up to the loft. Cleppetty, left alone with Sart, stopped his clumsy advances by stomping on his foot and then, when he opened his mouth to yelp, jamming a wheat cake into it. After several minutes, Jame returned.

"You always seem to be trundling Marc home," she said to Sart. "My thanks again. Now, what happened?"

"A trap happened, that's what," said the guard with a growl. "We're walking our balliwick, see, when we hear a shout for help. It's coming from a side lane, one of those rotting dead-ends near the Temple District Wall, where the stones crumble if you stare at them too hard. Me, I know the streets well enough to be suspicious, so I hold back, but Marc goes charging straight in before I can stop him. Then the bricks start to fall. I look up and see that the whole wall over his head is giving way. So I let off a bellow. Luckily there's a doorway handy, or he'd have gotten more than a broken head. It was no accident, either. I saw the bastard looking down as the dust settled, the lever still in his hands, wanting to see most likely if his work was well done. Well, it wasn't, and now he'll squirm on the Mercy Seat for injuring a guard—as soon as we can lay hands on him, that is."

"On whom?"

"Why, didn't I say? On that creep-thief Hangrell. He won't be easy to find, though, not when it sinks into his tiny little head that every guard in the city—aye, and half the thieves, too—will be after him. The gods only know what made him do a damn-fool thing like that."

"If they don't," said Jame grimly, "I do. Wait here, Sart. No one knows the hiding holes in this city better than I, except my master. Be ready to come when I send for you."

"Now just a minute, Talisman," he protested, stepping between her and the street door. "This man is our meat by law, and we've got to make an example of him. If we don't, no guard in Tai-tastigon will ever be safe again, or any thief, come to that, with the ban against mutual violence broken."

Cold silver-gray eyes locked with his own. "I said I would send for you. Wait."

He had not meant to step out of her way, much less to stand staring foolishly after her.

"If I were you," said Cleppetty drily behind him, "I would do as she said . . . or do you want her mad at you too?"

Sart Nine-toes closed his mouth with a snap, sat down on the hearth, and began to wait.

The afternoon light drained away. Dusk glowed and faded into night. When the message came at last, four guards were waiting at the inn.

Across the city, in the catacomblike cellars under a gutted mansion on the edge of the Lower Town, someone else also waited, nervously, starting at every hollow echo the subterranean spaces threw back. Water dripped, torches sputtered, the voices of others in hiding murmured confusedly in the distance. Thief! Surely someone had called his name. Here I am, here, here . . . no, nothing. Hangrell sat down again on the brick floor, snivelling a little in the dark.

Again and again, he told himself that here, if nowhere else in the city, he should be safe. Although the hand of every honest thief would be against him now, those who shared this dank, dark refuge were outcasts like himself, breakers of Tastigon or Thieves' Guild law. Both codes forbade the injuring of a guard. Hangrell would not have risked his petty revenge if he hadn't been sure (oh, so mistakenly) that he could get away with it, and that it would be applauded by the one person in Tai-tastigon whom he most wished to impress. Even now, with all plans gone awry, he hoped desperately that that individual would acknowledge the gesture and send help. He must know that it had been done to please him. Oh, why had it all gone wrong? A simple accident—that was what everyone would have called it except for the appreciative few who knew better. If it weren't for that second guard (damn him!) whom he had not seen until far, far too late . . .

Someone was shouting. Voices boomed through the halls. People were running, torches going out. "The guards!" a boy shrieked in the darkness. "The guards!"

Hangrell jumped to his feet, heart pounding. They were coming this way. He backed up, stumbling over debris, turned, and fled. Somewhere in this part of the cellar, there was supposed to be a way out. He had searched for it all afternoon in case of just such an emergency and, failing to find it, had hoped more desperately than ever that someone would be sent to show him the way.

Stone grated on stone. Ahead, the shadows on the wall fell away into a widening blackness through which a figure stepped. The thief's welcoming cry died in his throat.

It was the Talisman.

"Well, friend," she said in a quiet, almost pleasant voice. "You've really done it this time. If you had dealt with me directly, as Scramp did, we might have come to some understanding; but to injure a guard . . . that wasn't very bright, now was it?"

He backed away from her, panic clawing at him. Say something, anything. "It wasn't my fault!" he heard himself squeal. "He made me do it. It's his fault that your friend was hurt!"

"Whose fault, sweetling?"

"Bane's!"

"I . . . see." Her tone jerked his attention back from the shouts of the approaching guards. "So. This was how you bought your way into his favor. Cat's paw for a coward. I was going to hold you for the guards and the Mercy Seat, my dear. Instead, I'll give you a choice, a . . . chance. Do you see the stairs behind me? They lead to the sewers, to safety. All you have to do is pass me."

The shouts were closer, almost at the mouth of the passageway. Hangrell looked wildly behind him, whining, then at the slim, shadowy form that barred the way.

"Come along, little one," it said, its voice slipping into a deep, full-throated purr. "I wait—without a knife, without gloves."

With a choked cry, he spun about and ran straight into Sart's arms.

JUDGMENT SQUARE LAY SLEEK in the moonlight. The stalls that had freckled its surface by midday were gone now and their owners with them, leaving the great, triangular flagstones to wind-whirled debris and the small group gathered in front of the Mercy Seat. The Master of Mercy was arguing with four guardsmen while his assistant crouched behind him, tending a brazier whose coals sparkled fitfully. The wind bore none of his complaint upward. Knowing his reputation as a perfectionist, however, it was easy enough to guess that he was bitterly protesting the conditions under which these hulking guards expected him to work. What did they know of craftsmanship? What did they care? To them, only results mattered, and now they were set on creating an example. At last the Master shrugged and opened his tool case while his assistant took an iron from the fire and spat on it experimentally. The pale, thin form that sprawled on the Seat did not move as the two men bent over it. The drugs had done their work well; once again, the Master had justified his title.

On the south side of the square stood a rich merchant's house with a turret ornamented, in imitation of Edor Thulig, with three huge stone bats in high relief. On the head of the one facing north sat Jame. She was no longer regarding the scene below but her own hands, which rested, still gloveless, on her knees. With an expression of mingled disgust and fascination, she raised one and stared at it, as though it were some wild, unidentified creature that she had found scurrying across the forest floor. The abnormally long fingers flexed and arched. At the tip of each was the nail, razor tipped, fully extended.

Would she really have used them on Hangrell? Yes. Again, she heard her voice dripping black honey, felt the savage, exultant lust for blood. It had taken all her self-control to offer that wretched boy a choice at all, if only of deaths.

Ivory claws, black rage—both were a part of her Shanir nature, that terrible openness to a divine will as ruthless as it often was incomprehensible. But if it was truly another's will, how could she be accountable for its actions? Remember Ishtier, she told herself: he was a Shanir too, as every priest must be; but could she forgive him, even on those grounds, for what he had done to her? No. It was unthinkable. And yet clearly he had no influence over the god's voice when it spoke through him. It simply used him. Was she also being used when these murderous rages fell on her, and if so, to what purpose?

"No," she said out loud, recoiling from the thought. "*No.*

I will *not* be used. Let me be a monster in my own right if I must, but not the puppet of some damned, indifferent god. I will be responsible for my actions, whatever prompts them. I will be free.''

Such freedom would be hard to bear, but she might not have to live with it for long, Jame thought with sudden wryness. Her words in the cellar had been addressed less to Hangrell than to those others hidden in the shadows, and through them to that wretched creature's patron, who would learn soon enough what she had said and done. Defiance, insult, challenge—if she knew him half as well as she thought she did, he would swallow none of them. The uneasy, unaccountable friendship between them was at an end and war declared, her hand against his. She had no illusions concerning her chances for survival.

Meanwhile, there was no point in watching more of the sorry spectacle below. Jame climbed down and set off for home.

The Res aB'tyrr was brightly lit but ominously silent as she crossed the square to it. A sleek young man wearing a d'hen of a rich, dark fabric waited for her in the doorway. He stepped aside as she approached and bowed mockingly. Inside, seven more men leaned against the walls or slouched negligently in the best chairs. Bane sat by himself at the center table, his long, elegantly booted legs stretched out before him and a small goblet of golden wine at his elbow. He looked up as she entered and said, smiling, ''I got your message.''

Jame had known that this meeting must come, but had somehow never thought of it taking place here, in her home. One of Bane's companions was lounging on the kitchen threshold, another in the room itself by the street door. Cleppetty stood white-faced with anger by the kitchen table, one arm thrown protectively around Kithra's shoulders. A slow, deadly rage swelled up in Jame.

''Get those men out of here,'' she said to Bane in a low voice. Her hands had already gone cold, her body slipped to the inner rhythms that precede violence.

''Don't be a fool,'' he said sharply, reading her intentions in her stance. ''I would kill you.''

''Get them out or you'll have to. Now.''

He regarded her intently for a moment, then suddenly laughed and dismissed the others with a wave of his hand. Surprise broke the stride of Jame's growing, probably suicidal anger. She had not seriously thought that she could blackmail him with the threat of her own death.

"Sit down, sit down," he said when they were gone, gesturing to the opposite seat. "Have some of this excellent wine and do, please, stop glowering at me. For once, I'm not to blame. That imbecile Hangrell was acting on his own against my wishes, whatever he may have thought they were. I would have dealt with him myself if you hadn't gotten to him first."

"Why?" said Jame, warily seating herself. "If you didn't order it, what concern is all this of yours?"

"Do you mean to say," he said, regarding her with raised eyebrows, "that you still haven't guessed? Well then, here's a little story for you that may make it clear. About thirty years ago, a group of refugees came over the Ebonbane, fleeing from war and kin-strife, following their mad lord into exile. He died in the mountains. They went on, passing Tai-tastigon in the night, and turning northward into the unnamed lands. Nearly a year later, two of them came crawling back. One, a priest, entered the temple of the Three-Faced God and has not left it since. The other, once mistress to the old lord himself, was taken to wife by a high official of the Thieves' Guild. What no one knew then, or has guessed to this day, is that she crossed his threshold already quick with child. Ah, now you begin to understand."

"You're telling me that you also are of the Kencyrath," said Jame slowly; and somehow, she was not really surprised. "But no Kencyr I've ever known would behave as you do."

"None?" he said, giving her a sharp look. "Remember the Mercy Seat. You know as well as I what sort of inner darkness leads to a thing like that. I fought it for years, as you do now. I bound myself in secret to the rituals of our people and dared them to break me. Trinity, but that was hard. Then, seven years ago, my foster-father told me that I must be apprenticed to the Sirdan and become a thief. A thief! Oh, I didn't rush into the arms of the Guild like some others," he said with a bitter laugh. "Ishtier pushed me. Honor would be served no other way, he said. I owed it to Abbotir, my benefactor. Neither he nor the priest seemed to understand that if they made me go that far, whether I ever stole or not, nothing would ever hold me back again. It was a nice little paradox, really: how to save one's soul by losing it, and in a sense, that's exactly what I did. I've confused you again, haven't I? Do you like stories? Then here's another one, much older than the first:

"Once long ago, in a time of great danger, a randon warrior went to his lord and said, 'Master, our enemies hem us in, we die by the hundreds daily. I can deliver us, but only by such acts as will damn me forever in the eyes of our people and our god. Take thou my soul, so that it at least will be untainted, and loose me on the foe.' And so it was done. The Three People were saved, but by deeds so foul that no man would record them. Then, in the great hall, the warrior reclaimed his soul. Its purity consumed him, as if he lay on his pyre alive, and so he died at last with honor. . . . Do you have any idea what I'm talking about?"

"I understand this much at least," said Jame slowly, regarding his hand and the candlelight that glowed on the polished table top beneath it. "You cast no shadow. So Ishtier's is double then, but are you sure you can trust that priest to keep it and your soul safe?"

"I have reason to think so. Besides, who else could have done such a thing for me?"

"I could."

He stared at yer, then let his breath out slowly. "Oh, my lady. Yes, you could, and would—if it weren't already too late. But now you must follow me. Give up the struggle and let go, as I did. What good is honor in life to either of us? The very weight of it twists us. Better to fall. Yes, it's terrifying at first. Life loses all boundaries, then begins to expand, seeking new ones. You never find them. No one can tell you where to stop. Honor no longer matters, no, nor the lack of it. Then, in the end, you take back your soul and let its purity immolate you and your deeds. An honorable death wipes away all stains. But before that, the *freedom,* lady, to do what you will, be what you are, outside the coils of the law, beyond the touch of man or god—that is the course for you, as for me. As for that hulk of a Kendar or Dallen, that whelp's son, you are ill-matched with both or, if it has come to that, worse mated with either. In the end you will see that and turn to me. Until then, m'lady."

He sketched a formal salute and was gone, stepping lightly into the night.

Jealousy hung raw on the air behind him. Had Hangrell overheard such remarks as these last and posted eagerly off to his death on their strength? The poor fool, to have measured Bane's pride by his own petty standards.

But she had underestimated Bane too, in more ways than one. No need to have sent a message at all; the deed itself, like the smell of fresh-spilt blood, would have drawn him to her. Marc might be safe, but nothing would ever protect her again, now that Bane's interest had been thoroughly aroused. But perhaps she didn't want protection. Why else offer him the greatest intimacy possible between two Kencyrs . . . and since when had she even known that such a thing lay in her power? At every turn, her voice had answered his, darkness speaking to darkness. He might be the dead, consumed with hunger for the living, but it was her own face she had seen staring back at her over the table, monstrously mirrored in those odd, silver-gray eyes.

"Mother of Shadows," she said out loud to herself. "What will come of all this?"

"Probably a hall full of angry customers," said Cleppetty loudly, making her start. The others, who had been locked in the cellar, all came flocking in after her, except for Tubain, who had stayed below on a sudden impulse to inventory the rose wine. "Those flash-blades have been turning everyone away for the last hour *and* drinking our best wine without so much as a copper put on the boards. I ask you," the widow concluded, setting loose all her stored wrath at once, "is this any way to run an inn?"

"No, it's not," said Jame, "and I'm at fault. It's time Jorin and I left. He's grown too big, and I too dangerous."

The junior staff burst into loud protest.

"Bustard balls," said Cleppetty, cutting across the tumult. "This is your home. When the time comes to leave Tai-tastigon, you'll leave us too, but not before. You've fought for us in your way; we'll fight for you in ours. Besides, the B'tyrr has promised to dance tonight. After a start like this to the evening, the gods help us if she doesn't."

Jame at last acquiesced, glad to give in but still uneasy. She was on her way up the stairs when the widow called her back, holding up a folded paper that she had picked up from the central table where Bane had sat.

"Notes, yet," she said, giving it to Jame, then, more sharply, "Is anything wrong?"

"I—don't know," Jame said, frowning at the wax seal. "Probably not." But to avoid more questions, she turned quickly and ran up the steps with the note still unopened in her hand.

In the loft, the big Kendar lay face up on his pallet, snoring. She knelt to check his condition, then sat back on her heels beside him, broke the seal, and read. A frown gathered on her sharp young face. She sat there for a long moment with the paper in her hands, biting her lower lip, looking down at the guardsman. Left to himself, he would remain deep in *dwar* sleep for another twelve hours. It would be wisest to leave a message with Cleppetty, but something in her balked at the idea. This was Kencyr business, however strange, and not meant for other ears. She bent over the sleeping man and shook him. At last his eyelids slowly peeled back.

"Marc, listen to me," she said, taking his graying head in her hands. "I've been summoned to the temple of our god by Ishtier, Trinity only knows why. If I'm not back by the time you wake up again, I suppose you'd better come after me. Do you understand?"

"Issshtier . . .?" Marc struggled up on one elbow. "You can't do that . . . he hates you."

"That's no distinction. He hates everyone. Now go back to sleep."

"Ha!" said Marc with a cheerful if somewhat blurry grin, climbing unsteadily to his feet. "You've raised the beast right and proper, and now you'll have to put up with him. I'm going with you."

Jame swore under her breath. Of course he would say that. It was as natural for him to think of himself as her protector as it was for her to be constantly caught off-guard by the fact. With a sigh, she helped the big guardsman to find his truncheon (which, of course, turned out to be under a cat), and they set off.

THE TWO CAME ON THE TEMPLE of their god from its western approach, with the fire-stricken Lower Town close by to the south. The sounds of the living world followed them through the wasteland of deserted houses, but fell away to the soughing of wind in empty doorways as they emerged on the circle of dust.

"What a mess," said Marc, staring at the desolation around the temple. "Folk were beginning to move out when I was last here, but who would have thought that Ishtier would let things go so far?"

Then, absentmindedly, he rapped his companion on the back of the head for luck as though they were shieldmates going into battle together and strode down to meet the enemy. Jame followed, gingerly rubbing her head.

Inside, she took the lead. Even though she knew what to expect this time and had all her mental shields up, the currents of power were so swift that it was hard to walk the halls without reeling. Instinct, not memory, led her forward. There was the door she had crashed into, and beyond it, Ishtier.

The priest stood as before in the shadow of their god, looking as though he had not moved since that distant night. His yellow eyes too were as they had been before, cruel and haughty; but this time Jame met them. So this was the Highborn to whom Bane had entrusted his soul. Was it really safe with him? Bane might think so, but what would he say if she told him that this man had already proved faithless to his own younger brother by abandoning him to madness in the Haunted Lands? After hearing Bane's story, Jame had no further doubts that Ishtier was the priest who had fled the keep before her birth. She would indeed never forgive him for Anar's plight, but since he had not also deserted his lord (who, after all, was dead), his honor was intact as far as she knew.

Therefore she gave him a formal if wary salute and said: "You wished to see me, my lord?"

"You, yes. Not him." The words were brusque but power, licking at their edges, blurred them.

Jame tensed. Would he play at singeing her again? She had no time to consider it, for just then Marc, despite a commendably brisk start half an hour before, began to sway. She slipped an arm around his waist to steady him and punched him in the ribs to forestall a rising snore.

"Pardon, my lord," she said to the priest, getting her shoulder under Marc's armpit and heaving him upright. "We come as a set. If you try to put him out now, I shall tip him over on you."

Ishtier scowled at the swaying giant for a moment, then, unnervingly, a thin, secret smile flickered across his face.

"I have a mission for you, thief," he said.

Jame stared at him. "You want me to steal something? You, who all but spat in my face when I came to ask counsel before joining the Guild? Priest, you have a strange sense of humor."

"Hunzzaagg," said Marc.

"What?" snapped Ishtier.

"Never mind him. He thinks he's awake. It's a common delusion."

"Humph. Listen to me, you insolent, young . . . guttersnipe. I said nothing of stealing. Look here." He stepped aside. Behind him stood the small altar on which the temple's copy of the Law usually rested. It was not there now. "You see? The scroll is gone. Without it, only I, the priest, stand between the people of the Kencyrath and their god, all dread be to him. I want you to retrieve it."

Jame struggled with an answer. Suddenly, tendrils of power were slipping past her, sliding over her mind, numbing it with their touch. It was the nightmare of that first meeting all over again . . . but this time it was something else, too. For an instant, she seemed to see the faces of the tavern audience turned up eagerly. A bow, the first step of the dance, and they were hers. Not the mists of desire but tongues of ice and fire licked at her now. Still immobilized by Marc's weight, her mind shied away from them, instinctively tracing the first moves of a wind-blowing kantir. To her amazement, she felt the energy flowing past her, back into its natural channel over the tessellated floor.

The ultimate power, the ultimate dance. She had at last found the true outlet for her strange talent.

The priest was staring at her. "Shanir," he said, almost to himself. He must be one himself to wield hieratic power, but there was no dawning welcome in his face. Rather, Jame had the uncomfortable feeling that he was really seeing her for the first time, not just as a plaything or a tool but as an individual dangerously like himself who could only prove a threat.

But there was more at stake here than their mutual hatred. It was neither priest nor god she was being asked to serve, but the Law and the code of honor it embodied. Bane's abyss had opened up behind her. If she turned her back on that empty altar, as he undoubtedly hoped she would, it would be beneath her feet.

"Where is the scroll?" she asked in a low voice.

"Look in the temple of Gorgo. Did you think you could trifle with a priest—any priest—and not pay for it? Swear before our god that you will bring me the scroll that lies in the arms of the false idol there. Your word on it, thief."

"Priest," Jame said grimly, "death break me, darkness take me, the scroll will be in your hands tonight. My word on it."

ALL THE WAY ACROSS TOWN, she tried to talk Marc into turning back. Not only was he hurt, she argued, but unsuited by virture of sheer size for the job ahead. Moreover, since the guards of Tai-tastigon had no jurisdiction over the city's priests, his official status would be of no use to either of them. Obviously, the only fit place for him was at home in bed, with as few cats asleep on his chest as possible.

Marc only laughed.

This one-sided argument went on street after street, through the twining ribbons of the courtesans' district, over the Tone, past the Tower of Demons, ending only within sight of Gorgo's temple itself, where Jame at last yielded to the inevitable with a sigh.

The sound of ritual mourning rolled down the steps as they paused in the shadows of the opposite building.

"How do we get in?" Marc asked, staring up at the bright entrance.

"The most obvious way," said Jame. "Put your hood over your head like a proper worshipper and try to wail a bit."

They went up the steps together and joined the celebrants within. All were gathered in the outer chamber, waiting for the evening ceremony to begin and working themselves into the approved tearful state. The high priest himself perched precariously on top of a pillar beside the door to the inner chamber with his long silver-gray robe flowing down to the floor on all sides of it. From below, one might have supposed him to be either a very tall man with a very small head or a street performer on stilts. The combination of his loud, simulated grief and the wild circling of his arms every few minutes to maintain balance added considerably to the liveliness of the assembly.

Jame began to edge her way through the crowd with Marc at her heels, trying to make his seven-foot frame as inconspicuous as possible. She had not been in Gorgo's temple since the experiment with the water ducts some time before, which, presumably, had triggered Loogan's vengeance on her now. She wondered why he had waited so long, and where he had found an agent so bold as to plunder the house of her own god, whose very existence he had often so vehemently denied. On the surface, it didn't make much sense, but when had she ever had dealings with any priest that did? Each had his own subtle, tortuous patterns of thought, worn as deep into his mind as riverbeds on the earth's face by the power that flowed through him. Even the clownish Loogan must have his share. As for Ishtier, there was a man so eroded by the force at his command that hardly any of his original nature must be left at all. Small wonder that his code of honor was not her own or that she had so little protection against the wiles that had now maneuvered her into this nest of enemies. Bodies brushed against her, voices pounded in her ears. Her uneasiness rose as she approached the inner door, remembering suddenly with what ease Loogan had spotted her the last time she had infringed on his hospitality.

The priest had stopped his wailing. Incautiously, Jame glanced up and met his eyes as he crouched on the pillar, staring uncertainly down at her. The little man straightened up with a yelp.

"The blasphemer, the defiler of our temple!" he howled, pointing down at the slender, hated figure. "Take her, take her! A sacrifice, a sacrifice for the great Gorgo!"

Scores of faces turned toward Jame, contorted in rage. Scores of hands reached out. The mass of humanity in the room seemed to rise about her like the crest of a tidal wave, poised to come crashing down.

"Sweet Trinity," she heard Marc mutter under his breath, and then his rathorn war cry boomed out almost in her ear.

The human wave froze. Up on his pedestal, Loogan did a

passable imitation of an unbalanced statue. The inner chamber door opened and the buck-toothed acolyte, startled by the sudden roar, peered out. Marc reached past Jame with a muttered "Excuse me," caught the boy by the front of his robe and threw him over his shoulder. Instantly, the room was bedlam. Loogan pitched head-first off the column with a squeal. Roaring, the crowd of worshippers rushed forward. The big Kendar grabbed his companion by the collar and threw her into the inner room. A stride carried him across the threshold after her. Turning, he pulled the door shut and dropped the bar into place across it.

"Well," said Jame, picking herself up off the floor, "here we are."

The inner sanctum of the temple was just as she remembered it—high, dark, and dank even in this time of drought because of the hand-filled reservoir on the roof. Benches, moss velveted walls, the giant image of Gorgo looking, if anything, more woebegone than usual, and, balanced on its hands over a bed of old ashes, a roll of parchment. Perfect, if one discounted a minor host of enraged celebrants hammering on the door . . . or was it? Something about the length of the scroll, the color of its paper . . .

"Marc, see if you can find another way out. I think something is very wrong here."

While the big guardsman began a slow circuit of the room, Jame took the scroll out of the stone hands and carefully unrolled it. "EYES THAT READ, BEWARE," she began out loud, struggling with runes' meaning. "BE STILL, TONGUE . . ."

She recoiled from it, teeth closing with a snap. The words of Forgetting swept through her mind, drowning thought and memory. When she looked at the scroll in her hands again, cautiously this time, not translating, the marks on it were mere lines, their deadly power locked in. She stood there biting her lip for a moment, then looked around for her companion. He was not in sight.

"Marc, where are you?"

There was a scraping sound and a muffled grunt from behind the statue.

"What are you doing?"

"There's a lever back here. Maybe it controls a secret exit. I think I can . . ."

There was a sharp crack, then a deep-noted gurgle. Jame sprang back as the glass eyes of the idol flew out of their sockets, closely followed by two thick jets of water.

Marc emerged from the shadows, looking sheepish. He held out a metal bar and said, apologetically, "It broke off."

"Never mind that. Look here." She held out the parchment. He stared at it, making an obvious effort to focus. Like most Kendars with their faith in memory, he had never learned how to read.

"Is that the Law Scroll?"

"Not unless they've started writing them in the Master Words of High Runic. No, this is something else, older than any temple copy and far more deadly. See how the figures start out crisp and clear, then here, halfway down, begin to falter? Despite himself, the scribe must have begun to see the words forming under his quill point, and the race began to the end of each line. More speed, less control, ink spattering, lines shaking . . . and here it simply ends, in midsentence, in midword. Well?"

She glared up at Marc, oblivious both to the water now swirling about their knees and to the irate pounding on the door which had settled down into the steady, bone-jarring blows of some makeshift ram.

"Tell me I've the imagination of a street balladeer. Tell me the annals of the Kencyrath are full of such stories. Tell me this thing isn't Anthrobar's scroll, the only copy, partial as it is, of the Book Bound in Pale Leather. Go on, tell me!"

Marc blinked owlishly at the roll of parchment. "How did it get here?"

"God knows!" She was beginning to lose patience with him. Here they were, faced with a genuine crisis, and this nodding giant with his bandage slipping down rakishly over one eye was only half-awake. "We may find out later if—*if,* I say—we ever get out of here, but don't you see what a dilemma we're in now? Short of the Book itself, can you think of any more dangerous document ever entrusted to the Three People? Creation, preservation, destruction—this thing is the key to every power planted in us for good or ill. How many times have our wisest scrollsmen and greatest lords, in the best of faith, nearly destroyed us all by using it? And who wants his talons in it now? Ishtier! Why, the man doesn't even use the power he has properly. Marc, I can't turn it over to him."

"It isn't the Law Scroll," said Marc, beginning to sway gently. "You don't have to."

"Idiot that I am, I swore to bring him the scroll—*any* scroll—in the arms of the idol. My word binds me."

Marc shook himself fiercely. "Aaaugh! But listen: when we thought it was the Law Scroll, freshly stolen, it was all right for you to recover it. Now—how long has this thing been missing? Over two thousand years?—even for something so valuable, the period of jeopardy must have run out centuries ago. Originally Kencyr property or not, under the laws of the city it now belongs to Loogan, and if you steal it, *my* word as a guard binds me to turn you over to the Five . . ."

". . . who will be delighted to dethrone Hangrell in my favor. If you're a thief, as they say, never get too attached to your own skin. Oh, what a trap that priest has sprung on me, and all without telling one direct lie. If I take him the scroll, think of the power he will gain; if I'm killed, he will at least have the satisfaction of my death; if I refuse, I'll be breaking my word to him and he will declare me a renegade, which may be what Bane hoped for when he consented to be Ishtier's messenger. Between them, those two have given me the choice of being dishonorable, irresponsible, or dead. Beautiful! The only consolation is that matters can't possibly get any worse."

At that moment, three things happened more or less simultaneously: the whole face of the image gave way, releasing a torrent of water into the already half-flooded room; the rings holding the bar across the door, jolted loose, fell away on one side; and Marc suddenly fell asleep, standing up.

Jame looked around the room with raised eyebrows, then back at the scroll in her hand. One complication would have been manageable; two, a calamity; three, ridiculous; but four? It would be an excellent time to burn the manuscript and drown herself, but then there was Marc, who didn't deserve to die alone, much less asleep on his feet. She reached out and rapped the swaying giant on his chest.

"You'd better see to the door," she said. "I think we're about to have company."

"Zaugh . . . oh!" said Marc, blinking at her. He turned and waded through the water, which now reached almost to his waist, over to the opposite wall. While Jame took refuge on the statue's right kneecap, the big Kendar raised the bar back into place and began to hammer the ring bolts in again with the head of his truncheon. Suddenly he froze, looking startled, then spun about and came splashing back across the room.

"Lass!" he bellowed over the roar of the water. "I've got it! You can't steal the scroll, but I can!"

Jame saw his hand sweeping up at her out of the corner of her eye. She had been deep in thought and had only half heard what her companion had said. Instinctively, she twisted away from what, from almost anyone but Marc, would have been a threatening gesture. The stone beneath her was slick with spray. Her sudden movement threw her sideways off her perch and down, scroll and all, into the surging water.

Marc fished her out and set her sputtering on her feet. She swept a streaming lock of hair out of her eyes, shook herself, then froze.

"*What* did you say?"

He shifted his weight uncomfortably, as if he would have liked to have shuffled his feet if only there hadn't been so much water on them. "I wouldn't be stealing from a Kencyr, you know," he said, half pleading. "I wouldn't be breaking the Law, just—uh—bending it a little. After all, if that wasn't honorable, you wouldn't have been doing it yourself all thse weeks."

Jame's stunned gaze dropped to the soggy piece of parchment in her hand. At the sight of it, she caught her breath, then threw back her head with a shout of laughter. Marc stared at her. She held the scroll out to him. Streaks of ink twisted down it into a muddy lower margin. Not a letter remained legible.

"By Trinity, m'lord Ishtier may be subtle, but he's not omniscient," she said. "This is one solution he could never have foreseen. Here, take the damn thing! Just this once, I'll let you steal for me. Now, in all the names of God, let's get out of here."

"Uh, lass . . . short of staging a massacre, how? I've no taste for these peoples' blood."

"It needn't come to that. Look here: where there's fire," she gestured to the wet ashes in the cupped hands, "there's usually smoke. Where there's smoke, there had better be some sort of ventilation." Her finger traced a line from the offering bowl to the ceiling far above. There among the shadows was a square of lesser darkness, through which the eyes of the Frog constellation sparkled fitfully.

Her hands had been busy as she spoke, pulling small pieces of metal out of her full sleeve and fitting them into the familiar form of a Cloudie's grapnel. To this she snapped the line that had been wound about her waist. On the third try, the hook shot straight through the hole and caught firmly on something outside on the roof.

Marc went up first, by some miracle not falling asleep halfway to the ceiling, although he had begun to nod again. Jame, following him, heard the door at last give way as the bar dropped off altogether. The shouts of the celebrants changed timbre as the wall of dammed up water came crashing down on them. It was fortunate, she thought, as she scrambled up onto the roof, that they had all come expecting to get wet anyway.

So much for Loogan. Now, to get Marc safely home, and then to settle with m'lord Ishtier.

"FOOL, DO YOU KNOW WHAT YOU'VE DONE?"

Jame had come prepared for the priest's anger, but the violence of it drove her back a step, flinching.

"The key to our future was in your hands, and you threw it away. How many ages have you added to our exile? How many eons until night falls at last?"

"Night? Exile?" She had expected his rage to fall on her for denying him (and, unfortunately, the Three People as well) the means for escaping Rathillien to the next threshold world if the barriers here against Perimal Darkling should fall. Why was he looking backward to lands already lost?

At the sound of her voice, the old man stiffened, as though suddenly aware that he had said too much. The shriveled lips moved again. This time not words but raw power whispered in from the outer corridors, ripping into her, blocking thought, freezing motion. She knew that he meant this to be her death.

"BE STILL, TONGUE THAT SPEAKS . . . TO THE CHOSEN LEAVE THE HIDDEN WAYS."

Afterwards, seated by a sleeping Marc in the loft, Jame touched her sore throat. Yes, she had said that, one hand thrown up to shield her face . . . or perhaps, futilely, to seal in the words. But whatever had possessed her to raise it higher, fingers curved, nails unsheathed, beckoning as did the image of Regonereth, That-Which-Destroys, towering over both her and the priest? Sheer defiance, probably. It was dangerous to mimic the god, but well worth it this once to see Ishtier blanch. He had not hindered her leave-taking.

Jorin was pacing from one end of the loft to the other. She needed no mental link to know his thoughts as he turned his blind, moon-opal eyes to her with each pass: *the hills? Now? Now?* Soon, kitten, soon. As she had told Cleppetty earlier, it was clear that he was rapidly outgrowing these cramped quarters and would soon have to be moved elsewhere.

The knapsack lay on her knees. All this time it had been there, and she had been trying to ignore it, as though hoping it would somehow vanish or she would think of an excuse to return it to its hiding place unopened. No such excuse had occurred to her. With a sigh, Jame threw back the flap and drew out the large, flat package.

She unwrapped it gingerly, folding back the cloth, layer by layer, to reveal at last what appeared to be simply an old book, remarkable only in the unexpected warmth of its soiled white binding. Fixing in her mind the patterns she hoped to find but not their meaning, Jame opened it. The first page was covered with hieroglyphs of a completely unknown nature. So were the second, third, and fourth, up to the twenty-fifth; and every one of them was written in a different, equally unfamiliar language. The damn thing was playing with her.

"Stop it!" said Jame sharply, rapping it with her knuckles.

The next page was composed of Kencyr Master Words. On it, she found the second set of runes that she had been looking for and, turning back, located the first where before there had only been an unreadable tangle of lines. When she closed the volume, its binding was no longer dingy leather but something finer grained and warmer, with little white hairs and faint blue lines running just under the surface.

So. Now she knew not only why she had been so sure the

scroll in Gorgo's temple was Anthrobar's and why its destruction—a potential catastrophe for her people—had not dismayed her, but also why she had been able to quote to Ishtier both a section she had just read and one she had not.

Because the original was in her possession.

Marc's voice sounded again in her mind against the memory of falling water. "How did it get here?" he was asking. "How?"

There was only one way. When the elder world fell, the renegade Master of Knorth had kept it with him in the deepening shadows, dedicating it as he did himself and his sister-consort Jamethiel to the service of Perimal Darkling; and there it had stayed for time out of mind, becoming no more than a legend to most of those Kencyrs who had fled. If the Book was in Jame's hands now, it could only mean that she herself had brought it out of darkness. Those lost years, so long a mystery to her, must have been spent in the Master's house, in Perimal Darkling.

"Well?" she said out loud. "Tell me where else they could have sent you from the middle of the Haunted Lands—south to Rathillien, or north, across the Barrier. Idiot, it's been staring you in the face all this time."

But she hadn't seen it, had not, perhaps, wanted to see it. There, presumably, they had taught her to dance, fight, read the runes, and Trinity knew what else; yet even now not a memory of it remained. Nor did she know how she had come into possession of the Book. Clearly she was familiar with its contents, had perhaps even used it to flee Perimal Darkling, but once here in Rathillien all recollection of that had faded too . . . until tonight. Now at last the Book Bound in Pale Leather was on its way back to the Kencyrath, in her charge, as the widow would say, for lack of anyone more sensible. Or perhaps not. Such objects of power were said to fulfill their own destinies. If this one had been using her, one might even ask if she had stolen it from the Master's house or it had stolen her. One thing at least was certain: Gerridon of Knorth could not have been pleased to find it missing.

Might he, in fact, have been displeased enough to have come after it?

. . . dead, all dead under the twilight sky, within the broken walls: Anar, her father . . . Marc's demon warriors riding down from the north on East Kenshold, blood already on their armor as though fresh from battle, looking for something—or someone . . .

"Jame!"

She started violently. Ghillie's head had popped into sight around the spiral stair's newel.

"What's the matter with you? Don't you hear them? Aunt Cleppetty says come down quick before they start breaking things, or by all the gods, she'll break *you!*"

She jumped up as the boy disappeared, hearing clearly for the first time the steady, rhythmic pounding below, not hooves on the iron hills but tankards on tabletops, beating an impatient tattoo. A year ago, yet just that evening, she had made a promise; now they were here to see that it was kept. Let the dead wait, she thought, hurriedly returning the Book to its hiding place and stripping off her street clothes. The living would not.

At the stroke of midnight, as Marc lay on his pallet snoring happily and far away the temples of Tai-tastigon heralded the new day with bells, chants, and laughter, the B'tyrr walked down the stairway to be greeted by the waiting crowd with a roar of welcome.

Tubain, who had been considering a hasty retreat down to the wine cellar, beamed at her across the room. Trust a Kencyr always to honor her word.

CHAPTER 10

The Feast of Dead Gods

THE RABBIT'S HEAD jerked up, green shoots dangling from its lips. Jame froze. A stealthy movement seen past the quarry's alert ears helped her to spot Jorin, crouching behind a clump of late daisies. It had taken them over an hour of patient stalking to reach their respective positions, all for one stupid rabbit, which, it seemed, was not even going to let them get within striking range. Would it bolt? Yes, dammit, it was—away from them both.

Jame sprang up. The rabbit had broken to the left, but her wild dash set it jinking back toward the daisies. Jorin erupted from the heart of the clump, narrowly missing a perfect pounce. The rabbit was doubling back now toward Jame's original position. She pivoted. Sprinting to turn it, her foot hit something in the grass, and she fell, fingertips almost grazing the white tail as it flashed past.

She was lying flat on the ground with most of the breath knocked out of her when Jorin gave the top of her left ear a tentative lick. "Has it ever occurred to you," she said in exasperation, rolling over to look up into his face, "that you might just once go on without me?"

Apparently, it never had.

The ounce gave a conciliatory little chirp and flopped down beside her. Relenting, Jame ran her hand down the length of his back, feeling muscles flex under the richness of his late summer coat, now tinged with gold where that odious brown dye had worn off. Jorin stretched, purring, and rolled over on his back in a most Boo-like fashion to have his stomach rubbed. Jame sat up with a laugh and obliged. Then she groped back through the grass for the thing that had tripped her.

It was a helmet, rust-pitted, ancient. They had been stumbling over similar armorial remains all afternoon, and once over the top half of a skull in which a family of grass snakes had made their nest. Despite the depredations of scavengers, such things were fairly common here on the Plain of Bones, where the last and most vicious battle of the Skyrr-Metalondrian war had been fought. Jame felt fortunate not to have landed on someone's sword or spiked mace, quietly rusting in the grass. In her opinion, she had tried her luck quite enough for one day. She and the ounce both rose and set off westward into the shadow of the mountains.

It was late afternoon on the last day of summer.

Three nights had passed since they had come up into the hills, escaping the city's heat and bustle. No rain had fallen there all summer to lay the dust or ease the citizens' minds. Here too the land was parched, the leaves brittle on the bough; but a fitful wind off the Ebonbane rustled through the grass, and the evenings were cool. They had set up camp in a shallow cave on the banks of the Tynnet. Despite increasing skill, however, their hunting luck in the foothills had been uniformly bad. So, in the little time left, Jame had decided to see if the game to the east was any better. It wasn't. Now she must take the ounce back to their camp and return to the city, leaving him in the wilds.

This had not been an easy decision to make. She had watched his restless pacing in the loft too long, however, not to realize that he must have more freedom. She would visit him, bringing food, as often as possible, but how much better it would be if he could learn to fend for himself. One kill, just one, might be enough to start him out.

"Well, we'll make do, whatever happens, won't we, kitten?" she said, looking down at the young ounce.

His ears pricked sharply, but not to the sound of her voice. She stopped, surprised, then also listened, wishing for the vanished mind link to let her hear what he heard. Crickets sang in the long grass, a solitary thrush whistled once, and then, from far away to the southeast, came the sound of horns blowing for a hunt gone astray.

The stag seemed to explode over the crest of the next hill, all foam-lathered muzzle and wild eyes. It was in the hollow before it saw them. Jame saw it leap sideways, then stagger as Jorin's weight struck its hindquarters. The needle-pointed tines, the sharp hooves—if the ounce lost his hold . . .

She plunged down the slope after him. Her hands closed on the antlers, and all three—girl, ounce, and deer—fell. God, if she should land on the points . . . twisting in midair, Jame saw earth, then sky between the branching horns. For the second time in an hour, the ground slammed into her.

Something cracked loudly.

For a long moment she lay there, afraid to move, and then realized that the stag was also motionless. The angle of its head told the tale.

Jame eased herself out from under the dead beast. By morning, there should be some spectacular bruises from the feel of things, but nothing seemed to be broken. Jorin was crouching over the stag's haunches, looking vaguely amazed at himself and uncertain of what to do next. Then, abruptly, he tensed and began to growl. Jame got quickly to her feet. A moment later the grass on the crest of the opposite hill parted as two hunting leopards slipped through it in quest of their prey. They were magnificent beasts, with sleekly groomed coats and collars that glowed with gold. It did not please them to find others already on the kill.

The horns sounded again, nearer this time.

Jame slipped her knife out of its boot sheath, wondering how much good it would do.

Someone was clambering up the far side of the hill, whistling and calling hoarsely. Then he was on the crest, a thin, harassed-looking man carrying two leashes coiled in one hand and a short whip in the other.

"Away from that stag, you!" he shouted, wrathfully down at Jame. "This is my lord's land and his kill."

All four below snarled at him.

A man on a tall gray mare pulled up beside the cathandler. "What's this?" he demanded, regarding the scene below. The answer was long, impassioned, and apparently reached back to the beginning of the chase hours ago. Meanwhile, another rider appeared on the rise, and another and another until the hollow was ringed with them. Jame, still watching the leopards warily as they circled her, began to feel very conspicuous.

"All right, all right," said the first horseman suddenly, cutting short the other's tirade. "I'll grant it wasn't your fault . . . this time. You down there, the hunt is yours. Will you be so good as to grant my cats a cup of blood? They'll never settle down without it."

"My lord," said Jame, thinking quickly, "let me present you with the whole deer. I didn't know we were trespassing."

"Well! That's most kind of you," said the other. From his tone, which was light and waspish, she couldn't tell if he was being sarcastic or not. "Such generosity should be rewarded. Come back to my camp and share a cup of wine with me." Without waiting for an answer, he turned and rode away.

Jame saw that his followers had no intention of letting her decline this invitation. She retrieved her cap, dislodged by her fall, then stripped off her gloves and gathered as much stag's blood as her cupped hands would hold. Jorin lapped it up, rough tongue rasping her fingers clean, while the cathandler sullenly rewarded his own charges nearby. Then one of the riders impatiently gave her a hand up, and they all galloped off after the man on the gray mare.

The camp was small but heavily guarded, blood-feud and kin-strife being the major social conventions in Skyrr. Recent years had seen some lulls in the violence, mostly due to the new Archiem, Arribek sen Tenzi, but things never stayed quiet in the hill cantons for long.

Seated on a low stool in her host's tent, Jame watched the man as he moved restlessly about the room, discoursing on various hunting trophies in it. She wondered who he was. From his clothes, which were of good quality but much patched, she decided that he must be the impoverished head of the local ruling family. His sharp, covert glances were beginning to make her fidget. Obviously she had not been invited—no, ordered—here simply to listen to a monologue on local hunting conditions. The guards had taken her knife at the door. She dropped her hand onto Jorin's head as he leaned against her knee, drawing confidence from his presence.

The man abruptly pivoted to face her. "Enough of this," he snapped. "Confess! It's the link, isn't it?"

Jame stared at him.

"No matter where I go or what I point at, if your eyes follow me, so do your cat's, and any fool can see that he's blind as a brick."

"Well, I'll be damned," said Jame, looking down at the ounce in amazement. "Do you mean to tell me, you young imp, that all this time. . . . No wonder our hunts have always ended when I've fallen behind! You can't chase what I can't see."

"One way only, is it?" the man said, at last perching on the stool opposite her. "That may change. I've heard that these links can take years to form properly, or sometimes only seconds. I envy you the experience. But one thing still puzzles me. Why would anyone stain a Royal Gold that ugly stain of brown? One might almost suppose," his voice went on, almost purring now, "that you didn't come by this valuable beast legally."

Jame swallowed, remembering her promise to the man at the cattery. "I'm afraid I can't explain, but I didn't steal this cub," she said carefully. "I give you my word on that."

"And if I won't accept it?"

"Then I must defend my honor with my life . . . although I'd just as soon you didn't make it necessary."

"Indeed," he said drily. "The race best known in Rathillien for a certain—ah—inflexibility in matters concerning honor is also the only one that can form mind-links. Check and double-check. Therefore, having established your veracity, tell me how things go in Tai-tastigon, Kencyr."

This was a formidable request, but Jame did her best, thinking that news must be at a premium here in the hills. In time, her summary came to the doings of the Five. Here as elsewhere, he plied her with shrewd questions, mostly about his countryman, Harr, Thane sen Tenko.

"Would you say," he asked suddenly, "that the man is honest?"

Jame hesitated. For all she knew, her host might be related both to Harr and Marplet sen Tenko. "Well, there are rumors," she said cautiously, "I don't know if anything could be proved, though, even in the Skyrrman-Res aB'tyrr clash."

"Ah, I've heard of that affair," the lord said, adding pettishly, "you needn't look so surprised: *some* news filters into this back country, especially when it has to do with our own people. It's an undeclared trade war, from the sound of it. A boy has been beaten and a servant blinded, I understand; also some of the Skyrrman's property has been destroyed—some puncheons of wine contaminated with salt, a pile of bricks smashed, and so forth."

"Bricks?"

Oh, that must have been when Niggen dropped the beam. Jame described the incident to him, likewise the events that had led up to Niggen's thrashing and the mutilation of Bortis. There was no explanation she could offer, however, for the spoiled wine, which had come to light recently in a rash of petty vandalisms at the rival inn. In connection with these, she could only protest the Res aBy'tyrr's innocence.

"And Harr sen Tenko—according to rumor—has let all this happen? Why?"

"You didn't know, my lord? His brother-in-law is proprietor of the Skyrrman."

"Ah!," said the other, and promptly changed the topic.

Soon after that, the interview ended. Jame accepted some cuts of venison and set out with Jorin for their own camp to the west. It was early evening when they arrived. She put most of the meat in the cave and slipped away, leaving Jorin to his feast. She tried not to think how he would react when he discovered she was gone.

Tai-tastigon was in a state of subdued bustle. Last minute shopping was being done, children called in from the streets and pets secured within doors. Many houses already presented sealed faces to late passers-by, betraying no glimmer of light in the growing dusk. Silence gathered, flowing down the narrow lanes into the thoroughfares. Summer had ended. Autumn's Eve, that benign and neglected festival, sank under the shadow of the year's darkest night. Soon, soon the Feast of Dead Gods would begin.

Jame found Canden and Dally waiting for her at the inn. While the inn staff scurried around them, preparing for the host of old customers who traditionally spent this night at the Res aB'tyrr, she described her experiences in the hills.

"M'lord Harr seems much in the light these days," said Dally when she had finished. "I wonder why your ragged noble was so interested in him."

"Politics," said Kithra, sweeping down on them armed with a damp sponge just in time to hear this last remark. "Up glasses, all. Everyone in the high country knows that if that miserable Harr can buy enough support, he may well become a serious threat to the Archiem. Yes, madam . . . coming!"

"So it's money he'll be after now," said Dally thoughtfully as the servant girl darted away. "At the moment, he has access to the city treasury, but that will end when his appointment does."

"Mightn't he dip out enough before he leaves to do the job?" Jame asked.

"I expect he'll take all he can without getting caught, but a backer or two later wouldn't hurt him either. Yet, it looks as if he's doing the backing now, while he can," Dally went on. "Or at least everyone will think so after the way he embarrassed Theocandi by trying to get Mistress Silver's son executed. I don't think anyone knows how she's going to vote now that the Sirdan has only managed to get the boy exiled, not acquitted."

"And when Men-dalis is elected and pays Harr back from the Guild treasury seven-fold," said Canden suddenly, with unusual violence, "what will happen to Grandfather?"

Jame and Dally looked at each other, startled. They had been playing a political guessing game not unlike a hundred others in the past and had actually forgotten for a moment how personal their own involvement was.

"Why, then he'll be able to retire and live out the rest of his life in peace," said Dally kindly. "After all, he's an old man. The Sirdanate must be a terrible strain on him, however much he clings to it."

"And do you really think he will—live, I mean? They say it isn't like it used to be in the Guild—all the violence, the assassinations, the intrigues—we're more civilized now. But neither you nor your brother were here at the last election. Ask Master Tane's family—what's left of it—about that."

"My dear Can!" Dally protested. "Beg pardon, but even if that shadow-thief rot is true, that was when your grandfather won. Things will be very different when it's Mendalis's turn." Something in Canden's face made him stop, badly flustered. His idealism had never had to cope with the things that this boy had seen, growing up in the Palace of Thieves' Guild itself. "At any rate," he said rather desperately, trying to evoke a lighter mood, "whatever happens, I'll see that you don't end up bobbing in the Tone—not, at least, without a few more swimming lessons."

"You might be able to do that," said Canden miserably. "But if your brother doesn't win, I won't be able to return the favor. I've no influence in the Palace or the Guild to help friends, family or myself. There'll be nothing I can do . . . nothing."

"Well, I'm sure it won't come to that," said Dally awkwardly, embarrassed by the other's distress. "Mendy will carry the election, Silver's vote or no, and then everything will be all right. You'll see. In the meantime, it's getting late. C'mon Can; I'll walk you back to the Palace."

"No . . . go on, Dally, please. I'd like to talk to Jame for a minute."

"Oh. Well then, good night, all—Dalis-sar's blessings on you." And he was gone.

"Would you mind talking on the move?" Jame asked Canden. "I have an errand across town."

"Tonight? Is that wise?"

"No, but when has wisdom ever stopped me?"

He laughed, and they went out into the night together.

The two walked in silence almost as far as the Tone, their footsteps ringing hollowly in the deserted streets. Though the Feast proper would not begin for another two hours, few residents were taking any chances of being caught out in it. It must have been about this time a year ago when Jame had first stumbled into the city.

Canden cleared his throat, startling her. "The expedition for Tai-Than leaves in two weeks," he said. "Master Quipun has asked me to go with him."

"Splendid! Have you told your grandfather yet?"

"I tried to. He wouldn't listen. Jame . . . I-I think I may go anyway."

For a moment, her step faltered, then she went on without speaking. He was not a Kencyr. He had not been taught how unforgivable it was to desert one's lord in time of peril. On the other hand, supposing Canden stayed and the worst came to pass, what could he do about it? As he himself said, nothing. She had heard stories about the violence, supernatural and otherwise, that followed most Guild Councils, when the loser was no longer protected by Guild law. For the first time, she faced the possibility that if they both stayed in Tai-tastigon through the election, at least one of her friends might very well die.

They neared the Tone. Canden was darting anxious, sidelong looks at her, and Jame suddenly realized, with alarm, that whatever she said next would probably decide the whole matter for him.

How in all the names of God was she, a Kencyr, supposed to solve such a dilemma? Among her own people, the question itself would never have arisen. All such flexibility had very nearly gone out of Kencyrath with the withdrawal of the Arrin-ken, whose function it had been to unravel such moral conundrums. Yes, and think of the havoc *that* had wrought over the last two millennia in the lives of those, like Bane, who lacked her own dubious talent for finding chinks in the Law. And what was this boy asking for now but a way to adapt his own code of honor to survival, as she had tried to do with hers? It was not simply an escape from death that either of them wanted, but life: she, somehow, among her own people, and he in his chosen work. How her own quest would end, she had no idea, but as for his . . .

Canden started as she suddenly turned on him and said, with a vehemence that surprised even her, "Go! Don't think of your grandfather or the Guild or Tai-tastigon again. I take responsibility for the consequences, if there are any. Just get out while you can—and be happy."

A few minutes later, Jame watched the boy walk briskly away, homeward bound, and wondered what had possessed her to speak as she had. To make oneself accountable for something before the fact was about as intelligent as agreeing to carry an unknown soul, and yet she felt she had done the right thing. He would do well, that boy, if the past would leave him alone. She envied him his future and wondered if she would ever learn what he had done with it.

Meanwhile, it was getting late. She looked once more after Canden's retreating back, noting with satisfaction a lightness in his stide that had not been there before, and then turned and crossed the Tone in pursuit of her own fate, which waited for her in the Temple District.

SOON AFTER THEIR SOMEWHAT HECTIC EVENING in the house of the lugubrious god, Jame had thought it only fair to tell Marc why Gorgo's high priest had been so eager to see them both dead. It was the first time she had spoken to the big Kendar about either her experiments or her doubts, and it irked her that he listened to the account of both so calmly.

"Don't you see," she had finally said in exasperation, "if I'm right about faith creating reality in this city, what is the truth about our own god? Do we believe in him because he's real, or is he real because we believe in him; and what about all the other deities? If even one of them is genuine, then our own holy terror is a fraud, and we as Kencyrs can't honor a lie. How can you be so calm when the foundation of our whole culture may crumble out from under us at any minute? Living here all these months hasn't your faith been shaken even once?"

Marc had considered this for a minute, then said slowly, "No, I can't say that it has. I never thought we Kencyrs had much choice in the matter, not, at least, since old Three-Face got us by the short hairs. An acolyte did tell me once, though, that some people can decide whether to believe or not. Free will, he called it, and said that faith could be even stronger with it than without, not that I quite see how. You're clever, though; perhaps you understand."

"Clever!"

Moving through the silent streets, Jame remembered her bark of laughter and winced. That afternoon, she had been to the Lower Town to see Taniscent, and the former dancer had hidden from her under the covers, sobbing wildly.

"If I were even halfway intelligent, would I act the way I do? Is there one thing I've done since coming here that hasn't had disastrous consequences? Marc, despite all the time we've spent together, you don't know me. You don't even know my name."

He had looked at her, perplexed. "Why, Jame, short for Jameth."

"No. For Jamethiel."

"Oh." For a moment, it was as if he had just eaten something of a suspicious nature and was not sure how it would agree with him. "Oh!" he said again, stiffening. "What could your sponsors have been thinking of? Better to curse a child outright at birth than to give it such a name!"

"They may have done that too, for all I know," Jame had said wryly, beginning to be ashamed of herself for snapping at him. "Still, there's some distinction of being probably the first to bear that name since Jamethiel of Knorth turned renegade to follow the Master nearly three thousand years ago."

"Snare-of-Souls, Dream-Weaver, Storm's Eye . . ." he had run through the epithets thoughtfully, checking them off on his fingers. "Priest's-Bane. The name is an omen in itself. Servants of God, any god, will be bad luck to you, and you to them. I should have as little to do with them as possible, if I were you, especially with such a one as Loogan. He's too vulnerable."

And she had promised to try.

THAT HAD BEEN WEEKS AGO. Now here she was in the Temple District again, preparing for another raid on Gorgo's house. Somewhat reassured by Marc's refusal to be alarmed, she had given up testing Loogan; but the matter of Anthrobar's Scroll still haunted her. It was perhaps legitimate to say that the copy as well as the original of the Book had, for some obscure reason, been destined for her hands, but that didn't explain the mechanics of the thing. How in all the worlds had that long-lost manuscript come to be in Gorgo's temple? That was the question that drew her back now, on the one night of the year when she thought she could count on a minimum of interference from both god and priest.

However, the District was not as quiet as she had expected it to be. A murmur filled the air, seeming to rise from all directions and none; low, wordless, urgent. Rapid footsteps coming up from behind made her start. A man slipped hurriedly past and in at the door of a humble temple just ahead, letting the sound roll out around him for a second before the portal closed. The faithful held their vigils, praying for the safety of man and god alike, while the dead prowled outside the gate.

Jame had expected none of this. A year ago, she had entered the District later at night and had supposed, incorrectly, that it was deserted. This time she was spared the feverish power that would soon throb through these streets, but could her errand succeed in the face of so much hidden activity?

At any rate, here was Gorgo's temple. She tried the door and found it unlocked. The hinges protested piercingly. She froze, listening. Cool air slid past her face from the dim interior, bearing no sound. Had no one come to keep watch here through the long night? The outer chamber was empty. She crossed it and listened at the inner door. Nothing. Pushing it open a crack, she slipped through into the sanctuary.

It was cool and dark inside, as she remembered it, but no longer with the feeling of a woodland cave. The moss was brittle on the stones and the walls were dry. A fine patina of dust lay on the ranked benches. It had not occurred to her before what a difference the draining of the temple's reservoir would make.

The image of Gorgo loomed at the far end of the chamber, its shoulders hunched against the upper darkness. Some loving but clumsy hand had mortared together the ruined face. One had the impression that if there had been any water, the lopsided mouth would have drooled. Jame approached it, drawn by the sight of something in the idol's hands. It was another scroll. Wondering what on earth she had stumbled on this time, she carefully lifted it out and unrolled it. The writing was Kessic, the substance, a single column of unrelated objects. It appeared to be someone's shopping list.

She was still staring at it when the sanctuary door opened. Loogan stood on the threshold.

THE HIGH PRIEST had been in his quarters above the outer chamber, darning his best under-tunic. His acolyte should have tended to it that afternoon but had clearly been too unnerved by the approaching Feast to wield a needle, so Loogan had sent him home. It wasn't likely that there would be work enough to justify keeping him around tonight anyway. There hadn't been, to tell the truth, for several weeks. Soon the boy's father would probably be after him to terminate his son's contract. Well, let him go, let them all go . . . no, no, he didn't mean that. What was a priest without his people—and who would follow him now, with his personal demon, that willow of a girl (or was it a boy?) popping up every few days to sow chaos? Dear Lord of Tears, what had he done to deserve such a fate? It was just as the Reader of Bones had prophesied the very day that gray-eyed imp had first come into his life; but even the Reader had not been able to foresee the end of the matter. Would some of the faithful come tonight? They *must*. He wasn't sure that his god could survive the Feast without them.

What was that? The hinges of the front door. Someone had come after all.

Hastily, Loogan snapped short the thread and donned the tunic, then a neck cloth, the alb with its embroidered cuffs (merciful god, would he ever get the thing right-side-out on the first try?), the stole, the wool chasuble with its elevated shoulders and contingent of moths like a fitful nimbus, and finally the whole collection of rings, chains, and clinking amulets to which every one of his hieratic ancestors had made a contribution. Quick now, anything else? Ah yes, the diadem. He snatched it up and hurried down the stairs, threw open the inner chamber door—and found his nemesis standing by the altar.

For a moment, astonishment fixed Loogan to the spot, then rising anger broke the trance. He snatched up the tall candlestand near the door, ignoring the clatter as half the candles fell on the floor, and said, "Now I've got you, you thieving blasphemer."

"Why do you always call me that?"

The voice was quiet, even polite. Loogan stopped, blinking. It was his special curse that he could never ignore a question.

"Because you and all your kind profess the Anti-God Heresy."

"What is that?"

"'The belief that all the beings we know to be divine are in fact but the shadows of some greater power that regards them not,' " he heard himself say, automatically quoting the New Pantheon catechism.

"How do you know that this belief is false?"

"Because the gods *do* exist."

"Prove it."

The priest stared at her. Then, with an almost convulsive gesture, he threw aside the candelabrum and said shrilly, "All right, I will!"

Few preparations were needed, and Loogan went about them hurriedly, trying not to think what a rare and dangerous thing it was that he meant to attempt. So the congregation would stay away tonight of all nights, would it, and this artful tempter come in its place? Well, he would show them, he would show them all . . . but merciful god, how long was it since this ritual had last been performed? Not since Hierarach Bilgore's day at least. He lugged the benches aside, too distracted to notice that another pair of hands helped him. The space before the idol was now clear, and the two basins of water set on their tripods on either side. Loogan gave the small area one last, despairing look, then sank to his knees, took a deep breath, and began to chant.

At first, nothing happened. The singsong voice rushed on, gaining speed as it went like that of a reciting child who hurries lest he forget the words. Then bit by bit the air above the right basin and then the left seemed to thicken as a haze formed. Wisps of mist were reaching down from both sides toward each other. They met before the idol, merging into a slow, vaporish swirl. A form was taking shape. It seemed to move fitfully, and more mist wrapped itself around the half-gesture. Loogan chanted on, eyes closed, the sweat running down his plump face. Once he faltered, and the ghostlike thing before him appeared to flinch. Then he was done, suddenly, on a rising note as if he had not realized until the last second that the end was so near. Cautiously, the priest opened his eyes.

The figure that cowered before him at the feet of the great idol was about his own size and just as pale. Elaborate vestments and length after length of neck chain bowed it halfway to the ground. Webbed fingers, their upper joints encrusted with rings, fumbled helplessly at the enormous diadem that had slipped down over one bulging eye and apparently stuck there. Its wide mouth, drooling a bit, opened . . .

"No!" Loogan heard himself shriek. "No, no, no!"

Gorgo, with a stricken look at his priest, gave a thin, piping wail, sank to the floor, and dissolved.

Loogan was not aware that he had fainted until water from one of the basins hit him in the face. He lashed out wildly at the hand that had thrown it, at the face beyond, drawing blood with one of his heavy rings. Then his wrists were caught and, with difficulty, pinned to the floor. His rage died as suddenly as it had been born.

"I killed him," he said in bewilderment, looking up into those odd, silver-gray eyes. "I killed my god."

"No . . . we did. But don't think about that now. You need a drink, and I'm going to find you one. C'mon."

Near the Temple District was an inn which, like the Res aB'tyrr, stayed open at least until midnight on Autumn's Eve. Within minutes Jame had secured her charge in a private room with two glasses of neat wine already in him and a third waiting at his elbow.

As the little priest emerged from his daze, he began to talk—rapidly, without a pause, as though afraid of silence. Jame quickly learned that he was not the imbecile she had always taken him for. In fact, there was an excellent brain in that round, balding head; but years of bondage to the often ludicrous rituals of his god had taught him that his only possible dignity lay in unthinking obedience. Now all that effort and self-denial seemed to have been wasted.

"I've let them all down, my god, my ancestors, myself," he said, and then startled Jame by suddenly shouting, "Let them go, let them all go!"

"Quiet!" hissed the innkeeper, sticking his head through the curtains. "D'you want to bring every dead god in town down on us?"

"No, just one of them," said the priest.

Noting that the hour candle on the table had almost burned down to the twelfth ring, Jame hastily paid the reckoning. Loogan tried to break away from her at the door. He wanted to search the streets for Gorgo. She finally managed to get the priest back to his temple and forcibly put him to bed. He was snoring almost before she turned her back.

The front door snicked shut behind her, locking, and she stood at the head of the stairs, shivering slightly, staring at nothing. Somewhere up in the night above the District's architectural tangle, a bell struck, its single, deep note echoing down the corridors of the sky. Another, farther away, joined it, then another and another until all were in full voice. The boom of their combined tolling made the stones beneath shake. Then the lead bell subsided, its course rung through at last, the others following it as their turn came. At last only a treble was left, its silvery note shivering against the dark, faltering, dying away.

The Feast of Dead Gods had begun.

Jame left the District and took to the rooftops. Dry thunder grumbled in the mountain passes to the west, lightning edged the ragged clouds with tarnished silver as they came scudding over the peaks. The wind hunted where it pleased. Below, indistinct forms were wandering through the streets, sometimes pausing to scratch softly on this door or that, sometimes fumbling at a key hole, whispering in the dry, worm-gnawed voices of the dead. Corpse lights flickered in ghostly procession through the crossroads, over the roofbeams. Wisps of song and lament rose to mingle with the wind's rushing.

Jame went on. Cloudies in hiding who saw her pass thought she must be mad to walk so slowly on such a night. She didn't even bother to take the shortest route home. Once a water pipe down-roof gave way with a screech, as though something too heavy had tried to climb it. Once a great, misshapen shadow swept over the gables after her, barely missing, and a nightbird, caught under it, tumbled down dead at her heels. She paid no attention. It was long past midnight, nearer to dawn, when she at last came to the back roof of the Res aB'tyrr.

As Jame swung a leg over the loft's sill, she happened to look back and saw a muffled figure standing on the roof below her, looking up. Thinking it was some old woman of the Cloud Kingdom who had been caught away from home by nightfall, Jame signaled her to climb up to the dubious safety of the open loft. Then she crossed to her own pallet, sat down, and was quickly lost again in her own dark thoughts.

Sometime later she looked up. The shrouded figure was sitting opposite her. This surprised Jame because she had not heard the other's ascent. Regarding the stranger more closely, she realized with a sudden tightening of stomach muscles that she was not so much looking at her guest as through her. It was the night of dead gods, and death, at her invitation, had just entered the loft.

Seconds passed, then a full minute. The other still had not moved. The face, tilted downward, was hidden in the shadow of the cowl. The shoulders slumped. Even in this short time, the gnarled hands, hanging limply over the peak of shrouded knees, had become thinner and more transparent. Mortar began to rattle down behind the motionless figure. The poor creature was dying even out of death, and she was taking part of the inn with her.

How far would this go? Jame saw faint lines of erosion begin to furrow the opposite wall. She sensed that the stranger hadn't the strength to leave unassisted and knew that she dared not touch her. For a long moment Jame sat there, watching and thoughtfully gnawing her lower lip. Then she rose slowly and edged past her peculiar guest to the head of the spiral stairs.

The guest rooms on the third floor were empty, their lodgers undoubtedly below in the hall with the rest of the company. Jame descended to the second floor and slipped out onto the gallery. From there, she went down by the far stair to the court and crossed it stealthily to the kitchen door. When Cleppetty left the room for a minute, she quickly entered and took what she required. Actually, the widow would have begrudged her none of it, but it seemed best not to let anyone know who was in the loft or what, with luck, was about to be done about it. Clutching the ends of the large napkin in which her booty was wrapped, Jame retreated to the upper regions.

The drooping figure had not moved. The stones behind it were more visible than before, and more decayed. Dry rot was well advanced in the floor boards, with tendrils of it reaching out into the room.

There was no proper fireplace in the loft, so Marc had built a small one out of bricks against the north wall to be used for warmth. Jame soon had a blaze going in it. Then she unwrapped the napkin and began to separate its contents. By the time she was done, lined up in front of her were morsels of raw venison, beef, and pork, brie tart, two oysters, fried artichokes, a pear coffin filled with cooked lentils, spiced capon, marzipan toads, and finally the soggy piece of trencher bread (colored green with parsley) on which the whole mess had rested. The trick, of course, was to find out if any of these assorted fragments would make an acceptable sacrifice. Jame took the nearest at hand—a ragged chunk of pork—and put it on the grate. Then she withdrew to watch.

The meat began to sizzle over the leaping flames, the odor or its cooking reminding Jame forcefully that she had had nothing but a cup of wine in the hill lord's tent since early that morning. Then it began to burn. The hands of the spectre twitched once, but it made no further move. Several stones fell out of the wall and through the rotting floor. Eventually the bit of pork, reduced to a cinder, fell through the grate and was gone. Jame put the venison in its place.

This process seemed to go on for hours. It must be almost dawn, Jame thought, but she doubted if either the loft or her guest would last that long. The roof groaned and began to sag over the silent, nearly invisible figure. Dust drifted down. The beams overhead had started to disintegrate. Fighting an impulse to bolt below to safety, Jame tried to figure out what she was doing wrong.

"Of course!" she said suddenly. "You idiot, you've got the whole thing backward."

True, most of the dead gods craved sacrifices, but it was lack of faith, not food, that had killed them in the first place. Poor Gorgo's sudden demise proved that. Therefore, offerings were valuable to such beings only for the sake of the devotion that prompted them. That was why it did those out prowling the streets tonight so little good to devour whatever they could find or catch, and why her guest did not prosper now.

This presented a new difficulty.

"Goddess," said Jame to the figure, after a moment's hard thought. "I think I know now what you need, but not if I can provide it. I'm a Kencyr, a monotheist, it seems, whether I want to be one or not. If that wasn't true, I would have been able to accept this city on its own terms long ago. As it is, your kind, living and dead, have been a nightmare to me. I still think that in the end I'll find a way to explain you all away, but not entirely. In some quite alien way, you *do* exist.

I believe that now. So, to a certain extent, I suppose I believe in you too, goddess. That's the best I can do. I hope it's good enough."

And with this, she broke the last of her provisions, the soggy piece of trencher bread, over the fire.

It blazed up in her face. Half-blinded, choking, she threw herself back from it. The loft stank of burned hair. Through the after-image of flames, she saw the shrouded figure bending over the fire. It opened its hood and the smoke billowed up into it. The hands stopped trembling as the veins sank on them and the flesh returned. The outline of the stones beyond showed only faintly through the figure when it at last turned toward Jame. She shrank from it, wondering belatedly if she had outsmarted herself again. But no. It merely sketched what might have been an obeisance and drifted past her. Somewhere beyond the Old Wall, a cock shut within doors began to crow and was stifled in mid-note. Facing the sun that still swam in seas of mist below the horizon, the goddess raised her hands in welcome to the gray light of dawn and vanished.

Jame sat very still for a long moment, then sprang to her feet and practically threw herself over the north parapet. She could never remember afterward if she had used the b'tyrr in her descent at all. It was the beginning of a cross-town rooftop sprint that was spoken of with awe for years to come by the few early rising Cloudies who witnessed it. Jame only remembered its start and finish when she fetched up gasping in front of Gorgo's temple, suddenly jarred out of her haze of plans by the solid reality of a locked door.

Fifteen seconds later the lock was picked and she was tearing up the stairs to Loogan's quarters. Here she pounced on the unfortunate priest and began to shake him vigorously.

Loogan woke suddenly with all that had happened the night before clear in his mind, a roaring headache, and someone shouting in his ear "Get up, you lie-a-bed. We've work to do!"

"Please stop that," he said plaintively. "My head is about to fall off . . . what work?"

"Break out the jubilee wine, old man," cried Jame, doing a double backward somersault that made him wonder if he was still dreaming. "We're going to resurrect your god!"

CHAPTER 11

The Storm Breaks

"WOULD YOU PLEASE," said Loogan, "go over that again?"

Jame did. It was midmorning by now on the day after the Feast. She was explaining, for the third time, the series of experiments that had led to Gorgo's sudden demise and the theories that had prompted them. Then she told him about her adventures in the loft.

"As soon as I realized that the dead gods weren't beyond help," she concluded, "it occurred to me that something similar but more extensive might be done for Gorgo. I think your god can be resurrected if only we can restore his peoples' faith in him."

"That's all very well," said Loogan, "but how do we accomplish that when I wasn't even able to make them keep what little they had left?"

"That *is* a problem," Jame admitted, "but I can't help feeling that there's a way. After all, Gorgo must have been a fairly important deity once to have rated even a small temple in the District. Perhaps our answer lies in the past. What was he like in the beginning?"

"Foolish as it sounds, I don't know. Back during the

Skyrr-Metalondrian War, Great-great-great-great-great-grandfather Bilgore, who was high priest then, seems to have made some fairly extensive doctrinal changes. Then, to make sure there would be no turning back, he destroyed the early records and forbade the acolytes and celebrants ever to pass on the old ways again."

"*All* the old documents were destroyed? What about those two I found in the idol's hands?"

"Oh, those," he said. "They have nothing to do with Gorgo directly. You've been interested in them from the start, haven't you, or at least since the night the reservoir was drained. They're part of a secret that only the high priest of the order is supposed to know, but it doesn't matter any more, does it? No secrets, no priests, no god. If you really want to know, come with me." And he led the way down the stairs, a plump, oddly dignified figure in a darned undertunic.

They went across the outer chamber and into the little courtyard beyond, with its now-silent fountain. Cracks of blue sky showed above between the overhanging buildings. In the farthest corner, in the deepest shadows, Loogan bent and slid his fingers under the edge of a large flagstone. Obviously counterweighted, it rose easily, disclosing the first steps of a spiral stair dimly lit with light spheres. They descended.

It was a dizzying way down, farther beneath the streets of Tai-tastigon than Jame had ever imagined that one could go. Plaques set in the outer wall indicated the burial slot of many a hierarch, while squares of rock crystal gave distorted, highly unwelcome glimpses of each occupant. At the bottom, tucked into a widened sweep of the stairs, was a high, conical room lined with shelf after shelf of scrolls, extending up out of sight.

"These," said Loogan, with a gloomy sort of pride, "are the elder archives of Tai-tastigon. They were hidden here during the last battle of the Skyrr-Metalondrian War when it looked as if the winner, whichever side it was, would celebrate by razing the city. The only ones who knew about the transfer besides the novices who effected it were the Senior Archivist (who was one of us) and Great (times five) Grandfather Bilgore. The novices were given a very handsome wall slot each for their pains. The battle ended quite suddenly when the Archiem of Skyrr and the Metalondrian king decided it would be better to make Tai-tastigon a charter city and have it pay them both for the privilege than for one side to slaughter the other and then destroy the place. The Senior Archivist was brained by a flowerpot upset by a lady on an upper terrace while both were watching events below on the plain.

"That was when my ancestor began to change things. He seems to have had the idea that just in case anyone else did know where the documents were, the alterations would make them that much harder to find. Also, I think, it was an excuse to arrange affairs more to his liking. He got away with it too, on both counts. You're the first outsider to see this room in nearly two hundred years."

"But if it was such a secret," said Jame, "why risk betraying it by taking manuscripts up into the temple?"

"Had to," said the priest with a shrug, beginning to slide back into the depression from which his bit of story-telling had temporarily roused him. "They have to be resanctified regularly to stay here . . . or did. One a day, twenty-two years to a cycle. If you want to stay, stay. I'm going back to bed."

He departed. Jame heard his slippers shuffle up the steps and felt the dead, earthen silence close in in their wake. She was alone in the midst of one of the richest troves of its kind in all Rathillien.

THE SHROUD-LIGHT OF DAWN lay heavy on the southern plain, giving it the texture of a singularly dull tapestry woven with shadows. Birds flitted over it under a pewter sky. The road to Tai-Abendra, a ribbon of silver in the gloom, stretched away to the south, following the Ebonbane's dark curve. The small caravan was already a long way away. Jame and Dally stood on the battlements of the outer wall, watching it go.

"Do you suppose," said Dally, "now that Canden's gotten safely away, the old man might simply let him go?"

"I doubt it. He'll probably have about two days' grace before his grandfather finds out he's gone, and then maybe two hours more if the Sirdan's spies are slow about picking up his trail."

"Then we shall have to muddy it a bit for them. There are

plenty of people who will be glad to lay some false scents for the Sirdan's hell-hounds. Damn!" he said suddenly, torn between exasperation and amusement. "All these intrigues, all this deceit. Of course, we'll do away with the lot after the election; but Canden is well out of it for now. I almost wish I were going with him."

"I wish you were too," said Jame, "and myself as well."

Dally glanced at her sharply, hoping to see one thing, finding another that confused and disconcerted him. What had he said now?

"Well, it's time we were getting back," said Jame, turning from the parapet. "After all, if we're going to be dragging bagged foxes around town for the benefit of the pack, it won't do to be seen waving good-bye from up here."

They crossed over to the inner wall on the same rope walk Jame had used when she plunged to Jorin's rescue. There was the cattery, there the pool, but (thank God) no man carrying a sack from one to the other. Out in the foothills, the ounce would probably be wondering where she was, since this was the time when she normally brought him some food to supplement whatever he might have caught. He would have to wait a little longer.

They were on the Rim now.

"What a night!" said Dally. "I thought they'd never get everything packed. Canden's going to have a fine time with that lot if they're always so disorganized."

He found he was talking to himself. As he turned to look for his companion, there was a sudden scuffling sound in an alley that he had just passed and then a loud yelp. Running back, Dally found Jame seated on a small rodent-faced individual whose right arm and wrist had achieved an unusual angle in her grasp.

"Look what I've caught," she said, adding in a dangerously pleasant tone to her victim: "Must I promise to nail the ears of every spy who comes crawling after me to the nearest door in order to be left alone?"

The little man made violent signs to the negative. By now, virtually no one in Tai-tastigon took the Kencyr's word lightly.

"But Jame, it's all right," Dally protested, approaching them. "It's only one of the Creeper's men."

"*What?*"

The spy, taking advantage of her start, twisted free and sent her tumbling back into the wall as he scrambled to his feet. She was up almost as quickly as he, but ignored him as he scuttled away.

"How long has that creature had people following you?" she demanded. "Does your brother know?"

"Why, I suppose so," said Dally. "It's for my own protection, after all. Mendy worries about me. Stop looking at me like that—it's true. Listen, it's been a long night. Let's go to the Moon and have a drink. Then I can start being devious and you can go on with whatever it is you've been doing in the Temple District this last fortnight. Come on, let's."

"LET'S SEE," Raffing was saying owlishly, "who else will be up for promotion when the Guild Council convenes? You, Darinby, for one. Drink to all candidates for master!"

"Including Bane?" asked Patches mischievously.

"Man's a rogue," said Raffing, twisting about in his chair and scowling horrifically at the rest of the Moon's common room, which as usual at this early hour was full of thieves relaxing after their night's work. "A rogue, I say! Bought his commission. Everybody knows it."

"So they do, old chap," said Darinby soothingly. "You needn't shout it at them. I suppose," he added, trying to return the conversation to its original channel, "that the Talisman will be on the lists too, for a journeyman."

"Same difference," said an apprentice from the Rim. "Theocandi's pupil uses his father's money; Penari's, his master's secrets. Either way, it isn't fair."

"Oh, come now. Secrets? What master doesn't pass along his own, if the student is worthy?"

"You know what I mean," said the other stubbornly. "Look at the work he's done: the Sky King's britches, the Peacock Gloves, and half a dozen other things that no one else has even been able to touch, much less take. That's not common, honest skill, no, not any more than Penari's theft of the Eye of Abarraden was. There's sorcery in it, or worse."

"Jealousy too, I should think. It may be only a game to him—I mean to her," he corrected himself with a grimace, "but by all the gods she plays it fairly and well."

"Drink to the Talisman!" roared Raffing, echoed by Patches.

"I still say it's not right," muttered the Rim apprentice, "and what's more," he added, on a surge of false courage, "if he turns up here tonight, I'll tell him so to his face!"

"Then let us hope 'he' doesn't," said Darinby softly, remembering the death of Scramp. "For both your sakes."

"ON SECOND THOUGHT," said Jame, "let's not go to the Moon after all. We're closer to home here anyway. If we ask her nicely, maybe Cleppetty will make us honey cakes for breakfast."

IN A ROOM HUNG with silver and blue, Men-dalis was pacing back and forth. Wherever he walked, the light went with him, clinging softly to his hair and clothes, the god-glow of Dalissar's true son. For the thousandth time, he was counting up the odds.

Masters Gold and Shining were Theocandi's; there was no helping that. Mistress Silver still kept her own council, but was said to be furious with the Sirdan over her son. A pity the boy had only been exiled. The four Provincials were, of course, his. (He would not learn until much too late that one of them was not.) Jewel? The man might jump either way. A show of confidence would have more weight with him than bribes, but not so with Glass or the master thieves' two representatives. There was the crux, for those four votes might well decide the election. Theocandi thought he had bought them. Men-dalis knew that, with the proper backing, the old miser could be outbid; and that backing he would have, although not until the very day of the Council. His supporter had been inflexible about that. His integrity was under suspicion, he had said, and he must establish it at least in the public eye before daring to draw such a sum from the city treasury. Something about dispensing justice in an undeclared trade war on Winter's Eve . . .

With a start, Men-dalis found that the Creeper had entered the room and was walking with him nearly at his elbow. The thin, scratchy voice began its whispered report. Men-dalis listened to most of it without comment, asked a few questions, then suddenly turned on the master spy and said, quite loudly, "What?"

The information was repeated. He began to pace again, frowning.

"Well, what of it? If Dally helps that Kencyr hoyden to embarrass Theocandi, all the better. A pity the old man's grandson got away, though; we might have found a use for him later. . . . Yes, yes, I realize that her master is the Sirdan's elder brother. Those two have been at dagger's point for a dog's age. . . . You think their rivalry is all a ruse? Yes, if that were true, the Talisman would make a good agent for Theocandi. No one would ever suspect her of it, not with the old men constantly feuding. . . . Dally? The boy's not very bright, but he can be trusted—I think. Besides, there's been talk of Penari's professional secrets again. If Dally can worm them out of his 'prentice, it will bc quite a gem in our crown. . . . In *love* with her? Well, well, I don't know . . ."

Back and forth he went, arguing as though with himself while his familiar kept pace one step behind him, its avid face out of his sight. The whispering voice went on and on, and bit by bit the room began to dim.

JAME THOUGHT AT FIRST that she had begun to hallucinate. In that silent, underground room, time might have stopped for all one could tell. How many hours had it been since she had parted with Jorin on the hillside and Dally (who had gone out with her) at the gate? Two? Ten? And nearly twenty-four awake before that, helping Canden prepare for his flight. No, one didn't begin to imagine things in that length of time. She read the manuscript again, then rolled it up and went quickly out of the room and up the stairs with it in her hand.

Loogan was sitting on the steps to the upper apartment. "Well, it's happened," he said gloomily. "My acolyte's father has gotten the Priests' Guild to annul his contract to me. I can't say that I blame him."

"Never mind that now. Listen: *'By day and night, the battle raged, wheels of fire clashing over the seared plain while the heavens burned. Lances of lightning had Heliot and Dalis-sar, the moon for a shield. Their swords were tongues of flame, of woven comet's hair their armor. The earth trembled when they met, and the old gods fled to the deep places thereof to shiver in the dark.'*"

"Why read me all this?" said Loogan wearily. "What difference can it possibly make?"

"Listen, dammit! *'One alone stayed, saw through the green roof of his home the terrible conflict, felt the earth's agony, the forests burning, the waters boiling. And when Dalis-sar had won, Gorgiryl came from his sea-deep house to plead for the scorched earth. Taking pity on him and on the blackened land, the new lord of the sun raised him to the heavens so that his tears falling might restore the sunken seas, bring life to the charred fields.'*

"Now, is that or is that not, in unscrambled form, part of the ninth canticle of your evening service?"

"Yes," said the priest, looking puzzled, "but the name isn't right."

"That's just the point. It is. Look, I've been going over the religious tracts in your collection this past fortnight, and so far I haven't found one reference to Gorgo, which is ridiculous considering his obvious antiquity. Gorgiryl, however, gets at least a mention from nearly everybody because he was one of the few deities to make the jump from the Old Pantheon to the New essentially unaltered. Then along came your multiple great-grandfather Bilgore. It wasn't just Gorgo's name that he changed, either . . . you're looking remarkably blank. Am I going too fast for you?"

"N-no. I'm told I always look that way just before the rotten eggs hit."

"Well, this is more on the order of a spinach custard—just as messy but potentially more nourishing. As I was saying, the old attributes seem to have been kept, but not with the same emphasis . . . and that's where things began to go sour for poor old Gorgo—pardon, Gorgiryl. Instead of the tears of life—rain, that is—you have sterile salt water; instead of the world's salvation, endless sorrow. It's the whole myth frozen in the wrong place, with everything distorted to make its lowest point look like its proper end. What easier way to turn a simple, rather dignified religion on its ear? You're still looking blank. Come, I'll show you an example, the best one of all."

She took him by the arm and led him half against his will to the threshold of the inner chamber. Neither had entered it since the night its occupant had died. The basins were still there, also the short scroll peeking over the idol's webbed fingers; but more vivid than either was the memory of the bowed, bewildered figure in its garish finery that had stood trembling before them for so short a time.

"As the man that Bilgore made him," said Jame, "he was ludicrous." Then she pointed at the statue looming dark and cool in the shadows. "But as a giant frog . . . ?"

IT WAS EARLY EVENING on a day some three weeks into autumn, and the light was failing rapidly. Marc put down the tiny figure he had been carving. The rough form was there—the cowled head, outstretched arms, even some folds of the enveloping garment—but he didn't trust himself with the finer details at this time of night. Ah, but it felt good to have a bit of work in his hands again. He had almost forgotten the pleasure of making small, cunningly fashioned objects, not to mention his old dream of becoming a master craftsman before necessity and his own remarkable physique had defeated all such gentle ambitions. If he had a hearth of his own, he might have retired to it now to perfect this skill. Instead, all he possessed after a long life of service was his honor—and a few friends to brighten the way.

Still, one might do worse.

A mouse scurried across a beam overhead. Boo was getting lazy, Marc thought, staring up contemplatively at another sample of his handiwork. He and Rothan had had quite a time repairing the loft after its midnight visitor. Matters could easily have been worse, though: without Jame, the top two stories would probably have collapsed into the hall.

She was clever, that lass, but more than a bit strange. Marc knew how afraid many Kencyrs were of people like her, but he himself had seen too much of life to take fright at something a little odd. He wondered idly how much Highborn blood she had, all Shanirs necessarily possessing at least a trace. A quarter at most, probably. Pure Highborn women and even many half-bloods were strictly sequestered and used by their menfolk to bind together the ruling houses of the Kencyrath. Those with less Highborn blood, especially if it came with Shanir traits, could receive some pretty rough treatment. That might explain Ishtier's initial hostility toward Jame.

Ishtier. Strange things certainly happened to Kencyrs in this city, Marc thought, shaking his head. Here he was carving the image of one dead god for a small household shrine while Jame acted as temporary acolyte to another and their own priest set traps to snare them both. Then there was Bane, who acted like a Shanir, but (as far as Marc could tell) wasn't one, and that old Kencyr, Dalis-sar, deified. No wonder few of the Kencyrath stayed in Tai-tastigon longer than they could help.

So what arc you doing here now, old man?

A wail split the air, breaking his line of thought. Someone's baby? No, cats—squaring off in front of the inn directly below. There was a covered chamber pot near at hand. Marc flipped off the lid and tossed the contents over the parapet without bothering to look down.

"Hey!" said a familiar voice below in sharp protest.

JAME HAD BEEN in the Lower Town that afternoon, checking on Taniscent. Dusk was gathering and the byways were rapidly clearing of their shabby traffic when she left Patches's home. To save time, she turned down a narrow side street, which, according to the patterns of the Maze, should have been a short-cut to the fosse that bounded the area. Several turns in, however, the lane was blocked to shoulder height with the debris of a collapsed wall. Jame climbed the mound and set off along its spine, expecting the way to open up again somewhere beyond. Eventually it did, but only into a wasteland of fire-ravaged buildings and thoroughfares so choked with rubble as to be quite invisible. To her exasperation Jame realized that she was lost. Her knowledge of the city, theoretical and practical, had made her careless, here where the lack of all customary landmarks made caution most necessary. She had forgotten how quickly Tai-tastigon could revenge itself on those who took its mysteries lightly.

It was getting dark. Silence clung batlike to the charred rafters, swelled up out of the shadowed hollows in the heaped debris. A rat scratched and snuffled in the ruins, claws scrabbling briefly on a bone-white board. To go back or forward—return to the heart of the lower Town or press on toward the deadly circle of her own temple? Night breathed in her ear, waiting to pounce.

"Salutations."

Jame started violently. A dark, elegant figure had appeared on top of a broken wall above her. "Well, look who's perching on the battlements," she heard herself say in a shaky voice. "Come down, gore-crow."

"Gladly," said Bane, and leaped.

Jame sprang backward into a defensive pose. Water flowing met fire leaping, channeled its force aside with a blur of moving bodies once, twice, and again. They broke apart, regarding each other, now that the initial shock was past, with something like satisfaction. Neither had been so well matched in a long, long time. When they met again, it was not in the whirlwind fashion of the first round but with more subtlety of attack and response on both sides. Darkness gathered about them, two lithe, shadowy forms tracing the patterns of ritual combat as old as their ancient race.

Jame could never afterward say when the fight ended and the dance began. No need to ask then where in the night her partner was, for his movements had become an extension of her own. The kantirs flowed together, water and air mingling with touches of dark fire to smolder and nerves' end, fingertips tingling with a nearness that never became contact.

Where had she done this before, and with whom? . . . a vast chamber as dark as this place was now, surrounded by blazing tripods, a canopied bed, a man dancing, his face . . . no!

Cloth ripped, and Bane sprang back in a startled exclamation. The left sleeve of his d'hen was split from the inner elbow to the wrist. On the forearm beneath, black in the moonlight, was a thickening line of blood. He regarded it with a slow, secret smile. Jame's throat tightened. Without a word, she turned and climbed the wall of jumbled beams. As she set off through the wilderness beyond, Bane was walking by her side.

"The old man knows that you helped his grandson escape," he said, as though nothing had passed between them. "I've never seen him so furious."

"Damn. That will mean assassins lurking under every flowerpot, I suppose."

"Oh, he wouldn't be so angry if it were as simple as that. At the moment, he's afraid to interfere with you at all. The bones have warned him. According to them, if he's going to win the election, you'll have something to do with it."

"What, for God's sake?"

"I shouldn't stop here if I were you," he said. "It's following us."

"It? Oh." Jame looked back, saw nothing but jagged, darkening shadows and the cusp of the old moon rising. Nevertheless, there was only one thing "it" could be, here in the Lower Town. "You don't seem very concerned," she said, resuming her pace.

"M'lord Ishtier tells me that I shouldn't be," he said cryptically. "I'm to trust in him and all will be well. But I don't think it is, even now. If that man has betrayed me, kin or not, the next time he deigns to give me an order, the results may surprise him."

"Bane, I haven't the faintest idea what you're talking about. Now will you please tell me how I'm supposed to help Theocandi retain his power?"

"If he knew, he would have found a way to get rid of you without endangering his own future long before this, if only to stop the nightmares. Remember the statue at the prow of Ship Island? Every night for the past month, he's dreamed that it had your face and was brandishing his head. Have you noticed," he said, examining his arm, "that every time we meet, someone ends up bleeding?"

"I've noticed. Not very auspicious, is it?"

"That depends," he said, with an ambiguous smile. "This much at least is clear: If you stay in Tai-tastigon after the election, there'll be trouble—regardless of who wins. Don't trust Men-dalis anymore than Theocandi, despite that baby brother of his. Something nasty is brewing in that quarter, though no one seems to know exactly what. Beware of the Creeper, and also of m'lord Ishtier. Not only does our esteemed priest hate you, but there are rumors that he had more to do with the Sirdan during the last Council than either cares to admit."

"Oh? In what way?"

"My spies suggest an exchange of information, probably arcane. Theocandi is a fair Kencyr scholar, and I know that he has several of our 'lost' documents in his library that Ishtier might well have wished to see. Of course, the reverse is true too; remember, this was just before the appearance of the Shadow Thief.

"And now," he said with a sudden laugh, "having uttered my share of warning croaks, I'll flap off to the nearest rookery. Your way lies in that direction, over the fosse and home. Our murky friend will follow me, I think; it always does. But there's no point in tempting it."

On the other side of the little waterway, Jame suddenly turned. "That statue of yours . . ." she called after him. "I've just remembered. It carries two heads, not just one. In Theocandi's dream, whose was the other?"

Bane paused, a black silhouette against the sky. "Oh, didn't I tell you?" he said, the now familiar smile coming back into his voice although the dusk hid his face. "The other head was mine."

KITHRA SANK HER JUG into the public fountain and heaved it out again, full of water, to balance on the limestone rim. Pretending to check it for cracks, she peered over its round shoulder at the Skyrrman.

What was that man Marplet up to? He had dragged out the construction of his precious inn for nearly two years, and now, suddenly, everything must be finished at once. Even at this time of night, there were craftsmen at work inside, fitting inlaid panels around the walls. What was he readying the inn for? Kithra checked off the major, upcoming public events in her mind; the Thieves' Guild Council, several festivals in the Temple District, the biennial meeting between the Archiem of Skyrr and the Metalondrin king . . . of course, that must be it. Everyone knew that while their heralds exchanged ritual insults, the two rulers usually slipped off to spend Winter's Eve going from one tavern to another. Marplet must be hoping that they would honor him with a visit.

Ah, if she could only get the Archiem's attention for half a minute, what stories she could tell him about his "honorable" countryman! Gods, what a chance to gut that sleek pig of an innkeeper . . .

Niggen dashed out of a side street with a howl. Although he was feigning terror, Kithra recognized that detestable giggle welling up under all his clamor and wished savagely that the Talisman could be induced to knock out a few more of his teeth.

And here, as though in answer to her thoughts, was Jame herself, standing hands on hips at the mouth of the street from which Niggen had just bolted. The boy was in front of the Skyrrman now, loudly begging his father's servants for protection and casting looks of mock terror back across the square. The apparent cause of this scene regarded it with raised eyebrows and a look oddly compounded of perplexity, amusement, and distaste on her handsome face. Kithra found herself wishing, not for the first time, that the Talisman really was a boy.

At that moment, two other voices joined the uproar, cutting across it with their undisguised notes of raw hatred. Fang was stalking Boo on the very threshold of the Res aB'tyrr.

"Oh, for pity's sake," said Jame, and went to the rescue.

At the last moment, something made her look up. She saw what was falling from the loft and, with a shout of protest, leaped for the doorway, snatching up Boo en route. Fang was not so fortunate. Drenched, he backed rapidly away, shaking his head, then turned and dashed off.

"Sorry," said Marc, looking down.

Jame lugged Boo up to the loft, hoping to keep him out of further mischief. The cat continued to whuffle ferociously at nothing in particular up all three flights of stairs. He gave the impression that when set down he would bounce for some time like a clockwork toy.

When Jame had told Marc about Bane's warnings, the big Kendar said, "He's right, you know. It isn't safe for you here even now, nor for anyone else, I sometimes think. Too much is coming to a boil too fast. We Kencyrs are used to trouble, but this time most of it isn't even our own; and I'm getting too old to enjoy the thing for its own sake. What are we doing here, lass? We don't belong in this city, however entangled we're become with it. We should be going home."

Home—the broken walls, the doorways that gaped, the waiting dead—no. The images touched Jame's mind only for a second, then faded away. Home . . . no longer a place but a people whose face she barely knew but suddenly wished very much to see. The sun on spear points and the moon on shields, the rathorn cry and the charge that makes the earth shake; scrollsmen walking in their cloisters, thirty millennia of knowledge lying cool and deep in their minds; the hearth on a winter's night when friends meet; Tori . . . a place to belong. It was calling to her here in the dark, stirring her blood as the moon does the sea, and at last—after days, weeks, months of hesitation—she answered its summons.

"Yes," she said, "we should go home. Trinity knows what will happen to either of us when we get there, but we should go. Soon."

"Over the Ebonbane? The passes won't be safe for months."

"True. How about going south, either cross-country or down the Tone to Endiscar? The storm season will end soon. Then, dead water or not, we can take ship around the Cape of the Lost and reach the Central Lands by the sea route."

"You don't know what it's like down there," said Marc, grimacing. "The land is as rotten as the water, and as haunted as the north in its own way. Still, it may be our best chance at that. When should we leave?"

"Say, as soon after the election as we can manage. I'd like to set something right before I go, and it will probably take me that long at least . . . if I can bring it off at all," she added to herself, a worried look settling on her face in the darkness.

THE EVENING SERVICE HAD ENDED. Jame, by the door, watched the congregation file out, then went down to the front where Loogan was putting his cue cards back in order. Each scrap of paper had part of the revised ritual on it, gleaned from any one of a dozen different sources. With their help, supplemented by some vigorous pantomiming by Jame at the back of the room, he was attempting to replace the old, corrupt words—engraved on his memory by thirty years of use—with the new ones.

"That went quite well," said Jame, coming up to him. "I'd say that the people were impressed and pleased. They're taking the changes much better than I'd hoped. Gorgo"—they had decided to keep the old name—"probably hasn't been this popular in years."

"It helps to be a rain god in the middle of a drought," said Loogan. "Up to a certain point. You know, the people of the

Far Isles have a priest-king who they believe can summon the rains at will out of his belly. If he fails, they rip him open."

"In other words, an impressive performance isn't enough. Hasn't it made any difference, getting all these people to come back?"

"None," said Loogan heavily. "He's as dead as ever, poor thing, and all that we do in his name is futile. Only a miracle can help him now."

"Hush."

A stranger was standing on the threshold, his broad shoulders nearly filled the doorway. "Are you the high priest?" he demanded.

Loogan drew himself up, some of his old authority returning. "Yes, I am," he said. "How may I serve you?"

"Huh!" said the man, giving the modest interior of the temple a quick, scornful glance. "I'm part of a delegation of farmers from the Ben-ar Confederation, come up river to petition all the appropriate gods for rain. Damn waste of time, I say, but there you are. We must have it before Winter's Eve or the wheat crop will fail, and that will mean famine throughout the Eastern Lands. I hear that this Gurgle of yours is a rain god. What d'you charge for extra prayers?"

"Sir," said Loogan stiffly, "Where the good of the community is involved, we charge nothing."

"I should damn well hope not," said the other in a tone of satisfaction mixed with contempt for a fool who drives a poor bargain. "After all, it may be our wheat, but it's your bread." And with that he turned on his heel and stomped away. They heard his heavy boots clumping on the tiles, then the slam of the front door.

"What an odious man," said Loogan with distaste, "and what an odd sight you make, capering like that. Whatever for?"

"An idea. You wanted a miracle? Well, so did that oaf, and I think I see how we might be able to provide it!"

THREE WEEKS BEFORE the Thieves' Guild Council, ninety-nine of the hundred landed masters—one for each district in the city—converged on the Guild Hall to choose their two representatives. Eleven candidates vied for these honored and potentially lucrative positions, six promising if elected to vote for Men-dalis at the general meeting, five for Theocandi. Each needed two-thirds of his colleagues' votes to win and was dropped from the running if his share fell to less than half that. At the end of each round in which no victor was forthcoming, all the ballots were gathered up, wrapped around the shaft of an arrow, and sent—blazing—into the sky as a sign to the rest of the thieves' community of a null vote.

This had been going on since midmorning. By nightfall, twenty-six such votes had been taken, eight candidates eliminated (one by assassination) and two citizens injured by spent arrows. Nerves were raw, tempers flared. Emotionally as well as physically the city of Tai-tastigon was tinder, waiting for the first careless spark.

Jame had gone up into the hills the night before upon learning that her master really did not intend to join his peers in the Guild Hall. This had come as a jolt to her. She had always assumed that Penari would support the Sirdan in the end, despite the former's professed neutrality. Instead, he stayed home and she fled temporarily into the countryside, not wishing to defend the old man's actions among her fellow apprentices. Her affection for him had not changed, but there was nothing in her nature that helped her to understand, much less explain, the failure of a man to stand by his own brother, however unworthy the latter might be.

Another arrow, a pinprick of light at this distance arcing into the night sky. Even with a glum Cloudic sitting on every roof with a bucket of water, didn't those fools at the Palace realize how easy it would be to set the whole town ablaze?

Here in the parched hills, she would not have dared to start a cooking fire, even if she and Jorin had found any game to prepare on one. Nonetheless, there had been food for both: hers, from the city; his, from a more puzzling source. On arrival the night before, Jame had found the remains of a stag in the back of the cave, a far larger animal than Jorin could ever have pulled down by himself. Besides, it had died with its throat ripped out, an unlikely way for an ounce with its short canines to dispatch its quarry. She could only think that he must have stolen it from a larger predator, but what beast in all the hills was big enough to have left such marks on its prey?

The grass under her hand crackled drily. The hills on all

sides lifted seared slopes the color of Jorin's fur as he lay beside her. When would the rains come?

"*It must be before Winter's Eve,*" she had told Loogan, "*for the sake of the wheat and, by extension, to serve our own purpose. Remember, you're going to tell the people that if they believe Gorgo can make it rain, he will. The threat of famine should be enough to get them involved. I don't know if the faith-creating-reality aspect of this city will actually work that way, but if it does, or even if the rains simply fall in the course of nature, enough faith may be restored in Gorgo to resurrect him.*"

"*But if it does rain, won't every god in Tai-tastigon claim the credit?*"

"*Let them. Gorgo is still the most likely candidate, since it was just such a miracle that made him a New Pantheon god in the first place. His people will remember that. They must . . .*"

Hullo, flames—a viper's knot of them growing red and vehement in the darkness. Had those idiots managed to set the city alight after all? If so, they had started with their own house, for surely that fantastic roofline could only belong to the Palace itself. Now there was a sound coming from below, fainter than the crickets that called on all sides but somehow rising above their clamor and growing louder each moment. Shouts, cheering. So the representatives had at last been chosen. Now the real fun would begin.

THE RIM APPRENTICE was on his feet, glaring down at Raffing. "Take that back," he said through his teeth.

"Why?" said the other, giving him an insolent, somewhat blurry grin. "Everyone knows it's the truth. Your master may have been chosen as Theocandi's man, but we all know that he'll vote for whoever pays him the most."

"Liar!" screeched the apprentice, and he leaped forward with steel bright in his hand, as the startled Raffing went over backward off his bench, feet in the air.

Darinby was between the two. As the Rim thief lunged over the table in front of him, the journeyman caught his knife hand and twisted. Turned over in midair, he crashed down on his back. Tankards flew in all directions. The members of both factions, some with knives already out, froze, staring.

"Let me remind you all of something," Darinby said quietly in the sudden lull. "Open conflict between factions can be interpreted as the beginning of an undeclared guild war. If your side starts one, the Five will fine you out of existence. If they can't decide who's to blame, both parties will suffer. If, despite all this, any of you still want a fight, I suggest that you start it with me, for by all the gods I most assuredly will finish it."

There was an awkward silence. Then, one by one, the thieves sat down again, glaring at Darinby if they had the nerve to face him at all and muttering among themselves. The journeyman watched them, casually flipping the Rim thief's knife end over end. When he was sure nothing more would happen for the moment, he tossed the blade back to its owner and said pleasantly, "If I were you, I should leave. Now." The apprentice shot one last venomous look at the bemused Raffing and slipped through the crowd toward the door. Darinby resumed his seat, signaling for a new tankard to replace the one now somewhere under the table. Slowly, his heartbeat returned to normal.

In ten other public houses, three younger brothers, two nephews, and five cousins—Guild-men all—waited as he did now, with a timely warning and, if necessary, a ready blade. With luck and considerable impudence, they just might get Tai-tastigon through the night.

THEN AGAIN, THOUGHT JAME, surely there were still a few sane people left in the city. Things would be bad from now until the election, but there would always be those, longer-sighted than the rest, who would try to hold the Guild together despite itself for the future's sake.

Jorin was dozing beside her, his chin on her knee. Suddenly he woke, head jerking up, ears twitching. Jame also tensed. She seemed to smell something, a wild, musky scent not at all unpleasant but oddly stirring. No odor had ever evoked such a response from her before. She wondered briefly if it was reaching her through the filter of Jorin's senses. Then she remembered the stag carcass in the cave and leaped to her feet.

They had been sitting on a slope. The hilltop above them was crowned by a huge thorn bush whose branches spread from a solid black core out to a nimbus of fragile spikes. At its center were two points of light about five feet off the ground. They moved. The whole dark heart of the bush moved, detached itself, became a great, shadowy form gliding along the crest. Jorin, with an excited chirp, bounded up the slope to meet it. Gravely, the huge head bent to touch noses with the ounce, then lifted again, turning toward Jame. It winked, and both were gone, leaving the night empty in their wake.

Jame stared after them. "An Arrin-ken," she said out loud with awe in her voice. "I've just seen an Arrin-ken."

THERE WERE ISOLATED CLASHES in Tai-tastigon that night after word spread that Theocandi's chosen representative had secured one position and Men-dalis's the other, but none of these were witnessed by the guards or resulted in the death of anyone particularly notable.

Patches, on her way home, found Raffing in an alley near the Moon. Only his clothes made identification possible. Of the many knife blows struck, it was to be hoped that the first had brought death.

"I'M SORRY," said the secretary, "but Master Men-dalis doesn't have time to see you today."

"So you've been telling me for the last week. Are you sure? I'd just like to talk to him for a minute."

"Sorry," said the man again, beginning to shuffle through the papers he carried. "We *are* busy here, you know. The election is only a fortnight away now. Try again tomorrow. Good day."

Out again on the steps of the New Faction headquarters, Dally paused. Had someone just ducked back out of sight around the corner? Another of the Creeper's agents, probably. *"Watch our for that man,"* Jame had told him. *"I think he wants your brother all to himself, and you're in his way."* He knew now that he was followed everywhere. Mendy wouldn't tell him if this was by his orders or not. Mendy wouldn't even see him. What had gone wrong between them? When the election was over, perhaps all would be well again. Yes, of course—it was only tension that made his brother act this way.

But if so, why was Dally suddenly so frightened?

Someone was shouting and others rushing about inside the Skyrrman calling to each other in excited voices.

"What now?" Ghillie said to Rothan as they stood at the Res aB'tyrr's front door, listening.

"I smell smoke," said Rothan suddenly. "Look. Something is burning, perhaps in the kitchen."

Behind the front wing of the building, a horse screamed in terror.

"No," said Ghillie the hostler sharply. "It's in the stable. Here, you!" he shouted at a servant who had come running out to the public fountain with a bucket. "D'you need any help?"

"From you?" the man replied with scorn, hurriedly dipping his vessel in the water. "Think you haven't done enough already, do you? Well, just wait. You'll pay for this, you'll pay!"

"Pay?" Ghillie repeated in confusion. "For what?"

"Quiet," said Cleppetty. She had come up behind them unnoticed and now stood fists jammed on hips, scowling at the activity across the square. "I don't like this," she said. "I don't like this at all."

And then, at last, it was the dawn of Winter's Eve. Jame was asleep in the loft. The gray morning light touched the sharp line of her cheekbone and jaw, but failed to erase the darkness under her eyes. Over the last few weeks, her triple role of thief, dancer, and acolyte had taken its toll. She had lost weight and slept badly, with the growing foretaste of failure to poison her dreams. The deadline was almost here, and still it had not rained.

She was dreaming now.

Images came and went; faces whirled past like drowned rats in a river. Scramp, Hangrell, and Raffing; Theocandi and Men-dalis; Marplet and Tubain; Gorgo and Loogan dancing together, both so horribly alike. They froze, staring at each other, than shrieked and simultaneously melted away. "The Anti-God Heresy?" croaked the idol. "Don't know, couldn't care (ribbet) less. Excuse me—my constellation is rising." And it jumped, up through the smoke hole in the sky. Beams came crashing down, mounds of debris grew. A dark, elegant figure was walking across them under the old moon, an unnaturally swollen shadow at his heels. He turned, and his face was Tori's. "Shanir!" he cried. "Priest's-Bane, see what you've done!" A figure crouched before her, rings, chains, and amulets raining down from it; but surely that wasn't Loogan's corpulent form. Bent back, narrow shoulders, hooded visage, and then an altar, tessellated floor, her own ungloved hand raised as though in summons. The figure looked up. Ishtier. Shocked recognition, then hatred and something not unlike fear ripped the remaining shreds of humanity from his skull-like face.

Jame woke with a start, gasping for breath.

What time was it, she wondered confusedly. Ah, dawn . . . but if so, why was the light steadily failing, and what was that distant sound, like rocks cannoning down the mountainside? She threw back her blanket and sprang up. The sun was indeed rising, but toward it rolled such a mighty rack of clouds from over the Ebonbane that it was as if a great shroud were being pulled across the earth. Lightning flickered within the black billows, tingeing them with silver; and the thunder sounded again, closer this time. It was growing steadily darker. As Jame stood by the parapet, the wind came, slipping through the loft, lifting the black wings of her hair, and then the first chill drops of rain struck her face.

At first she could hardly believe what was happening. Then she threw back her head and gave full tongue to the great war cry of victory, waking every sleeper in the house. Before they could even ask themselves what on earth they had heard, she was gone, flying across the rooftops northward toward the Temple District, pulling on her clothes as she went.

The rain was falling harder now. Slates were slick with it, and every gutter held a raging torrent. Soon it was hard to see, even to breathe in the downpour. Jame got as far as the River Tone, then was forced down to street level opposite Edor Thulig. Both arms of the Tynnet were roaring around the island on which the Tower of Demons stood, its upper heights lost in the driving rain. When she came to the first bridge after that, Jame found that the high gates that gave access to the side streets on either side of it were shut. Puzzled, she crossed over to the north bank and loped westward toward the next intersection.

High above, a man struggled with a shutter loosened by the

wind. Looking down, he saw the lone figure making its way up an avenue already half awash and shouted at it, "Get out of the street, you fool! D'you want to drown?" The shutter closed with a bang.

Jame caught her breath, realizing at last what she should have guessed immediately. She began to run. At the next bend in the road was another closed gate, but this one had a rickety ladder nailed to it. Jame sprinted for it. Already she could hear the approaching roar. Her foot was on the first rung when a wall of water twenty feet high appeared around the street's next bend. She climbed frantically, hearing it smash into the opposite houses and cannon off them. Her leg was over the top of the gate when the flash flood boomed into it.

Every board shook. A sheet of spray, exploding upward, lifted Jame neatly off her perch. She tumbled down on the far side, more through water than air, to the hard cobbles below.

It was a thoroughly bedraggled, badly limping figure that at last presented itself on the threshold of Gorgo, formerly the lugubrious god. Loogan darted across the outer room, grabbed Jame's hand and half dragged her, hopping on one foot, to the door of the sanctuary. It was raining inside almost as heavily as out, from a private miniature bank of clouds up near the ceiling. A grotesque, indistinct form cavorted about in the middle of the room, bouncing over benches, splashing boisterously in the growing puddles.

"He—ah—isn't very big, is he?" Jame said.

"No," Loogan agreed, beginning to grin, "but he's very, very green."

Solemnly, they drank to the health of the newborn god in rainwater from cupped hands.

BOOK III

SHROUD OF DAYS

CHAPTER 12

A Flame Rising

ON THAT DAY, the whole city rejoiced. The rain ended in the early afternoon, and the sun came out to shine on the remains of a sparkling day. The dust that had lain everywhere was washed away. Gilt towers glowed in the light, and red tile roofs and mosaic prayer walls of turquoise and chalcedony. Bitter enemies met in the streets and went off together laughing; thieves who had not exchanged a word in weeks, except to curse, toasted each other in the taverns. The thoroughfares were full of people walking together, singing, dancing. Whatever tomorrow might bring, today was unanimously declared a high holiday and all set about gathering sweet memories for the troubled times ahead.

Jame and Loogan went out to celebrate with the rest.

In the distance, they could hear the music of trumpets and tabors in Judgment Square where the Archiem of Skyrr and King Sellik XXI of Metalondar were meeting in a blaze of pageantry. Jame wanted to go and see, but her bruised knee hurt too badly. Instead, at Loogan's suggestion, they drifted from tavern to tavern, drinking at each. The afternoon slipped away in a growing vinous haze. At dusk, Jame found herself in the same tavern to which she had taken Loogan on the night that Gorgo had died. The priest had just poured her another cup of wine, spilling half of it on the floor, when Ghillie appeared at her elbow.

"They taunted me about it at the fountain," he said rapidly, ignoring all offers of wine or a seat. "They aren't even trying to keep it a secret anymore, they're so confident, and Aunt Cleppetty says they've got reason to be . . ."

"Ghillie, you're making my head ache. Who are 'they' and what is 'it'?"

The boy took a deep breath. "Harr sen Tenko is bringing the Archiem to the Skyrrman tonight, as though by accident," he said with great care in a brittle voice. "If the service is good—and the gods know it will be—according to custom, the Archiem will ask Marplet what payment he will take for it. Marplet means to ask for a judgment against the Res aB'tyrr. He'll accuse us of spoiling his wine, terrorizing his servants, starting that fire in his stable—in short, of waging an illegal trade war against him. His cellar is full of oiled bales of straw, ready to stack around us and set ablaze. The Archiem needn't hesitate for the city's sake, now that there's been rain. We'll be burned to the ground.

"Please, Jame," he burst out, all control vanishing. "Stop gaping at me like that and come. We need you!"

JAME PAUSED in the courtyard of the Res aB'tyrr, drew a bucket of water from the well, and dumped it over her head. Somewhat clearer in mind, she entered the kitchen. Cleppetty turned to stare at her.

"Why is it," she demanded, "that every time we have a crisis, you turn up dripping wet?"

"Force of habit, I suppose. What's to be done?"

"Damned if I know," said the widow in disgust, to the others' horror. "The way that devil Marplet has arranged things, we might as well all be bound and gagged. Even if we could force our way into that mock court he's setting up over there, who would believe us? It's his game this time, and no mistake . . . if he can really pull it off."

"Can he?"

"How should I know?" said Cleppetty again, violently. "Do I look like an oracle? No, no, I haven't given up hope.

It's just that I don't know what to hope for. Ghillie has already gone to fetch Marc, and Tubain is up with Abernia. If the worst happens, Jame, you're responsible for getting the two of them out; Rothan, for clearing the stables; Kithra, for seeing that no one is left upstairs. Save whatever else you can, but be sure that you get out yourselves. That's all we can do. Now, out into the hall, all of you, and see that it's in order. Whatever happens, I'll not have this inn go to glory with a dirty face."

They went. Word of the impending conflagration had apparently spread throughout the neighborhood, for few of the regular customers had come in that night, despite the prevailing carnival mood in the streets. Jame helped with the table wiping, floor sweeping, and tankard polishing, painfully aware, as the effects of the afternoon's debauch wore off, of her throbbing knee. Then she joined the others at the front door. The Res aB'tyrr waited.

"Does this situation seem at all familiar to any of you?" Kithra asked suddenly.

"Hmmm. Too bad it isn't Marplet's thugs this time. Even given the chance, we couldn't drug two royal courts—or could we?"

"Hush," said the maid sharply. "Listen."

The sounds of the outside world were coming nearer. They heard voices—some laughing, some singing—and saw shadows begin to leap on the house fronts of the square. Torchbearers were coming down the main avenue from the north. A brilliant crowd followed them. At its center walked three men, one decked out grandly in scarlet velvet, one wearing the insignia of the Five, one clad in patched jerkin and leather britches.

"Why," said Jame, "it's my ragged hill lord."

Kithra boggled. "Your *what?* You fool, that's Arribek sen Tenzi himself, the Archiem of Skyrr!"

"Look," said Rothan, "They're arguing about something. Harr pointed at the Skyrrman, and the Archiem shook his head. Now what . . . gods preserve us, they're coming here!"

There was a precipitous general retreat from the front door. When the first guest entered, they were all at their posts except Jame, who had been sent tearing across the courtyard and up the stairs to fetch Tubain. Explaining the situation to Abernia through the keyhole took longer than it did for the innkeeper to emerge more or less in his proper attire once he understood what had happened. Jame followed him down the steps, ripping off the random bits of feminine apparel that he had not had time to remove. Luckily, he had on most of his own clothes beneath them, and, due to a wrangle between King Sellik and sen Tenzi over who should enter first, managed to beat both of them into the great hall.

Great confusion followed as the liegemen of both rulers trooped in and settled themselves, shouting orders for everything from honey wine to buttered eggs. Most of them were already in the exhilarated stages of drunkenness, including the monarch of Metalondar, who turned out, at close range, to be a foolish-faced young man with a stammer. Of them all, only the Archiem and Harr, Thane sen Tenko, seemed fairly sober, although each kept urging the other to drink deep. Through their veil of courteous conversation, it was clear that sen Tenko was extremely annoyed about something, and that Arribek enjoyed his rival's discomfort.

Tubain rather timidly entered this poisoned atmosphere to inquire if all was to their satisfaction.

The Archiem's answer, delivered in his clear, sharp voice, easily reached Jame as she stood beside Cleppetty at the kitchen door: "We have been informed that an exceptional dancer, the B'tyrr by name, is attached to this inn, and I have persuaded my colleagues to enter in hopes that she might be induced to perform for us. Can this be arranged?"

Tubain looked across at Jame, and Jame, in despair, at the widow.

"I know, I know," the latter said, more gently than usual. "You're exhausted, your leg is about to buckle under you, and, to tell the truth, you aren't quite sober. Still, will you try? Everything may depend on it."

Miserably, Jame agreed, and Tubain passed on the good news.

Up in the loft, she combed out her long black hair, now nearly dry, and put on her costume. Then she tentatively tried a few dance steps, stumbled, and banged her sore knee against a stool. Almost in tears with pain and vexation, she sat on the floor hugging it. She would never get drunk again, never, never, never; but remorse wouldn't help her now. She was about to let them all down—Cleppetty, Tubain, Ghillie, all of them—after everything that they had done for her.

The memory of all the times she had danced successfully rose up to haunt her. That first night here at the inn, in Edor Thulig, in the temple of her own god; but that last time it had been different. She hadn't just manipulated a score of half-drunken patrons then but, in some obscure way, the power of the godhead itself. Jamethiel, her namesake, had also danced before their god and before men the night two-thirds of the Kencyrath had fallen. Clearly, hers was a dangerous, easily perverted talent, but it also had surprising potentials. If she could only tap the right one now, darkness damn the consequences.

"Oh, brave, brave thoughts," she said out loud with a sudden, bitter laugh. "You fool, you can't even stand up."

But while she had stood that last time in the temple, she hadn't moved. The Senetha pattern that had channeled the power had been performed only in her mind. Exactly how that could aid her now, she didn't know, but it seemed marginally possible that more of the same mental exercise might help her prepare for the work that she knew she must at least attempt in the hall below. Consequently, she eased herself into the formal kneeling position, closed her eyes, and concentrated.

It was remarkably difficult. Not only to visualize the kantirs but to sense them—the tension of balance, the play of muscle on bone, the rhythm of movement . . . try to encompass them all, and they blurred; focus on one, and awareness of the others began to slip away. For an endless time she struggled with them in the dark, then music came. Behind closed eyes, she seemed to see the spiral stairs, the third floor landing, each step of the way down to the hall just as she had each time in the past, descending to the call of Ghillie's flute. Confidence seeped back as concentration became easier. Now she simply danced, beyond pain, beyond reflection, weaving the ancient tapestry of motion and dream. Then, when the sequence was complete, she bowed, opened her eyes, and found herself on the center table under the chandelier, with King Sellik, the Archiem, and Harr sen Tenko all staring at her.

There was a moment's silence, then a burst of noise so loud that even when she spun about and saw for herself, she could hardly believe that it was only applause. The performance was over. Her knee felt as if someone had put a live coal under the cap.

"Well!" said the Archiem, his sharp brown eyes regaining their customary glitter. "I was told to expect something unusual, but *this!* Thana B'tyrr, I had intended to ask this of your master, but in view of the honor shown us tonight, with my colleague's permission"—he glanced at the king, who was still sitting open-mouthed, oblivious to all but memory—"I'll ask you instead. What pay will you accept for this most exceptional service?"

Jame stared at him. She was still trying to figure out how she had gotten from the loft to the hall.

"Well?" repeated the Archiem sharply. "Speak up, girl. What shall I—we give you?"

"Justice," she said in a whisper.

Harr sen Tenko glared at her. "What impudence!" he exclaimed angrily. "My lords, this is an insult to us all. Such a request should be made through the Five. To address it to you personally is to imply that the normal channels of government—*your* government, administered by *your* representatives—are not capable of handling it properly."

"And yet I believe your kinsman wished to ask for something similar," said Arribek softly. "Think of the opportunity this gives you to demonstrate your skills as a judge before the most important men of two nations. Come, set up the court. Let the trial begin."

Harr had been getting steadily redder in the face during this short speech, but now visibly took himself in hand and did as he was ordered. Salt and a fresh loaf of bread were hastily procured from the kitchen and a cockerel from a neighbor's coop. With these, he perfunctorily mimicked a sacrifice to the nameless gods of hill and mountain.

"We are met to determine the culpability in an undeclared trade war," he announced, holding up the indignant fowl by its feet, not deigning in his own anger to pretend that he knew nothing of the matter at hand. "Let the accuser speak first."

Marplet had come quietly into the hall, forwarned, it seemed, of what to expect. Before anyone from the Res aB'tyrr could react, he stepped up to the notables' table, swore by bread and salt to speak the truth, and began to lie most convincingly. After all, he had had weeks to prepare his story. This was not the setting he had envisioned, but what of that? He had the judge of his choice and all his witnesses primed and waiting, including the two stolid guards he had called in when Niggen had been thrashed. One by one he presented them, heard their evidence, and dismissed them with growing satisfaction. He loved a thing well done.

The staff of the Res aB'tyrr listened, dismayed. They had no experience with this sort of smooth mendacity and felt themselves increasingly helpless before such a citadel of lies.

Jame also listened, with a sense of nightmare. In order to give her the justice she had demanded, the Archiem must convince both his followers and Harr's that Marplet, their countryman, was a perjured liar. They would neither like that nor accept it without proof. Arribek was sharp enough to know in what general direction the truth lay, but how could even he find his way through Marplet's wilderness of falsehoods without a guide?

With a jolt, she suddenly realized that all this time, out of the corner of his eye, the Archiem had been watching her. "*Therefore, having established your veracity* . . ." My God, he was taking his cues from her reactions. Once again, as in the hills, her Kencyr honor had become the guarantee of her truthfulness. Gulping, she began to pay closer attention to the proceedings.

Soon after that, Marplet finished and stepped back, a slight, self-satisfied smile on his face.

"Let the accused speak," intoned Harr sen Tenko.

There were sounds of confusion in the kitchen. The drunken nobles craned, curious to know what was amiss, but Jame could guess easily enough. Tubain had bolted again. Hosting dignitaries was part of his profession, but the crisis he had been asked to face now was so alien to him that it probably had not registered at all. Hence, the inn had lost its rightful spokesman.

"Let the accused speak," repeated Marplet's brother-in-law impatiently.

Marc came up behind Jame and gave her a light, reassuring rap with his knuckles on the back of her head. The big guardsman took up a position flanking her just as Kithra, unbidden, stepped forward to speak for her adopted home.

It was obvious from the start that the girl had a strong personal grievance against Marplet. Her spitefulness compared unfavorably with his smooth air of injured innocence, and many Skyrr noblemen began to hiss at her. But the Archiem, and now Marplet himself, covertly watched Jame as she winnowed the grains of truth from Kithra's malicious chaff with slight gestures of assent or denial. Despite everything, she found herself trying very hard to be fair to the rival innkeeper.

At last Kithra ended her diatribe and stepped down to drunken catcalls from the audience.

''Well!'' said the Archiem lightly. ''There you have it: two totally contradictory sets of facts. Which to believe?''

''Why, surely that's obvious,'' said Harr sen Tenko with surprise, real or feigned. ''One believes and supports one's own loyal servants, in this case, the two guards who have testified for our countryman.''

''And what penalty shall the offender pay?''

''Let the victim name it, according to our oldest traditions.''

The Archiem looked at Marplet with raised eyebrows.

''I can ask for the vengeance of fire,'' said the innkeeper tranquilly. ''Let this house be burned to the ground.''

Oh God, thought Jame. Was I wrong? Is sen Tenzi going to let them get away with this? She had never supposed that the current dispute mattered to him one jot beyond the chance it gave him to embarrass his political rival, but now realized that whatever his ambitions might be in this respect, he had committed himself—at her request—to achieve them legally. The room was full of supporters with whom he would lose face if he did not.

The Archiem was speaking again. One by one, he listed the major incidents in the conflict between the inns as Kithra had described them, omitting only those with which Jame had disagreed. ''Now,'' he said at last, turning suddenly to her, ''do you swear to the truth of these facts?''

''I so swear.''

''So do I,'' said Marc unexpectedly, startling everyone.

''Ah, good,'' said the Archiem with a thin smile. ''You are

a Kencyr too, aren't you? You know, it's an odd thing about these people: they never lie. And they will fight to the death to uphold their word. You there by the door, you guards, can you say the same? Will you do battle for your honor?"

The guards looked at Jame and Marc, then at each other. "No, sir," said the bigger of the two flatly. "We weren't paid enough for that." And they turned and tramped out of the inn.

"Where is your case now?" said the Archiem to Harr sen Tenko, purring. "'According to our oldest traditions,' the judge is responsible for the trustworthiness of the witnesses whose word he decides to accept. You are a false magistrate and a corrupt one as well for letting this situation ever develop. Your position here is forfeit. Now, get out. All honest men are sick of your sight."

Harr, Thane sen Tenko, did not deign to reply. His group gathered about him as he stalked out into the night, passing his kinsman without a word or glance. There would be war in the hills again over this; but whatever its outcome, his part in the affairs of Tal-tastigon had ended.

"And as for you," the Archiem said to Marplet, "let your fate be from your own lips. Someone, bring me fire."

A torch-bearer stepped forward, offering his still-blazing brand while the retainers drunkenly shouted their approval. Arribek accepted it, beckoned Jame forward, and put it in her hand.

"The hunt is yours—again," he said in a low voice. "Now go and draw the blood."

She walked out into the square, dazed by the uproar, hardly believing the rapid turn of events. The mixed courts of Metalondar and Skyrr followed her. There stood the doomed inn, bright, open, and empty. Hearth and candlelight shone on crystal goblets set out on the tables, the rich gloss of the new panelling, the beautiful proportions of the great hall. The wind came, pushing at her back. Overhead, flames leaped hungrily about the brand, a halo of fire. Surely it was all a dream. No sound came from behind now, nor from Marplet who had stepped forward and stood quietly some dozen feet from her. Their eyes met. She could read nothing in his, nor he, perhaps, in hers. The fragile bond of understanding they had shared was gone.

They were still staring at each other when the brand was snatched from Jame's grasp. Kithra darted forward and thrust it between the bars of a cellar window. Orange light glowed behind the grate, then the flames themselves appeared, glowing brighter as oiled bale after bale of straw, prepared for the Res aB'tyrr's immolation, caught fire. The dry underpinnings kindled eagerly while steam began to roll off the damp outer walls. For a long moment, all was as it had been in the great hall: then a wilder light than any shed by candle or hearth began to grow there. The tapestry-hung end walls were in flames.

Marplet watched it all, with a strange little smile. When the upper stories began to burn, he turned to Jame, gave her a slight, mocking salute and walked into the blazing tavern. The hall beams came down behind him.

THE SKYRRMAN BURNED most of that night. The next morning, one of the Creeper's spies thrust a note into Men-dalis's hand as he was climbing the Guild Hall steps.

> *The Talisman, acting for Theocandi, has caused the downfall of Harr sen Tenko* [it read]. *Ask your brother how she rewarded him for betraying your secret backer.*

For a long moment, Men-dalis stared to the southwest at the thin pall of smoke still rising there. Then he turned and entered the Hall without a word.

Routine business kept the Council occupied all that morning, afternoon, and well into the evening. Consequently, it was quite late when the Conclave of Electors finally gathered in an inner chamber. Odalion and one of the masters' two representatives entered looking disgruntled: both had hoped to reap greater rewards from this business. Abbotir, Bane's foster-father, came in all his massive dignity; Jewel, in terror lest he choose the losing side; the Provincials, loud-voiced with self-importance and secretly filled with awe. Chardin, unhappily climbing the outer steps, heard that Mistress Silver had not come at all, choosing to abstain rather than vote for or against the man who had secured her son's life but not his freedom.

"Now why didn't I think of that?" said Master Shining to himself, and joyfully returned to his beloved workroom.

The chamber was at last sealed, and the Conclave convened. Half an hour later, it was all over. By a vote of eight to four, Men-dalis had lost to Theocandi on the first ballot.

CHAPTER 13

Three Pyres

ON THE AFTERNOON following the conflagration, Jame went to the Lower Town in response to a message from Patches. She found the area in a state of chaos. Having no intact river gates, it had suffered badly from the flash flood two days back, and so far had made little progress in sorting itself out. All the rickety houses along the Tone had been swept away, while others, seriously undermined, continued to fall with little or no warning. The homeless thronged the streets, terrified at the prospect of another night in the open, but unable to seek shelter elsewhere because of the barricades erected by the remaining four of the Five, who feared riots and looting. Meanwhile, each dawn saw more children ill or dead. The thing that stalked in the dark fed well.

Marc had been in the area since early that morning, alternately helping to keep order and searching through the rubble for the dead. When Jame found him, he put down his crowbar and, with his captain's permission, went with her.

They found Patches's house still standing but befouled inside and out with river silt. Patches herself was there, assisting her mother and siblings to clean away the muck. Though all had been drenched, none were the worse for it except Taniscent, who had developed an inflammation of the lungs. It was for her sake that they had come. At last, the dancer was returning to the Res aB'tyrr.

Marc carried her home wrapped in a blanket while Jame limped along beside him. There, they put her in her old room. She didn't remember anything that had happened to her since the night of the near-riot almost a year before and was very confused. The sight of her own hands, knob-knuckled and blue-veined, upset her badly. She kept asking, in a thin, querulous voice, for a mirror, which no one was so foolish as to give her.

Jame stayed nearby all that long day and well into the night, taking turns with Kithra and Cleppetty at nursing the invalid. Sometime well after midnight, she excused herself from the sickroom and, with a plate of scraps, crossed the square to the fire-gutted Skyrrman in search of Fang.

Someone was huddled on the doorstep. Moonlight shone on Niggen's tear-swollen face as he jerked it up. Misery gave way to terror. He scrambled to his feet, lashing out wildly at the hand that she held out to him. Only after he had lurched past her into the night, fleeing as if for his life, did she realize that he had thought she was about to strike him.

She did not follow him, nor did any ragged feline form slink out of the ruins in answer to her call as it had the previous night. The city had swallowed Marplet's cat as it had his son.

Jame put the plate of scraps on the ground for whomever might claim it and walked back to the Res aB'tyrr. As she reached the front door, someone called her name. Turning, she saw a shadowy figure approaching her across the square. It was Dally.

"Well, it's all over," he said. "We lost."

Almost with a start, she remembered the Guild Election. "I'm sorry. What happens now?"

"I hardly know," he said. "Even now, I can scarcely believe it happened. Mendy's secret backer failed him at the last minute. If it weren't such an odd idea, I'd almost have thought that he blamed you for that. Now . . . I just don't know. My brother is used to getting what he wants, usually when he wants it. He might try again in seven years or when

Theocandi dies, I suppose, if the Sirdan's assassins don't get him first. Canden was right,'' he said with a bitter laugh. ''It isn't easy to stay alive once you've lost. He almost died tonight after the Conclave, coming down the Guild Hall steps.''

''The Sirdan is working fast.''

''Oh, I don't think he ordered this particular attack. It was just some little 'prentice trying to curry favor. I killed him.'' An odd look crossed Dally's face. ''I've never killed anyone before,'' he said. ''I didn't like it. Anyway, word has gone out that Theocandi has something else in mind, something far surer. There's talk of the Shadow Thief again.''

''Oh?'' said Jame. ''The last time that name came up, you weren't even sure that such a thing existed.''

''Nor am I now, but a good many other people are, and some of them—Canden, for instance—are no fools. They say Theocandi's such a traditionalist that he would never have threatened Mendy before the election (candidates being sacred), but now. . . . Of course, there's still a chance that he could touch off a guild war; but if he were to get Mendy first, my brother's remaining supporters would disband immediately to save themselves, and there'd be no one left to bring charges.''

''Not even you?''

''Who would listen to me?'' said Dally bitterly. ''Without Mendy, I'm nothing in this town, not even a practicing thief. I can't help my brother, myself—or you.''

''Me!'' said Jame in surprise. ''Why? Do you think I need it?''

''Yes . . . if what I've heard is true. It's rumored that the Shadow Thief will have a double assignment this time. You're the second half of it.''

''I'm honored.''

''Jame, please! Be serious. This is no ordinary assassin. We're talking about a . . . a 'temporarily detached soul of special malignancy and power,' or so the Guild archivist tells me, 'a psychic vampire that steals the soul and kills simultaneously with the touch of a hand.' No one knows who it was seven years ago, but your friend Bane's name has been mentioned, and you've told me yourself that he consigned his soul to Ishtier at about that time. Perhaps the priest loaned it to

Theocandi. I've heard rumors too about how cozy he and the Sirdan were during the last Council session. If that was the case then and again now, don't count on Bane's friendship—such as it is—to protect you. The Shadow Thief has no will but his master's, and in this case, that's Theocandi."

"I'm still honored. Look, Dally, when Canden left, I told him that I would take full responsibility for any consequences. If they only involve a game of 'tag-you're-dead,' I'll consider that I've gotten off lightly. But what about you? What are *your* plans?"

"They hardly matter now, do they?" he said, startling her with his sudden note of hopelessness. "I'll wait, and see what role Mendy wants me to play."

"Just the same, it can't be very healthy to be his brother just now. Stay here awhile. The inn is safe enough. Stay with me."

He gave her a quick glance of surprised gratitude, then looked away again, the light fading from his face. "I wish I could," he said dully, "but I can't desert him, now least of all, when everyone else is. I should be getting back to the party's headquarters in case he needs me for anything tonight."

"Well, at least take some precautions," she said, touching the sleeve of his royal blue d'hen. "You shouldn't go around wearing his color, tonight of all nights. Change jackets with me. This one should fit you; after all, it used to be yours."

"N-no. . . . somehow that would be almost as bad as staying here. I'll be all right. Good-bye, Jame. My father's blessings on you."

He took her hands and stood looking at her for a moment, then turned and walked away. She watched him go, wondering at her sudden impulse to follow him. Then Kithra called, and she went in to help.

DALLY CROSSED THE SQUARE, thinking about the boy he had killed. The thin form darting forward, the sudden scuffle on the steps, the boy's astonished face as steel slid home between his ribs . . . then Men-dalis looking at him over the still-twitching body, cold, remote. *Do you think this changes anything?*

What had gone wrong?

He turned westward onto a narrow side street, a nameless despair gnawing at his heart, eating it away. The corner light sphere shone down on him, startling a flash of blue from his d'hen as he passed.

Two men muffled in their cloaks watched from the shadow of a doorway. "Yes, that's him," said the larger one heavily when the boy had gone by, "consorting with the chief agent of my enemy, just as you said. I believe it all now." He stepped out into the street, closely followed by his wizened companion.

Some instinct made Dally turn. He saw the two standing there and recognized both his brother and the Creeper despite their disguises. A sense of unreality and hopelessness deeper than words swept over him. When the others emerged from the shadows all about and closed in on him, he didn't even struggle.

TANISCENT LIVED FOR TWO MORE DAYS. At first, deep in some dream of the past, she called out from time to time for her dancing costume, wine, or Bortis, but then the long silence fell, broken only by the gurgling sound of one who drowns slowly within herself, beyond the help of man.

Patches came to the inn several times during this period, bringing news from the outside world. The Thieves' Guild was not settling down properly after the excitement of the Election. Usually by this time the loser had either fled or fallen to some assassin's wiles, but Men-dalis refused to do either. He had withdrawn into the fortresslike headquarters of his party and from there held together his followers apparently by the sheer fact of his continued existence. It was almost as if he had not yet given up hope of obtaining the sirdanate, although by what means no one could guess. The entire Guild was on edge, sensing the potential violence that lurked beneath this strange state of affairs.

"One wrong move now and bang!" said Patches at the end of her last visit. "Guild war. That sort of thing, no one wins."

"Sounds like a good time to go hide under a haystack. What about Dally? How's he managing?"

"Wouldn't know. No one's seen him since the Election. I expect he's holed up in the fortress with his brother. Oh, before I forget, this is from your master.'' She handed Jame a folded square of paper, begrimed by the dozen or so hands through which it had passed. Naturally, its seal had long since been broken.

''Time I was scooting,'' the Townie said, standing up. ''If you do go out tonight, Talisman, walk wary, won't you? You've a lot of enemies out there, the Sirdan not least, just waiting for you to break cover.''

She left. Jame read the note, smiling slightly both at its contents—which, in part, rather surprised her—and at the thought that Patches, illiterate as she was, had still found a way to familiarize herself with the message.

Early that night, Taniscent died. They laid her out in her own room with fire and iron at both door and window and the usual effigy, hastily carved from a bar of soap, in the next room. The Keepers of the Dead would come for her in the morning. Kithra unearthed the dancer's little rosewood box of cosmetics and tried to make her more presentable, but nothing could disguise the network of wrinkles, those sunken eyes with their blue-veined lids or the shriveled lips. It was very hard to remember just then that Taniscent had only been twenty-five years old.

Jame found that she couldn't face the prospect of an all-night wake.

''If you can spare me,'' she said to Cleppetty, ''I'm going out. Penari sent me a note this afternoon. It seems that despite everything, I've been promoted to journeyman, and he wants to celebrate.''

''Do you think that's wise?''

''No, but it's the only chance I may get to say a proper farewell to the city. This is Marc's last night on guard duty. In a day or so, as soon as I can find out what's happened to Dally, we'll be off down the Tone, bound for the Eastern Sea.''

''I keep forgetting you two are leaving us so soon. It will seem strange here without you. I've almost forgotten what peace and quiet are like.''

Jame laughed and went.

She found Penari up a spiral stair in the Maze, chucking rare manuscripts over his shoulders onto the floor far below in an irate search for some ancient tract probably devoured by mice a quarter century before. He would never acknowledge the ravages of time, here anymore than out in his beloved Tai-tastigon, which made housekeeping rather a problem. In fact, as he came rattling down from the heights, Jame suddenly remembered that the stairway he was on, an infrequently used one, had several broken treads near the top. Before she would shout a warning, however, he was at the spot and past it without missing a step. It must have been the wrong staircase after all, she thought, helping the old man to find his cloak, which Monster had tried to convert into a nest. Then they set off.

Penari had not been out of the Maze since the night he had taken her to be enrolled at the Guild Hall. For the most part, he lived quite comfortably with his memories and the supplies left weekly by arrangement inside one of the Maze entrances, only emerging himself on special occasions, such as the time Monster had chosen the previous Feast of Dead Gods to come down with a sore throat, which required physic. Paddling through the streets with him now, Jame wondered if the unspecified tavern of his youth, for which they were bound, was still in existence. It would be just like him to burst into some private home built on its ruins and demand service. Soon, however, she saw that she needn't have worried. Ahead of them loomed the Cross'd Stars, an inn that had stood for better than two hundred years and was good for as many more.

Penari's sudden appearance there caused a considerable stir. He was quickly absorbed at one of the main tables in a babble of greetings, some from friends whom he had apparently not seen in decades.

Jame quietly took a seat a little back from the others. Just as the Moon catered to apprentices, the Stars had masters and high officials of the Guild as its primary clientele. There wasn't another journeyman in the room, and most of the men at the table were arch-partisans of Theocandi, who had probably done everything in his power to prevent her own promotion. Some celebration this was going to be.

She was trying to think of an excuse to slip away when the trouble started.

Someone had congratulated Penari on Theocandi's success, and he was responding in a typically sharp-tongued way when one of the Sirdan's lieutenant's slammed down his tankard.

"Thal's balls, man!" he exclaimed thickly. "What sort of a brother are you not to have helped the Old Man when he needed it? What are a few secrets compared to the sirdanate? 'Greatest thief in Tai-tastigon'—ha! If you really had anything worth knowing, it would have come out long before this."

"Are you trying to say," said Penari in a dangerous voice, "that I don't deserve my reputation?"

"D-damn right. Name one thing you've stolen lately, 'greatest thief.'"

The old man scowled. "Name one thing—anything—and I *will* steal it. Now. Tonight."

"Sir, no!" hissed Jame at his back under cover of the commotion that had broken out at the table.

"All right: the other Eye of Abarraden. Steal *that,* if you dare."

"Done!" cried Penari with glee.

"Oh, God," Jame said, putting a hand over her face.

THE ARGUMENT CONTINUED all the way to the Temple District, waxing steadily.

"Look," said Jame at last, catching the old man's arm and making him stop in the shadow of the gate. "Even if that man back at the Stars was as drunk as he seemed (which I doubt), look at the situation you've let him maneuver you into: no time to scout the land, even less to lay out escape routes, and enough publicity to make an escort of trumpeters superfluous. You think the guards are deaf? One word in the wrong ear and your venerable hide is up for grabs."

"I tell you, I know what I'm doing," said Penari petulantly. "Remember, this isn't the first time I've been on this particular errand. Besides, no one will betray me. Such things simply aren't done."

"Someone did it to me when I took the Peacock Gloves to the Moon. All right, at the very least, I'm going with you."

"Huh! You just want to nose out my secrets."

"If I hear that word one more time, I'm going to take a flying leap at the nearest brick wall. Has it ever occurred to you that I simply don't want that scrawny neck of yours to get broken? Loyalty is the only virtue I happen to possess; kindly stop throwing it back in my face."

"You mean it, don't you, boy?" he said, peering at her. "Well, come along, then. I suppose you've earned the right."

The temple of Abarraden was one of the largest in that part of the District still held by the Old Pantheon. Its front loomed over a small, sun-starved square from which eight minor avenues radiated, two of them sweeping back at an angle along its outer walls to form the boundaries between the old gods and the new. The temple immediately behind it had been burned down the previous year, as the last blow in a temple war dating from the overthrow of Heliot by Dalis-sar nearly two and a half millennia before; many of the huge, decaying temples beyond that were still engaged, however feebly, in similar struggles.

At the height of her power, Abarraden's house had expanded seven times in as many decades, on each occasion gaining a newer, larger, and more shoddily ornate shell. The temple was now like a series of boxes sitting one inside the other with a warren of rooms between each major set of walls.

Once, the whole place must have hummed day and night with activity; now dust muffled Jame's footsteps as she followed Penari through the passageways. Over the weeks since Gorgo's accidental demise, she had become increasingly aware of the gods of Tai-tastigon as a community in their own right, dependent on faith for their creation and specific characteristics, yet often capable of independent thought. And she sensed that they were increasingly aware of her, the godstalker and theocide, in their midst. It was partly for this reason that she had insisted on accompanying her master, hoping to frighten off Abarraden or at least to divert her divine wrath. It was clear now that that would not be necessary. The goddess slept, her deep breath flowing through the empty halls. Like Taniscent, she would never wake again.

They reached the sanctuary without incident, having seen only a handful of caretaker monks, all easily evaded. This innermost chamber completely occupied the original shell of the temple. It was high, dimly lit with light spheres, and one-third filled by the giant image of Abarraden, once the all-seeing, now the single-eyed. Like most of the Old Pantheon deities, she was a composite of human and animal features—

the latter, in this case, predominantly bovine. At her cloven feet lay a broad ring of dark water, the usual barrier against demons. Only bolt holes were left of the spell-shielded bridge that should have spanned it. A constellation of luminous disks floated just under the water's surface. Jame leaned forward for a closer look, but Penari hastily pulled her back. He took a dusty piece of sausage out of a pocket and tossed it out over the water. A dozen ribbon-thin tentacles whipped up, snatching it out of the air. The eyes blinked once, simultaneously, and waited. Human warders came and went, but the Guardians of the Pool remained.

"This is so ungodly simple," the old man said in a whisper, "that I'm almost ashamed to do it. Still, a challenge is a challenge. Go keep watch at the door."

Jame went. When she looked back, Penari was above the pool with the tentacles snapping futilely up at him, halfway across a bridge that no longer existed.

She was still staring at him, mouth agape, when the sound reached her. Men, a considerable number of them, had entered the temple. She listened a moment longer, hearing the muffled tramp of boots, the low voices arguing which was fastest, then hissed across the room; "Sir, guards!"

"Damnation," said Penari irritably. He was standing on one of Abarraden's full breasts with the white eye-gem from her bowed head already in his hands. He pointed to a doorway in the far corner.

"Up the stairs to the roof, quick, but first douse these lights."

Jame did as she was ordered, extinguishing sphere after sphere with a breathless, "Blessed-Ardwyn-day-has-come," all the time hearing the voices draw closer, grow louder. She paused at the last light, waiting until the old man had gained the stairs, then threw the room into darkness just as the first of the guards burst into it. The others piled up behind him, from the sound of it, then came spilling into the room helter-skelter, cursing loudly. At least one fell into the pool.

Good night vision notwithstanding, Jame could see as little in this blackness as any of them, but had the advantage of knowing the room's layout. She had almost reached the stairway when, to her amazement and horror, a strong pair of arms suddenly locked about her. With all her breath, she gave tongue to the rathorn war cry—a shocking thing to do to anyone at close range. The arms released her instantly. Sprinting for the door, she ran head-on into one of its posts, recovered, and scrambled upward. A spirited free-for-all seemed to be going on below. Then the guards were on the stairs. She half fell out onto the roof, heaved the trap door shut, shot home the bolt, and collapsed on it.

"What kept you?" demanded Penari.

The rooftops of the Temple District stretched out in all directions, a jagged landscape slashed with fissures through which the streetlights far below shone. Penari held up the stolen gem to the moon, turning it over in hands so sensitive that they more than made up for his failing eyesight.

"What a great deal of trouble," he said with a dry chuckle, "for a piece of glass."

"What?"

"That's what it was fifty years ago, and it hasn't changed since. I examined both eyes then and took the genuine one. Mind you, that was no such plush job as tonight, but I never have understood why people made such a fuss over it. Fools, the lot of 'em. Why, anyone could have walked out with this bauble anytime since then"—provided they could cross a spell-bridge that was no longer there, Jame thought—"but the imbeciles managed to convince themselves that it was impossible. This is a city for odd beliefs. Maybe you've noticed."

"Yes, sir. But how did Abarraden get a glass eye in the first place?"

"Who knows?" he said impatiently. "Probably some rogue priest made off with the other real one centuries ago. It doesn't look as if the sect survived losing them both."

The boards of the trap door groaned, one of them beginning to bend under the pressure of a crowbar applied from beneath. Jame shifted her seat hastily. "Uh, sir, glass or not, these gentlemen are still after our hides. What do you suggest we do about it?"

"Why, leave, of course," he said, standing up. "A good thief never overstays his welcome."

"By what route?" she asked, with a premonition of disaster.

"How many choices d'you think we have up here?" Penari said irritably. "Across the rooftops, of course."

He was pointing toward the back of the temple, across the gaping void left by the building that had burned down.

The bridge had been real to him, perhaps those missing steps in the Maze as well, and now—this was hardly the time to shake his self-confidence, but oh lord . . .

"Are you—uh—sure it's all right?"

"Of course I'm sure," he said petulantly, and stepped off into space. He slithered down several feet, regaining his balance with difficulty. "Reasonably sure, anyway. But what are a few rotten shingles? Come along, boy, and mind the holes."

She watched him carefully pick his way across the abyss, probing ahead into emptiness with his staff. That solved his problem, at least, provided he didn't slip. But as for her own! She made a rapid circuit of the rooftop, noting the smooth, sheer walls; the opposite buildings, well beyond reach; the distant ground, which a grapnel line would have reached, if she had thought to secure one in her dress d'hen. On the whole, it was not a particularly favorable situation.

"Well, come on," Penari shouted impatiently from the opposite roof. "D'you think they'll take all night with that door?"

Patently, they would not. Wood splintered. A hand came through the jagged hole, groping for the bolt. Theoretically, there was no reason why she should run from them at all. Having never touched the stolen object, she was innocent of its theft according to the laws of the city, but something told her that tonight such fine distinctions would do no one any good.

"Well?" shouted Penari, beginning to grow hoarse with exasperation. "If I can do it, by all the gods, so can you!"

Perhaps he was right. There was no question that he believed what he said; and with this old man, belief was obviously a very potent thing. Jame stood there a moment, ignoring the sounds at the door, Penari capering with impatience on the far roof, forgetting everything except what she had learned over the past year about faith and reality in Tai-tastigon. Then, with eyes tightly shut and infinite caution, she took a step forward, over the edge.

There had to be something there, because her foot slipped on it. Like Penari minutes before, she found herself sliding sideways down what felt like a slick, sharply pitched surface. Eyes still squeezed shut, she checked her descent and began to creep forward along the incline. The surface over which she blindly groped her way had no particular texture at first, and an unnerving tendency to melt away whenever the growing commotion to the rear caused her concentration to waver. She recalled vividly how Penari had so often had her describe a route through or over a house she had never seen—often because it no longer existed—and the kind of imaginative reconstruction necessary for such work. This wasn't all that different, really, discounting the possibility of a hundred-foot plunge. Ah, there *were* shingles. She traced the outline of one, then jerked back her hand with a hiss.

"What's the matter now?" demanded Penari's voice, very near.

"Of all the . . . a splinter, I think. What did you say about . . ."

"Talisman!"

The bellow came from behind, incredulous protesting, and unmistakably from the powerful lungs of Sart Nine-toes. Startled, Jame opened her eyes. There was nothing beneath her, nothing, and she was falling. Her hands flew out wildly as though with a life of their own, and clamped on the edge of the opposite roof.

"I *told* you to watch out for those holes," said Penari, hauling her up by the scruff of the neck.

After that, Jame insisted on escorting her master out of the district and home, through back alleys, at as fast a pace as the old man could maintain. Although his trophy was only glass, so worthless that by rights the period of jeopardy should have elapsed by the time its length could even be determined, she suspected that there were those who would refuse to treat it as anything less than the genuine article. Someone was out to get Penari, and perhaps herself as well. If it was the Sirdan, he would not hesitate to bend the law as he had already bent the thieves' moral code in betraying them to the guards. Under the circumstances, the best place for Penari was the Maze, and for her, the hills to the northwest of the city, waiting either until things settled down or she and Jorin could rejoin Marc for the trip south. Consequently, she said goodbye to her old master at his front entrance and then set off hurriedly for home by the rooftops, meaning to collect her possessions and get out of town as quickly as possible.

REACHING THE RES AB'TYRR, Jame climbed hastily up to the loft and froze, one leg thrown over its parapet. Inside, the floor was strewn with shreds of clothing. The two pallets had also been gutted, and the bricks of the fireplace were scattered everywhere. In the far corner, stones had been pried out of the wall, revealing the dark, secret cavity behind them. The knapsack lay sprawled on the shambles of her bed. The sword shards lay beside it, and the little package that contained the ring was just visible in the folds of the blanket, where it had apparently been overlooked. The Book Bound in Pale Leather, however, was gone.

Jame sat quite still for a moment, taking this all in. Then she swung her other leg over the parapet and went quickly down the inside stairs. Just as she entered the kitchen, Sart Nine-toes appeared at the street door.

"Now wait a minute, Talisman," he said hastily, seeing that she was about to bolt. "Believe it or not, it's Marc I'm looking for, not you."

"Marc?" Sudden alarm sharpened her voice. "Has something happened to him?"

"That's what I'm trying to find out."

Cleppetty had come up from the cellar as he spoke and now advanced on them purposefully. Before she could say anything, however, Sart swept her off the ground and clamped his hand over her mouth.

"We're on patrol just outside the Temple District," he continued, ignoring his squirming captive, "when the captain comes trotting up with a dozen or so of our lads behind him and says, 'Someone is robbing Abarraden. Fall in.' So in we fall, and off we go to that puzzle-box of a temple; but someone (in a minute, m'dear) douses the lights just as we come into the idol room. I grab hold of Marc's sleeve, knowing that you Kennies have a way with the dark, and get hauled right across the room. Then someone lets off a godawful yell just about in my ear (wait, love, wait) and the next thing I know, Marc has swung about and is wading into our lads like the last typhoon of summer. I bash a few heads too, just to be companionable, then go pounding up the stairs with the rest and out onto the roof."

He paused, eyeing her doubtfully.

"You really were standing on air, weren't you? It wasn't just too much ale? Anyway, so I turn to point you out to Marc, and he isn't there. I haven't seen him . . . ouch!"

Cleppetty, at last losing her patience, had bitten his hand. He dropped her.

"You may not have seen him since, but I have," she said grimly, smoothing her apron. "He stopped by about an hour ago. Whatever's going on, I'm afraid it's serious. Jame, he asked me to tell you that 'An honorable death wipes away all stains.'"

"Oh, God. It's serious, all right. I've got to go after him. Sart, would you mind staying here until I—we get back? I've an odd idea that the inn shouldn't be left short-handed tonight."

"Glad to," he said, grinning at Cleppetty. The widow, unaccountably, blushed.

It was obvious what had happened: those had been Marc's arms around her in the dark. By releasing her, a supposed thief, as soon as he had realized who she was, the big Kendar believed that he had broken faith as a guard. For him, that constituted a massive loss of honor, more than any Kencyr would expect him to survive. Consequently, he had gone to restore his good name in the surest way possible, by seeking a death in accordance with the ancient rites at the hands of a Kencyr Highborn. In Tai-tastigon, that could only mean the priest, Ishtier. She must stop Marc before he reached the temple or, somehow, cut short the rites, which could destroy an innocent man as readily as a guilty one.

Once again, the rooftops provided the fastest, safest means of travel. Jame sped over them, following the route that Marc was most likely to have taken, anxiously scanning the streets below. Dally might be somewhere down there too. She would not leave the city until she had seen him, Jame decided, even if it meant invading his brother's fortress; but that must wait until Marc was safe. Nothing else mattered now.

Nothing? Not even the Book? Sweet Trinity, she'd completely forgotten about that. Some guardian you are, she thought, negotiating a treacherous stretch of thatching far too fast.

Her feet shot out from under her. She went cannoning

down the slick straw into space, caught someone's laundry line, circled it once, let go and bounced off a shop canopy, somersaulted twice onto the opposite balcony and swarmed up again to the rooftops.

"Next time, bring down a pigeon!" someone shouted from the street below.

It was a night for essentials and establishing priorities. Darkness damn the Book, and her too, if she failed Marc now.

Then she saw him, a tall, unmistakable figure striding along far down the street. He was almost to the circle of decay that surrounded the temple. She swung down to the ground and ran after him, calling. He didn't seem to hear. In another minute, she would be close enough to touch him.

Then, in complete silence, a figure glided out of the shadows to stand between them, one hand raised.

Jame skidded to a stop, staring at it. The night was dark, but even so she should have been able to make out some detail of the stranger's face, or at least of his garments. All were featureless, black, a mere silhouette . . . no, a shadow—upright, solid, reaching.

So she had not been the second half of Theocandi's assignment at all but the first; and here was his assassin, nameless, faceless, come to execute its commission.

She retreated, shouting again after Marc. His step did not falter. This time he must have heard, but as far as he knew she could say nothing that would redeem his honor or save his life. She must explain the truth to him, she must, but death stood in her way. Too dangerous to try ducking past . . . she sprang sideways into an alley and ran for both of their lives.

Fleet as her own shadow, it followed. The byways twisted and turned, choked with rubble, treacherous underfoot. It would not let her double back. What obstacle would stop it? Ah, between two sagging walls, the moon-glint of the Lower Town's western fosse. Jame raced for it. One leap and she was across, dashing northward toward the temple. The other kept pace on the far side. They were coming to a bridge, just short of the temple's ring of dust. If it could cross . . . Jame sprinted. It *had* crossed. She saw its outstretched hand from the corner of her eye and dove forward, out from under it, to roll over and over in the crumbling debris, sending up billows of dust. Coughing, on her knees, she saw that it had stopped, just as that other nightmare had done so long ago, at the edge of the poisoned circle. She rose and ran toward the temple, noting with a little spasm of panic that its door was wide open. Marc had already entered.

She finally caught up with him in the central chamber. He was kneeling before the altar, his big, gnarled hands frozen in a gesture of resignation. To her alarm, he responded neither to voice nor touch.

"You're too late," said a thin, dry voice. Ishtier stood beside the statue, looking like a pale excrescence on its granite form. "He is already deep in the death-trance and will sink farther still before the end. Never before have I encountered a man so eager to greet oblivion."

"But he mustn't! It's a mistake, all of it: he's done nothing to make this necessary."

"So you say. Nonetheless, I abide by his wish in this matter, not by yours. All your cunning can't save him from himself, anymore than it helped you to retain possession of the Book Bound in Pale Leather. Ah yes, I guessed that you had it," he said, coming down a step, his face alive with triumph. "'BE STILL, TONGUE THAT SPEAKS . . . TO THE CHOSEN LEAVE THE HIDDEN WAYS.' You remember that, do you? The first half is indeed from Anthrobar's scroll, which you contrived to destroy, but the second is not. Only someone familiar with the contents of the original would have been able to add that quote. There are a handful of priests and scrollsmen who possess such knowledge—little good it does them without the runes themselves—but none of them have ever been near East Kenshold, your home; and it was to East Kenshold that the Master himself came, looking for something so valuable that he entered the corrupt air of this world in an attempt to reclaim it. A guess, you see, but I was right, wasn't I? Well, it's out of your hands now, and soon to fall into some appropriate ones."

"Yours, I suppose," said Jame, trying to conceal her dismay. "Might I inquire how?"

"You have a friend to thank for that," he said with malicious relish. "As soon as Penari's message to you was intercepted, Theocandi laid his plans and I, mine. Bane is responsible for your loss."

"And perhaps for yours as well," said Jame, sudden alarm in her voice. "When I saw him last, he spoke very bitterly of you and said that the next time you gave him an order, the results might surprise you. How long overdue is he?"

"He would never betray me," Ishtier said, more to himself than to her. "He couldn't, even if he has been less obedient of late than usual. I have you to thank for that too," he added, shooting her a venomous glance. "But this . . . this would be a betrayal of the whole of our people. No, no, it's unthinkable."

"To him, *you* are the Kencyrath, and when he spoke of vengeance, it was because he thought that he himself might have been betrayed. You know better than I if you have any reason to fear him now."

"I deny any reason," said the priest furiously, "but I acknowledge my foolishness in trusting someone so unstable. That boy is capable of imagining anything. Assume the worst, then, as he undoubtedly has: what will he do next?"

"In his place," said Jame slowly, "I would do the most injurious thing possible. I would give the Book to Theocandi."

Ishtier drew his breath in with a hiss. "The man's a savant of sorts, as I have cause to know. And he is ambitious enough to devour the world. If the Book is there, we must get it back. *You* must."

"I, m'lord? And what of my friend here? If I do this errand for you, do you swear to bring him out of this trance so he can hear the truth and change his mind?"

The priest struggled with this for a moment, then made an ill-tempered gesture of assent.

Jame got as far as the chamber door when a thought struck her. "Uh, m'lord . . . a slight problem. The Shadow Thief is waiting out there to kill me. How does one dispose of a demon?"

"Nothing to it," said Ishtier irritably. "All you need is its true name and then a great deal of fire or water. That should be easy for you, theocide."

Water she could provide, Jame thought as she stood just within the temple door, waiting for her chance. As for a name . . . ah, there the thing went, passing her narrow line of vision through the door's crack as it began another patient circuit of the circle's rim. Wait, wait . . . *now*. She threw open the door and dashed out, racing for the fosse.

It was marginally faster then she, but with a head start, Jame managed to get to the other side of the little waterway before it closed with her. Almost all the way to the Tone, this slight lead allowed her to shift banks just ahead of her pursuer whenever a bridge gave it access to her side. Then, within sight of the Tone, she stumbled. The assassin cut in front of her. She sprang sideways into a ribbon-bedecked street of the Silken Dark, deserting it as soon as she could for the rooftops of the courtesans' district.

The chase ended on the crest of a house whose upper stories overhung the swift-flowing Tone. Jame, at bay, turned to see death slipping toward her along the roof's spine. She had one chance now.

"Bane?" she said tentatively.

It rushed at her. She barely had time to block the reaching hand, forearm to forearm, and to get a grip on something that felt like a collar before it was on her. She went over backward, one foot in its stomach, and threw it over her head. Something hard, swinging down from the shadowy form, hit her in the face. Tears of pain blinded her momentarily. When she could see again, there was only the rooftop, the Tone, and something dark on its surface, being borne swiftly away.

Jame sat on the roof, getting her breath back. On the basis of Dally's description, she had gambled that only the creature's hand was deadly, but as for the name. . . . Even now, she could hardly believe that she had guessed that correctly, too. As Dally had pointed out, Bane had entrusted his shadow to Ishtier seven years ago, during the priest's "exchange of information" with Theocandi and just before the Sirdan's erstwhile rival, Master Tane, had fallen prey to the Shadow Thief. If Ishtier (who was supposed to be keeping Bane's soul safe) had lent it then and again tonight for such a foul purpose, he had betrayed his trust indeed. Well, she had put an end to that; but Sweet Trinity, what an end.

The sound of angry voices below broke in on her thoughts. A group of men clad in Men-dalis's royal blue were forcibly restraining one of their number, while Theocandi's supporters jeered at them.

"Quiet, man," a friend hissed at the angry man. "D'you want to start a war?"

Jame suddenly realized that the street below was full of thieves—far too many of them. Instead of lying low like their master, the partisans of Men-dalis were out in force, much to the delight of their enemies, who lost no chance to taunt them. If they responded violently, so much the better: an undeclared guild war would bankrupt the side that struck the first blow. But why was the New Faction abroad tonight at all? Its members had the air of waiting for something without knowing exactly . . .

What was that?

The sound grew, a low, hoarse roar, almost a groan, rising nearby to the north. The thieves below exchanged looks. They began to move, slowly at first then faster and faster, toward the firelight outlining the houses that looked down on Judgment Square.

Puzzled, Jame swung down to the cobbles and joined the flow. Crossing a bridge to the north bank, she saw a familiar figure in a cream velvet d'hen walking blindly toward her.

"Darinby!" she called, fighting her way through the crowd to his side. "What's happened?"

"Talisman?" He hardly seemed to see her. "Don't ask. Don't go to look. Just get off the streets. There's nothing anyone can do . . . nothing."

She stared after him, shocked, then turned and ran toward the Square.

It was full of men, swarming about the Mercy Seat. Torch flames leaped over their heads, casting a demonic light on the upturned faces, on the back of the Seat where something blue was draped. Jame paused on the edge of the crowd, some touch of prescience sickening her. Then she began to force her way through the press of bodies, pushing and kicking at first, then using her nails with an abandon which would ordinarily have appalled her. Then she was through the front line and saw.

"Oh God . . . Dally."

The world narrowed to the two of them, one sprawling negligently on the marble throne, the other on her knees before him, vomiting again and again. The emptiness of her mind ached with the buzz of carrion flies. Slowly, their insectile hum became words, repeated over and over, each time drawing a louder response.

"This is Bane's work!" a man in a blue d'hen was shouting. "This is war!"

Could the dead do this to the living, she wondered, still half-dazed. But even if she had just destroyed his soul in the Shadow Thief, it couldn't change what had happened here—it might not even change him at once. A slow, withering death, Darinby had once said.

Around her, Theocandi's supporters had drawn back, surprised, frightened by the mob's response. Jame guessed before Men-dalis's rabble-rousers could name it, how this growing sense of outrage and violence would be channeled. The intensity of it almost brought her to her feet, shouting with the rest, but a sudden doubt stopped her. She looked again at what sprawled on the Mercy Seat, taking leave of it, then rose and slipped out through the crowd. At its edge, she began to run, then to climb.

"Why, Talisman!" exclaimed the dark figure that had suddenly appeared at the roof's edge. Its hand, raised to strike, swooped down to help her up. "What's going on?"

"Sparrow, I haven't time to explain. Any second now, that mob is going to march on the Thieves' Guild Palace, and I've got to get there first. Can you and your people delay them?"

"The Palace? Fleshshambles Street to the river is the best route, with the north bank tangle mazes on either side. Yes, we can do something about that, if you don't mind us maybe dropping four tons of stone bull on a few heads."

"Smash every one of them, for all I care. Just give me five minutes."

"You've got them," said Sparrow, and darted off.

Jame remained a moment, looking down. Below, they were already on the move, torches streaming toward the mouth of the street the Cloudie had indicated. The sound that rose was hoarse, grating, scarcely human. This was what Dally's death had unleashed on the city. Jame stripped off her gloves and let them flutter down into darkness. So be it: nothing hidden, nothing held back.

The roofs of Fleshshambles Street were ornamented with an array of stone animal heads, meant to propitiate the spirits of the beasts sold piecemeal below. One of these, a particularly massive bull on the corner of River Street, already had a dozen Cloudies active at its base, chipping away the few patches of good mortar that held it in place. Jame waited until the mob had nearly reached the Tone, then raced for the corner. The Cloudies shouted a warning as she sprang to the bull's broad head, feeling it bow under her weight, then off again, barely in time, over to the opposite roof. She did not look back either at the sound of that great weight crashing to earth or at the screams that followed it.

Ship Island rode at peace behind its vengeful figurehead.

Jame came into the Guild Hall shouting for Bane and was promptly collared by one of his followers. This man took her back into the Palace and up to the richly furnished apartment from which, so long ago, she had seen the corpse of a boy flung.

Bane turned away from the fireplace into whose flames he had been staring. "So you've come to me at last," he said with a smile.

"Never mind that. Did you do it?"

"Let's just say I had it done. Forget the Book, m'lady. It's a filthy thing. You're better off without it."

"*Damn* the Book! Dally is out there on the Mercy Seat, half flayed in your own favorite pattern, and his brother's men are on their way here now to make you pay for it."

Bane's henchman swore out loud and hastily left the room to check. His master's smile, however, hardly flickered.

"You have more casual cruelty in you than anyone I've ever met," said Jame to him fiercely, trying to break through his composure, "but God's claws, man, you aren't stupid! Whoever did this must have known what would happen. It's the first blow in an undeclared guild war, and right now you look like the instigator. Tell me you haven't been such a fool, especially not for my sake. Tell me!"

Bane's man reappeared at the door. "The minx told the truth," he said breathlessly. "They're coming! What shall we do?"

"Whatever you like. I'm a fool, certainly," Bane said to Jame, stepping between her and the door, "but not in this, m'lady."

"Damn it, then *do* something! I don't want to lose you both in one night . . . oh God," she said, suddenly paling. "I'm going to anyway. Bane, I-I think I've just killed you."

"What on earth do you mean?" he said, looking amused. She explained. To her amazement, he burst out laughing. "Indeed, you've out-guessed yourself this time. No, look farther away and yet near at hand for your thief of souls, m'lady."

"What do you mean . . . and why do you keep calling me that?"

"You'll have to get used to it, you know. After all, it's probably the least of your titles."

"What?"

"Do you mean to say that you didn't know?" he said, surprised at last. "No one ever told you? How very odd."

"Wait a minute," Jame protested. "How do *you* know all this? Have I got a sign on my back that says, 'Kick me, I'm Highborn?'"

"Go around offering to carry other peoples' souls, and you might as well have. All Shanirs must possess at least a touch of the Highborn strain, but soul-carriers like you and Ishtier need blood as pure as it comes. Besides, how many Kencyrs are there, even among the Highborn, with your talents or training? For such a clever person, you really are remarkably ignorant. What a pity I shall never have the chance to educate you."

Below, the Guild Hall door crashed down. Someone screamed. Now many feet were thundering through the passageways, many voices howling on the trail of blood.

"You know," said Bane, turning back to her with a smile, "this may not be quite how I envisioned our last meeting, but you must admit that for us, it *is* at least in character. Farewell, my lady. Remember me."

His hand slid up to the back of her neck and he kissed her, fiercely. Through sudden pain, she heard a sharp click behind her, then staggered backward as he pushed her away. The wall beside the fireplace was not where it had been. As she came up hard against some further surface, the panel swung shut again, sealing her in.

From the chamber beyond came the screech of wood as its outer door gave way.

Jame tore at the panel with her nails, raking up splinters, knowing all the time that it was hopeless. A spot of light touched her hand. Hurriedly she knelt and peered through the spy hole.

They were in the room, a semi-circle of them almost facing her, with more pressing in behind, all held at bay. Even now, with their overwhelming numbers, their prey terrified them. In that brief, petrified silence, Jame heard him quite clearly no more than inches away on the other side of the wall, laughing quietly as though at some private joke. Then they closed in on him.

He fought with the knife and the Senethar, with consummate skill and savage joy. Within a minute, the dead lay thick at his feet and the living drew back, appalled at the carnage. Jame heard his quiet laugh again.

"Dogs," he said softly, advancing on them, drawing their eyes from the secret panel. "Is death sweet? Jackals, come and lick the blood."

There was a movement on the floor behind him. Jame saw the hand of a fallen thief stealthily close on a dead neighbor's knife. She cried out, but too late. The man sprang up. He caught Bane around the throat with an arm and plunged the knife up under his ribs. Bane shook himself free. With a movement too fast even for Jame to follow, he broke his assailant's neck. Then, almost contemptuously, he jerked out the knife. Blood poured down. Something like a sigh went through the room. They were waiting for him to fall. Instead, he advanced on them again, one step, two, and then he went down on one knee, a hand pressed to his side. He looked up at the spy hole and smiled. Then they descended on him.

Not a man there struck less than once, and some many, many times, but Jame could hear Bane's ragged breath as clearly as her own long after it should have ceased. He was still breathing when they took him away. A man who has lost his soul dies very, very hard; and a Kencyr hardest of all.

Jame found herself sitting on the floor, leaning against the panel. Pain had roused her. In a half-dazed fashion, she raised a hand to her face, then held it up to the arrow of light from the peephole. The fingertips glistened darkly. Bane had bitten nearly through her lower lip.

She was still staring at her raised hand when something came between it and her face. Jame threw herself sideways with a cry of horror. The other's fingers almost brushed her cheek. No amount of river water would suffice if the name was wrong, she thought wildly, springing to her feet. It had tracked her down again; she was alone with the Shadow Thief in the dark.

She ran. The secret passageways formed a maze within a maze, twisting past all the Palace's major rooms. Shafts of light from many spyholes pierced them. Jame raced on, seeing little ahead and nothing behind but the swift, silent darkness that broke each beam of light as it passed. This was not the Tower of Demons nor was the thing that pursued stupid Thulig-sa, whom this obscurity would have baffled. Despite its name, it meant to touch her, not her shadow, and was perilously close to doing so. Desperately, she put on a fresh burst of speed, rounded a corner, and ran head on into a wall.

Half-stunned, she saw the dark form bending over her, haloed by the furtive light of the peepholes.

Then, far away, someone screamed.

The Shadow Thief froze, its hand inches from Jame's face, then incredibly, it whirled and was gone. She marked its rapid progress down the corridor. Some instinct brought her unsteadily to her feet, sent her after it, stumbling at first, then moving more swiftly and surely. The hunter became the hunted, both now racing in the direction of that terrible, un faltering cry. God, how could anyone sustain such a ghastly sound so long without once pausing for breath?

Ahead, the end of the corridor was rimmed with light, momentarily obscured as the other passed through it. The scream, very close now, sank to a hideous gurgle. Jame, skidding to avoid another collision, came up against a soft, yielding surface, the back of a wall tapestry. She swept it aside, and stepped into Theocandi's private study.

The Sirdan himself sat at his desk, his gnarled hands gripping its edge. His head was thrown back, his eyes wide, wide, open. Eyes? He had none, just dark holes punched out under the bristling brows, opening into greater darkness. A thin, hissing noise still escaped between his clenched teeth. Under its heavy chain of office, the frail chest continued to contract until the ribs themselves collapsed with a flesh-muffled crunch. And all this time, the Sirdan's returning shadow grew darker on the pages of the Book Bound in Pale Leather, spread out open on the table before him.

"A savant of sorts," Ishtier had called this man. Clearly, he had been enough of one to summon the Shadow Thief and to unlock the runes, but the latter had proved beyond his control. Anthrobar must have looked much like this when the Book had finished with him.

"It is a filthy thing, isn't it?" Jame said to the motionless figure. "For what it's worth, I'm sorry that this happened."

She closed the Book and gingerly rewrapped it in its old linen cloth, shuddering at its obscene warmth. Then she slipped out into the main corridor with it in her arms.

The hallways of the Palace seethed with people, each one intent on saving himself from the coming holocaust. No one paid any attention to the slight figure clutching a flat white parcel, who joined the general flight out into the cool night air. Frantic as they were now, how much greater the rout would be when word of the Sirdan's death spread among them.

At the prow of the island, the figurehead brandished its grisly trophies over the swift water, the sky turning red with flames behind it.

CHAPTER 14

The Untempling of the Gods

IN THE QUIET of the temple, Jame hesitated, looking at Marc's motionless form. Then she put the Book Bound in Pale Leather in Ishtier's hands.

"Now," she said, "keep your word. Wake him."

But the priest seemed to have forgotten both her and his victim. With trembling fingers, he unwrapped the Book and cradled it awkwardly in one arm, his free hand turning the heavy pages slowly as he gloated over each one.

"At last I have it," he murmured, with barely suppressed excitement. "The power, the power to set things right, to bring down the Barriers and restore my people to their rightful lord under shadow's eve. I have it, I have it, I . . ."

"What in Perimal's name are you talking about? Will you rouse him or not?"

"Rouse him?" The priest drew himself up, staring coldly down at her. "You petty-minded little fool, what does that matter now? You don't understand what has happened, do you? Then I will explain it—in Perimal's name—if you think your weak wits can stand it. After all, you still believe that the Kencyrath is the chosen champion of God against the ancient enemy, Perimal Darkling, Devourer of Worlds. Like the rest, you spit on the name of Gerridon, Master of Knorth, whom most call renegade and traitor because he withdrew his loyalty from your divine monstrosity and gave it instead to the Lord of Shadows. But he was right to do so. I went into exile with the Gray Lord. I saw the face of darkness and know that in all the Chain of Creation there is nothing to equal it."

"Wait a minute . . . are you saying that the Gray Lord survived the crossing of the Ebonbane?"

Ishtier flinched away from the question. "Nothing to equal it, I say!" he repeated, his thin voice becoming noticeably shriller.

Jame sensed a change in the flow of power around them, a growing element of instability. The priest's control had begun to slip.

"M'lord . . ." she said sharply.

"Then I came to Tai-tastigon," the priest continued, overriding her, rushing on. "Gods everywhere, hundreds, thousands of them, when we are taught that there is but one. But you think, you presumptuous guttersnipe, that you were the first to ask questions, to experiment with the fabric of reality in this wretched town? Before you were born, I was here, wrestling with the enigma. Seven years ago, the answer was mine at last."

Again, he drew himself up, and an ominous tremor passed through the room. Out in the hallways of the temple, a low moaning began.

"The force embodied in the Three-Faced God, which we are taught to fear and obey, which has controlled the fate of our people these last thirty millennia under the pretense of being the sole source of divinity in all the worlds, this force, I say, is not unique! For three hundred centuries, it has used us, deluded us, kept us from the truth. All this I have proved," he said with a wild laugh. "I! Of what worth is the Kencyrath if it continues to serve such a fraud? What price is godhood itself when any man can create it?"

The chamber door groaned softly. At its foot, the tiles had begun to ripple.

Jame stared at the priest. So his doubts had paralleled her own, but how had he come to such a conclusion? Then, almost against her will, she understood.

"Oh God. So the Townies were right to blame us for their misery. While Theocandi was calling forth the Shadow Thief, you used the same knowledge to create the Lower Town Monster. But Ishtier, it's demon, not god! It lives off the life-force of children, and as for its soul . . . Trinity! No wonder it always followed Bane like a shadow: that's exactly what it was. The timing is right, the characteristics . . ."

Butcher of children, are you thinking of me?

The image of a marble seat, dark with blood, crawling with flies, suddenly filled her mind. Once again, perhaps for the last time, her thoughts had crossed his.

"Theocandi couldn't die until his shadow returned to him," she said with rising horror, "and neither can Bane. Ishtier, we've got to help him! He's still alive, and they're taking him to the Mercy Seat."

"Serves him right," said the priest with a malicious snicker. "He should never have betrayed me."

"You betrayed him first, by agreeing to carry his soul and then by using it in such a damnable manner," Jame cried, unconsciously shifting into High Kens as shock changed to fury. Cat's paws of power rippled through the room. The patterns on the floor changed at their touch. "He trusted you because you brought his mother, once the Gray Lord's mistress, down out of the Haunted Lands, because he thought—and you let him think—that you were his father. But Ganth Gray Lord was alive when you deserted him, wasn't he? You've betrayed not only Bane and Anar, your younger brother, but your liege-lord as well. I brand you coward and lack-faith for what you did then, and renegade now for trying to pull down the Kencyrath so that you might hide your shame in its ruins!"

"Who are you," he almost shrieked, spittle flying from his lips, "to pronounce sentence on me? A petty thief and a tavern whore, an outcast from East Kenshold!"

"I am not from the east," she cried, enraged beyond all control. "Like you, I came from the north, and from the same place. The lord you betrayed was my father, the man consigned by you to torture on the Mercy Seat, perhaps my half-brother, and I—I am Jamethiel Priest's-Bane . . ."

". . . WHO SHALL YET BE THY DOOM."

With a look of horror, Ishtier dropped the Book, hands flying to his mouth as though to seal in the words he had just spoken. The god-voice flowed unimpeded, uncontrollable, through his spider-thin fingers, booming prophecy to the far corners of the room.

Jame scarcely heard him. She had suddenly become aware of the changed atmosphere of the room, the growing fury set loose. A demonic howling had begun, the sound of trapped energy moving faster and faster. The walls groaned. Cracks began to lace their smooth surfaces. The three Kencyrs were in the eye of the storm here, protected only by one slowly disintegrating door. Already power flowed around its edges. The floor mosaic shifted again, throwing Jame off her feet. Triangles of green serpentine, lapis-lazuli, and ivory moved under her hand.

". . . WHO MAY YET SAVE THE CHAIN OF CREATION OR DESTROY IT . . ." Ishtier's altered voice was crying, each word like some great weight crashing down. The priest was on his knees now, hands scrabbling at his face, staring wildly at nothing. The power that he had scorned had him by the throat. No help would come from him now.

Through all of this, Marc had not stirred. Jame staggered to her feet, clinging to him as to a rock in storm-maddened seas. His broad shoulders were warm and steady to the touch. Her dazed mind slowly cleared, then began to focus on what she must do next. When her self-control had fully returned, she carefully stepped away from him, bowed to the towering image of her god, and began to dance.

It was like weaving through fire. The dark joy she had felt in molding the dreams of men turned to agony, a flaying of body and soul. This was the maelstrom where god and man met. The god-head itself was flowing through her, consuming what it touched. She struggled to control it, grimly, desperately.

". . . CHAMPION, FRATRICIDE, TYR-RIDAN . . ."

Tyr-ridan?

No, ignore it, concentrate, concentrate. . . . So much power and no place to channel it. Had the floor begun to shake? They would all die unless she found an outlet here, beyond . . . yes, there was a place, many of them, waiting, filling the night with their hunger. No time to ask what they were, no time for anything but to send the power spiraling out to them through the movements of the dance.

"... TORRIGION ..."

That-Which-Creates. (A roaring noise ...)

"... ARGENTIEL ..."

That-Which-Preserves. (Quickly now, increasing, louder ...)

"... REGONERETH."

That-Which-Destroys. (Done.)

Ishtier, in his own voice, began to scream. The sound pursued her, ringing down the halls of her failing consciousness until at last the final echo died away. Then all was still.

MARC HEARD THE SCREAM TOO. It seemed to come from a great distance at first, weaving through his trance-numbed mind, growing rapidly louder. Then he forgot it as memory returned. Was he dead and his pyre somehow neglected? While the body remained, so did the shadow, a soul trapped by death, held naked in the presence of the hated Three-Faced God—or so Marc had been taught. Cautiously, fearfully, he opened his eyes.

A book lay before him, its pallid cover uppermost. The mosaic of ivory and semi-precious stone beneath it had been shaken loose from its pattern. Vaguely, he remembered some upheaval. That must have been when the animal got in, for assuredly there was one somewhere in the room now, its voice raised in a yammering frenzy, broken at intervals by a slobbering sound. He turned stiffly to look for it.

What first met his gaze, however, was a crumpled figure several yards away, lying at the center of a large, well-defined spiral, which certainly had not been there before. Recognition and alarm cleared his wits instantly. He rose painfully, cursing the cramped legs, limped over and knelt beside the still figure. A moment later, Jame's eyes fluttered open.

"Are you all right?" he asked, helping her to sit up. "You look a proper mess."

"I'll bet I do," she said with a shaky laugh, wiping blood off her face. "Like something the cat threw up, probably. I ought to be dead."

"So should I."

Jame gave him a startled, remembering look, then launched into a rapid explanation of the night's misadventures. "And now that that's been cleared up,'' she said at last, ''what in Trinity's name is making that uproar? It scarcely sounds human.''

They went to look, and found Ishtier crouching on the far side of the altar, quite mad, trying to gnaw off the hand that had touched the pages of the Book Bound in Pale Leather.

''What do we do about him?'' Marc asked, eyeing the priest doubtfully.

''Nothing.'' The cold hatred in her voice surprised him. He had not, after all, been there to hear her speak to Hangrell in just such a tone. ''He brought this on himself and more besides. Let's just get out before something else happens.''

She picked up the Book, grimacing at the feel of it and at the darkening patch on the binding where it had hit the floor. ''One man dead because of this, another insane, and all it has are bruises,'' she said with disgust, much to Marc's confusion. ''I've a mind to throw it into the first fire we come to, but I won't. Guardians never get off that easily. Besides, the damn thing would probably find some way to come crawling back.''

They went out through the ruins of the door, which crumbled to dust at a touch. The outer halls were quiet. Though the directing influence of the priest was gone, it would be weeks before the power here built up again to a dangerous level. By that time, Jame hoped, help would have been sent out by those sensitives in the Kencyrath who, however distant, could scarcely have failed to note the chaos unleashed in Tai-tastigon that night.

She and Marc began to get some idea of it as they stepped out of the temple.

''Something's wrong with the skyline,'' said Marc, pausing uncertainly on the threshold. ''We should be able to see the Tower of Bats near Judgment Square from here, and Fumble's Folly, and look: Edor Thulig is gone.''

There were in fact many unfamiliar gaps in the city's skyline, especially near at hand, where whole rows of deserted houses had tumbled down, greatly increasing the circle of ruin about the temple. Beyond, most structures except a few of the tallest still stood—or at least leaned—though over all hung such an unearthly air that it was hard to think of the whole as Tai-tastigon at all. Odd lights played out across the sky, blooming silently from the labyrinth of streets and quickly fading back into it. Hollow, booming sounds were heard in the distance, almost but not quite resolving themselves into words. The odors of incense, burning, and death rode the cross-winds.

The two Kencyrs looked at each other, baffled, then back at the strangely altered city. Marc gave a sudden exclamation. A light was coming toward them, growing steadily brighter. Within seconds, they could distinguish over the intervening rooftops the spark that flew upward from it and the tower of smoke that rose at its heels. Jame gripped her friend's arm.

"Dalis-sar!" she said.

Before he could react, she had thrust the wrapped Book into his arms and was gone, racing off through the mounds of dust toward the approaching blaze. He followed as quickly as he could, with a curse at his still-cramped legs. Jame disappeared around a corner at the circle's rim. When Marc caught sight of her again, she was at the far end of the street, silhouetted against an inferno whose brilliance made him look quickly away, seeing nothing but gigantic wheels of fire rolling slowly on, hearing only the roar of the flames and Jame's voice shouting over and over:

"Bane! Its name is Bane!"

Then the greater light was gone, southward bound. In its wake, everything burned—houses, rubble, even the slight, dark figure that had thrown itself face down on the ground, arms wrapped about its head.

Marc was hobbling to the rescue when something else came down the street. It was about half the size of the first apparition and appeared at first to be nothing more or less than a small ambulatory storm cloud, complete with fitful flickers of lightning and sharp little thunderclaps. The rain it let fall extinguished most of the flames its predecessor had left behind. When Marc came up to Jame, she was on her feet, slapping at the patches of her soaked jacket that still smoldered. Staring down the street after this strange procession, Marc saw that there was something in the heart of the retreating cloud, something that hopped along jauntily in time to its own warlike music and seemed, by what light there was, to be a particularly vivid shade of green.

"Gorgo?" he said incredulously. "But how? What in all the names of God is going on?"

"They're on their way to the Lower Town to destroy its monster," said Jame, still slapping at her clothes. "Armed with fire, water, and its true name, they ought to succeed. Dalis-sar has waited a long time for this. I suspect he sensed from the start that it was a Kencyr affair, but there was nothing he could do about it as long as he remained securely templed. As for Bane, now at last he can die. I suppose in a way it will even be an honorable death, what with Ishtier, Dalis-sar, and myself all contributing to it. Perhaps that was all he ever really wanted from me. Now I will never know."

Marc was still staring after the two gods.

"How did they come untempled?" he asked, bewildered. "I've heard tell of one god breaking loose before, but two at once?"

"I think I know," said Jame, "but let's go home. If I'm right, we'll find out soon enough."

At the first step, she stumbled. Marc, hastily catching her arm, realized then that the light of Dalis-sar's war chariot, so painful even to him at a distance, had temporarily blinded her. Well, if she didn't want to speak of it, they wouldn't, nor of her torn lip, which was clearly the work of someone else's teeth. All in good time. They set out for the Res aB'tyrr with his hand on her shoulder.

The streets of Tai-tastigon presented a curious spectacle. At first, much of the damage there suggested natural causes: an earthquake, perhaps that had left downed buildings, fissured roadways, and fires casually gutting homes from which all occupants had fled. But there was more to it than that.

Vast, shadowless forms prowled the thoroughfares. Some pulsed with light; others seemed like holes cut out of the fabric of space; many were so nebulous that nothing could be said of them at all except that they moved and, somehow, lived. Whole blocks crumbled with their passage, if they did not turn from stone to crystal, sprout flowers from every cranny, or perform some other unnerving if temporary transformation. Voices boomed in the distance. Overhead, an enormous, grotesque creature scuttled along the walls, leaving a phosphorescent trail and, at intervals, triumphant proclamations in schoolboy Kessic that "Edolph the Bat-Wing was here . . . and here . . . and here."

More often, however, the two Kencyrs came across scenes of consternation. One indistinct form raced wildly around block after block, cutting through the corner houses to the great dismay of their occupants; another frantically tried to creep into a lay-temple half its size; a third simply huddled at the end of a blind alley, whimpering. What had happened was now clear enough, at least in general terms: *All* the gods had come untempled, and most were finding the experience profoundly unsettling.

"'All the beings we know to be divine are in fact but the shadows of some greater power that regards them not,'" said Jame suddenly as they neared the inn, interrupting Marc's description of a shimmering form that he had just seen flutter past the end of the street, closely pursued by a priest brandishing what appeared to be a giant butterfly net.

"It's the Anti-God Heresy in action," she explained. "When I channeled energy out of the temple tonight, it entered the so-called gods of Tai-tastigon. They must live on it. In fact, I'll bet that they were created out of it in the first place, with their worshippers' faith to give them form and life. Why, they're nothing but parasites, so insignificant that their host doesn't give a damn if they exist or not! The senior priests must have discovered that and called it a heresy to keep their power intact. I don't think the gods themselves knew the truth until tonight, when they suddenly got more power than they could comfortably swallow. Poor things, no wonder they're so upset."

"Look," said Marc abruptly.

They had come to the edge of the Res aB'tyrr's little square, and he was pointing across it at the inn. Jame, whose sight had by now returned, stared in disbelief. Golden light streamed out of every window and up like a beacon from its courtyard into the night sky.

Everyone was in the kitchen, clustered around the open courtyard door, staring out of it incredulously. Cleppetty swung around sharply as they entered the room.

"Bloody, singed, *and* dripping wet," she said, regarding Jame with fists jammed on bony hips. "Now I know we've got a crisis."

Jame ducked under Sart's arm, around Rothan, and between Kithra and Ghillie, who made room for her without once taking their eyes from the scene outside. A familiar figure was walking back and forth over the flagstones. The black, hooded robe had not changed, but through it shone a golden light, outlining the lithe body within and playing about the beautiful hands as they traced wide circles in the air, as though ecstatically embracing all before them. There was still no face within the hood, only light and more light. When it touched the b'tyrr figures on the wall, they wriggled with joy, stone lips parting in silent laughter, ivy-bound hands flexing, bursting their green bonds.

"I've just one question for you, missy," said the widow's voice belligerently at Jame's elbow. "The last time we had that lady for a guest, the roof almost fell in. So now when does it catch fire?"

"After this," said Jame slowly, "probably never. She's returning your hospitality. I think you've just acquired a resident goddess."

"Look!" said Ghillie suddenly. "She's disappearing!"

They watched as the light slowly faded, the moving figure becoming less distinct. The same thing was probably happening all over the city, to everyone's great relief. It was to be hoped that the other deities would withdraw to their own temples now that they had expended enough energy to fit into them; but the Res aB'tyrr's still nameless guest had no place else to go. Indeed, even when her form had vanished entirely, it was clear that she remained because the walls of the inner court continued to glow, and would, as it turned out, for years to come.

While the others exploded into a babble of excited conversation, Jame tried to explain to the widow what had happened.

"Well," said Cleppetty at last, "with Theocandi out of the way, at least you won't have to go rushing off. A few days' rest will do you good after a night like this."

"I expect it would, but it isn't that simple. Too many people know I was in the Palace trying to get something back from the Sirdan just before he died. No, I've got to leave now, tonight, before the Guild gets its breath back."

"The Talisman is right," said Sart. "If Men-dalis takes power now, he'll need something to get folks' minds off that odd business with his poor brother. A hunt for the murderer of a sirdan should suit him just fine, especially since he seems to hate you anyway. Off-hand, I can't think of anything that would pull the Guild together faster. What I don't see," he said, scratching an ear, "is how you're going to get far enough away fast enough. Come the dawn, they'll be down the Tone after you like a wolf pack."

"Then I won't go that way. There are still the mountains."

"In the middle of the storm season? You haven't a hope of a guide," said the widow, sounding outraged. "And as for proper clothing . . . !"

"There's an outfitter's shop near the Mountain Gate. I'll raid that. As for a guide, one of my own people, an Arrinken, lives up there. He may help . . . if I can find him."

"If we can, you mean," said Marc.

She gave him a searching, hesitant look. "You're sure?"

"I never try to commit suicide twice in one night," he said with a slow smile. "We'll get through all right. Anyway, I'll not have it said in the houses of the Kencyrath that you shook me off so easily."

TWO HOURS LATER, he was still smiling slightly as they left the Vale of Tone and began to climb up into the lower reaches of the Ebonbane. Decked out in a preposterously small mountaineer's jacket (the largest, nonetheless, that the outfitter's shop could provide), he might well have been quietly laughing at himself or at Jame, who, by contrast, looked as if she had been swallowed alive by her new, oversized clothes. The little mound of coins they had left on the counter was probably too large for such dubious comfort, but Jame had been determined that, as a parting gesture, it should be large enough. She never meant to steal again.

Still, awkward fit or not, it was a pity nothing similar could be done for Jorin. He was trotting beside her now, as he had been ever since her silent, anxious call had drawn him to her down from the foothills to the north. She slid a gloved hand over his winter coat, noting its richness. Perhaps, after all, he was better prepared than either of them.

Already the air was much colder.

Jame turned on the slope, looked down through the valley of the Tone for the last time at the city below. At the world and the people she had known, Penari, to whom she had not even said good-bye. Though perhaps he, of all people, would best understand why she left. Every detail of the Res aB'tyrr's warm kitchen came back to her, every word spoken in those last hurried moments; but most of all, she remembered Cleppetty's sudden, almost defiant announcement that since it was a night for surprises, she would contribute one of her own: during the course of their long vigil that evening, Sart Nine-toes had proposed to her and she had accepted. What was more, she believed that Rothan and Kithra had come to a similar understanding.

One leave-taking, two engagements and three—no, four pyres. Jame hardly knew whether to laugh or cry.

She had said good-bye to Tubain through the locked door of his "wife's" apartment. To her astonishment, the innkeeper and Abernia had both answered from inside, speaking simultaneously. Taniscent, of course, had had nothing to say at all. Standing at the door, Jame had taken a last, silent farewell, seeing on that narrow cot the symbol of all the lives lost—friends' and foes'—since she had first slipped through the Warrior Gate on that night so many, many days ago.

A very different emotion went through her now as she regarded not memory but Tai-tastigon itself, that marvelous city, flayed with fire and prostrate with terror. A great fissure had split Judgment Square in half, swallowing whole the Mercy Seat and whoever had occupied it, Dally or Bane, in those last minutes when the mob still ruled. She was tired of feeling responsible for things beyond her control, and angry at those whose schemes had unleashed the chaos below, especially at that one who, if her instincts and Sart's were correct, was getting away with murder. But not forever. There would be an accounting for that someday, if she lived to bring it about.

This certainly remained as all else began to slip away, an entire way of life flowing back into the darkness. Was the Gray Lord really her father and she Highborn? In the temple, the thought had seemed almost inspired, but here the possible reality of it was harder to grasp. If it was true, then in Torisen Black Lord, leader of the Kencyrath, she might find her long lost twin brother Tori—miraculously ten years older than herself. Well, stranger things had happened, even within the last hour. Perhaps time moved at a different pace beyond the Barrier, or even near it. Perhaps she had even first fled Perimal

Darkling to someplace other than Rathillien: after all, the Master had come searching for his precious book a good two years before her own arrival with it in this world.

Questions, always questions. Still, some answers were at last beginning to emerge. Soon she would know them all, and no longer be a stranger to herself.

Marc was calling her from farther up the path. She took one last look at the city, settled her pack, and turned to follow him. A sudden feeling of happiness lightened her step. Despite the uncertainty that awaited them both, despite fire, ruin, and the snow that had begun to fall, they were going home at last.

APPENDIX I

The Thieves' Guild

THE THIEVES' GUILD is the most powerful professional organization in Tai-tastigon, so much so that it usually has a representative on the city's governing council, the Five. Guild members obey both Guild and municipal laws (the latter rather peculiar, in some cases) and are considered respectable citizens—unless they get caught. Then the penalties range from fines to the loss of a finger for a first offense to the removal of one's entire hide, usually for a robbery involving undue violence or the injury of a guard.

The Sirdan is high lord of the Guild. Under him are five officials, each one in charge of a court where a certain type of stolen goods is assessed to determine the duty that the thief owes the Guild and also the period of jeopardy during which possession of the stolen object is punishable by law. These courts handle gold, silver, jewels, and glassware (a highly prized commodity in the Eastern Lands). The fifth court specializes in fur, fabric, and works of art. At the time of this story, the following officials are in charge of these courts:

Gold Court: Abbotir *(Bane's foster-father)*

Silver Court:	Carbinia
Jewel Court:	Thulican
Glass Court:	Odalian
Shining Court:	Chardin

The Sirdan appoints these people, so they tend to support him—unless someone makes them a better offer.

Next in importance are the one hundred master thieves who each have been granted one of the city's districts as his territory. There are landless masters too, but they haven't the right to take on apprentices or to vote.

Every seven years, a Guild Council convenes on Winter's Eve to elect a new sirdan or to reinstate the old one. Three weeks before, the landed masters meet to select their two representatives to the Council. Each of these men has one vote. Four more votes go to the Provincial representatives, who come from affiliated thieves' guilds in Endiscar, Tai-Abendra, Tai-Weir, and Tai-Sondre. The real power, however, remains with the lords of the five courts, who have two votes each. Guild elections tend to be quiet before the fact and violent afterward, when the unsuccessful candidates for high office are no longer protected by law.

APPENDIX II

The Tastigon Calendar

Tastigon Dates	*Equivalents*
Spring's Eve (new year begins)	March 1
Summer's Eve	May 1
High Summer's Day	July 1
Autumn's Eve	September 1
Feast of Dead Gods (begins at midnight of Autumn's Eve and lasts until dawn)	
Winter's Eve	November 1
Mid-Winter's Day	January 1
Feast of Fools	February 29

360 days = a year (361, actually, but the Feast of Fools is never counted)

Autumn = 60 days
Winter = 120 days (60 to Mid-Winter's Day)
Spring = 60 days
Summer = 120 days (60 to High Summer's Day)

1 week = 10 days

The novel spans just over a year, beginning with the Feast of Dead Gods and ending a few days after the next Winter's Eve.

APPENDIX III

The Kencyrath

SOME THIRTY MILLENNIA ago, the entity known as Perimal Darkling first breeched the barrier between the outer void and the series of parallel universes called the Chain of Creation. It began to devour universe after universe, entering each one in turn through a threshold world. These special worlds existed in different dimensions but overlapped each other so that parts of each extended into the two adjacent universes.

Whatever Perimal Darkling touched began to change. The animate and the inanimate, the living and the dead, grew closer together in nature. Good and evil began to collapse in on each other. Many men chose to serve the spreading darkness, and so became extensions of it. Others fled, or were enslaved.

The Three-Faced God stood in opposition to the dark invader. As inscrutable in his own way as Perimal Darkling itself, he chose three races from different threshold worlds to be his champions and forged them into the Kencyrath.

The original Kencyr—renamed (by themselves) the Highborn—became the leaders of this new people. They were quick-witted and proud, blessed (or cursed, as some thought even in those days) with an unusually close relationship with their god. Those especially affected were called the Shanir. These individuals possessed strange powers and had a tendency to go mad. They often became priests.

The warriors and craftsmen of the Kencyrath were the strong, easy-tempered Kendar. These capable, self-reliant men and women found that their god had altered their basic natures so that they must now either serve a Highborn lord or suffer great emotional distress. This ensured the Kencyrath's continued existence. Of all the ways in which the Three-Faced God manipulated his people, however, it was perhaps the most cruel.

In contrast, the Arrin-ken retained most of their independence. Not even a god would have cared to tamper much with these folk, who were themselves nearly immortal. Unlike the Highborn and Kendar, the third of the Three People resembled great cats. They served as the Kencyrath's judges, interpreting the laws that the Highborn priests pronounced when their god chose to speak through them.

These, then, were the defenders of the Chain, the champions of their god, whether they wanted to be or not. But when the first clash with the servants of Perimal Darkling came, the Kencyrath found itself fighting for its life, alone. The Three-Faced God had left his people to fend for themselves. No one knew why. The demoralized Kencyrath was defeated.

This was the beginning of the long retreat. On threshold world after threshold world, the Three People made a stand, defending each in turn until forced to withdraw again. As their fighting skills increased, their numbers dwindled and their bitterness grew. They felt betrayed by their god, but were unable to refuse the role that he had forced on them. Stubborn pride and a fierce sense of honor alone upheld them.

Then one man rebelled. Gerridon, Master of Knorth, Highlord of the Kencyrath, offered his soul and that of his followers to Perimal Darkling in exchange for immortality. He induced his sister and consort, Jamethiel Dream-weaver, to pervert the great dance used in the temple so that instead of channeling the god-power, it would suck out the souls of all who witnessed it. Two-thirds of the Kencyr host fell. The rest fled into the next threshold world, Rathillien.

On Rathillien, the remnants of the Three People struggled to reestablish themselves. They became obsessed with honor, feeling that Gerridon's fall from grace had somehow tainted them all. Much of their bitterness was taken out on the Shanir, whom many of them blamed for their current plight. After all, hadn't both the Master and the Mistress been of the old blood? Because of Jamethiel Dream-weaver, Highborn women also fell under suspicion. Their lords stripped them of all civil power and confined them to special halls.

The Arrin-ken disapproved of these changes, but their influence was dwindling as their number, too, declined. The handful of them that remained withdrew into the wilds of Rathillien to consider what should be done next.

During the long absence of the Arrin-ken, contention grew among the Highborn. By now, nearly 3,000 years had passed since the Kencyrath's arrival on Rathillien, and in all that time there had been no significant clash with Perimal Darkling. True, the barrier between the uninvaded areas of Rathillien and the parts now claimed for Perimal Darkling by the Master grew weaker each year and large areas near it, like the Haunted Lands, had been contaminated. But that hardly seemed as serious as the recurrent attacks by the native rulers, most of whom still considered the Kencyrath itself an unwelcome invader.

The Highborn no longer agreed on their priorities. They couldn't entirely abandon their traditional role as the guardians of the Chain, but they could divert much of their energy toward carving out a place for themselves on Rathillien—or so many of them argued. This debate came to a head when Ganth of Knorth was invested as Highlord. Ganth lead a great Kencyr host against its enemies on Rathillien, but he was betrayed and the host broken. Ganth Gray Lord presumably died on his way into exile.

A time of near anarchy followed as the remaining lords vied for power.

Then a young man came out of the Eastern Lands, claiming to be the Gray Lord's son. His name was Torisen. Although he had neither Ganth's sword nor ring to prove his identity, the war-weary Highborn proclaimed him their lord so they might have at least a season's peace. No one thought he would last longer than that. But Torisen Black Lord proved himself so superior a leader that his rivals lost heart. They would have been astonished to learn that while Torisen dismissed them almost contemptuously, there was one rival whom he feared, even though he had not seen her in over twenty years. Somewhere out there was his twin sister, Jamethiel—cursed at birth with the name of an arch-traitor, driven out into the Haunted Lands as a child by Ganth, their father.

But she would come back. She was already on the way. Torisen waited, wondering what would happen when he at last met her face to face.